Praise for *Driven*

'A great plot … a great read … I couldn't put it down'
Murray Walker

'Author Toby Vintcent takes inspiration from F1's
on-track action and off-track paddock politics in
weaving together a page-turning conspiracy thriller. His
attention to detail captures the spirit of current F1'
F1 Racing magazine

'*Driven* – it howls along like Lewis Hamilton
round the streets of Monaco!'
Boris Johnson

About the Author

Toby Vintcent served as an officer in the British Army with the 16th/5th The Queen's Royal Lancers during the Cold War as part of NATO's Rapid Deployment Force. He then had a successful career at Merrill Lynch, and has been Director of International Affairs at the British Equestrian Federation. Toby Vintcent's lifelong passion for Formula One resulted in his first book, *Driven*. He lives in Oxfordshire, the heart of F1 country, with his wife and son.

DRIVEN

TOBY VINTCENT

A

Arcadia Books Ltd
139 Highlever Road
London W10 6PH

www.arcadiabooks.co.uk

First published in the United Kingdom by Moreton Street Books 2014
This B format edition published by Arcadia Books Ltd 2015
Copyright © Toby Vintcent 2014

ISBN 978-1-910050-71-2

Typeset in Garamond by MacGuru Ltd
Printed and bound by CPI Group (UK) Ltd, Croydon CRO 4YY

Arcadia Books supports English PEN *www.englishpen.org* and
The Book Trade Charity *www.btbs.org*

ARCADIA BOOKS DISTRIBUTORS ARE AS FOLLOWS:

in the UK and elsewhere in Europe:
Macmillan Distribution Ltd
Brunel Road
Houndmills
Basingstoke
Hants RG21 6XS

in the USA and Canada:
Dufour Editions
PO Box 7
Chester Springs
PA, 19425

in Australia/New Zealand:
NewSouth Books
University of New South Wales
Sydney NSW 2052

For Anne-Marie and Sammy.

Dedicated to my parents.

About the Formula

The Formula referred to in this story is a fictional composite. While it includes authentic elements used by the FIA over the last few years, no similarity with any given year's Formula should be looked for or expected.

PART ONE

SAINTE DEVOTE

ONE

Remy Sabatino's heart rate held steady at a hundred and forty up the hill from La Rascasse and through the exit of Turn Nineteen as the Ptarmigan Formula One car entered the pit straight. Screaming up to eighteen thousand revs, the engine was throwing off seven hundred and twenty horsepower. Such fierce acceleration affected the timbre of Sabatino's voice – heard in a message over the team's radio:

'This time, Andy,' sounding juddering and strained, 'I'm … in the zone.'

The Ptarmigan hit one hundred and seventy miles an hour as it crossed the line – to start a flying lap.

Images flashed down either side of the extraordinarily narrow Monaco street circuit – trees, lampposts, overhanging balconies, and an astonishing array of advertizing hoardings. All of this would have melded into a blur if Sabatino had even *tried* to take any of it in: the driver's gaze was boring between the convergent barriers either side of the road ahead, flicking down only once to check the LED display on the steering wheel.

Sabatino held top speed for as long as possible, on a line to the left of the circuit. Less than one hundred metres from the upcoming right-hand corner, the driver braked dramatically, changing down from seventh to second. Turning in at the last possible moment, Sabatino accelerated – with total commitment – through the apex of Sainte Devote, feeling with hyper sensitivity for any slide in the back end – the first sign of power spilling over, traction being lost – and the extreme risk of slamming into the steel Armco around the outside of the corner. But, here – now – the Ptarmigan's grip was converting all its immense power into forward momentum.

Changing up again and then again, the engine howled up to

eighteen thousand revs before each gear change as the car rocketed up the snaking rise, through Beau Rivage – the only section of the Monégasque circuit passing as a geometric straight – to hit seventh gear. Unevenness in the road surface sent violent jolts up through the suspension, frequently blurring the vision. Sabatino hung right as the car unweighted momentarily over the slight crest before taking some pace off, the engine management system pulsing the revs on each of the three rapid downshifts before slicing the corner of the open left-hander of Massenet below the Hotel de Paris, practically brushing the Armco barriers with the wall of the left-rear tyre. Sabatino's heart beat reached a hundred and sixty as the car pulled four G, while the breathing rate remained deep but steady.

For no more than a fraction of a second the car straightened up – before Sabatino timed the acceleration through the following right-hander past the Casino, pulling G-force in the opposite direction, and on down the hill from Casino Square. Racing back up the gears, Sabatino jinked right then left within the narrow street to miss the destabilizing hummock on the true racing line to the left, and powered on down towards Mirabeau. One hundred and twenty – one hundred and thirty miles an hour.

A call came over the team radio.

Sabatino barely heard the race engineer's voice before it crackled badly.

The message was lost.

'Say again?'

Another transmission came from the pit lane in response – but only as a deafening crackle.

'Damn it,' shouted Sabatino into the visor. What the hell's going on?

There was no time for clarification.

Timing to brake as late as physics would allow, Sabatino began decelerating, changing down, before starting to turn in. But the car did not respond quickly enough, wasn't turning enough.

Understeering badly.

Sabatino felt the front right lighten even further with the camber of the road – and feared a lock-up of that wheel and flat spotting the tyre. It began to feel too late. Was there enough road to slow down?

Steel barriers loomed straight in front.

Sabatino's heart rate surged above one seventy, while fighting with repeated flicks of the steering wheel to the right, to slow, stabilize and turn the car, all at the same time.

They were going too deep.

In an instant, the driver opted to do something completely counter-intuitive – to accelerate.

Accelerating far earlier than usual, Sabatino sought to use the outward swing of the rear through the corner to help turn the car. The Ptarmigan did indeed react – its back end trying to step out – so tightening the rate of turn. Slewing onto three tracks, Sabatino turned into the slide. It worked. But the car exited the corner far wider than desired. Correcting quickly, and already shutting such a close shave with the barriers out of mind, the driver punched blistering power into the short slope down towards Loews Hairpin.

Massive deceleration followed – the engine surging the power on each gear change down to first – before Sabatino put on full left lock through the slowest corner in Formula One. This time, the car didn't understeer. For some asymmetric reason, the balance – to the left – was okay. Sabatino straightened up, laid the power down hard, drifted across the road to the left – changing up before cutting right through Mirabeau Bas, down towards the sharper corner of Portier.

Another right-hander.

How would the car respond this time? thought Sabatino – probably better, being slower and camberless.

It was.

Straightening up through the exit, full throttle was unleashed – the chunky rear tyres giving the car all the mechanical grip needed to accept the huge acceleration. A few hundred yards later it was already doing one hundred and ten miles an hour as it entered the tunnel. From the brightness of the Riviera sun, Sabatino was momentarily blinded, plunged into darkness under the Fairmont Hotel. But that didn't stop any of the drivers racing on up through their gearbox to eighteen thousand revs, seventh gear and up to one hundred and seventy miles an hour, all while pulling two-and-a-half G on the long gliding right-hander.

Matt Straker stood on the quarterdeck of the 1930s super yacht, *Melita*, out in the marina – basking in the velvet air of a Mediterranean summer morning, particularly enjoying the sun on his face. Looking over the dark blue waters of the harbour, and up at the array of pastel-coloured houses spread across the hillsides of Monte-Carlo, he thought this had to be one of the most glamorous places in the world. The Principality of Monaco had it all. And with this escapist weather, she was blessed with the climate, too. Straker suddenly felt a pang of conscience.

Revelling in the distractions of this scene, he felt awkward – still not sure how his skills could be of any use here. How could he justify his pay and rations in such an extravagant setting? He hated the thought of merely being along for the ride.

That was professionally.

Personally, he just hoped this assignment – whatever it turned out to be – would be enough of a diversion from his troubles.

Straker's introspection was instantly shattered – pierced by a band saw-like shriek. As a reflex he turned his head. It was coming from the right as he looked at the view. The sound got louder – the noise – reverberating in the acoustics of the harbour, hills and buildings.

'There,' said the elderly, distinguished-looking man standing beside him, pointing at the end of the Fairmont tunnel with the cigar held loosely in his fingers. Most people in their mid-seventies would have long-since wound down their career and lessened their work load, taking things easier. Not this man: Dominic Quartano, head of Quartech International – Britain's largest defence contractor and recent saviour of the Ptarmigan Formula One Team – was as active, and as fired up by the prospects of the next business deal, as ever.

And the deal to be done – here – was a game changer.

Its significance was energizing Quartano's bearing – his presence – giving him an aura. Wearing a beautifully cut blue blazer, open-necked pink shirt, white chinos and handmade loafers, his lived-in Mediterranean face radiated conviction and command. Quartano switched his attention to the car's telemetry on the iPad he was holding. 'Up point-three in sector one,' his rounded baritone announced to those around him.

Straker, following the streak of brilliant turquoise, caught glimpses of the Grand Prix car between the rows of yachts as it flashed – right to left – down the slope from the tunnel along the harbour wall. The engine note rose and fell rapidly several times as the car decelerated hard before it flicked between the raised kerbs of the Chicane. Immediately, power was laid down again – in a rising scream – as it hurtled on along the waterfront towards Tabac. Straker didn't just hear the noise – he felt it. His entire frame seemed to resonate with the sound.

He, too, switched his attention from the car to Quartano's screen. An on-board camera – mounted above Sabatino's helmet – showed the road ahead. At death-defying speed, the car was hurtling down the impossibly narrow track between the steel barriers, through the sharp turns around the Swimming Pool complex, juddering sharply over the apex of each corner as the driver clipped the red and white kerbstones, before powering on towards the sharp right-hander of La Rascasse. Overlaying the TV image were columns of data from the car's telemetry, relayed from the team's computers in the pit lane; at that moment, they all showed the car to be running well, comfortably within limits.

A matter of a few seconds later the Ptarmigan had completed the lap, crossing the line.

There was excitement all around.

In practice, at least, the car was performing as competitively on the Monte-Carlo street circuit as it had on the very different track in Bahrain a fortnight earlier. During the intervening two weeks, the four hundred-man Ptarmigan team had clearly worked effectively on this very different set-up. So far, their car was fast. Blisteringly fast.

The lined, rugged face of the hard-to-impress Dominic Quartano, the team owner, said it all. Running a hand through his silver hair, his expression exuded a mix of vindication and potential triumph. Ptarmigan had just gone fastest by four tenths of a second.

That promised exciting things for his prospective deal – and for the Monaco Grand Prix in three days' time.

TWO

A few minutes later a figure approached the *Melita*, walking along the marina pontoon. Recognized by the burly security man standing guard on the quayside, the new arrival was readily invited aboard. He was soon walking purposefully across the gangplank, and up onto the yacht's quarterdeck.

'Ah, Tahm, could I have a quick word?' said Quartano, holding out an arm behind the visitor to show him into the art deco saloon.

Tahm Nazar, Team Principal of Ptarmigan Formula One, was in his late fifties, but seemed completely unlike the typically determined-looking F1 team boss. More the appearance of a professor, he had a near-white moustache and wispy flyaway hair, both of which contrasted with his mahogany-toned skin.

The two men enjoyed their car's performance for a few moments.

'Tahm,' said Quartano after offering Nazar a drink from the steward. 'I'm sorry for our loss of Charlotte Grant.'

'Very sad.'

'Not for public consumption, but she proved to be a right pain in the arse.'

Nazar looked a little surprised at the tycoon's unexpected vocabulary.

Quartano nodded his confirmation. 'We discovered that she had been leaking Quartech blueprints for a state-of-the-art rifle to a rival company; at the same time she was trying to sabotage a defence contract we were negotiating in the Middle East – which nearly cost us billions.'

Nazar took a sip of his drink. 'You'd never have thought it possible.'

'No one's more shocked – and let down – than I. But I am concerned, Tahm. Charlie was doing a lot of sensitive stuff for you

– intelligence gathering on the other teams. Just to be on the safe side, I need to be sure she wasn't doing Ptarmigan any harm.'

Nazar looked unconvinced. 'Are you sure you want to go to that much trouble and expense?'

Quartano looked at his watch. 'I'll know for certain in just over an hour – after our meeting with Mandarin Telecom. Putting that opportunity at risk – because we weren't prepared to be vigilant – would be insanity. I'm assigning you one of my best people, Matt Straker … I'll introduce him to you in a moment.'

'From Charlie's team?'

'Competition Intelligence and Security, yes.'

'An industrial spy, then?'

'My eyes and ears on our markets and competition.'

'And you rate him?'

'Completely. He has one hell of a CV. Colonel in the Royal Marines until a couple of months ago. Quite a guy. Afghanistan, DSO, several tours with Special Forces. He was the one who saved the Buhran deal – and his investigation flushed out Charlie as the traitor. I want him to be your eyes and ears until we're absolutely sure Charlotte Grant didn't leave Ptarmigan any nasty legacies.'

'Okay, Dom.'

'Make sure you only introduce him around the team as a research resource, though – helping you to keep an *outward*-looking eye on other teams' developments and innovations, etc. For morale reasons, best not to mention our internal suspicions.'

Nazar nodded his agreement.

'Good man. Come and meet him now – we've a few minutes before the Mandarin Telecom directors arrive.'

Quartano led Nazar out of the saloon back onto the quarterdeck, walked him over, and introduced Matt Straker.

'Welcome to Ptarmigan,' said Nazar, shaking hands.

Straker was in his mid-thirties, six two, medium-to-slim build, with wiry dark hair and eyebrows. Nazar, taking in his face, thought it strong and intense – an intensity reinforced by the bridge of Straker's nose, which seemed to run in a straight line – almost vertically from his forehead to its tip: Nazar was put in mind of the warrior-on-a-Greek-urn kind of profile. From Quartano's description of him, at least, the warrior association seemed right enough.

That was all until Straker smiled.

At that point his face lost all its edge and intensity – radiating warmth and a genuine readiness to engage.

'Thank you,' said Straker. 'Given our concerns about what Charlotte might have done here, I hope I end up doing absolutely nothing for you – whatsoever.'

Nazar smiled warmly, moved by the younger man's modesty.

A Quartech aide appeared from the saloon and politely attracted Quartano's attention. 'Sir, the directors from Mandarin Telecom are here.'

The boss nodded and, drawing his team forwards with a series of inclusive hand gestures, bade them all make for the stern of the yacht.

Quartano took a moment.

He inhaled more deeply, his nostrils flaring slightly:

This was it.

This was *the* meeting.

Several Chinese businessmen were walking somewhat tentatively across the gangway. 'Dr Chen, thank you for coming,' said Quartano, with an authentic air of welcome.

Dr Chen, the CEO of Mandarin Telecom, was a dark-haired man in his sixties with heavy-rimmed glasses, dressed in an immaculate, handmade, charcoal-grey suit. The two men shook hands very formally, Quartano investing their greeting with due ceremony. 'May I present the Principal of the Ptarmigan Team, Mr Tahm Nazar?'

Moving forwards, Nazar shook hands with Dr Chen.

Quartano continued: 'And this is my Marketing and PR Director, Mr Bernie Callom.' The artistic communications specialist walked forward and bowed deeply to greet the Mandarin Telecom chief executive. 'I'd also like you to meet Colonel Matt Straker, our Competition Intelligence Director, who'll be helping me look after you and your colleagues during your stay in Monte-Carlo.'

In turn, Dr Chen introduced the three members of his board. All hands were shaken before Quartano invited their guests into the yacht's saloon where he offered them a drink. Small talk ensued for several minutes before the Chinese visitors were invited to sit in the nest of elegant art deco armchairs. Monaco's harbour, yachts, hillside, and morning sun were visible through the picture windows all around them.

'Dr Chen,' said Quartano running a hand through his mane of silver hair. 'We are honoured that Mandarin Telecom is prepared to consider sponsoring the Ptarmigan Formula One Team. Mr Callom has prepared a presentation to indicate the benefits we feel this would bring your company. Before he elaborates, I'd very much like to offer you a few preliminary observations of my own.'

Dr Chen took a sip of his orange juice and gave a perfunctory nod.

'Mandarin Telecom is exceptionally well placed to break out of China and establish a global presence. Your mobile phone technology is leading-edge, while your distinctive style – embodied in your eye-catching handset design – resonates well with younger consumers all over the world. China chic, we would call it. We've conducted extensive market testing which we're keen to show you,' said Quartano as he looked over his shoulder as the cue to one of his aides. A weighty, bound document, emblazoned with Mandarin Telecom and Ptarmigan logos, was soon handed forward. Quartano took it and smiled his thanks.

Dr Chen's attention appeared to lock on to the research document, seeming surprised that Quartech should have done so much work – unprompted – in advance. The effect was not lost on Quartano.

'Formula One fits your brand and markets – almost perfectly,' he went on, deliberately placing the document in clear view on the armrest between them. 'Sponsoring Ptarmigan will give you immediate access to the global television audience – put conservatively at 400 million – who watch each race. And, with twenty Grands Prix now on the calendar, the geographic spread of the season would give you a significant advertizing presence in every key consumer market around the world.'

Dr Chen placed his glass on a table decorated with heavy marquetry beside him. 'Mr Quartano,' replied Dr Chen. 'I'm impressed by your appreciation of our marketing needs. However … The 400 million you mention is appealing, hence our interest. But that is for Formula One as a whole. The question we have to answer is why we should sponsor the Ptarmigan Team, and not one of the others?'

Quartano smiled warmly and added with conviction: 'You should sponsor Ptarmigan, Dr Chen – precisely,' he said deliberately pausing for effect – 'because you were … *impressed by our appreciation of your marketing needs.* We do offer something different. Quartech acquired Ptarmigan for business purposes. We see enormous crossover benefits of the team's technological innovation to our other companies – and, *most* importantly, we see huge value in the marketing reach of this sport. We understand – we would say better than any of the teams – that you need to see a substantial commercial return on any sponsorship money you might invest.'

'Ptarmigan was bankrupt at the beginning of this year, Mr Quartano,' offered Dr Chen – verging on a challenge. 'It suffered financial failure, collapsing with sizeable debts.'

'Quite so. Except all that happened before Quartech bought the team. Since then I have replaced the management, bringing in Tahm, here, as one of the world's most respected team bosses in motor racing. I've written off the debt you mentioned and provided the team with a substantial budget – £100 million this year. I've built Ptarmigan a new factory in Oxfordshire. I have made all Quartech's leading-edge technology and management expertise available to the team. We've signed a four-year deal with Benbecular, to supply

Ptarmigan with engines. And, with the recruitment of Remy Sabatino as our number one driver, not only have we risen close to the top of the Constructors' Championship, but in Sabatino we have a phenomenal communicator and media personality to front the team – widely acknowledged as a major benefit to the sport as a whole.'

Quartano waited until he met the visitor's eye directly. 'Dr Chen,' he continued authoritatively, almost sternly: 'Ptarmigan is going to win this year – because of Quartech. Our backing – technical and financial – sets Ptarmigan apart. We're ready to offer Mandarin Telecom a unique opportunity to be part of this turnaround story – and to help you grow your business around the world on the back of the ground-breaking publicity we are going to generate.'

Quartano, the master negotiator, chose this moment to stop talking.

The yacht's saloon fell silent.

The *Melita* gave the slightest hint of movement in the wash of a passing boat.

Dr Chen looked straight back at Quartano for several seconds. For all his intended Chinese inscrutability it was obvious the power of the message had struck a chord. 'I would be interested to hear more of what you propose,' he said.

Quartano smiled genuinely but with restraint – realizing they had just moved the relationship significantly on. 'Excellent. I'll ask Mr Callom, now, to go through his joint marketing proposal with you.'

'Thank you,' said Dr Chen. 'However, we will want our own marketing department to do an assessment of the television impact of this potential relationship. We have brought a freelance journalist with us. We would ask that he film a test interview with your star driver – and we, ourselves, would like to meet Remy Sabatino.'

THREE

Matt Straker was looking forward to that meeting too. While only a casual motor racing fan, he was well aware – through mainstream press and television coverage – of its more prominent figures. Getting to meet someone he had only known through the media was an intriguing prospect. What would Sabatino be like in real life? he wondered.

Within the hour, Straker and Quartano were walking the Mandarin Telecom directors along the Monaco pit lane towards the Ptarmigan garage. Bernie Callom's presentation seemed to have gone down well; the Chinese businessmen had not flinched when – at the end of it – Quartano put a price tag of $750 million on their proposed three-year deal.

For Quartech, given the capital it was risking to back Ptarmigan, the Mandarin Telecom sponsorship would be a sizeable payback and represent a substantial – and rapid – return. But that wasn't Quartano's "deal".

Quartano had been trying to break the Chinese defence market for years. Commercially, of far more value to him was the access this relationship could afford his company to the highest level of the Chinese business community: Mandarin Telecom's client list included every organization that meant anything in China. And of those, Quartano's holy grail was the PRC's Ministry of National Defense. Through the Mandarin relationship, and Ptarmigan's corporate hospitality, he expected to find himself in a unique position to promote the full range of Quartech's defence equipment and satellite services to the largest military organization on the planet.

Quartano would not have been able to capitalize on any opportunity Ptarmigan might create had the car and team not been competitive. That made the biggest decision he had taken even more rewarding.

His choice of leading driver.

A few moments later, even at the modest limiter-speed of eighty kilometres per hour, the bright turquoise Ptarmigan Formula One car seemed to hurtle down the pit lane towards them. Its noise was overwhelming. Sabatino swerved deftly into the bay – as in a racing pit stop – but instead of the crew diving in around the car, the engine was soon cut. The driver unfastened the steering wheel, and started to climb out.

Sabatino released the elastic straps of the HANS device on either side of the helmet, took it off, then undid the Velcro at the top of the turquoise tunic to pull the fire-retardant balaclava up and over the head. Straker watched the striking features of Remy Sabatino appear – before she ran a hand through her short, nut-brown hair, set her black-rimmed glasses squarely on her face, tugged out her earplugs, turned to face Quartano and acknowledged his presence with a nod of her head and a flash of her dark brown eyes. She signalled politely with a hand gesture that she would be with him shortly before pointing rapidly back and forth between herself and her race engineer. Half-turning away, she spoke with Andy Backhouse, a squat British man in his forties with dark thinning hair, hairy arms, and heavy glasses – who had just joined her from the pit wall.

'I'm getting understeer into Mirabeau and Rascasse,' she stated. 'Hoped it was just a dirty surface, and would rubber up. That's not happening. The track's still pretty green.'

Backhouse nodded and then squinted badly against the head-splitting screech of a car flying down the straight on the other side of the pits behind them. 'The fronts were cooler than we thought. That's why we suggested the brake trim,' he said in his pronounced Birmingham accent. 'Why didn't you make the adjustment?'

Sabatino looked surprised. 'What trim?'

'I radioed you down into Mirabeau.'

'Never heard a word of it. All I got was static. You kept cutting out. Interference.'

'That's weird,' said Backhouse. 'That radio's brand-new – we've only just replaced all its circuitry – since Bahrain.'

Sabatino noticed the unexpected expression on her race engineer's face. 'Can we check it over, then? We don't want that happening again.'

'Sure…' he said, regaining his focus, '…and, on the tyres, we're already checking the temperatures with the manufacturer.'

'If they're going to stay that cool, can we warm them by dropping a PSI or two – and try a click on the front wing?'

Sabatino smiled her thanks to Backhouse before breaking away to meet Quartano and his guests, now standing in front of the team's garage. 'Sorry about that, Mr Q – nearly always better to be debriefed immediately afterwards, while it's still fresh.'

Quartano gave her a that's-no-problem smile – before saying proudly to his visitors: 'Gentlemen, may I present Ms Remy Sabatino of Malta, Ptarmigan's number one driver, currently lying second in the Drivers' Championship.'

Most of the Chinese directors smiled coyly and bowed even more politely than usual. Sabatino, at five feet two, was easily absorbed into the gaggle of Chinese businessmen as she shook hands and acknowledged them all individually.

'Remy, we've had a promising discussion with our friends about Mandarin Telecom sponsoring Ptarmigan.'

Sabatino nodded and smiled directly at each man in turn. Dr Chen and his colleagues smiled back.

'They have asked that Mr Li, here, a freelance journalist, might record an interview with you to be evaluated by their marketeers back home?'

Sabatino nodded immediately. 'Sure. How about now? Would now be good?'

'Excellent,' replied Quartano. 'Tahm, can we find them space somewhere inside the garage?'

Five minutes later Mr Li had set up his camera, tripod and cameraman ready to begin the recording. Sabatino, perching on a stack of her tyres, faced the group of businessmen who were semicircled around her.

'Miss Sabatino,' said Mr Li somewhat formally, in heavily accented English. 'How are you coping as the first woman driver in Formula One?'

Sabatino smiled broadly. 'Actually, Mr Li, I'm not the first. There have been several. Italy had two – Maria Teresa de Filippis in the 1950s and Lella Lombardi in the 1970s. Divina Galica, British, was also on the scene in the mid-70s, around the same time that South Africa's Desiré Wilson competed at her home Grand Prix. More recently, Giovanna Amati drove for Brabham in the early 1990s.'

'But how many of them won any races?' asked Mr Li dismissively. 'None.'

The journalist seemed to sneer: 'Doesn't that prove you're at a disadvantage – being a lady driver?'

With a dazzle of her trademark smile, Sabatino said: 'I'm lying second in the Championships – you tell me, Mr Li,' and gave him a wink. Then, a little more seriously, she added: 'As with most things, it comes down to technique, feel and judgement. I have a degree in engineering, so I understand the car. I've won races in everything from karts to GP2, so am comfortable with my car control. And judgement? Well, I negotiated myself into the best seat on the grid, so I'm pretty happy with that too, Mr Li.'

Straker revelled in the way Sabatino handled herself. He had seen her sparkle many times on TV but it was clear that her charisma wasn't some kind of media affectation or any sort of favouritism the camera bestowed on some people. Her televisual and media personality – a major component of any prospective sponsorship package and, therefore, a significant part of its overall value – was completely authentic.

'And what about physical strength?' continued the Chinese journalist, sounding slightly irritated at her nonchalant, unforgiving answers.

Sabatino maintained her smile while a little forced patience crept into her voice. 'There's a physical difference between men and women, sure. Strength, of course. Stamina, perhaps. With semi-automatic gearboxes these days – worked by fingers on the steering wheel – we don't need heavy foot-operated clutches anymore. For the steering and brakes, the car has to carry a certain amount of hydraulics, anyway – even to help the men – so we tweak them a little. As for increasing stamina and resistance to G-force, etc., methodical preparation can condition anyone. After all, it's *women* who have the strength to give birth, Mr Li – not men.'

Sabatino gave the interviewer a thanks-for-asking-and-enjoy-the-rest-of-your-day kind of smile; she looked up to see the enthralled faces of the Chinese directors who had been listening attentively.

Quartano smiled with barely-contained pride.

Behind them another figure approached, also wearing the striking turquoise livery of the Ptarmigan Team. 'Ah, Helli!' said Quartano warmly, offering his hand. 'Let me introduce you to some of our friends?' and turning to the group of Chinese businessmen, Quartano added: 'May I present Herr Helmut Cunzer, from the Republic of Germany – Ptarmigan's esteemed number two driver.'

Helli Cunzer, a pint-sized man in his twenties with fine facial features, bronzed skin, and close-cropped blond hair, gave their guests a boyish smile. 'Helli came to the team having been runner-up in the GP2 Championship last year. We have great hopes for his phenomenal talent.'

Cunzer, yet to be spoiled by the attention and praise of Formula One success, smiled again, not quite sure how to take the compliment. 'Thank you, Mr Quartano.'

To save him any further embarrassment, Quartano suggested that Cunzer and Nazar show the Mandarin Telecom directors around the rest of the garage. The Chinese gentlemen nodded enthusiastically, not least with so much to see going on all around them.

After they moved off, Quartano turned and said: 'Remy, you won't have met Matt Straker – who works with me in London.'

Sabatino turned and, looking up to Straker's six-feet-two frame, shook hands politely. 'So you're the army guy Tahm was talking about?'

Straker smiled back less than fully, slightly unsure why she had chosen to pick up on his military background. 'Was ... with the Royal Marines.'

'That's just what we want,' Sabatino said looking at him intently, '*more* testosterone around here.'

'Matt's a colleague of Charlie's,' Quartano chipped in.

Sabatino's expression palled slightly. 'I was sorry to hear the news. Tragic. It's been hard to imagine such an accident. Easier here, maybe,' she said with a flourish of her hand indicating Formula One, 'but not out on the road.'

Straker must have looked momentarily nonplussed as Quartano quickly volunteered: 'Such a waste to be killed by a drunk driver.'

So that was the line, thought Straker. Whatever the deceit, it had to be easier – and quicker – than the truth.

'We all liked her. She seemed very *popular*,' said Sabatino with the flick of an eyebrow.

'So I gather,' said Straker. 'I'm hoping to pick up where she left off.'

Sabatino studied his expression with exaggerated curiosity, before giving him a look that indicated they both really ought to know that was going to be unlikely.

Andy Backhouse reappeared. 'Mr Quartano?' he said as an apology for butting in. 'Remy – the tyre people are doing some more work for us. Meantime, they're happy with your idea of dropping two PSI on the fronts, and we'll combine that with your suggestion of a click on the front wing.'

Sabatino nodded her approval. 'Great. We'll give it a try in a mo',' and, nodding her exit from Quartano and Straker, disappeared into the back of the garage.

Once Backhouse had called out the adjustments to his mechanics around Sabatino's car, Quartano introduced him to Straker as Ptarmigan's new Competition Intelligence and Security officer – the replacement for Charlie.

'So you're the company spook?' said Backhouse in his Brummie accent.

'I expect to feel right at home here,' Straker said with a smile, 'given how much you all spy on each other already.'

'Ah, yes. On the back of things like the Spygate scandal, perhaps, it's not difficult to see why you might think that!'

Straker accepted the concession with a smile.

'Well, I'm glad to have you with us,' said Backhouse genuinely. 'I've heard great things about what you do. When do you want to get started?'

FOUR

It was vivid – so vivid. It always was. Cold – freezing, blustering air. He could feel it cut his skin – could hear it whistling all around him.

Then came the blinding lights. Thunderous – body-shaking – sounds. Screaming people. People dying. *His* lights, his sounds. His doing.

The scream of ground-attack aircraft – four Tornado – howling into the valley below. Condensation clouds and vortices flowed along their wings – as they rolled and skimmed between the craggy mountains – flying between the narrow valley walls towards the tented camp. Seconds later there was a series of brilliant flashes and explosions. The tented camp on the hillside plateau, the suspension bridge, were destroyed, collapsing down into the furious river hundreds of feet below. The air strike was working – the Taliban resupply caravan, strung out for several miles along the pass, was strafed. Taken out. Only a handful of surviving Afghans attempting to flee, desperately trying to scramble away up the steep sides of the valley.

The aircraft and their noise soon faded into the distance.

Then a different sound.

A deep thumping beat – echoing, bouncing off the mountains – the unmistakable thump of helicopter blades. He could even feel them now. Only one kind of aircraft made that sound: the awesome double-rotored Chinook. Three dark, sinister shapes swooped in along the Pakistani valley, noses up, looking to put down. Snow and sand swirled up as they hovered above the small plateau and remnants of the Taliban's camp. Doors opened. Sticks of the 506th Infantry Regiment – part of the 101st Airborne Division – debussed, fanned out and laid down fire at the fleeing Afghans.

The Screaming Eagles set about taking the valley floor.

Now his mission was over, extraction by helicopter had to be a whole lot quicker and easier than his planned two-hundred-mile yomp down through the foothills.

He felt his hands rising above his head. He gingerly broke cover – indicating his presence to the US fighting patrol.

No! he screamed, as if to try and stop it all – now that he knew what was coming.

It was no use.

He felt he was looking down on himself, from somewhere above. A figure dressed in native Afghan clothes – with twenty days of beard and rank body smell – was approaching the US soldiers. Shouting heatedly, four of the Americans kept him covered – rifles aimed directly at his head and chest – while the figure, as he now saw himself, was cajoled and manhandled down off the mountain side.

He heard the first of the deep southern accents. The 506th company commander didn't buy his identity, role – as a Forward Air Controller – or even his dog tags, dismissing such "props" as to-be-expected fakes, with a tone of do-you-think-we-were-born-yesterday. He then saw himself roughly hooded, bound, and thrown up and onto the floor of a Chinook.

Water – now there was water – gushing water. He fought to breathe. Cold water filling his mouth, hitting the back of his throat, flowing up his nose. He started to choke. He coughed violently. Couldn't clear it.

How and why? The water stopped. The coughing was all-consuming. He still couldn't breathe properly. He was gasping. Gagging.

That southern accent came back to haunt him: 'You look Taliban. You talk Taliban. You were picked up near a Taliban patrol. Mister, if something looks like an elephant, moves like an elephant, and shits like an elephant – hey, it's probably an elephant.'

Water gushed again. Then came the horrific cycle: water, gasping, barked questions, protest; water, gasping, barked questions, protest. How long was this going to go on?

Matt Straker lurched bolt upright. His heart pounding, thumping in his chest, neck and ears. His chest was also heaving, heavily and quickly, his breath rasping through his nose, mouth and teeth.

Why did he keep reliving this? Why the fuck couldn't he shake it off?

Any torture was bad – bad enough. But his torture seemed worse.

Tortured by his own side.

The intelligence-equivalent of friendly fire.

Cretinous stupidity.

He opened his eyes.

Darkness. Looking into the blackness, he saw a hint of light bleeding round the edges of the curtains – it was plainly night time. Over the throbbing in his ears, he couldn't hear anything. Straker breathed in hard, held his breath, trying to hear better. Nothing. There seemed to be nothing to hear. If anything, he thought he detected a low gentle hum – the hum of a building asleep. His breathing started again, back up to rapid.

Straker's circumstances and location began to dawn on him. He looked across at the glow from the electric alarm clock by his bed. Three forty-two a.m.

Fuck.

His heart still pounded. Angrily, he threw back the covers, and became aware of the dampness of the sheets. Swinging his legs over the side of the bed to stand up, he felt the cooling effect from even that limited movement – confirmation that he was covered in sweat. As he stood up, cold beads of moisture rolled down his temples, chest, onto his flanks from under his arms, and into the small of his back.

Still in the dark, Straker walked across the large high-ceilinged room, making for the tall curtains, and heaved them apart. Fiddling with the ornate Charles III latches and handle, he opened the heavy glass-panelled double doors, and let himself out onto the balcony.

The night air was surprisingly warm – much warmer than the air conditioning inside had been. A gentle breeze blew into his face and across his chest, coming off the vast dark void of the Mediterranean, which stretched away into the night beyond the darkened roofs of Monte-Carlo below him. Fiercely gripping the wrought-iron railings of the balcony with both hands, Straker continued to breathe deeply, trying to calm himself down.

The principality was quiet. Sound asleep.

Lights, mainly on the outside of buildings and along the streets, were burning – the more distant ones seeming to flicker in the humidity. Traffic could be heard, but was so slight he could even hear individual cars in different directions at the same time. Gradually, his heart rate and breathing began to slow.

Straker knew comrades had returned from active tours with limbs and faculties missing, and continued to suffer physical disability and pain. He knew he was lucky. Even so, his experiences and subsequent trauma had not been without their painful consequences. They had cost him his career – even his marriage.

Civvy Street should have signified a new beginning, particularly his recruitment by Quartech. Working for its Competition Intelligence and Security team looked like filling a large part of the gap left after resigning his commission in the Royal Marines. His new role was certainly stimulating – it demanded imagination, intelligence, resourcefulness, persistence and the taking of calculated risks. Contributing further to this sense of recovery, Straker's first assignment for Dominic Quartano – salvaging a multi-billion-pound weapons contract with a Middle Eastern state – had been a triumph. So, fuck it, why the regression now? Why tonight?

Standing on the balcony overlooking dark and sleeping Monte-Carlo, he tried to make sense of the episode. In therapy, he had been encouraged not to see each episode as a flashback to the original emotional scarring – but to see any such reversion being triggered by more recent troubles. Straker went through his encounters, conversations, experiences and feelings of the previous day, as he had been taught.

What, then, had caused this?

He could only conclude one thing.

This relapse *had* to have been tripped subconsciously by the mention, yesterday, of someone's name.

Charlotte – "Charlie" – Grant.

FIVE

Straker found it impossible to get back to sleep that morning. Rarely, if ever after such an episode, could he do so. He knew that, invariably, his only solace under this torment was to purge his soul through the pain of physical exertion. At half-past four in the morning he found himself – like so many times before – out in the darkness, trying to run off the disturbance in solitude. This time, it just happened to be along the streets and across the hillsides of Monte-Carlo.

As they went, this attack had been a bad one. Despite the energy expended in his two-hour run, its effects completely suppressed his appetite.

Not having any interest in breakfast, Straker dragged himself down to the harbour, still fighting to regain his composure – barely even noticing the Riviera paradise all around him.

As arranged, Backhouse was waiting for him at the main entrance to the paddock. Engagement with the race engineer was Straker's first proper distraction following the episode.

Walking along the waterfront on the western side of the harbour, they passed down the line of the teams' massive and jaw-droppingly expensive motor homes and mobile headquarters. Ptarmigan's own – an articulated eighteen wheeler with extendable sides and smoked-glass windows – was dressed overall in the team's brilliant turquoise livery.

Punching a code into the security key pad, its door hissed open; Backhouse led Straker up and into Ptarmigan's mobile command centre – equipped as high-tech as a moveable platform could allow. The team set-up was impressive. Straker was relieved it was all so engrossing. His mood began to change significantly for the first time that morning.

Everything in the motor home was striking – it was decked out in rosewood, chrome and glass, with pale turquoise-coloured leather seating, edged with navy blue piping. Down one side, a row of eight turquoise-liveried team members sat at a bench-like desk that ran the full length of the truck. Each member wore a set of Ptarmigan-branded headphones and sat at a console, with a keyboard and bank of plasma screens in front and above them. It looked to Straker like a – small-scale – cross between Mission Control and a City dealing floor. A meeting table ran down the other side of the truck, surrounded by a curved bench.

'Let me introduce you to Oliver Treadwell, Ptarmigan's Strategy Director, who'll run through what's going on,' Backhouse said. Treadwell was in his thirties, slightly shorter than Straker's six two, and had a mop of blond hair. Straker moved forward to shake hands.

'For the race on Sunday, we have the prat perch – our command centre – on the pit wall,' said the Strategy Director in a noticeable Australian burr. 'But this set-up, in here, is our eyes and ears on the track and pit lane in the build-up to the race. We collect all the data and information we need to decide our drivers' race strategy – the number of pit stops, what kind of tyres to use, and when.'

Straker's eyes ran over the array of screens. CCTV pictures from the Ptarmigan cars were displayed, along with various digital channels from the sport's commercial rights holder.

'These guys here,' Treadwell indicated, bracketing them with outstretched arms, 'are watching all the telemetry from both our cars on these screens. We can measure, remotely via on-board sensors, upwards of two hundred and fifty aspects of the car – temperature, pressures, loading, etc. – and all this real-time data can be called up instantly via our touch-screen menu system.'

'So who's that?' asked Straker, pointing to a face shown on a video conferencing screen with whom one of the team was clearly conversing.

'That's the factory back at Shenington, in Oxfordshire. All the data we collect is simultaneously fired back there and fed into a simulator. We then extrapolate all the discernable trends on the cars while they're racing to see what effects they could have. Those findings, too, help us adjust our strategies and, hopefully, afford us better reliability and performance.'

Treadwell used his arms again. 'These two guys are monitoring the weather. Rain's our biggest concern, although we're hopefully looking okay this weekend. Even so, atmospheric pressure, temperature, humidity and wind speed all have a huge influence on the workings of the cars. So, we monitor the weather closely and adjust our set-up accordingly.

'And here,' said Treadwell walking further down the row of consoles to the far end, 'is our Intel headquarters. All the teams keep an eye on what the other teams are up to. These guys are trying to work out the strategies – number of pit stops – the other teams will adopt for the race, while over here,' he said pointing with splayed fingers at a bank of recorders, 'we aim to collect every bit of VT footage of all the other cars and their crews – filmed by ourselves or captured from the official broadcaster, whether external or on-board. We then collate, scrutinize and analyse everything we can. Assessments will be made of any unexpected components – or actions by drivers or crews – that we notice, any of which might give away an innovation they might have made. We also record the engine noise of every car for analysis, and listen for anything unusual. And then, when we do come across something interesting, we brief our director of the relevant aspect – engines, gearbox, brakes, fuel, tyres, aerodynamics, pit crew, strategy – showing them what we've found.'

'All *very* sportsmanlike.'

'Yeah!' said Treadwell with an exaggerated tone of Australian. 'Everyone does it, though, so I guess it's a level playing field.'

'Anything interesting come up recently?'

'Kind of. We think Massarella's diffuser is non-compliant. We've written to them about it this morning – and are waiting to hear back.'

That evening Straker was invited by Quartano to join the Ptar-migan Team in hosting Dr Chen of Mandarin Telecom at a gala dinner held in the Casino in Monte-Carlo. Although not officially connected with motor racing, this was now *the* annual charity fixture of the Monaco Grand Prix weekend, attended by everyone who was anyone in Formula One.

Dressed in black tie, the Quartech party alighted in front of the institution which first put the principality on the map. What greeted them outside the Casino seemed more like a night of film-industry awards than a fund-raiser. Red carpet ran from the kerb to the main entrance. Banks of photographers were corralled down one side, while television cameras and glamorous TV presenters were gushing down the other.

Once inside, and between the marble columns of the baroque atrium, they were met by the official receiving line and presented to His Serene Highness. Quartano conversed with the Prince and introduced Dr Chen, Nazar and Straker. After a polite but formal welcome, they moved on down the line.

Quartano then introduced his party to the President of the Fédération Internationale de l'Automobile – FIA – the interna-tional governing body of motor sport and the organization that set the "Formula". Straker thought Bo Mirabelli, the Marquis of San Marino, one of the most patrician and distinguished looking men he had ever met. Mid-sixties with wise, piercing blue eyes, and swept-back hair off his round forehead, he had the appearance of a 1950s Hollywood star. But looks weren't Bo San Marino's only appeal. Famed for his charm, he greeted Dr Chen and Straker as if they were long-lost friends, investing their conversation with that rare gift of making it seem the most important moment of the evening.

After Bo San Marino, Quartano introduced them to the other power axis in motor racing – the boss of the commercial rights holder and, therefore, the controller of the multi-billion-dollars-a-year Formula One revenues. As head of the recently formed Motor Racing Promotions Limited, Joss MacRae was, indirectly, the successor to the legendary Bernie Ecclestone. By way of a briefing beforehand, Nazar told Straker that MacRae had been a former PR director with two of the teams in the paddock. He had taken over as the Tsar of Formula One, having been lauded for breaking the key Asian markets – India and China – in the early noughties. Nazar was not so generous in crediting MacRae with such achievement. He attributed the breakthrough in Asia to have been more down to necessity – down to Formula One's desperation at losing the bulk of its revenue from the then impending Europe-wide ban on tobacco advertizing.

Straker was also told that MacRae had been involved with a Finnish rally driver. Nobody knew he was gay until news broke over the internet, despite – but probably because of – the superinjunction MacRae had taken out in the UK. Straker did not take to him at all. MacRae was all over Dr Chen and Nazar to the point of being obsequious, but there was none of the genuine warmth of San Marino, while, he, Straker – an unknown – was barely acknowledged.

Twenty minutes later the five hundred guests were invited through into the majestic setting for dinner – the Salon de l'Europe. There, they were surrounded by onyx columns, endless gilding, and were dazzled by the eight – vast – Bohemian crystal chandeliers.

On the way to their table, the Quartech party encountered the bosses of two other teams. The first was the Earl of Lambourn, owner of Lambourn Grand Prix.

'Dom, my dear fellow,' said Lambourn to Quartano genuinely. 'Wonderful to see you.'

Straker instantly warmed to Lambourn – and detected an authentic friendship between him, Quartano and Nazar.

Straker had read countless articles on Lord Lambourn over the years. The British press seemed obsessed with him, probably because he was the very last of a dying breed – the dashing, playboy aristocrat – able, through the good luck of birth, to indulge his passion for cars, speed and women. He was tall, slim, with a full head of well-groomed hair and had the easy manner and effortless conversation of a natural host. Suave was definitely the word. Lambourn offered his hand with a gentle bow, saying: 'Dr Chen, I'm delighted to meet you. Thank you, sir, for gracing our sport, should you decide to do so. Ptarmigan is one of the finest marques in motor racing. I hope you enjoy a successful association, and that Formula One serves to grow your brand around the world.'

Dr Chen, somewhat thrown by Lambourn's lack of competitiveness – particularly as one of his drivers was leading the Drivers' Championship – gave a slightly confused smile indicating, perhaps, that he did not quite understand the English.

Moving on through the dining room Quartano encountered another team principal. He introduced his party to the Afrikaner Eugene Van Der Vaal, team boss of Massarella.

Dr Chen shook hands.

'You don't want to be wasting your money on Ptarmigan,' said Van Der Vaal without levity, his guttural Boerish accent giving his comments a barbed and abrasive edge.

Straker likened Van Der Vaal, with his closely-shaved head and broad physique, to a rugby prop forward. His brutish expression added to the look. Word had it that he never smiled – let alone laughed – unless it was at someone else's expense.

'Britain is old world,' said Van Der Vaal. 'Tired, complacent and of the past.'

Straker was getting a first-hand feel for why the team bosses might have been referred to en masse as "the Piranha Club". Quartano's composure, however, did not waver for a second. 'That's very interesting,' he said to the Massarella man. Turning to his guest, he said: 'And yet, Dr Chen, isn't it strange that all of Mr Van Der Vaal's key team members – Massarella's COO, designer, and both race engineers – happen to be British.'

Dr Chen's face broke into a smile. This, perhaps, was a bit more like it. 'We Chinese, Mr Valley, have an old saying for someone who says one thing … and does another…'

It was Quartano's, Nazar's, and Straker's turn to smile.

Reaching their table, Straker and Quartano were left alone for a moment while Nazar escorted Dr Chen to find a lavatory. The tycoon, certain they could not be overheard, turned and asked discreetly: 'How are you holding up, Matt?'

Straker shook his head. 'Fine,' he said dismissively.

Quartano looked at him carefully, almost intently.

Straker found himself turning away. 'Incidentally,' he said, looking back towards one of their encounters on the way in, 'talking of Massarella – Ollie Treadwell said he had written to them this morning about their diffuser. What does *writing to* mean, exactly?'

Quartano smiled and raised an eyebrow, inhaling deeply. 'This is a funny – and I mean funny-peculiar – sport. It's best to remember that, in reality, Matt, Fı's more or less – no, I'd say largely – about rules. The interpretation of rules.'

'Largely?'

'Without the rules – or the *Formula* – a Grand Prix car could easily do over three hundred miles an hour and pull so much G-force round the corners that the drivers would actually black out. Modern cars are not primarily limited by physics or the laws of nature. They're limited by arbitrary, man-made rules. Interpretation of those rules, therefore, is everything.'

'Doesn't that make the limits rather subjective?'

'Oh, completely. Because of this, a number of teams have signed the equivalent of non-aggression pacts. Massarella's signed one with nearly every team, including Ptarmigan. If either party believes the other is pushing the rules for unfair advantage, these agreements are meant to encourage resolution of a dispute between themselves – bilaterally – before anyone runs off to the FIA to bad mouth the other in public.'

'Do they do any good?'

'Hardly. They're like signing an NDA – they're more about declaring an intent than a legal bond.'

'How many times do they get exercised?'

'Between us and the other teams – never.'

'So what's with Massarella's diffuser? Why've we thought it significant?'

'No idea. And I'd be quite sure it isn't. If it *is*, then, what the hell, the FIA stewards in Parc Fermé will pick it up.'

'So why bother *write* to them at all?'

Quartano's lived-in face broke into a contended, mischievous smile. 'Massarella never stop whingeing, sniping and causing trouble. We use their stupid pact to yank their chain from time to time.'

Dr Chen returned and was introduced by Quartano to the other guests at their table before a fanfare heralded the Prince's arrival into the dining room.

Straker's pang of conscience, over not being able to justify his presence in the luxury of Monaco – let alone his concern about how this assignment could use his particular skills – was about to be shattered.

SIX

During coffee and port Straker was distracted by his phone vibrating. Looking down at the screen he saw a message from Andy Backhouse:

Can you come to HQ urgently? Something you need to see...

Straker showed this to Quartano, who, reading the message, encouraged him to go.

Still wearing black tie, Straker strode round Monte-Carlo harbour in the balmy evening humidity. Soothed by the gentle breeze off the Mediterranean, he made the Ptarmigan headquarters truck down by the waterfront twenty minutes later. Just before midnight.

From the outside, Straker could see little more than dim light through the smoked-glass windows. Inside, he found the lighting matched by the mood. Backhouse sat alone at the small meeting table. 'Matt, thanks for coming. I need you to look at this.'

Backhouse held out his hand to offer Straker a tiny object. 'Yesterday afternoon – in practice – Remy complained of a crackling radio. Our signal kept breaking up. It seriously affected our ability to make adjustments to Remy's car. As a result, I went through all her radio circuitry. While I was lifting it all out, I found this.'

Straker squinted, given its modest size. 'It looks like some kind of chip?'

'It's a transponder.'

'Hang on ... why do you say *found*? It's not one of ours?'

'Absolutely not.'

'Where was it?'

'Hidden in the foam lining of Remy's helmet.'

Backhouse could not miss the change in Straker's expression. There was suddenly a gleam in the hooded eyes.

'I thought you encrypted your radio traffic,' said Straker.

'We do. But that wasn't wired to our system – it wasn't transmitting *from* her circuitry.'

'You mean it was picking up her voice independently?'

'Being halfway between her mouth and right earpiece – it would have been able to hear and relay her incoming traffic too.'

'Somebody's been listening in?'

'But that's not all,' said Backhouse. 'The reason we were looking at the radio circuitry in the first place was because Remy complained of radio crackle. Matt, the radio crackle was *not* a malfunction.'

Straker's eyes widened. 'You mean it was induced?'

Backhouse nodded slowly. 'By that device.'

'She was *jammed*?'

'It disrupted her radio signal, yes. Yesterday afternoon we were jammed. Matt, if we are jammed in the race – preventing us from making tactical, ad hoc adjustments – it would be absolutely critical to our chances. It could be catastrophic.'

'You're saying, then, our communications were *sabotaged*?'

'I am.'

Backhouse went on to say something else but Straker's mind was whirring. 'Hang on. Was this blanket jamming?'

'Meaning?'

'Was it constant or intermittent?'

'Intermittent. On and off – come to think of it – whenever I talked.'

'Only when *you* talked?'

'Yep.'

'So it was being activated deliberately each time.'

'Seemed that way.'

Straker looked pensive. 'Do we know if these people – whoever they are – have got other ways to do us harm?'

Backhouse's face registered the sinister implications. He shook his head.

'Then we've no idea if this is our only foreign body on either car,' said Straker. 'First off – and absolutely critically – we have *got* to double-check everything, before Remy or Helli get in them again.'

The Race Engineer nodded at the unpleasant corollary of Straker's logic. 'Of course. I'll bring the guys back in right away.'

'Don't tell them why. No one's to know there's a sabotage threat. We've got to be careful who *does* know about this – it could cause suspicion and mistrust, and seriously damage team morale. Can you invent some other reason why the cars might need a total examination?'

'I'll come up with some paranoia about the FIA.'

'Good. We've no time to lose.'

Backhouse, grabbing his phone, started ringing people, waking them up, calling them in from bars around town – down to the garage – to start going over both cars immediately. When he finished the call-out procedure he returned his attention to Straker. He could see the other was still deep in thought.

'I take it you have no idea who's behind this?' Straker asked distantly, before looking up.

Backhouse shook his head emphatically.

'Have you found the activation frequency of the bug?' Straker asked.

'Of its transmissions? Yes.'

'No, I mean the frequency that activates the jamming signal.'

Backhouse looked blank. 'Why would we? Better we've found it and got rid of it.'

Straker gently shook his head. 'Do we know who put this there?'

'No.'

'Exactly. We've got to find out who's behind this.'

Backhouse nodded tentatively, knowing he should agree, but he wasn't quite sure how knowing the jamming frequency was linked to identifying the perpetrators.

'Okay,' said Straker, delicately handing the bug back to Backhouse. 'Here's what we're going to do. I want you to find the activation frequency. Then, I want you to put this thing back *exactly* where you found it.'

SEVEN

Straker phoned Quartano immediately. It was ten to one in the morning. He was still at the charity dinner. Quartano was incandescent at the news.

'Bloody Charlie. I don't mind being beaten fair and square. To eavesdrop on our team is bad enough. But to try and sabotage us is something else. Out*rage*ous.'

'Charlie could well be the culprit,' said Straker calmly. 'She'd certainly be the most obvious choice – and most convenient – but we can't be sure yet. If it was her, then we don't know whether this was her only legacy, or whether she was working with someone else on the inside? One thing's for certain: that bug could only have been planted by an insider. She's out of the picture, now, and can't do any more damage – so we'll only know it was her if we don't suffer any further incidents. But, we do know someone else *is* involved.'

'How?'

'From Backhouse's description of the jamming yesterday, it wasn't blanket. It sounds like somebody was manually activating the interference each time.'

Quartano grunted at the logic. 'What's your plan for combating this?'

'To keep news and discussion of it as quiet as possible. We don't want to give the saboteurs any warning that we know about them. I don't want to frighten them off before we find out who they are – and we get the chance to nail them.'

'Who knows about this so far?'

'You, me and Backhouse. We'll have to tell Tahm and the drivers.'

'Okay, and you'll also need to tell Treadwell.'

Straker hummed. 'If you're sure about him?'

Quartano grunted. 'What else are you planning?'

Straker didn't miss a beat. 'Generally, heightened vigilance all round. I've suggested to Backhouse that we do a full examination of both cars before Qualifying – which is happening as we speak – but the guys have not been told why.'

'Good.'

'And my own priority,' Straker went on, 'is to set up a range of countermeasures – and to try and trace whoever operated that device.'

'You can do that?'

'Yes, sir. Ironically, we're in luck the bug in Remy's helmet *is* a jamming device. Had they simply been listening in, that bug would only have needed to be a transmitter and it would've been impossible for us to detect a receiver at the other end. Their eavesdropping could have been electronically passive.'

'But being a jammer, they have to send out a signal, of course?'

'Precisely. It's because it is a jamming device – and requires a direct transmission by the operator to activate it – that we have a slim chance of being able to detect that signal and use it to find the saboteur.'

Quartano's tone hardened. 'Do what you have to, Matt, but find them.'

'I'm going to need some Quartech surveillance kit.'

'Whatever you want. Straker, find and stop the people who are sabotaging us. Don't let these bastards do *anything* to risk that sponsorship and market access to China.'

For the second night running Straker got inadequate sleep.

His head was spinning. Not just with the sabotage developments, but with the realization that Charlotte Grant could have struck again. Surely the time had now come, he thought, to look at her phone. Sensitivities over invading her privacy were nothing more than an indulgence. After all, she was dead now. And a suspect.

Moving over to the safe in his hotel room, Straker unlocked the door, picked out the sleek black iPhone and made to turn it on. Try as he might, he couldn't prevent images of Charlie appearing in his mind.

How that woman had beguiled him – professionally, in one sense, and sexually, in another. His encounter with her, at the time, had seemed so spontaneous. So innocent.

Straker met her seemingly by accident, or so he thought. He'd been out in Buhran for that first assignment with Quartech. It seemed like luck – luck that he should meet and enjoy talking with a beautiful woman by the poolside of his hotel. After chatting in the afternoon sun for some time, casually – easily – Straker and Charlotte arranged to have dinner.

They got on. Really got on. Straker was transfixed. She was punchy, intelligent, provocative, funny; she could talk about a host of different things, and seemed to have opinions on all of them. Not only that, she was physically captivating too: five eleven, slim, with the smoothest of tanned complexions, long dark hair and radiant grey eyes.

Even in that, their first evening together, Straker's self-control had been sorely tested. There was palpable physical and sexual chemistry between them. Her body language – and tone – implied she was drawn to him, and why not? He was six two with a powerful and obviously fit physique, dark eyes, and a naturally severe expression that indicated confidence and purpose – but which, when he smiled, was transformed to unexpected openness and ready engagement.

Straker's marriage, heavily strained at the time because of the aftermath of his rendition and torture, might have provided a justification of sorts, but he had not succumbed. For the rest of the night following that dinner, though, he had got no sleep, as he mulled, moped, and paced his hotel room thinking about this striking woman.

But that was until he was jolted and even panicked from holding such thoughts. His assignment – and very liberty – was threatened. It became dangerous enough for him to need to get out of that despotic country in a hurry. With all the concentration, urgency and tension that escaping involved, Straker found himself with more pressing matters to think about than a stunning woman he might have met by a pool.

Until – having managed to get out – a few evenings later, completely unannounced, she showed up on his doorstep in London. Straker's wife, by then, had moved out, taking with her the last of the fidelity he felt he still owed her.

He and Charlotte Grant had had an amazing night together. Such passion, such excitement, such arousal – such technique.

And so, to Straker – Charlie and he having been lovers – rooting through her private messages was prompting severe levels of discomfort.

He looked down at her phone. It seemed chock-a-block with emails and texts, too many for him to take in right this minute. He would need to go through all the contents methodically later. Even so, he couldn't help noticing two of the names – at the bottom of two texts – sent just a few days earlier:

Charlie, my darling. Call me when you get in to Monte-Carlo. Can't wait. Budge XX.

While the second one read:

I need a pit stop, my lover! Splash and dash, no? Adi.

Straker felt a consuming stab of jealousy. Charlotte Grant had been having intimate relations with other men. And how! And who! The Lambourn Formula 1 team boss *and* the Massarella Grand Prix driver, Adi Barrantes.

At the same time?

Straker forced himself to concentrate, not easy against his surge of adrenalin and mounting anger. He quickly skimmed through her phone's contacts directory. He wanted to see what other names might be loaded in there, apart from the intimate and painful text messages from Lord Lambourn and the Massarella driver. Indeed there were many, mostly nicknames by the looks of things, but none of them meant anything to Straker. He quickly realized her phone was not going to be of any immediate help.

A little after two-thirty in the morning Straker took a shower, changed into working clothes, and made his way back down to the pit lane.

Walking in from the dark, the Ptarmigan garage – harshly lit by glaring fluorescent lights – was frenetic with activity. Backhouse had secured a special dispensation from the governing body for the team to work overnight. Both cars were being dismantled and their components thoroughly scrutinized, tested by their respective crews for any signs of damage or abnormality.

With all that in hand, Straker worked until daybreak – moving back and forth between the garage and the headquarters truck – to set up his own counter-espionage measures. The jamming device had been replaced in Sabatino's helmet, and confirmed to be still serviceable. The same went for the team's original radio circuitry. Now, though, Straker had advised for a second radio to be installed in both cars, but set on very different frequencies.

To establish the team's other defences, a number of people were woken at godforsaken hours. Some of Quartech's specialist military surveillance equipment, along with the necessary operating teams, was even flown out by chartered plane from England.

As all this was assembled and deployed, Straker was increasingly sure they were ready to fight back.

But he needed something more.

He felt he needed some bait.

Backhouse warned him, though, that this could be a difficult conversation.

EIGHT

'What do you mean – you've put it back?' snapped Sabatino. 'How can it be as serious as you're trying to make it out to be, if you're not getting rid of it?'

Straker and Backhouse were meeting her, in private, first thing the next morning in the cabin of the motor home. 'And what do you mean, you want some *bait*? I've got a car to drive – I don't need the distraction of this sort of spy-game crap.'

Because of Backhouse's advance warning, Straker was not fazed by her reaction. Speaking noticeably softly, he said: 'Doing this is the only chance we've got of identifying the people who are trying to sabotage you.'

Sabatino shook her head. 'You've made a massive leap from the crackle of a defective radio to sabotage. You might be ex-army, but don't think there's an enemy under every bush. I won't be distracted by your need for self-justification.'

Straker smiled tolerantly and simply let the jibe pass. 'The last thing I want is to cause you any distraction. All I need is one ploy – which I've discussed with Andy – and which, in any case, might only be needed when you're coasting, and certainly not when you're racing.'

Backhouse said nothing but looked at Sabatino. Very gently, he nodded, simultaneously indicating his assent and assurance.

'Sorry about that,' said Backhouse to Straker after the meeting broke up. 'Drivers are notoriously focused people. They don't like anything that can possibly distract them.'

Straker patted Backhouse on the shoulder, and went straight back to work.

By mid-morning, nifty negotiation had resulted in two rooftops in different parts of Monte-Carlo being rented, on which a number of direction-finding dishes were quickly erected and tuned to the activation frequency of the bug. Two more dishes were installed on the superstructure of Quartano's yacht, out in the marina.

An hour before the start of Qualifying, Straker was checking his network of equipment. Sitting in the Intel area of the Ptarmigan headquarters truck, he was wearing a pair of headphones, with Sabatino's radio net in one ear, and Helli Cunzer's in the other. In front of him was a computer screen displaying the networked output from the dishes. This showed a wire diagram of the principality – outlines of the buildings in line-of-sight of the Grand Prix circuit, as well as all the boats berthed in the harbour.

Straker's set-up meant that any transmission to activate the bug in Sabatino's helmet ought to be picked up by one or more of his direction-finding receivers. Each detection would then be vectored and instantly shown as a line on his display. Where any two or more such lines triangulated – crossed – that would give him the location, to within a few square metres, of any signal trying to jam their radios. Straker would then be able to plot out, and print off that location on his wire diagram of Monte-Carlo.

At one o'clock that afternoon, Qualifying started.

Straker felt he was ready.

His trap was set.

NINE

Immediately after Qualifying started, there was a surprising lack of activity. For all the anticipation, it felt like an anticlimax. Few cars were in a hurry to get out, and only a handful were even out of their garages. Everyone seemed to be waiting to see what the others would do. This was not unexpected, though. Q1 was not the high-pressure session. For this first round of Qualifying, the drivers only needed to finish in the top sixteen.

Eight minutes in and the level of activity was a very different story. Most of the cars were then out on the track or ready to leave the pit lane. England's Paddy Aston in one of the Lambourns, the current Championship leader on 44 points, set a challenging time. Simi Luciano from Italy, Massarella's number one driver, soon went six tenths faster, while the Argentinean Adi Barrantes in the other Massarella was clearly struggling with a poor set-up. Straker, watching the main TV broadcast pictures, saw a fleeting shot from a camera zooming in for a close-up of team boss Eugene Van Der Vaal's face. The Afrikaner was clearly not impressed by the way one of his cars was performing.

Midway into the qualifying session Remy Sabatino headed out onto the circuit. The air was warm and humid. She put on a burst of acceleration up through Beau Rivage to bring the car up to temperature, and felt content. Aerodynamically, the car was performing well. And by the time she rounded the corner at Mirabeau, she was reassured their adjustments of yesterday afternoon were mitigating the understeer. It hadn't gone completely, though.

Straker switched his TV channel to the on-board camera above Sabatino's helmet. As she coaxed the car round the out-lap, he saw her rolling her head gently, flexing her neck and relaxing her shoulders. The car accelerated and braked in rapid succession; he then saw

Sabatino weave extra violently left and right through the Chicane – trying to work temperature into her tyres and brakes.

As Sabatino approached Tabac in the middle of the harbour complex, Backhouse's voice came up over the radio: 'You've got a window in thirty seconds. There's traffic around Loews, but by the time you're hot they'll be long gone.'

Straker began to feel himself drawn into the live picture of the road ahead as Sabatino cranked up the pace around the Swimming Pool. Pulling up the hill after La Rascasse, she shot past a Ferrari and a Lambourn peeling off into the pits. Through Anthony Noghès, into the pit straight, she floored the throttle and let the Ptarmigan go.

Because of the suspected sabotage, Straker couldn't help but feel apprehensive. He watched the TV picture even more closely, listening out intently over the radio for any kind of trouble.

The car was clearly on top of its game.

Sabatino went two tenths up in the first sector, four tenths up in the second and, even with a minor lift to pass a Red Bull around La Rascasse, still clocked up the fastest time of the weekend so far.

At the end of Q1 Sabatino was comfortably through to the next round; Helli Cunzer in the second Ptarmigan was also through, as were the two Lambourns and both Massarellas.

Straker sat back in his chair and squinted at the screen. This was not good.

Nothing. No sign of the saboteur. At all.

He stepped out of the motor home and, making sure he was not able to be overheard, telephoned Backhouse in the pit lane. 'No sign, Andy, I'm afraid.'

'That was only Q1, Matt. No one would expect our cars to fall out this early.'

'Okay. Can we do the tease on the first in-lap of Q2?'

'She's not going to like it.'

Qualifying Two started seven minutes later. This time, the field was to be reduced from sixteen cars to ten.

Sabatino put in a good lap early on. They were confident it would be fast enough to get her through, so she wouldn't need to pound the car unnecessarily. Coasting home on her in-lap, she reached the tunnel. Straker heard Backhouse come up on the radio again: 'Remy, we're looking at the hard compound and a three-stop strategy.'

Straker waited to see how well she would participate in their ploy.

'Okay,' was all she grunted in response.

Backhouse kept going with the pre-agreed script: 'We've just run the numbers, Remy. If we go for three, we'd need to make up nine seconds per stint. What do you think?'

Sabatino did not reply.

'Remy?'

Straker groaned.

Finally, she mumbled: 'Okay. Go for three.'

'We might have to play with your brake balance midway through Q3…' Backhouse went on.

There was no further response from Sabatino.

Straker sucked his teeth, not sure how convincing that had been. He hoped that with the competitive significance of their transmission, though, they might have done enough to bait his trap. The next – and final – round of Qualifying was critical.

The shootout.

For Q3, it was mandatory for cars to be in race trim – the very set-up in which they would start the race the next day – no fundamental adjustment being permitted under the rules from then until the start of the Grand Prix itself. Backhouse's and Sabatino's discussion over the radio, therefore, was meant to sound like they were finalizing their set-up for the race. On a three-stop strategy, the Ptarmigan would be considerably lighter than the other competitive cars, giving it an advantage. However, running that light would alter the car's balance; the team's only chance to test and adjust the set-up would come over the air during this last Qualifying session. Straker hoped that news of the three-stop strategy – and expected radio exchange in Q3 – would excite the jammer to act.

When Sabatino got back to the pits, the soft compound tyres were replaced. Under Backhouse's instructions, the fuel rigger deliberately fumbled the hose – attaching it and removing it several times – to disguise the fact that he was actually fuelling for a two-stop strategy.

Towards the end of Q2, things were put dramatically into perspective.

Helli Cunzer, Sabatino's teammate, was out on a hot lap. Something wasn't quite right. The car was yawing noticeably under braking.

Straker quickly switched one of the screens over to watch the feed from Cunzer's Ptarmigan. Down into Mirabeau, the German clearly locked-up his front left, sending a plume of blue smoke into the air. Round Loews, he could be seen jabbing at the brakes again, and flat spotting the front right.

Through Portier, TV viewers could see the car's rear end step out and Cunzer snatching at the wheel, trying to keep the car from hitting the wall. He was clearly having a torrid time of it.

Under the Fairmont Hotel tunnel, the car finally seemed to settle. Cunzer wound the Ptarmigan up through fourth, fifth and sixth gears. Except that, as his speed increased round the long right-hander, he found himself wafting to the outside of the corner.

From the relative darkness of the tunnel, he was soon back out in the glare of the Mediterranean sun.

Was he momentarily blinded? Did he blink? Did he squint?

Did he take his eyes off the game – even for a moment?

No one knew for certain. Hurtling down the slope by the harbour wall towards the Chicane, though, the car suddenly jinked.

Badly.

The back end stepped violently out to the left.

Unweighted by the crest of the road there? Who knew?

Cunzer, himself, had no time to think about the cause.

Right then, all he could think about was one thing.

Survival.

As a reflex, the driver snapped the wheel the same way, to correct the slew. But too much. By now, though, the car was on the marbles – the small spheres of cooled molten rubber thrown off the tyres of the other cars and littering the edges of the circuit. On this dirty part of the track, the car became almost unsteerable.

Worse, the unweighting of the car had disturbed the natural airflow under the front wing. And, with the attitude of the car, its aerodynamics were not working. Air seemed to be getting underneath it. Instead of downforce, the wing started to generate lift – to fly. The car was soon imitating a blown piece of paper skimming across the surface of a table. Cunzer's car was starting to hover. Ground effect. Doing one hundred and eighty miles an hour in a confined space, surrounded by steel Armco barriers – he was completely out of control.

The world watched on in horror. The car skimmed on down the hill towards the Chicane, still not responding to any controls.

Its left rear hammered the barrier. Bits of the car exploded outwards. That collision saw the car bounce off, veering out to the right and back down the middle of the track. Viewers watched aghast as Cunzer's head whiplashed like a rag doll in the impact despite the restraint from the tethers of his HANS – Head And Neck Support – device.

Even after that ricochet off the barriers, the car was still travelling at over one hundred and fifty miles an hour. There was an ear-splitting crack and wrench as the car passed over the raised kerbs of the Chicane, ripping off parts of the undertray. That jolt also broke the suspension in the front right, causing its wheel to collapse inwards. Sparks scattered in all directions as the resultant lower ride height brought other components into contact with the road making it easier for them to be wrenched from the bodywork – bargeboards, the front wing, and fancy aerodynamic trimmings like fins and blades.

Everyone held their breath. Eyes flicked from the car and then on down the track and back again, it being all too easy to plot Cunzer's likely trajectory.

The outcome was all too obvious.

It was too horrible to watch.

But impossible to turn away from.

Cunzer was heading for the end of the solid, bewalled and tree-lined island that was the central reservation of the road normally used as the Avenue Président J. F. Kennedy. A tyre wall had been constructed for the race to soften the sharp point of this island in the road. A car hitting this on a slight angle was meant to glance off – be deflected away without serious impact – down either side.

But Cunzer wasn't going to glance off. Everyone could see that.

They could see exactly where he was heading – straight for the apex, perpendicular to the narrowest point.

His impact was going to be head-on.

It happened.

Blam.

Cunzer's car smashed into the end of the central reservation. From one hundred miles an hour it decelerated to zero in a millisecond. The G-force on the car – and the man – was unimaginable. Cunzer's head flopped around like a ball tied to the end of a stick. As the inadequate tyre wall did its best to absorb the massive kinetic energy – bulging and erupting under compression – it somehow started to lift the car, so that it was soon standing up – improbably on its gearbox, its front wheels held up like hands in surrender. It began to pirouette on its rear end. In agonizing slow motion, the car soon lost its balance and started to fall back, crashing down onto the road – upside-down, resting at an angle on the air intake above the driver's head. All the car's extremities were snapped off as it crashed down, creating a turquoise explosion of broken parts radiating out from the impact.

The car rocked back and forth, as the last of its energy slowly dissipated.

All that could be heard was Cunzer's very sick engine – just about turning over, but in the process of grinding itself to pieces. Soon, it, too, spluttered to silence. Vapour or smoke started billowing out from somewhere within the car. Finally, there was stillness.

Cunzer did not move. His body and head were simply hanging vertically – upside-down against his harness – from the upside-down car.

Marshals started running in immediately. Astutely, one of them ran back up the track towards the Fairmont Tunnel frantically waving double yellow flags as a warning to any cars still out on the circuit that might be racing down the hill towards the Chicane.

Marshals ran to Cunzer's stricken Ptarmigan.

There was still no sign of life from the driver.

Just as one of the marshals took charge and started directing the others, there was a massive explosion. Cunzer's fuel tank erupted, sending out a deafening shock wave and a huge ball of orange flame, engulfing the car and driver.

Cunzer was completely hidden by fire. Viewers were hit with instant déjà vu – of Jos Verstappen at Hockenheim.

Stoically, the lead marshal recovered from the shock of the explosion and retook command. Charging forward with a fire extinguisher, he blasted white foam in front of him as he waded into the fireball towards the cockpit. Other marshals, taking their lead from this astonishing selflessness, followed on – first, though, blasting their jets of white foam over their colleague, and then over the car and the stricken driver.

The flames were put out remarkably quickly.

Moments later blaring sirens could be heard. Two ambulances and a fire engine were belting down the Avenue Président J. F. Kennedy, while another emergency vehicle approached from the other direction, from under the Fairmont tunnel. Screeching to a halt, paramedics jumped out of the first ambulance and sprinted towards the crash.

With the fire out, one of the marshals had ducked under the upside-down car, cautiously peering up into the cockpit at the driver, dreading what he was going to find. Squatting beneath the car, he tried – still awkwardly – to look up underneath to assess the driver in the cockpit. A paramedic crouched down beside him. Attention was drawn to the blood pouring from the cockpit rim. Concerns of any danger from moving a suspected spinal injury, though, were surrendered to the greater fear of further explosions and fire – and the bleeding.

There was clearly no way to carry or support the driver's weight up under the car – given the cramped space available.

The two men seemed to agree on a plan. The paramedic lowered himself on all fours directly underneath the car.

The marshal pushed his head up into the cockpit and prepared to release the harness, awaiting the order from the paramedic.

Click.

Under gravity, the inverted driver slid down out of the cockpit and landed on the paramedic's back. Their plan seemed to have worked. Cunzer's fall had been broken. Several other medics clustered round, helping the laden paramedic reverse out awkwardly from under the car with Cunzer's limp body draped across his back. He crawled his way clear. A stretcher was brought up and put on the ground alongside. Foam blocks were placed around the driver's head and neck to immobilize him. Cunzer's vital signs were checked. Automatically, a mask, providing oxygen, was placed over his nose and mouth. Another medic, seeing the copious blood pouring from Cunzer's leg, quickly pulled a tourniquet from his pocket and, slipping the rubber strap under the driver's leg, connected the buckle assembly and pulled it flesh-distortingly tight around the top of his thigh.

Overhead came the high-pitched whine of a jet turbine. An emergency services helicopter swooped in over the harbour. It was able to put down on the area of road by the Chicane at a safe enough distance from the wreckage.

Seconds later, four medics lifted the stretcher and shuffle-walked the driver as fast as they could, subconsciously ducking under the rotors. Cunzer's stretcher was manhandled aboard. No more than a moment later, the pitch on the rotors steepened and, with a blast of air out from under the disc, the helicopter lifted off the ground, swung round to face the sea, dipped its nose, pulled more pitch, and climbed rapidly up into the air, out over the harbour.

By the time he arrived at the Princesse Grace hospital, Cunzer hadn't regained consciousness.

Understandably – and fittingly – Qualifying was suspended. It wasn't until three hours later, in front of a mass of media congregating around the main entrance of the hospital, that a spokesman finally emerged to make a statement.

Within a matter of minutes of his arriving at the hospital, the doctor explained, Cunzer had been rushed into theatre. After two hours on the operating table he had been moved into intensive care. Still unconscious, none of the medical specialists yet knew of his mental condition – whether he had suffered any brain damage in the trauma of the crash.

But at least he was alive.

Just.

The mood around the circuit and pits was extraordinarily subdued. Nowhere more so than within Ptarmigan. Not only had they seen their colleague and friend go through such a horrific ordeal – but all minds were concerned about the cause. What did this mean for the reliability of the Ptarmigan cars? Would the same fate befall Sabatino, driving an identical machine?

The effect of all this was worse on those who knew about the sabotage. Was there a connection? Was this hideous accident just an accident? Or was Cunzer's crash the intended result of malicious intervention?

Straker's phone went. It was Backhouse: 'What the fuck does Helli's smash indicate?' he asked. 'What if there *is* a connection between that and the radio sabotage?'

Straker realized he needed to strike the right balance here. He was anxious they maintained a high level of vigilance, but that they were not alarmist – not least given Sabatino's scepticism and irritation over the sabotage issue. 'We don't yet know the cause of his crash,' he said. 'Presumably we will carry out a full investigation on the wreckage?'

'So you *do* suspect a connection?'

'I do – if only for the sake of motivating us to take the right precautions. I would far rather we did something and were wrong than we did nothing and were proved complacent.'

'Should we not talk this through with Remy, then? To make her take the threat seriously?'

Straker couldn't deny that this accorded with his professional view. 'I'll leave that to you, Andy. You know her, and have the advantage of not being an interloper whom she seems to distrust.'

Straker wasn't told whether Backhouse did say anything about the possible causes of the crash. Sabatino had shut herself away in the back of the pit lane garage.

She sat with her head down, trying to shut the drama surrounding her teammate out of her mind.

She couldn't let it affect her.

If she did, she might never get back in a cockpit again.

TEN

After Helli Cunzer's horrific crash, there was much discussion between the powers that be. Eventually, the decision was taken to restart Qualifying – spun aggressively to the press, media and watching world as the sport paying tribute to the bravery and spirit of one of its most promising young drivers.

Qualifying Three finally got under way.

But Straker soon realized that Cunzer's crash hadn't affected everybody. It hadn't affected Ptarmigan's curse.

Midway through Q3, Straker got his first real scent of the saboteur.

Sabatino was out on track. Approaching Massenet.

Backhouse radioed that, with the lighter fuel load, the brake balance needed to be adjusted slightly to the rear. There was no acknowledgement from Sabatino until she was halfway down the hill to Mirabeau. But then, as she transmitted, and started speaking, the radio signal was jammed. She stopped transmitting and waited while she concentrated through that right-hander and the left-hand hairpin of Loews before transmitting again. When she did, her voice was drowned out completely by the crackle of white noise. Approaching the tunnel, she spoke once more, and the same thing happened. Straker heard exactly what it was immediately.

This wasn't blanket jamming – as Backhouse had observed on Thursday. This jamming was deliberate. Someone was transmitting – very precisely – to coincide each time, this time, with Sabatino's messages.

This was their saboteur all right.

He was back.

Straker's eyes bore into the screen. "Come on, pick him up!" he said to himself. "Where are you, you fucker?"

Suddenly, two vectors flashed across the wire diagram on his screen. And intersected. Mentally, he shouted: "Gotcha!"

The source of the transmission appeared to be on the promontory up by the Palace of Monaco. A printer whirred into life printing off the saboteur's location on a map of Monte-Carlo.

Grabbing a small digital camera and shoving it in his pocket, Straker darted out of the back of the headquarters truck, pulled on a helmet, jumped onto a Piaggio Scooter, fired it into life and hurtled out of the paddock towards the Palace on its rocky promontory above the harbour behind him, to the west of Monte-Carlo.

Getting through any part of the town, with the Grand Prix infrastructure and circus blocking the way, was hell. Weaving and snaking between the traffic, he swept round the back of Avenue de la Quarantaine before starting his climb up the inclined road cut into the cliff face.

Straker crested the plateau no more than eight minutes after detecting the jammer on his screen, and steamed down a few narrow streets before reaching Rue des Ramparts. Pulling off the road into a sightseeing lay-by, he stopped, extracted the map, orientated himself quickly, and confirmed his location. There was no mistake. He was in the very spot identified by the triangulation.

Straker looked up and down the road, squinting against the brilliant sunshine and scoured everything in sight for anything suspicious – any sign of someone with a radio or some kind of device. He studied a group of holiday makers traipsing along the road, but they seemed to be simply using the vantage point of the road to look down over the waist-high wall at the magnificent view of Monte-Carlo, the harbour, and its marina full of yachts bathing in the sun below. There was nothing else there.

No stationary cars. No one looking suspicious. No one with any kind of equipment.

No sign of a saboteur anywhere.

Straker made it back to the pit lane as Q3 finished. Simi Luciano in the Massarella had qualified on pole by a considerable margin – point-six of a second. A Ferrari was next to him on the front row in P2. Remy Sabatino was third, on the second row, while the Championship leader, Paddy Aston in the Lambourn, was alongside her in fourth. Adi Barrantes, the Argentinian in the other Massarella, was down in P7.

Straker walked back into the garage. Sabatino accosted him: 'Well? Any developments with the *so-called* saboteur?'

Straker forced a smile – despite the edge in her voice. 'Yes and no.'

'What does that mean?'

'Somebody was active. I got a fix. When I got to the location, there was no one there.'

Sabatino screwed up her face. 'What a surprise.'

Straker responded with a neutral expression and a shrug, realizing he wasn't going to get any support from her on the sabotage issue. 'Well done in Qualifying, then,' he said. 'Pretty impressive, given the circumstances and the scare with Helli. You pleased?'

'Sort of,' grunted Sabatino. 'Be warned,' she added with a pointed smile, 'if I get any grief from the Big Man about not being on the front row, I'll blame you and the distraction of chasing your non-existent spy.'

Straker, Quartano and Backhouse were in conference five minutes later.

'How's Helli?'

Backhouse looked shattered. 'Tahm's up at the hospital waiting for news.'

'I want to know immediately of any development,' said Quartano.

'Of course, sir.'

Quartano changed the subject, saying to Straker: 'What about the saboteur? Are you sure this bastard's still out there?'

'Quite sure.'

'What more can we do?'

'Nothing different, at least for the time being,' answered Straker confidently, despite not offering any new ideas.

'Remy remains unconvinced by any of this,' Backhouse reported, 'and is sorely irritated by the distraction of our countermeasures.'

Quartano shrugged his tolerance. 'We certainly don't want to affect her or the team's concentration in the race.'

Straker said quietly: 'I'm pretty sure I can do what's needed without interrupting her normal routine.'

'Okay, let's not disturb her race tomorrow,' summarized Quartano. 'Do all you can – but try and keep everything as passive as possible.'

That was all fine in principle. Straker had a feeling the saboteur was going to be *anything* but passive.

ELEVEN

Race day of the Monaco Grand Prix.

At five minutes to two the next afternoon, following a procession of carnival-like entertainment for the crowds – including the drivers being paraded round the circuit on an open-top bus, and the staging of the Formula Renault and GP2 support races – the long build-up to the most glamorous Grand Prix of the season neared its climax.

At the sound of the hooter, the chaotic-looking grid, teeming with brightly coloured overalls in each team's livery and their trolley-borne equipment, suddenly started to clear. Blankets were pulled off tyres. Umbrellas providing shade from the Mediterranean sun were lowered. Pit lizards, the scantily dressed dolly-birds carrying signs with the name and nationality of each driver, trooped off in procession. The mass presence of the media, TV camera crews and presenters withdrew. And the plethora of international A-Listers from rock, pop, film and the arts, drawn to the glamour of Monte-Carlo, Formula One and, above all, the Monaco Grand Prix, was escorted off the hallowed tarmac to their fiendishly expensive but highly prized hospitality suites and boxes overlooking the circuit.

In no time at all only the cars were left on the grid.

Then, as an ever-growing roar, twenty-one high-performance engines started to growl. Fifteen thousand horsepower – screaming – ready to do battle.

The lights on the race gantry went on, indicating the start of the slow formation lap round the 2.1 mile circuit.

The cars began to move.

Out in front, the pole sitter, Simi Luciano, flicked the launch control and throttle of his Massarella, lighting up his rear tyres as he hurtled off in a mock start towards Sainte Devote, laying down some rubber to try and improve his traction the next time round.

The procession of cars made their way round the circuit, each driver weaving, braking and accelerating to work temperature into their tyres, brakes and hydraulic fluid.

Three minutes later they had completed their warm-up lap and were forming up again on the grid. As the last car slotted itself into position at the back, the engine noise became deafening. All twenty-one cars were being blipped between ten and fifteen thousand revs, building up torque for that critical release at the start.

One red light went on.

The second light went on.

Then the third, then the fourth.

The fifth red light came on. The crescendo of sound in the narrow cavern of the street was utterly deafening.

Seconds passed. A pause.

Then, all the lights went out at once.

GO!

Twenty-one clutches were engaged within a fraction of a second. And the fleet of the world's most sophisticated automobiles screamed off the line, hurtling at breakneck speed down the street towards the impossibly narrow right-hander of Sainte Devote. It was a breathtaking sight.

How could so much energy, speed and hardware converge into that corner and hope to emerge on the other side without incident? There were puffs of blue smoke as tyres were locked-up. There was bumping, wheel to wheel. One car, interlocking its wheels between the wheel-base of another, made contact and was momentarily lifted off the ground. Anyone watching, let alone commentating on the race, could only focus on one tiny part of it, and just hope they could follow and understand even *that* minor segment of the story. It all happened so fast. Only with repeated replays afterwards would the full story of the start be clear.

A matter of seconds later, most of the field was through Sainte Devote. Commentators were frantically trying to call the race – to see who the emergent drivers were, who had got ahead, who had dropped back, and who, if any, was out.

The cars charged on up through Beau Rivage. Simi Luciano in the black Massarella had built a lead from pole. Remy Sabatino had had a blistering start. Although starting one row back, she had jumped the Ferrari into second place having the advantage of the clean side of the track. Paddy Aston remained fourth in the Lambourn, while Adi Barrantes, still having a miserable weekend of it, had been bumped in Turn One and was now down to ninth.

Straker watched the main broadcast feed as the cars streamed past the Casino and hurtled down the hill towards Mirabeau. As far as he could tell, there were no retirements. All twenty-one cars were still racing after the first half-lap.

He heard Backhouse radio Sabatino with an update on placings. There was excitement in his voice.

But there was a long way to go.

Around they raced, more or less as a high-speed procession.

So it remained for the next fifteen laps. No one was able to overtake, and there were no incidents.

Fortunately for the spectators, everything came to life shortly afterwards.

Simi Luciano in the Massarella had managed to build up a fourteen-second lead. Then, taking everyone by surprise, he pitted far earlier than expected. Straker heard the TV commentators getting thoroughly over-excited at the realization of his three-stop strategy. They'd all thought the Massarella was naturally quicker, not that it was significantly lighter than the others. Recalculations were swiftly done to try and work out how fast Luciano really was on a fuel-adjusted basis.

That was the first incident.

The second involved the other Massarella.

Well down the order, Adi Barrantes was having a feisty scrap with one of the Red Bulls. Heading out of the Chicane, Barrantes caught a good exit and was quickly up behind the Red Bull's gearbox. With some distance to run before the ninety-degree left-hander of Tabac, Barrantes, frustrated by his lack of opportunity to overtake, pulled out sharply and lunged down the inside. Relative to each other, it seemed like slow motion, even though they were both travelling at well over one hundred and twenty miles an hour.

Slowly, Barrantes's front wheel managed to pass the other's rear axle. Then the front wheel pulled level with the other driver. Barrantes was still gaining when the Red Bull started moving over to claim the racing line.

Was Barrantes alongside far enough? Did *Barrantes* now have a right to the line? Except at that speed, it was almost too quick for rational judgement.

As the Red Bull started to set itself up for the corner, Barrantes realized his space was disappearing. Bottling out, he lifted off and jabbed at the brake.

And that's when it all went wrong.

Barrantes's front left rolled over some white line markings on the normally public road. As he braked, that tyre was on shiny white paint rather than the rough, grippy surface of the track. It was no help in slowing him down. The skid started right there. Instinctively, Barrantes yanked the steering wheel to the left, trying to correct the resultant understeer, but the car simply continued straight on.

Adi Barrantes's Massarella would not respond. It was streaking across the circuit. And there was no way out.

No run-off.

It could only slam into the Armco on the outside of Tabac. Luckily, the angle was slight – more of a glancing blow. Even so, at that speed of impact, the front wing and carbon-fibre nosecone crumpled and splintered, as it was designed to. The front wheel hit the barrier. Again, the shock was absorbed in the car's construction, this time in the wishbones. Fragments of carbon fibre exploded outward from the impact. The car scraped its broken front end some distance along the bottom of the barriers before its kinetic energy was finally dissipated.

Barrantes came to a stop. He waved a hand immediately to indicate that he was conscious and not hurt.

From around that section of the circuit, race marshals jumped into action, waving yellow flags and radioing to the operator of the hydraulic crane, a short distance along the Armco.

Right behind the stricken Massarella, Formula One cars were still belting past only a matter of feet away. A lethal situation. Barrantes looked over his shoulder, hurriedly yanked off the steering wheel, pulled himself up out of the cockpit, and jumped up and over the steel barrier to safety.

In a matter of seconds, with extraordinary Monégasque efficiency, the marshals managed to hook the car to a crane and lift the dangling and broken Massarella clear of the track. The race was continuing, but under yellow flags.

Next to Straker in the headquarters truck, the Ptarmigan team members were animated – particularly Oliver Treadwell, the Strategy Director. 'Get a shot of Tabac,' he commanded, 'quick!'

Treadwell was soon able to study the CCTV image. 'Is that oil?' he asked the room.

'Looks like it,' replied one of the team.

'All stations, all stations: possible safety car.'

Straker heard the radio traffic buzz in both ears as the pit lane spoke to Sabatino. This was absolutely crucial. Tactically, the team had a huge call to make.

Was the safety car about to be called?

If so, Ptarmigan could take a punt and call their driver in immediately, and maybe grab a "cheap" pit stop. At full race speed, taking the twenty-five seconds out of the race to make a pit stop – when the field was travelling at one hundred and fifty miles an hour – was always expensive in time and distance. But to make a pit stop now – with the chance that the entire field might soon be bunched up and slowed to seventy miles an hour behind the safety car – would cost them a lot less time. Sabatino could dart in, pit, change tyres, refuel, and be out again with the opportunity to shoot round and quickly rejoin the back of the pack. If the safety car was then deployed, she would have stolen a march on her rivals – Race Control would close the pit lane for stops once the safety car was out. Her rivals could then only pit when the race was restarted and the field was back up to full race pace, costing the stoppers, then, considerably more speed, distance, possibly even track position.

On the other hand, if they called Sabatino in and the safety car was *not* deployed, they would have destroyed their planned strategy for the race.

Treadwell watched the CCTV screens showing the crash scene at Tabac. Two marshals, leaning over the Armco, were clearly checking for debris on the circuit as cars continued to hurtle past. Arms and fingers were being pointed at the middle of the track. One of them was speaking animatedly into a radio.

A camera zoomed in on the surface of the road.

It was clear that there was oil among the razor-sharp splinters of carbon fibre scattered across the road.

The team made its decision.

'Remy, Remy...' said Backhouse over the air, 'Boccrrgghh...' but the saboteur returned – jamming the radio – obliterating the message with white noise. There was total mush over the air – the message was completely blanked out.

This was critical. A spontaneous adjustment to race tactics was going to be thwarted if they couldn't co-ordinate things right now over the radio.

Another message was transmitted by the Ptarmigan pit wall. At precisely the same moment the jammer blasted them again with crackle. Sabatino's radio *could* be heard in reply. But only as static.

The CCTV showed more commotion at the trackside down by Tabac.

The Race Director wasted no time. The safety car was ordered to deploy.

Very soon the field started to slow down. The cars all began to bunch up. The crocodile started to form.

The pit lane was closed for stops.

Straker, though, heaved a massive sigh of relief. Despite the jamming, Sabatino *had* got the message – and *had* pulled in to pit. Ptarmigan had just pulled off a stunningly opportunistic stop and had got her back out – just in time. Straker's insurance policy had proved inspired.

Advising the team to fit second radios and setting the original radios to transmit only, meant the driver and pit wall were not hearing any of the white noise. Straker may have been. But the critical discussion about tactics and the call to "Box" had proceeded without interference – all conducted over the second radio net on a completely separate frequency.

Despite the enthralling drama on the track, and over the air, Straker had to pull himself away. He now had work to do.

Looking down at his screen, he saw that three of his dishes had actively vectored the saboteur's jamming transmission and plotted the direction of their signal.

He had a multiple fix.

Triangulation.

Straker had got him.

TWELVE

This time, Straker's radio fix seemed to be a location in the town, only three roads back from the circuit. "Got you, you bastard," he shouted to himself as he grabbed the printout and his digital camera, and set off on foot.

Running out of the paddock, Straker belted along the Avenue du Port, finding his way down Rue Saige, to reach Rue de la Princesse Caroline. He sprinted flat out. Because of race day, the streets were relatively free of cars, but were now full of pedestrians taking advantage of their short-lived freedom. Straker ran athletically, nimbly weaving his way between the ambling crowds, before turning right into Rue Louis Notari to reach Rue des Princes.

A few blocks later, he was there.

He reached the triangulation point, his chest heaving for breath. Pulling the printout from his pocket, he orientated himself as before, looking left and right to identify the exact grid reference.

It turned out to be a pinkish-beige, four-storey townhouse, built as a small apartment block. Trying to calm his breathing, he quickly looked it up and down.

Although its basic shape was box-like, it had some elegant baroque touches. An ornate overhang around the roof resembled a plaster architrave. Each floor level was distinguished with horizontal white moulding, which stood out from its flesh-coloured walls. A similar flourish surrounded the well-proportioned windows and their white shutters, and each floor had its own semicircular balcony edged with decorative wrought-iron railings, all of which were covered with a mass of flowers. Could this chic townhouse really be the place he was looking for?

Straker, now standing on the opposite side of the road, took a photograph of the building, unable to ignore the screaming sound of the Grand Prix cars only a few blocks away to the south and realizing that the safety car must be in and the race was back on.

If this house *was* the location, though, which floor was hiding his quarry? How on earth was he going to find out?

Straker moved across the road through some light traffic – dodging a scooter and a taxi – and trotted up the steps to the front door. To one side of the entrance, a brass panel of buttons to each flat was set in the wall. There were five in total, with a printed name for each – none of which meant anything to him. A sixth button offered the porter along with a telephone number.

Hang on, Straker thought, would a resident be involved in the Grand Prix?

Not that likely. Then he had an idea.

Entering the telephone number into his phone, and then jotting down the names of all the occupants on the back of a business card, he dialled the number for the porter. Luckily, the call was answered. An aged man came on the line who, thankfully, could at least speak some form of pidgin English.

'Hello, I've been told that you have apartments to let?' Straker said.

There was a grunt from the other end. '*Non.*'

'Oh, I heard that one of them was available for the Grand Prix?'

'*Non.*'

Straker thought quickly. 'I'm sorry. I thought someone had rented one this week?'

'Yes. That's why we don't have one now.'

Aha, thought Straker. 'And was that…' he said looking down through the list and picking a name at random, '…Monsieur De Lancy's apartment?'

'*Non.* For the race – this week – it is Madame Larochelle. Number 5.'

Straker grimaced as he made ready to try his luck: 'Thank you. And could you tell me who has rented it, please?'

'*Non!*' barked the porter, adding: '*Privé!*' and hung up immediately.

Straker shrugged, hardly surprised. At least he now knew that Apartment 5 – on the top floor – was occupied by a temporary visitor who seemed to have rented it for the Grand Prix. How was he going to get this person's name, or even identify him?

Straker soon thought of something.

He walked back up the street to a corner shop he had passed that had a large display of flowers on the pavement out front. He walked in and ordered a bouquet.

While it was being put together, Straker wrote out a small card to Madame Larochelle, the owner of Apartment 5 in his target block. Then, for a large-denomination euro note, he managed to engage the shop keeper's help.

Having thought through as many of the permutations of his wheeze as he could, Straker asked the newsagent to deliver in person the bouquet to the front door of the townhouse – straight away. He was clear in his instructions: The newsagent was to ring the bell and insist that the occupant come down to the front door to sign for the flowers. If the occupant referred the delivery to the porter, he was to say it must be signed for personally. And if the shopkeeper was asked to bring the delivery up the stairs, he was to refuse – complaining of a bad back. Finally, if the occupant did sign for the flowers, the shopkeeper was to ask for a printed name, to make sure he'd got it absolutely clear. To Straker's relief, the shopkeeper seemed taken with this charade and readily set off up Rue des Princes with the bouquet.

Straker, meanwhile, hurried up the road behind him, looking for a vantage point on the opposite side of the street.

The noise of the Grand Prix continued to reverberate through the air.

From across the road, Straker watched the newsagent approach the apartment block and ring the bell several times before getting any response. From what Straker could see, he was soon engaged in a fairly protracted discussion over the intercom, with the florist leaning in close to the loudspeaker grille. Finally, it seemed, the temporary occupant of Madame Larochelle's apartment had relented and was ready to receive the delivery.

A few minutes later the front door was opened. Straker waited to confirm that it was the person who had come down to collect the flowers rather than someone else who just happened to be leaving the building, and then took several photographs of the recipient. The telephoto lens pulled him in nice and close. He didn't know what to think. The man was in his forties, balding, slightly over-weight and dressed in casual clothes. Did he look like a saboteur? Was this really their jammer?

As the door was closed on the delivered flowers, and the newsa-gent turned to leave, Straker walked down the pavement on his side of the road to meet him as he crossed over.

'Here you are, monsieur,' said the newsagent handing him the receipt. 'He is Monsieur Michel Lyons, and that's his signature.'

THIRTEEN

Straker, with his freshly-garnered intelligence, sprinted back to the Ptarmigan motor home in the paddock. Having missed all the goings-on in the race since the deployment of the safety car, he was anxious to be briefed by Oliver Treadwell, Ptarmigan's Strategy Director, who was supervizing the bank of team members monitoring the race.

'What's happening?' he asked.

'You've missed some drama,' Treadwell said. 'Remy was in the Swimming Pool section when the safety car was called, so she hadn't crossed the start line. That meant Backhouse *could* call her in for a pit stop immediately. We got her in and out again, with a new set of boots, in just over nine seconds. Then Race Control closed the pits. Remy emerged from the pit lane as the field was backing up behind the safety car. She was obliged to pass it, circle round and form up at the back.'

'Hell, what place did that drop her down to?'

'Nineteenth.'

'Shit!'

'But no one else on a two-stopper had been able to pit by then. Our timing was immaculate.'

'How many laps under the safety car?'

'Six.'

Straker whistled. 'Any blow-ups?'

'Only the Championship leader.'

'Paddy Aston?'

'Overheated on lap twenty-one.'

'What then?'

'By lap twenty-three, the marshals had cleared the oil and shards of carbon fibre off the track. Race Control opened the pits and called in the safety car. There was mayhem over the next few laps, as every-one tried to pit before they ran out of fuel. Two cars even bumped in the entrance to the pit lane.'

'Where was Remy when they started racing again?'

'Twelfth, but because of the backing-up behind the safety car, there was less than eight seconds between her and Simi Luciano. Apart from him – on his three-stop strategy – everyone between the two of them had to pit as soon as possible.'

'What a bummer I missed all this.'

'Three laps later, everyone had made their first stop, putting Remy right up behind Simi.'

'In second?'

'Yep.'

'When did Luciano pit again?'

'Lap thirty-five.'

'And what kind of lead had he built up?'

'Being lighter, of course, he should've run away with it, but Remy was able to stay in touch. Eight seconds was all he could manage. The moment he was in, Remy had the road to herself – with lots of clear air – and off she romped.'

'Where did Luciano feed back in?'

'Best he could do was seventh.'

'And the order now?'

'Remy, Ferrari, Red Bull, Mercedes, Simi.'

Straker's face broke into a broad smile. 'How many more laps to go?'

'Ten.'

'Stops?'

'All done. Provided we don't pick up any residual splinters from Barrantes's car, we're looking good. Remy's running A-Okay. Anyway,' he said in hushed tones, 'how did you get on? Did you get anywhere?'

Straker nodded.

'You did?' To be discreet, Treadwell moved over to Straker's console. 'Any idea who's doing this?'

Straker nodded again.

'You got names?' he asked with impressed enthusiasm. 'Who?'

Straker whispered, 'Michel Lyons?'

Treadwell looked blank.

'You don't know him?' said Straker sounding a little disappointed. 'Nope.'

'Perhaps you'll recognize him,' answered Straker as he leant down to connect his camera to one of the computer's USB ports. Straker soon put the face of Michel Lyons on the screen. '*Do* you know him?'

The Strategy Director shook his head. 'Afraid not.'

'He's taken an apartment on the top floor of 25 Rue des Princes for the week of the race, which was the source of the signal jamming Remy's radio.'

Treadwell suggested, 'He could be attached to one of the teams, or be a freelance brought in from outside to do the dirty work?'

Lap seventy-seven, with only one to go.

Straker, still in the headquarters truck, was listening out on the radio, watching the race on one of the screens in front of him.

Desperate to spot any further sabotage interference, he called up the on-board shot from the camera above Sabatino's helmet.

She was crossing the start line. They all hoped she would be crossing it again in one minute and fifteen seconds – for the last time.

She reached one hundred and sixty miles an hour down the start/finish straight, before decelerating hard into Turn One. She glanced down at the lights on the steering wheel, willing the car to stay normal and reliable for just one more lap. Everything seemed to be operating within limits. Three laps earlier she had leaned off the fuel mix.

Her closest rival, in one of the Ferraris, was seven seconds down the road behind her.

The Championship leader, Paddy Aston, was out and going to

score no points to her prospective ten. She was trying desperately not to think about it, trying to shut the significance of this afternoon out of her mind. But it wasn't easy.

She was on the verge of winning here in Monaco – the ultimate race in Formula One – and being the first woman to do so. Not only that, she was about to go six points clear at the top of the Drivers' Championship.

Sabatino forced herself to disregard these thoughts. Don't blow it for a moment's lack of concentration, she screamed to herself.

Backhouse came up on the air. 'All's good, Remy. Just bring it home.'

Straker smiled as the jammer blocked out her message on her original radio frequency. Thankfully, the second radio was still clear and unaffected.

Sabatino went through Portier, Turn Eight, reaching the water-front. Heading under the tunnel, the race track was plunged into darkness. Seconds later, she appeared into the harbour and was bathed again in the glorious afternoon sun.

And that's when it started.

It was completely unexpected.

She felt it first, she could *feel* the noise.

Even over the engine, even through her helmet. She could hear the crowds. They were roaring.

Sabatino couldn't believe it. They were cheering her home.

Flicking through the Chicane, she powered on, down towards the narrow Tabac where Barrantes had earlier come to grief in the Armco. Once round there, the scene was quite extraordinary. Every-one in the stands – bang next to the track on either side – was on their feet. The circuit felt even more overhung than ever. Banners flew. Flags were waved above a sea of waving people. Air-horns blared. The Monégasque crowd was cheering the winner. They were saluting the winner of their race. Whoever won *their* race deserved to be saluted. But being a woman – the first woman – seemed to have captured the crowd's emotion even more than usual.

Sabatino, still moving at considerable speed, weaved effortlessly through the kinked turns of the Swimming Pool complex and on along the harbour towards La Rascasse. She accelerated up the hill towards Turn Nineteen, Anthony Noghès, the last on the circuit.

Then the significance of her drive suddenly struck her.

Sabatino's eyes welled up as she accelerated down the pit straight towards the line.

There it was.

The most prized sight in Formula One – the chequered flag of the Monaco Grand Prix.

And it was being waved in her honour.

She crossed the line.

She had won.

Tears flooded down her cheeks.

Straker was listening out on the radio. 'Fantastic,' he heard a choked-up Backhouse say over the air, the excitement broadening his Birmingham accent. 'Well done, Remy. Well driven. *Brilliant.*'

Straker could hear the emotion from the hard-bitten race engineer.

'Thank you, Andy,' she replied, with a clear catch in her voice. 'To you – and all the guys.'

Five minutes later Remy Sabatino brought her turquoise Ptarmigan to a stop in Parc Fermé, right in front of the Royal Box. As she killed the engine, the noise of the crowds hit her for real. There was jubilation – celebrating this unprecedented win.

She climbed out and stood up on the nose of her car before turning to face her team and punching the air with both hands. Everywhere around her the crowds were in raptures. Flags waved, banners swirled, air-horns sounded, and the cheers were deafening. Although she was still wearing her helmet and no one could see her face, her body language indicated that she was completely overcome.

Pulling off the elastic straps of the HANS device, she removed her helmet to a fusillade of camera shutters. She pulled off the balaclava to another rattle of shutters, giving the public and the world's media the expression on the face of the first woman ever to win the most male of races, the Monaco Grand Prix.

They were not disappointed.

The scene had everything for a modern media story. High emotion, tears, a striking face, cheering crowds, and the radiance of someone delighting in the moment.

Sabatino's mood was infectious. Photographers saw the euphoria as well as the significance of this story; working excitedly, they expected to see their images splashed across the front pages of the world's newspapers the next morning.

Andy Backhouse broke through the cordon and rushed over to congratulate her, lifting her off the ground in a hug. She was overcome once again as they shared the moment together. Cameras zoomed in for a close-up.

A minute later Remy Sabatino, wearing a baseball cap with a sponsor's name emblazoned across the front, walked up the short flight of red-carpeted steps into the Royal Box. His Serene Highness looked as pleased as she did. A court official gently indicated to Sabatino where she should stand as the Maltese national anthem started to play and the island's flag rose up the middle – and winner's – flag pole.

But Sabatino could hardly take any of it in.

The British national anthem then played, acknowledging the nationality of the winning constructor. As it finished, the crowds roared once more.

Sabatino was congratulated by the Prince who handed her the most prized trophy in Formula One. After receiving a few words of congratulation, she turned and held it aloft to show the crowd and the world's television cameras; there was an even bigger crescendo of noise.

Sabatino soon swapped the trophy for a jeroboam of champagne, which almost dwarfed her. Taking a hesitant sip, because of the weight of the bottle, she soon broke off. The Ferrari and Red Bull drivers – second and third – were bearing down on her, spraying her with champagne.

Hundreds of camera shutters clicked.

Sabatino ducked. One image caught *the* moment.

In glorious sunshine, with a huge smile across her face, Remy Sabatino had hunched her shoulders, trying to prevent torrents of fizz going down the back of her neck.

In an instant, that image became one of the most iconic sporting pictures of all time.

FOURTEEN

With Sabatino's win, the Ptarmigan Team was in a state of delirium. Corks popped in the headquarters truck as Straker and that contingent of the team were swept up in the moment. A win was always a win, and sparked celebrations. But Treadwell told Straker that this was very different. Remy's win, here, meant a whole lot more.

She was now the leader of the Drivers' Championship, six points clear of Paddy Aston – and, in the Constructors' Championship, Ptarmigan had pushed five points past Massarella to lead it, too, for the first time.

Straker put his various intelligence material, a digital recorder, and other findings into a large envelope, on the outside chance that anyone would want to talk about them that day, and made to join the pilgrimage towards the pits.

However, as he walked along the Monte-Carlo waterfront, he soon realized he was to enjoy no time off. His mobile rang.

'Matt?'

'Mr Quartano,' replied Straker. 'Congratulations. What a phenomenal result.'

'It certainly is. Come on board *Melita* when you're free, will you? I hear you've found something.'

There was clearly going to be no rest for the ambitious.

Straker met up with Backhouse in the Ptarmigan garage. It was jam-packed with people from up and down the pit lane. Champagne was flowing and the buzz was extraordinary.

'Congratulations, Andy,' said Straker, bawling above the noise.

Backhouse, already several large gulps of champagne into his celebrations, was almost too overcome to speak.

The noise got louder as Sabatino appeared through the doors

from the pit lane, having just finished her post-race TV interview. Straker watched as the victorious driver was enveloped by the Ptarmigan Team and other well-wishers.

Emerging a few minutes later, Sabatino walked over and gave Backhouse another hug, which lasted for several seconds. Then, turning to Straker, she held out her hand and gave his a perfunctory shake. 'Not too much sabotage to worry about in the end, then,' she said in an I-told-you-so kind of tone.

Straker just smiled and said, 'Congratulations, Remy. What a great result.'

Not long afterwards, the celebrations were transferred to the quarterdeck of Quartano's yacht, but Straker did not have long to enjoy them. He was approached by Tahm Nazar, the Ptarmigan Team Principal: 'Matt, DQ would like us to go through what you've got on the saboteur?'

'Sure,' he said putting his glass down and picking up the envelope he had left on one of the white leather benches.

He followed Nazar into the art deco saloon. Already inside were Quartano, Backhouse and Sabatino. One of the yacht's white-tunicked stewards was laying out some food and drink. He was thanked and asked to shut the door behind him as he left.

They all moved to sit at the dining table.

'What did you find?' asked Quartano with no time given over to revelling in the win.

Straker opened his envelope. 'Immediately after the Adi Barrantes crash,' he said, 'we were jammed. An attempt was made to sabotage our communications at a critical moment in the race.'

Sabatino's face seemed to set. 'When was that?' she challenged. 'I didn't hear it.'

'It was while you were all discussing the opportunistic pit stop,' Straker replied calmly.

Sabatino looked dismissive. 'I didn't hear anything like that.'

Straker nodded. He let the moment hang for a few silent seconds.

'All of this was on your original radio circuit, which was why we fitted a second radio, on a separate frequency, and turned your original radio down to zero. You weren't meant to hear any of it. You might all like to take a listen, though,' he said and pressed the play button on the recorder.

The implications of the recording were obvious.

Before it had even finished, Sabatino's whole demeanour had changed completely, as if someone had thrown a switch. She said, 'Not being able to speak over the radio – right then – would have scuppered me ... I'd have been denied that ad hoc pit stop. I ... *wouldn't* ... have won.'

Straker was pleased his methods might finally be being acknowledged. He hoped his expression conveyed none of his satisfaction, though, and to make sure, he lowered his voice: 'While the saboteur was trying to jam us, I got a fix – via triangulation.' Straker briefly outlined his strategy before sliding copies of a printout from the surveillance screen showing the intersection of the vectored signals across the table. 'The location, this time, turned out to be a block of flats in Rue des Princes,' he said, handing out photographs of the building.

Sabatino looked at the picture of the screen and then the photograph showing the block of flats, appearing increasingly surprised.

'It seems the saboteur is in a temporary let of Apartment 5,' continued Straker. 'His name is Michel Lyons and this is what he looks like,' with which Straker produced another sheaf of photographs and handed these around the table.

Backhouse looked staggered. 'How the hell did you *get* all this?'

'A few tricks of the trade,' replied Straker. 'Anyway, this isn't a complete story, I'm afraid. None of you seems to know him.'

Sabatino picked up one of the photographs and studied the face of the man she now had to acknowledge had been trying to sabotage her race. 'What do we do about this?' she asked, looking down the length of the table at Straker. 'How do we stop this arsehole doing anything like this again?'

'Several things,' he replied, 'but I wanted to go through a few thoughts with you before I discuss my action plan. First, we have no idea of the scale of this threat. Until we're all satisfied that Helli's crash was due to mechanical failure or driver error, I advise we see Ptarmigan – as a whole – to be under threat, here. That said, I didn't detect any jamming of Cunzer's radio this week.

'Second, we need to establish the source of this threat. The jamming device planted in Remy's helmet could not have been planted by an outsider. It could *only* have been put there by someone intimately connected with the team – someone close. An *in*sider. That creates all kinds of sensitive issues, not least suspicion – about whom we suspect and whom we should trust. We might be lucky, though – it could just have been a leftover from Charlotte Grant.'

'Charlie?' chipped in Sabatino. 'Are you serious?'

'Very, Remy,' replied Quartano.

'Yes,' agreed Straker. 'Long story. But, if it *was* her, the saboteurs, now, have clearly lost their mole, which makes things a lot simpler. We must be ready, though, for it to have been someone else – someone who may still be active on the inside.

'My final observation,' Straker went on, 'is to do with the intention of the threat. Your helmet device could have been intended for one of two purposes. Either to eavesdrop and gain advantage over us – learning about our design changes, technological innovation, tactics, pit-stop strategies, and so on. In other words, competitive espionage. Or it was intended for disruptive purposes to throw us off our game and damage our chances. Sabotage.'

'What's your read of their intention?' asked Quartano.

Straker paused. 'From the precise timing of each burst of jamming,' he said, 'I have no doubt that this was sabotage. They were quite clearly trying to damage Remy's chances.'

The room fell silent.

'Okay,' said Quartano, 'that might give us a hunch *why* they might be doing this, but we've no idea who.'

'Correct,' replied Straker, 'apart, that is, from the unknown Michel Lyons.'

'What about the tease you had me play along with during Q2 yesterday,' asked Sabatino, 'when Andy pretended we were going for a three-stop strategy?'

Straker shook his head. 'Inconclusive, Remy, I'm afraid. The tease certainly prompted a subsequent wave of jamming transmissions in Q3, while you discussed brake balances – and which led to my fruit-less intercept up by the Palace. The only car to start the race on a three-stopper was Simi Luciano's Massarella, but we can't be sure he did that because of the teaser message.'

'Right,' said Quartano in a chairmanship tone, as if to indicate the need to draw something from the discussion. 'As you say, Matt, none of this is conclusive, but at least we now know we've got a problem. Also, whatever motivated these people to do this can only be rein-forced by Remy's win here, let alone with her and the team currently leading both Championships. Let's heighten vigilance as much as possible – among the team out here, the mechanics, the roadies, and everyone back at the factory. Matt, I want you to go to Shenington as soon as possible and review all our security measures across the board. Right now – while the F1 circus is still in town – I'm going to ask for an unofficial word with Bo San Marino, to alert him to our problem.

'In the meantime,' said Quartano raising his glass in tribute, 'well done again, Remy – and Andy. A truly historic day and a totally deserved win, both strategically and tactically. Could you both go and make a fuss of Dr Chen and his directors? Make sure they all feel part of this.'

As everyone rose from the table to rejoin the celebrations on the quarterdeck, Quartano added: 'Matt, I'd like you to come with me to see San Marino, please? And be ready to talk through your collec-tion of evidence.'

An hour later Straker and Quartano were shown into Bo San Mari-no's suite in the stylish Columbus Hotel. The President of the FIA looked as patrician as ever, glowing from Formula One's triumphant afternoon.

'Congratulations, Dom,' he said in his soothing Italian lilt as he generously shook hands. 'Remy's win is truly a spectacular achievement for her – for you – for us – for the whole sport.'

'Isn't it, Bo. One of the great sporting stories. Sadly, though, we have to tarnish things, I'm afraid. We have some unnerving news for you.'

'About Helli Cunzer?'

Quartano shook his head. 'He's not yet come round, and it's still too soon to gauge the effects of his terrible crash. No, that's not our news.'

The Marquis of San Marino looked a little disappointed as he showed his guests to the table in the dining area of his suite.

Once settled, Quartano invited Straker to give an overview of their situation. Telling the story from the beginning, Straker produced Remy's helmet from a bag and showed him the location and nature of the jamming device. He then explained how he had detected the saboteur, and produced his findings. He played a recording of the team's radio traffic – to illustrate the precision of the jamming bursts both in Q2 and in the race when the safety car was being deployed.

At the end of the account, Bo San Marino looked at the photograph of Michel Lyons and sat back in his chair. The distinguished face – which had appeared so contented only fifteen minutes before – now looked decidedly troubled.

'Gentlemen, thank you for bringing this to my attention. I'm grateful to know what you've told me. Races, championships even – on which tens of millions of dollars ride – are won or lost by fractions of seconds. This jamming could quite clearly have had a material influence on the outcome of the race. If a team *is* involved in this, and is found guilty, they will face the most severe sanctions.

'However,' San Marino went on, 'as you have had the grace to state yourselves, this,' he said with a wave of his hand at Straker's material, 'while very impressive is not conclusive. You don't know who's behind this. There's not enough, now, for me to act on.'

Both men nodded. 'That's agreed, Bo,' answered Quartano calmly. 'We were just anxious that you be aware of what's going on.'

'Thank you. Can I urge you, at this stage, to be extra vigilant and make sure, for all our sakes, that nothing happens in Spa? You must let me know, immediately, if you detect any further sabotage attempts, or anything intended to thwart Ptarmigan's or Remy's performance.'

FIFTEEN

Straker rejoined the senior Ptarmigan officials on the quarterdeck of Quartano's yacht where, in the peachy light of the evening Mediterranean sun, the celebrations were ongoing. A television crew from a major international channel was granted permission to film an indepth interview with Sabatino on board. As part of the arrangement, Quartano persuaded the producer to include an interview with Dr Chen – so as to offer a perspective on this unprecedented sporting win from a different culture. That it happened to demonstrate the platform Ptarmigan was in a position to offer the CEO of Mandarin Telecom to broadcast to the English-speaking world at the same time was, of course, entirely incidental.

Straker, armed with a fresh glass of champagne, found his way onto the more-secluded upper deck where the interview with Sabatino was taking place. The Mediterranean, the harbour, marina, and hillsides of Monaco provided a luxurious and exotic backdrop. He watched Sabatino – under the lights and surrounded by paraphernalia and numerous technicians – conduct herself with characteristic flair and media savvy.

When it ended, and she emerged from the semicircular cluster of television equipment, Straker was surprised that she made straight for him. 'How did it go with San Marino?'

'As well as we might have hoped, I think. He's appalled, and completely onside. But, as we suspected, we haven't got enough for him to act on.'

Sabatino paused and looked up into Straker's eyes. 'Listen, I meant what I said earlier,' she said. 'I didn't know what you had been getting up to. But what you did helped *directly* with my win today. Without it, I would have lost radio contact – completely – at the critical moment of the safety car. It would have been catastrophic,' and, with that, she raised her glass in apologetic concession. 'I would not have won. I would not – we would not – now be leading both Championships.'

Straker said nothing but very gently chinked her glass and smiled in acknowledgment of her surprising change of heart.

'I'm afraid,' she said more dismissively than apologetically, 'that I thought you were yet another one of those good-looking bullshit-ters, you see – trying desperately to make a role for themselves around here. Believe me, there are plenty of them in Formula One. Now, though – seeing your skills in action – I get why DQ rates you so highly. He says you were quite a soldier.'

Straker looked uncomfortable. 'Hey, this is your day and evening. We should be talking exclusively about you. How many more inter-views like that have you got?' he said jerking his thumb in the direc-tion of the cameras.

'One more, for the Yanks. Americans don't get Formula One – probably because they didn't invent it. My win seems to have caused quite a stir over there, though, so it ought to be good for me commercially. Good enough, at any rate, to buy you dinner. You hungry?'

Straker found himself again taken by surprise. From Sabatino's initial resistance to his counter-espionage measures, to the surprising change of tone as she learnt of his success in identifying the jammer, to her acknowledgment of his helping her win, to this invitation to dinner, Straker was learning to be never quite sure what was coming next with her.

'Famished,' he said. 'Are you serious? I mean – on *this* evening, of all evenings? Haven't you got princes and moguls to schmooze?'

Her smile fell before she added: 'Yeah, probably – but you helped me win today. *You*'re going to keep me safe, aren't you? I'm the Championship leader, now, and I want to hear how you're going to get rid of this bastard saboteur before Spa.'

After her interview on US television, Sabatino and Straker went ashore in the increasingly orange glow of the setting sun. They walked along the pontoons in the harbour, leaving the celebrations aboard the *Melita* still in full swing. Street lamps and lights in shop-fronts were starting to come on along the waterfront. She led him straight to her chosen restaurant, Miguel's in Rue de Grimaldi, which was not what he expected at all. No Michelin star chef, no glitz, no glamour and no one in the place he would recognize. Miguel's was a small family-run affair with elegant décor, gentle lighting, white tablecloths and simple table-top decorations. On first seeing the place, Straker wondered whether Sabatino might have brought him here because she didn't want to be seen with him in public. After her win today, she was definitely media worthy. Any companion would likely prompt all kinds of press interest and speculation.

'I love this place,' she declared with such genuineness as she sat in the chair held for her by the maître d'.

'Mademoiselle Sabatino. A pleasure to see you again. And many congratulations.'

She nodded her thanks and smiled warmly. 'I've been coming here since my GP2 days,' she explained.

'No Monte-Carlo razzmatazz, then? I would've thought you'd be hanging out with all the F1 boys?'

The maître d' unfurled her napkin and laid it gracefully across her lap.

She smiled coyly. 'That's the thing, though, isn't it?'

'What?'

'Boys. F1 *is* a lot of boys. Boys and their toys — and the size of their penises.'

Straker gave a reactive laugh. 'What?'

'Formula One is *so* testosterone-laden. Ridiculously competitive. Even socially, you can't talk about anything — say anything — without someone trying to top it or turn it into a competition. Every story gets trumped. Every claim gets wilder. Every drink gets bigger — and more of a test.'

Straker frowned. 'Isn't that just the way they are?'

'Probably,' she said with an unconvinced shrug. 'Except I can't help feeling it's because I'm a woman.'

'There are loads of women around these people, aren't there – wives, girlfriends?'

'There are, but they all seemed resigned to being spectators. More hangers-on or fawning groupies. They don't seem to be *competed* with.'

'You're different?'

'I'm supposed to be on their level.'

'A threat, then?'

'Shouldn't be. No more than anyone else around those tables and bars, at any rate. I sense a woman doing their thing unnerves them, though. Makes them insecure. Somehow diminishes their masculinity.'

'Whoa, paranoia alert!'

'I *beg* your pardon?' she said sharply.

Straker paused, slightly taken aback by her apparent mood change. 'You're successful in a competitive environment,' he explained. 'They wouldn't be successful competitors if they didn't envy and resent someone beating them. Of course they're not going to like you – you're winning. Exactly the same dynamic would surround you if you were a man.'

'But I haven't been winning till now. It hasn't been resentment of any success. They've behaved like that ever since I started.'

'Of course they have,' he said almost unsympathetically. 'Just being *part* of the F1 circus means success – that you've arrived. You're all threats to each other at that rarefied level. Maybe your suspicion of chauvinism induces in you an awkwardness of manner. Maybe you behave with defensive offence when you're with them?'

'*Fuck* off!'

Straker leaned back in his chair and sighed: 'Q? … E? … D?'

'Fuck *you*!'

There was an awkward – deathly – silence at the table.

Crap, he thought to himself.

Whatever hopes he might have had of setting up a working relationship with this woman now seemed to be shot. Straker cursed inwardly. He hadn't needed to say so much; he hadn't needed to goad her. He looked down and rearranged the napkin in his lap. When he raised his eyes after a few moments' silence, though, he was once again taken completely by surprise. Sabatino was looking at him with a radiant glint in her eye.

'Not at all,' she said, her smile lingering. 'The men in Formula One imply they have big penises. That only a *man* can do what they do. Maybe a woman doing it proves it's not quite so manly as they'd like everyone to believe it is. Trouble, though,' she said slightly defiantly, 'is I know what a big penis *should* look like. *I* know how to measure one.'

Straker smiled, but was not completely sure whether she was being literal or not.

'Whatever the real reason,' she said, 'these boys seem to have to declare themselves whenever I'm around – well, that's how it seems to me.'

They were interrupted by their waiter introducing himself, explaining the specials, and taking their order for drinks. They asked for two Kir Royales. Reassured that the mood between them might have been restored, Straker looked to change the subject. 'How did you get into all this, anyway?' he asked as bread and olive oil was placed between them.

'F1? Slowly, then quickly.'

Straker offered Sabatino the basket. 'Sorry?'

She took a piece of bread and dunked it in the oil. 'Antonio, my elder brother – back in Malta – was a petrolhead. A car nut. Spent his entire childhood dying to get a drive in a go-kart. He stripped down cars, reconditioned parts, tuned up engines. He'd do hundreds of them to earn pocket money from a local garage. The owner's son raced go-karts, you see. But the son was crap – constantly crashing and damaging everything. Antonio earned pocket money – and brownie points – fixing up his engines and parts. As a treat, every now and again, the garage people would take him to the track, just outside Valletta. He hoped that, one day, they might give him a drive. They never did. Even so, Antonio would still enjoy going to watch.'

The waiter returned with their drinks. They ordered their food.

'One Saturday when I was about sixteen, Antonio asked me to go with him to the track. I went and loved it, you know? The whole scene – the noise, the smell of heat, exhaust, oil and rubber. But particularly the speed.'

'You had no interest in anything mechanical up until then?'

Sabatino shook her head. 'Ponies. Didn't have my own, but was completely obsessed. Used to do the same sort of chores as Antonio, but my hangout was the local riding stables. While he was fixing up parts from the rich boy's mistakes, to get my rides I'd be shovelling shit and grooming. Mother wasn't rich enough to buy us our fun – we had to earn it for ourselves.'

'How did *you* get to drive, then?'

Sabatino smiled wistfully. 'The garage boy fancied me. He kept asking me back – to watch him race. Suddenly, to Antonio, I was a little sister with currency. It looked like I'd be guaranteeing him a lot more tickets for race days. Anyway, over time, I got familiar with the scene. While standing around for hours, I started *watching*. I found myself wanting to understand why some karts were faster than others and, then, why some drivers were faster than others in similar machines. Without realizing it, I seemed to know how to read a track – and the dynamics of racing.'

'Very analytical.'

'Maybe, but it got me into serious trouble. After one race, I stupidly pointed out that the rich kid had been beaten by slower drivers and slower karts. Then I told him why. It was like kicking him in the balls. In a tantrum, he said: "Well if you think you're so fucking good, *you* do it!"'

'You did – and the rest is history?' offered Straker as a denouement.

Sabatino took a sip of her Kir Royale, and shook her head. 'Never so easy. I did drive – in the last race that day. But only as a laugh. I got bumped, overtaken, baulked – all sorts. There was *some*thing there, though. Definitely. The race was only ten laps, and I was only steady for the last three. But it gave me enough time to try out my observations – about line, timing, acceleration, braking and car control. And, bizarrely, in those last ninety seconds, I found a rhythm.'

'Which meant you displaced the rich kid and took his drive?'

Sabatino shook her head. 'The only displacement was me as the rich guy's girlfriend. He was so pissed off because I'd managed to clock a faster lap time than he ever had.'

'Within your first ten laps *ever*?'

'Amazing, huh? But me falling out with the boyfriend triggered a falling-out with my brother – because *I* had been given a drive in a kart and he never had.'

'All that pique from your brother and the so-called boyfriend.'

'Yep, all because of wounded pride and jealousy. It was harsh, but, as an experience, a great foundation.'

'For what?'

'Being a female doing something at the same time as a man. I realized that, for me, if I was ever to do anything in motor racing – or life, probably – I'd have to learn to cope with an additional set of dynamics.'

'Don't tell me – chauvinism?'

Sabatino scowled at him.

'What *did* you learn then?' asked Straker moderating his tone enough, he hoped, to prevent another "fuck you".

Their food arrived and was placed reverentially in front of them by two waiters.

'Certain things,' she said. 'I came up with one overarching mantra.'

'Which was?'

'To stay *me*.'

'*Very* deep.'

'It is,' she rebuked. 'The temptation was to become male – or masculine. To be one of them. To be what *they* want. I resolved very early on not to do that.'

'Not even if that helped you to understand them – or how to beat them?'

'Think like them, yes. But not *be* like them, no. That would never work. I could never *be* them. Trying to be them would only make me phoney.'

'If *staying you* was your main mantra, what others did you come up with?'

'Only my Machiavellian killer app!'

'What's that?'

'To treat people – particularly egotistical men – not as they are … but as they *think* they are.'

Straker frowned as he mulled this over. 'Doesn't that create phoniness too?'

'Oh yes!' said Sabatino with a broad smile. 'But in them, not me! With this approach, they're never directly threatened. They're disarmed. It helps me get their guard down – meaning I can read them much more easily and, ultimately, get them to do what *I* want.'

They ate for a few moments, Straker praising the food. 'If you were so completely ostracized by your brother and boyfriend, how did you get back into racing, then?'

'That first drive didn't go unnoticed. I was spotted by a rival team. The owner saw my rapid improvement in lap times. When his driver had an accident and couldn't race, he got in touch – probably because he liked the novelty of fielding a girl driver, more than me. It certainly caused a bit of a stir. I made it a condition of my agreement, though, to be given a proper budget for practice.'

'And that was the off?'

'In karting, yes. I raced for two seasons and notched up some good wins and results. It was then that I came up with my third tenet – nothing to do with chauvinism, you'll be pleased to hear.'

'Which is?' he asked with a concessionary smile at her taunt.

'Attention to detail. To leave nothing overlooked. The competitive difference between karts or F1 cars, particularly, in normal conditions is minimal – measured in hundredths of a second per lap, a matter of seconds over a two-hour race. Nothing, really. But working through the whole gamut of a race and race preparation I came across one potentially huge advantage.'

Straker's expression conveyed considerable curiosity: 'What was that?'

'It was so simple and obvious – to me, at least. Race cars and rain don't mix, right? In the wet, you can easily drop half a minute a lap. Also, because of the far higher likelihood of spins, bumps and crashes, the expected race order in the wet can be completely turned on its head. Wet conditions can easily turn a motor race into a lottery. So I thought: why be a hostage to the wet? Why not try and turn rain – wet conditions – into an advantage? In any season of racing, it's *inevitably* going to rain sometime. If I could *materially* bring it home when everyone else is cocking it up, I saw the possibility of creating enough of a margin – even in just one race – to make a difference to a whole season's results.'

Straker nodded and smiled appreciatively at the logic. 'How did you act on that?'

'Practice, practice, practice! Some people practise until they get it right; I wanted to practise until I couldn't get it wrong. Every time it rained – or even looked like raining – I rushed to the track and went out in a kart and drove – drove, drove, drove. I spun. I slid. I spun some more, got soaked, caught God knows how many colds. Nearly caught pneumonia – certainly had a bad bout of pleurisy. But … I kept pushing myself and, in the end … I got better. In fact, I got pretty good.'

'Doesn't everyone do this?'

'No, thank heavens. There's only one other who I discovered did anything similar – and I only learnt about him after I'd started in Formula One.'

'Who was that?'

Sabatino raised a self-effacing eyebrow. 'Ayrton Senna,' she said.

'But I'm convinced my obsession with rain also helped my general driving. Tuning-in to the hyper sensitivity of wet conditions, I guess, improved my car control. Must have. Because of that, I genuinely believe that I'm able to push myself harder in the dry.'

'Makes sense. Who spotted you for the bigger cars, then?'

Sabatino finished a mouthful of food. 'I soon moved to England, to study engineering at university – go-karting sparking my interest in mechanics – and picked up an occasional drive here and there. I seemed blessed by a series of one-offs. An injury to a driver at Brands Hatch gave me a chance drive in a Formula Ford. A disqualified driver at Thruxton opened up a seat in Formula 3000 for half a season. And my big break came at Donington at the end of last year where I was driving a GP2: I pulled off a coup against Simi Luciano, the runner-up in last year's F1 season, no less, who had turned up to give some sort of exhibition drive.'

'You beat him?'

Sabatino nodded coquettishly.

'What?'

Sabatino smiled at Straker's reading of her expression. 'That day, Donington was wet. Not just wet – it was *wet*, wet. Ceaseless torrential rain. Standing water across large parts of the circuit. To everyone's surprise I wiped the floor with Luciano. I went round *twenty-five seconds* faster than him – only four seconds slower than for a dry lap time. It caused quite a stir.'

Straker gave an I-can-see-why nod in admiration.

'*That*,' she said almost as a flourish, 'was lift-off – Mr Quartano being the reason.'

'Really?'

'He was there – at Donington. It all happened so fast. He made me an offer that very afternoon. I think it was about the time he was trying to buy Ptarmigan from the receiver. I guess I'd have to say that from that point on the rest is history.'

Straker shook his head in appreciation. 'Talent will out.'

'Maybe, and in the end, perhaps – but not immediately. It's not automatically meritocratic. Talent's still got to find its chance to shine. And so much of that's down to luck. Quartano, therefore, was my lucky charm.'

Straker nodded. 'Mine too,' he said as he subconsciously reached for his drink in a toast. 'Where do you think your driving talent comes from?'

Sabatino shrugged, taking a sip of her own. 'Who knows? Certainly not my parents – neither nature nor nurture. My father died when I was four, but had no mechanical bent, and Mother's practically a certified agoraphobic. She hates me racing – says it's far too dangerous. If she gets to hear about Helli Cunzer's accident yesterday, she'll have a fit. Where does any ability come from? Beats me. I enjoyed riding, and I suppose you enjoy things you're good at. Horses test you in all sorts of things – but certainly balance, feel, rhythm, and a sense of anticipation. A horse has an independent spirit. A mind of its own. You can get it to do certain things, but it can always spook, change its mind, lose its balance, or require help recovering, particularly jumping cross-country.'

'And you think those skills transferred to the cockpit?'

'They're pretty similar to the demands of car control, I'd say. In that respect, horsemanship and driving ability have a similar core. It's not for nothing, for instance, that Schumacher's a quite brilliant horseman – Western riding,' she said with a smirk. 'But still. None of those abilities are worth anything, though, without nerve. The key factor in F1 has to be a readiness to push hard and to commit.'

'Not the will to win?'

'Male drivers say that. Must play to the macho instinct, I suppose. To me winning's incidental. A by-product. If I get everything right, I normally come out on top. Winning's not my drug; getting it right is. You can win and still be rated as a human being.'

Straker was surprised by her tone of self-justification. 'Why do you say that?' he asked.

She looked almost apologetic. 'I was the only driver to go and see Helli Cunzer today. Twenty-four hours ago he nearly died. There but for the grace of God … Was it weakness to go? To support a man who got it wrong? Am I any less of a winner for caring about a friend who made a mistake?'

There was very nearly a tear in Sabatino's eye. Straker's opinion of this woman was changing by the minute.

Their plates were cleared away, creating a natural break in the conversation. Trying to divert herself from such frustration and disappointment, she said: 'I have a subject for you,' and gave him a knowing smile. 'I saw your reaction to it – in the pit lane on Thursday.'

Sensing a tone of mischief, he asked, with exaggerated hesitancy: 'Reaction to what?'

'The mention of Charlie Grant?'

Straker immediately looked down, somewhere towards his napkin.

'There's a personal history there, no?'

Straker dabbed his mouth.

'It wouldn't surprise me if there was,' she said with a verbal shrug in her voice. 'She was stunning to look at. All the men clustered round her like bees to honey. She knew how to work people; she had everyone eating out of her trousers.'

'Charlie was a menace,' Straker said, leaning back in his chair and looking Sabatino in the eye. 'For various reasons, she was out to do Quartech – and Quartano, personally – serious harm.'

Sabatino, struck by Straker's expression and tone of voice, was clearly keen to probe further: 'How?'

Straker reached again for his drink and took a long sip. 'By leaking company – and potentially national – secrets to a foreign rival. Because of that, Quartano's convinced she's behind this sabotage of you, your car – maybe even Helli's car – and the race.'

Sabatino looked genuinely surprised. 'How *did* she die then? I get the feeling it wasn't anything to do with a road accident?'

Straker shook his head. He paused. 'She died in Buhran.'

'Really?' said Sabatino, indicating that she believed there was a lot more to all this.

Straker shrugged before taking another sip of his drink.

'How close to her death were you then?' asked Sabatino, with a strange hint of bloodlust in her voice.

Straker put down his glass and looked her straight in the eye. 'Too close,' he said. 'Now,' with a clear edge to his voice, 'can we change the subject, please?'

This time, it was Sabatino's turn to be taken aback – by the sharpness of *his* tone. She backed off immediately.

SIXTEEN

The Formula One circus was on the move. Being a double-header, most of the artics and motor homes were making straight for the Ardennes to set up for the Belgian Grand Prix the following weekend.

Quartano, accompanied by Sabatino, flew the Mandarin directors out of Monte-Carlo to Mandelieu Airport by helicopter. After seeing them off from there, Remy flew in her private jet to Malta for a few days, to celebrate her win. Straker made his own way to the Nice airport by road, using the time to consider events and refocus on his task. He found himself motivated by something new. For all the pressures Sabatino had to put up with – technical, racing, physical, performance and media – he was troubled by how personally she was now taking the attempt to sabotage her.

Looking out of the window, as the taxi snaked its way through the rocky scenery of the Côte d'Azur in the early Riviera sun, he returned his mind to what he had by way of leads. Two things. One, a piece of physical evidence – the bug found in Sabatino's helmet; while the second was a name: Monsieur Michel Lyons – the temporary tenant of Apartment 5 at 25 Rue des Princes. What more could he learn about these? And how could either help him?

Straker had an idea. Pulling his mobile from his pocket he scrolled through his contacts directory and retrieved the telephone number for the porter of the block of flats. He asked himself: When would Michel Lyons be leaving Monte-Carlo? Taking a punt, he gave the number a ring.

'Could I speak to Michel Lyons, in number 5, please?'

'*Non*,' said the aged porter.

'Has he gone out?'

'*Non*. He has left.'

Excellent, thought Straker, exactly as he hoped. 'That's a nuisance,' he said. 'I have an important package for him. Do you have an address I could send it on to?' Straker asked.

There was a grunt from down the line.

'Please, monsieur, this is very important.'

'*Attendez*,' growled the porter.

Straker heard the receiver hit something hard and then the man's raised voice echoing in the background. He breathed deeply, hoping he would get lucky and be able to keep this lead alive. After several minutes of uncertainty, the aged porter came back on the line and, although sounding disappointed, he said: 'I have a home address.'

'*Merci, merci.*'

'Monsieur Michael Lyons, Flax Cottage…'

Straker's mind was already racing.

'…Prince Rupert Lane, Gaydon, Warwickshire, Royaume-Uni.'

Straker shook his head as he jotted down the details. '*Pardonnez-moi*,' he said as apologetically as he could. 'Did you say Michael, as M – I – C – H – *A* – E – L?'

'*Oui!*'

'*Monsieur, merci bien.* Thank you very much. I'll send the parcel on to him at home.'

Straker ended the call and smiled in satisfaction. 'Odder and odder,' he said to himself as he mulled this new information. Dialling his office number in Quartech International's London headquarters, he spoke to Karen, his department's research assistant. He could picture her in their office on the ninth floor of Cavendish Square, with its stunning views out over the capital through its floor-to-ceiling, plate-glass windows. He asked the quiet but superbly meticulous Karen to research Michael Lyons, of Gaydon – particularly in respect of any connection he might have with motor racing.

With this additional unexpected piece of the jigsaw puzzle, Straker considered his other potential lead. The physical evidence they had in the form of the jamming device found in Sabatino's helmet. What could they learn from that, if anything?

Picking up his phone again, Straker rang Andy Backhouse, who had flown out on the red-eye that morning and whom he expected to be back on the ground in England by now.

'Come up to the factory as soon as you like,' said Backhouse keenly.

'How about later today? I want to tackle this scumbag saboteur as soon as possible.'

'Sure. I'll be at Shenington within the hour. I'll be there till whenever.'

'Great. I'm due to land at Heathrow with DQ around lunchtime.'

'I'll send a car to meet you. See you this afternoon.'

Straker arrived at Nice airport, and, this being the wealthy Riviera, was processed airside through the large part of the Mandelieu complex devoted to private aircraft. With barely any delay, he was soon driven out across the apron to the steps of the waiting Quartech Falcon. It proudly boasted the company's logo on the tail fin: a crimson Maltese Cross within the circular part of a black letter Q – and the company motto, *"Si Vis Pacem, Para Bellum"*, underneath.

Quartano was already on board. The moment Straker appeared the doors were shut, the engines whined into life, and the plane sought clearance for take-off from the tower.

'I've just seen Dr Chen and his colleagues board their plane,' reported Quartano, spreading a linen napkin across his lap. 'Mandarin Telecom could not be more engaged, despite the horrors of poor Helli's crash. Remy's win seems to have sealed the deal. We've clearly exceeded their expectations from a marketing point of view. Hardly surprising. The press and media coverage from the weekend – around the first female winner of a Grand Prix, let alone Monaco – has been astonishing. We've agreed to sign a Memorandum of Understanding within two weeks, and the full contract in Shanghai at the Chinese Grand Prix. Mandarin have already offered to introduce Quartech to Chinese government – *Ministry of National Defense* – officials, no less. Priceless,' he said with a broad triumphant smile. 'Thank heavens for Formula One.'

Straker could see how much Quartano was fired up by the events of the weekend. 'Your absolute priority, Matt,' he said as the plane levelled off and they were served their coffee and breakfast, 'is to rid us of any further interference by this sodding saboteur. Thanks to Backhouse's team finding the bug, and your outstanding countermeasures, we denied them their interference in our communications, which could have done us serious damage. And what about Helli's crash? God forbid it was sabotage, as it was clearly life-threatening. If they and any bastard insider are still motivated to do us harm – and after the win in Monaco we have to assume they would be – this could get ugly. And now, with a sponsorship deal of $750 million and this phenomenal "in" to Chinese government circles via Mandarin Telecom, Quartech has a massive market position at stake.'

Straker nodded his appreciation of the situation. 'I'm on it, sir.'

Quartano looked reassured, but his expression seemed to demand elaboration.

'Backhouse is arranging a car for me from Heathrow,' Straker volunteered. 'I'm going straight up to the factory the moment we land.'

'Good.'

'I've also uncovered some *new* news.'

Quartano raised an eyebrow.

'I've managed to establish that Monsieur Michel Lyons is not actually *Michel* but Mr Michael Lyons. And that he lives in Gaydon.'

Quartano's expression darkened.

'Should it surprise us he's British?' Straker asked.

'Not really. If Mr Michael Lyons was to have *any* credibility in motor racing, it would certainly be enhanced by his being British. Seven of the eleven F1 teams are based in England.'

'And Gaydon?'

'Fits perfectly,' replied Quartano. 'Gaydon is home to Aston Martin and Jaguar Land Rover. Ptarmigan are minutes away. And within an hour you've got Lotus, Mercedes, Williams, Lambourn, and Red Bull, while not forgetting that Prodrive's one junction down the M40. And Silverstone, of course, is right there too. If you wanted someone to come from the heart of motor racing, Gaydon's pretty close to it.'

'Well at least it goes some way to confirming that the occupant of Apartment 5, 25 Rue des Princes *was* the source of the jamming. It would, I suppose, have been too easy for his geographic location to have told us something about his team affiliation?'

'It might have, if he lived in Maranello or Stupinigi – for Ferrari or Massarella. But, no. Ironically, he's geographically closer to Ptarmigan than any of the others.'

'I've got Karen in Competition Intelligence doing some digging on him.'

'Good. Now you know where to find him, I want to know everything about this arsehole – particularly who he's working for. Then, we will decide how to remove him, and take out anyone around him who fancies themselves as a threat.'

SEVENTEEN

Straker split from Quartano at Heathrow and was met by the car sent for him from Ptarmigan.

On his way up the M40, Karen called him from London. 'I have some info on Michael Lyons, but it's not much, I'm afraid.'

'Not to worry – anything might get us started.'

'It looks like he's an I.T. specialist. Graduated from Aston University, started out on a graduate traineeship with IBM. Was sent on secondment to MG Rover and then transferred to them permanently. Joined their electronics team but was made redundant just before the company went into administration in 2005. Strangely, there's no further information since then. Nothing about current employment. Whereabouts unknown.'

'Is that it?' Straker asked disappointedly.

'Afraid so.'

Just over an hour later Straker was driven onto the Shenington Airfield, one of Oxfordshire's long-abandoned RAF wartime air stations. Passing some of the derelict pre-fab concrete huts, and even the old control tower, they drove down a long straight approach road lined by an avenue of trees. Straker was greeted at the end by iconic architecture. Confident, proud and powerful were the adjectives implied by the brand-new Ptarmigan factory. It had nowhere near the self-belief of the Foster and Partners statement in Woking, but was impressive nonetheless.

They continued through a tunnel set into a broad, three-storey facade of reflective glass, emerging on the other side into a sizeable quadrangle and more reflective glass. Despite the sheen on the windows, there was some visibility into the buildings. Ghostly-looking figures could be seen working behind desks, at CAD work stations, poring over laboratory benches and, in one window, he saw a team working on a complete chassis. Straker's car circled round the sweep of the quad, which enclosed a large, heavily-landscaped ornamental garden, and pulled up under the awning in front of the main entrance.

Inside the reception area, he faced more glass, this time fronting a row of display cabinets holding all the team's trophies, which seemed to cover every spare inch of the walls.

Straker was greeted by Backhouse and handed a security pass.

'I daresay you'll want to study our security measures,' Backhouse said. 'Perhaps it might be helpful to give you an idea of the whole process so you could see where we might be vulnerable to leaks or outside interference?'

Straker agreed, slipping the turquoise lanyard over his head.

'Let's start in Design, then.'

Riding up two floors in a glass-walled lift, they moved through the cathedral of modernity to the design studio. As Backhouse swiped his card through the door panel, automatic doors let them into a vast open-plan office. Forty or so people were distributed across the space. Atmospherically, it was quiet and serious – not exactly what Straker had imagined from a creative team, particularly one that had enjoyed such a historic weekend.

While security was the main purpose of the two men's tour round the Ptarmigan factory, Backhouse inevitably found himself describing the practices in each room or workshop along their way. Straker soon gathered that, remarkably, Ptarmigan's aim was to reinvent the car on a continual basis – but always within the dimensional, weight and capacity constraints imposed by the FIA's Formula. Backhouse explained that in trying to work within those limits, they were faced with the classic trade-offs of any design; in this case, they had to balance any extra performance that might be enjoyed from a new component or configuration against any unwanted consequences – typically extra weight or size. Straker was told that paring a component to the bone might get it to perform better but doing so could reduce its tolerance, weaken it, and even invite it to fail, which would of course then threaten reliability.

Backhouse went on to point out that making their components and cars too reliable, on the other hand, would result in their being heavier than they needed to be, so slowing them down. 'But, as the legendary Murray Walker had it: "If you want to finish first, first you've got to finish". Except the last thing we want is any structural redundancy,' qualified Backhouse with a believe-it-or-not expression on his face.

Straker was led on through the quietness of the design studio, between the rows of designers, most of whom were working on large high-definition computer screens. Some of the operators were rotating wireframe diagrams, while others analysed brightly coloured thermal images of components in three dimensions via touch-screen commands. Backhouse indicated that the data recorded from the cars' two hundred and fifty on-board sensors, which Straker had seen being collated through the headquarters truck in Monaco, was fed into this redesign process. Conclusions drawn then allowed for each component to be redesigned electronically. Once done, the computer could then backtest any new design against a model using the actual load, pressure and temperature data of the last few races.

Straker was clearly impressed with the attention to detail and the capacity of the system. 'But won't reshaping one component have an effect on all the others around it?'

Backhouse gave him a smile of appreciation. 'Welcome to the Rubik's Cube of race car design.'

Backhouse led Straker on through the room to another set of automatic doors. Once he swiped his card, they passed onto a balcony overlooking a cavernous space that reached from the ground up into the three-storey roof of the building. Every surface of the room was white and gleaming. Here, there was considerable noise.

Several bulky machines were spread out across the workshop floor. This, Backhouse explained, was where the newly designed components were sent to be made. They walked down a flight of long white stairs to ground floor level, and across to one of the size-able machines. Backhouse indicated that one of them made alumin-ium components, while another did tungsten, and another titanium parts.

Leading him off into the next room, Backhouse told Straker: 'This is where we test samples of our new components to destruction.'

Inside, behind some sturdy-looking safety glass, several techni-cians were operating machines and applying force – percussive, com-pressive, torsional or tensile – to several components.

'And once you've made and tested something new – and it passes these tests – what happens if it *does* require a change in the shape of its mounting or its interface with other components?'

Backhouse explained the most likely consequence of a new com-ponent was a change in the shape or weight distribution of the car, albeit that the change might be small. Even so, the bodywork could be affected, necessitating remedial adjustment in the aerodynamics. Most problematic, he said, was a new component that threatened to protrude beyond the limit of the physical dimensions set by the Formula.

'And if you *do* break the Formula, what can that mean?'

'A *big* fine.' Backhouse described the penalties imposed by the FIA, and illustrated how the governing body meant their fines to hurt. The last one – for an infringement – had been five million dollars for a non-compliant diffuser on one of the Massarellas. But worse, the FIA could dock Championship points, which potentially cost the teams even more. Under the Concorde Agreement – the arrangement with the commercial rights holder to distribute some of the multi-billion-dollars-a-year revenues from Formula One spon-sorship, advertizing, TV rights and royalties – shares of that income were calculated using a team's standing in the Constructors' Cham-pionship at the end of the season. Being docked Constructors points as a penalty, therefore, could cost a team its placing in the standings, which would then hurt its share of the Concorde payout – to the tune of millions of dollars.

Backhouse led off into a smaller room. 'This is our carbon fibre workshop.'

In the middle was a large – twenty-or-so square feet – waist-high table. On it was a sheet of what looked like black cloth. Lifting up a corner, Backhouse extolled the virtues of carbon fibre as a remarkable material, showing a fascinated Straker that it came in flexible sheets and, depending on the direction of the fibres, could give enormous tensile strength while being remarkably light. This was coated in resin and fired in an oven. Backhouse leant down and lifted up a three-foot long nose assembly from Remy's car, offering it as an illustration. 'This is constructed of twenty-five layers of carbon fibre. It can withstand a head-on impact at one hundred and twenty miles an hour, absorbing all that force within it and so is capable of protecting the driver. This stuff most certainly saved Helli's life over the weekend. But feel the weight?'

Straker's arm almost shot up as he took hold of it, expecting it to be far heavier. It only weighed about the same as two litres of milk.

'The only trouble with carbon fibre,' Backhouse went on, 'is that you can't screw anything into it; it won't take the thread of a screw, for instance. The stuff just crumbles.'

'How *do* you fasten it to other materials then?'

'Good old-fashioned glue!'

After looking at the next workshop, focusing on hydraulic technology, Straker was shown the engine section of the factory. Backhouse explained that Ptarmigan did not make their own engines, which would be far too expensive – even with their sizeable Quartech budget. He explained how their engine partner, Benbecular, fitted in, and likened the power, quality and reliability of their engines to those of Mercedes, Renault and BMW. Straker learnt that Ptarmigan's only involvement with engine design was in engine management, working with an outside contractor, Trifecta Systems, to develop Ptarmigan's own bespoke operating system – a highly sophisticated optimizer which offered them various nuanced options and settings they could adjust during a race.

'All this is worked on in here,' said Backhouse as they entered a room that reminded Straker of a music studio. Technicians were working at something resembling a mixing desk, while through another sheet of safety glass an engine was bolted to a static mount and being run at what sounded like – even with the soundproofing of the glass – full throttle.

'Finally,' said Backhouse, as they made their way on through the Ptarmigan factory, 'we come to aerodynamics and our wind tunnel.'

They passed through a further set of security-controlled automatic doors, and entered another manufacturing section. Inside, Backhouse led Straker towards a man in a white coat who was studying what looked to Straker like a scale model of a Formula One car.

'Colin, can I introduce Matt Straker of Quartech? Matt, this is Colin Moore, Ptarmigan's Director of Aerodynamics.'

The two strangers shook hands. Straker took in Moore's intense expression which was enhanced by his closely – almost brutally – shaved head.

'Andy's giving me a crash course in how our cars are designed and built.'

Moore smiled and asked how much Straker knew of aerodynamics in the context of these cars. He admitted not much.

'Without aerodynamic surfaces,' said Moore inviting Straker to look at the model on the workbench, 'a Formula One car couldn't go anywhere near as fast as they go. Mechanical grip – the grip provided simply by the balance of the car, the tyres and their contact with the road surface – would not, on its own, hold a modern car on the track. Aerodynamic surfaces are critical.' To give Straker an idea of their effectiveness, Moore indicated that an F1 car travelling at ninety miles an hour generated enough aerodynamic downforce that it could run upside-down along the roof of a tunnel.

'However, the greater the downforce, the more the drag – and so the less quick we can go. But all of us are presented with numerous challenges. The first is set by the Formula, which limits the dimensions of the car – including the size and placement of any wings and fins. Second, the FIA – in trying to reduce the cost of F1 – has banned the teams from all testing, other than on the track during race weekends.'

Straker pulled an are-you-serious? face.

'And, third, we're allowed to simulate the aerodynamics in a wind tunnel, but – get this – we have to do it with half-sized cars. Our half-sized models are made of plastic rather than metal and carbon fibre, which of course requires a whole other manufacturing process,' he said with a wave of his hand at all the technicians and machine tools laid out across the bustling workshop.

After a few minutes looking at the model, Moore led them on to a nearby computer screen. 'F1 is an open-wheel formula. In other words, we can't smooth the shape by covering the whole body like a Le Mans car, and we have limits on the size of the aerofoils we *can* fit. When an F1 car punches a hole through the air,' he explained, 'its profile, wheels, and protuberances create drag – friction, resistance – which slows us down. Our aim is to minimize that drag, and help increase the ease with which it slices through the air.' The aerodynamicist tapped a few icons on the screen. Two images appeared. Straker saw the screen was horizontally split – top and bottom – each showing a silhouetted chassis. Blue smoke seemed to be flowing over each one. 'Here,' he said pointing at the upper image, 'is a simulation of our car's core body with no aero assistance at all.'

This top car, without any wings or surfaces, showed the blue smoke swirling frantically off the front wheels and bubbling the length of the car, with a huge cloud of turbulence behind. 'Every element of disturbed air slows us down,' said Moore. 'Now look at the bottom model, which shows our current aerodynamic package.'

This car, fitted with the wings and surfaces, showed the blue smoke – the airflow – over and around it was considerably smoother. Even where there were blunt bits of the car, the small blades and fins attached to various parts clearly trimmed and nudged the airflow preventing nearly all of the turbulence seen in the one above.

'Does this computer model analyze the airflows and then prescribe what changes are needed?'

'Sadly not for everything. CFD, Computational Fluid Dynamics, are getting better but – for reliability – if we want to try something new, we prefer to physically cut out a fin or wing, stick it on the model, run it through the tunnel and see what happens.'

'Pretty much trial and error, then?'

The aerodynamicist nodded and moved further down the workshop. 'Here, for instance,' said Moore, 'we're working on and testing a design for a new front wing we've come up with. It's quite a radical innovation. We've configured these three blades,' he said lifting up a model of the nosecone, 'to go on each end of the front wing.'

These, Straker saw, were curved and in different sizes, the smallest was about the same size as a paperback novel with the largest about the size of a piece of A3.

'As you can see, they're each curved and, when they're fitted together, have the effect of spiralling the air up and back off the end of each wing. We've nicknamed them our Fibonacci Blades.'

'As in the golden section?' offered Straker.

'The very same,' said the aerodynamicist with a nod of appreciation. 'It's uncanny how nature's arithmetic, so often, gets it right.'

Straker took the model and studied it more closely. 'When do you hope to have this on the cars?'

'Spa this weekend. We're testing it in the wind tunnel at the moment, if you want to go and take a look?'

Backhouse accepted the invitation and they thanked Moore for his time. Straker was led from the modelling workshop through another set of computer-controlled doors and into a vast room. This was filled with a deafening rushing sound. Above their heads was a twelve-foot diameter tube configured in a circle about thirty yards across. 'That's the tunnel up there,' said Backhouse as he led Straker up some stairs. 'Air is accelerated and then whizzed continually round that loop.'

'Like your own mini Hadron Collider?'

They reached a viewing gallery. Set in one wall was a sheet of glass which gave them sight of a half-sized model of a Ptarmigan racing car suspended from the ceiling by a complicated-looking hydraulic arm.

Backhouse provided a voice-over for Straker as he stared transfixed through the window: 'You will notice the floor under the car is being rolled extremely quickly, which is turning the wheels. We do that to simulate the airflow through and around a real car as best we can.'

'How long do you test each model for?'

'Each modification gets about an hour in here. The results are analyzed. We then play with a few alterations, which we hope will make a difference, and then go back and test it all again – and so on.'

'Good God, it sounds never-ending.'

'It is – because it's an iterative process. It shouldn't surprise you that this wind tunnel is running twenty-four hours a day.'

'No down time, then? How close to Spa will we be testing the car for *that* race?'

'Right up until Remy's car leaves here for Belgium tomorrow evening – hopefully fitted *with* our new design, the Fibonacci Blades, that Colin mentioned next door. You can see them, there, on the model,' said Backhouse pointing through the window.

Backhouse walked Straker back to his office. 'The fact is that if you don't make improvements to your car, with every other team constantly trying to innovate, you'll effectively end up going backwards,' summarized Backhouse. 'The Formula may get more and more restrictive from one year to the next, but, despite that, the developments we all make to our designs still make the cars go faster and faster every year.'

'The pressure to perform is absolutely remarkable,' declared Straker. 'We were lectured on competitiveness throughout training in the Marines, but I truly didn't fully understand what being competitive meant until I saw this. Your pursuit of every possible ounce of performance – in every single component of the cars – is astonishing. With all this effort and dedication, it makes the work of the saboteur all the more detestable.'

EIGHTEEN

Backhouse led Straker into his spacious office, which had a restful view through the reflective glass out over the Oxfordshire countryside. Its inside walls were festooned with pictures of racing cars, miniature replicas of trophies, models of Ptarmigan cars and other memorabilia. Unexpectedly, one wall showed an array of photographs from a time when Backhouse had clearly been a member of the Massarella team. Straker had been completely unaware of that association in Backhouse's past.

Turning his attention to the room, he was grateful to see a plate of shrink-wrapped sandwiches and several cans of soft drink waiting for them on the desk.

'Thanks for the tour,' said Straker. 'It's helped fill me in on the process, pressures, as well as our systems. Can we talk about overall security?'

'Sure,' said Backhouse, unwrapping the sandwiches and offering them to Straker. 'You saw our computer-operated doors around the factory. Every member of our four hundred staff wears a security pass and has to swipe in and out of everywhere they go, as we did. That would have to make it hard for anyone to be where they shouldn't, or do anything without being spotted.'

Straker acknowledged the statement with a nod.

'What about scrutiny of the team out on the road and while we've got people at races?'

'Not possible to be so tight,' said Backhouse. 'The road crew numbers about sixty, which includes the lorry drivers, those who travel with the cars, the kit, those who set up the garages in the pit lane, and the staff in the headquarter truck. Lorries can get left unattended, as do, sometimes, the cars and our kit – when things are being unloaded.'

'What can we do to tighten security away at races?'

Backhouse finished chewing and snapped open a can of Coke. 'The circuits operate very strict accreditation and pass controls, as you saw in Monte-Carlo. But they are not perfect and – here's the crucial flaw – they don't stop accredited members of other teams coming near us. We often find people wandering about – particularly, would you believe, in the pit lane?'

Straker frowned. 'Where, then, do you reckon we are most vulnerable to interference?'

'If these saboteurs have someone on the inside, Matt, it could be anywhere. I wouldn't know where to begin.'

Straker was surprised by such resignation. He hadn't expected Backhouse to be quite so fatalistic. 'What about external interference, then?'

'We have a number of external suppliers – not many – who we accredit at the factory visit by visit. There, though, I think the opportunities are more limited – as the risks are enormous. If the saboteurs *are* connected with another team, and they got caught, the fines they'd suffer from the FIA would pretty much put them out of business. So if it is another team, they have got to be *extraordinarily* careful, clever and discreet.'

'I think we need to face up to this being a very real and devious threat.'

Backhouse almost shrugged. 'What do you want from us then?'

'Enhanced awareness,' replied Straker. 'You have good security in the factory, which seemed to work well as we walked around this morning. We need everyone to stick to your existing rules, to the letter; it might be an inconvenience, but that will make it harder for any rogue insider. Also, at races, let's cut out all visits to the pits for non-team members. Let's set up our own internal checks into and out of our garage in the pit lane.'

Backhouse raised his eyebrows. 'You do realize there's an incompatibility between the spontaneity of a tactical racing team and the rigid processes of a security system.'

'Look what happened to Helli. Do we really want to take any chance with machines that go this fast? It's not just the lives of our drivers. It could be the crowds around the track. Next time the saboteurs strike, they could actually kill people.'

'Of course I understand that,' said Backhouse testily.

'So we'll tighten everything up?'

The race engineer nodded unenthusiastically. 'So what are *you* doing – about all this?' he said with just a hint of a challenge.

Ignoring Backhouse's frustrated tone, he said: 'Sabotage research. I want to learn more from the bug, which I'm hoping will tell us something. I also want us to go over what's left of Helli's car – to convince ourselves that his crash wasn't caused by anything sinister.'

Backhouse took another bite of his sandwich. 'The Monaco kit should be here by lunchtime tomorrow. We can examine the bug and begin the crash investigation then.'

'Okay.' Straker went on: 'In the meantime, I want to chase down every lead – particularly Michael Lyons. How far are we from Gaydon?'

'Ten or so miles.'

Straker looked at his watch. 'In that case I'd like to borrow two things?' Straker explained what he wanted to do. 'The first, therefore, is a version of whatever system you use to track the cars round a circuit?'

'A GPS tag. We can fix up some bits and pieces normally attached to an MES logger. What's the other?'

'A car?'

'We've got Ptarmigan courtesy cars. You can have one of those.'

'Are they liveried?'

'Turquoise, brand name, the works.'

Straker smiled apologetically. 'I'm looking for something inconspicuous – not flashy. Unmarked.'

'Not really, then. You can take mine, if you like?'

'What've you got?'

'A six-year-old Ford Focus.'

'Perfect.'

Later that afternoon, having spent some time with a Ptarmigan technician, Straker drove the nondescript Ford down the Edgehill escarpment, making his way to Gaydon. To his delight he saw four Aston Martins – being driven under trade plates – go by in the other direction.

He reached the edge of the village and started looking for the address elicited from the porter of that apartment block in Monte-Carlo.

A few minutes later Straker found himself driving down a very rural single-track road. Several hundred yards further along he saw a patch of mown verge and several white-painted stones marking the entrance to a driveway. "Flax Cottage" was painted, in an Old English typeface, on a plaque fixed to the gate.

Straker had reached his target.

Slowing to a walking pace, he crawled by – looking through the driveway to take in the small cottage, its thatched roof, neatly gravelled drive and wealth of colourful plants and flowers in the garden. There were no cars parked out front.

Straker found another house a few hundred yards further on, meaning that Lyons's home was isolated and fairly private.

Turning round, but hanging some way back from Flax Cottage – on a bend in the road – Straker pulled up onto the verge and positioned himself to have a partial view back along the lane towards Michael Lyons's driveway. This spot would allow him discreetly to observe anyone who came or went. He looked at his watch. It was nearing five-thirty in the afternoon.

So now he was sitting there, watching the house that he believed belonged to the Monte-Carlo saboteur. This address was all he had to go on to trace the people trying to do Ptarmigan harm. Straker had to smile to himself. How could this sleepy single-track road, and the modesty of this quintessentially English cottage, be so directly linked to the glamour, pace and wealth of the global Formula One industry? But it *was* – through an unknown I.T. specialist from Gaydon in Warwickshire.

Who *was* Michael Lyons? Who did he work for? And why the hell had he been trying to sabotage Remy Sabatino in Monaco?

Straker settled back in to his seat and waited for him to appear down this lonely country lane.

NINETEEN

It wasn't until seven o'clock that evening that anything happened. A Peugeot hatchback appeared, coming down the road towards him.

Straker sat up.

The car indicated left and shortly afterwards pulled in through the gate of Flax Cottage. Was this Michael Lyons returning home?

The evening was still bright, although with the cloud thickening to the west, the sun was long obscured and the light levels were fading fast.

Wanting to take a closer look, Straker climbed out of his car and walked along the lane towards Flax Cottage. He reached the gate and cautiously peered into the driveway. The small Peugeot was parked out on the gravel. Lights had come on in the house. Each window, Straker saw, had a curtain drawn across it. The occupant had clearly withdrawn for the day.

Straker walked in through the gate. Ghost-walking across the gravel – careful not to make a noise – he reached the back of the Peugeot. Bending down, he slipped a small magnetic container – the tag – up under the rear spoiler. But as he stood up, twisting slightly, his shoe made a crunching noise on the gravel.

Immediately a dog started barking from behind Michael Lyons's front door.

Straker froze.

He held his breath.

It kept barking.

For several minutes.

Would the dog never relent? Straker daren't make any more noise, in case of further alerting the dog. If he was quiet, surely the owner would dismiss the commotion from the animal as a false alarm. Straker remained crouching down, out of the sight of the windows, directly behind the car. He seemed to be there, motionless, for an age. The barking continued, but at last he heard a raised voice from the inside, shouting the dog down.

Finally, it shut up.

Straker, still in a crouch, slipped off his shoes. Easing himself up to full height again, he ghost-walked in his socks across the uncomfortable gravel to the grass beside the driveway. He made for the gate post. Nipping round the corner, he made it onto the verge, walked briskly to the end of the mown strip, put his shoes back on, and sauntered away slowly, back to his car.

Once inside and behind the wheel, he lifted a laptop he had left in the passenger well and turned it on. Within a matter of seconds, a satnav-like display showed a map on its screen with a flashing arrow indicating the location of the tracker.

Straker smiled to himself. He started his car and drove away.

Backhouse and Straker had supper at a local pub. After their early start that morning from Monte-Carlo, both were relieved to turn in relatively early – at Backhouse's two-bedroom terraced house in Tysoe.

Straker woke at half-past five the next morning and immediately checked the tag-tracker device on the laptop. He was relieved to see Michael Lyons's car still appeared to be parked out in front of Flax Cottage.

Straker drove straight for Gaydon and was back on his verge within view of Lyons's driveway by six-thirty.

At seven thirty-five, Straker's attention was caught by the white reversing lights of the Peugeot backing out of the drive from Flax Cottage. Simultaneously, the tracker beeped into life on his laptop, confirming Lyons's movement and that, more importantly, the device was working.

He waited until the Peugeot was out of sight before following on behind. Any sight of Straker, now, would draw attention to him, particularly in such a quiet country byway. Once they were on the open road, it wouldn't be so much of a problem; he could lose his presence among other traffic.

Straker eased along, past Lyons's home. Still out of sight, he saw on the tracker that his man was turning left towards the middle of the village. Straker followed suit.

Lyons headed for the motorway, turning north towards Warwick and Birmingham.

Hanging back, Straker followed him, observing the Peugeot from some distance behind, comforted by being able to track him electronically at the same time.

Lyons left the M40 and headed for Royal Leamington Spa. Straker followed him into the centre of the town, in amongst its surprisingly elegant white stucco Regency townhouses and dark green cedar trees.

Lyons parked by a meter in the town centre.

This was odd, thought Straker. Where was Lyons going? Not to his office, if he was on a meter. Was he there for a meeting or a trip to the shops? Still some distance away, Straker quickly came to a halt, pulling over on the opposite side of the road, hoping to observe the direction in which Lyons might be making on foot. Straker saw his man walk down the street away from him. Lyons reached the intersection with The Parade and turned right. Driving on again, Straker pulled up to the same crossroads. From there, he was able to wait long enough at the intersection – before anyone honked him from behind – to see Lyons crossing the road a little way further down the hill. Lyons, dodging through the traffic to the far side of The Parade, soon disappeared into the grand entrance of The Regent Hotel.

Straker needed to follow him on foot to be sure. Sod's Law had it there were no free parking spaces or meters nearby. Straker had to drive on down past the hotel and over the River Leam. It wasn't until he reached Bath Place – two turnings on and some distance later – that he found a parking space. Bolting back from the car over the bridge, and up to the hotel, he reached the main entrance and walked in.

Slightly out of breath, he ordered a coffee to be taken in the reception area. Asking for the lavatories, Straker walked on into the hotel past the dining room. He managed to spot Lyons over by the window having breakfast with someone. Straker looked around his immediate location to check whether he was being stealthy enough. Believing he was, he moved slightly behind a door, pulled out his phone, switched it to "camera" and, as surreptitiously as possible, aimed the lens at his quarry, zoomed in, and fired off a couple of shots. In one, he managed to catch Lyons's rendezvous almost face on.

Straker returned to his low table in among the armchairs of the reception area, where he helped himself to the coffee and, reading one of the broadsheets available in the hotel, kept a discreet but attentive eye on the main entrance in the lobby.

Michael Lyons walked out an hour or so later.

Straker, raising his eyes from the crossword, saw him go and, within a few seconds, had dropped a note into the leather bill holder, replaced the newspaper, and followed Lyons as far as the door. Through the porch windows to one side, Straker was able to watch Lyons make his way back up The Parade to Regent Street, and presumably his car.

Moving quickly from the main entrance of the hotel, Straker turned left and ran swiftly and easily down the street in the opposite direction, back over the river and to his own car in Bath Place.

Ten minutes later, Straker was three cars back from Lyons as he saw the Peugeot indicating left to turn into an industrial estate. Still some way behind, he followed Lyons through the business park before his quarry pulled up in front of a sizeable and impressive modern factory complex. Michael Lyons parked in what looked like a reserved bay, among the heavily manicured beds and trees out the front. Above the glass doors of the main entrance, Straker saw the name of the business. It rang a bell from his tour round the Ptarmigan factory the day before: Trifecta Systems. And, from the respectful nod Lyons received from the security guard standing by the main entrance, and a smile from a woman coming out of the building,

Straker felt comfortable in deducing that Lyons was well-enough known here for this to be his place of work.

Straker made it back to Ptarmigan shortly after nine-thirty, and passed on his findings to Backhouse. 'Michael Lyons had breakfast with a guy in the Regent Hotel,' he told him, 'and then pitched up for work at Trifecta Systems.'

'*Trifecta?*'

'Didn't you mention them yesterday?'

'I did – when we were talking about working with Benbecular. They provide our bespoke EMS – engine management system.'

'What else do Trifecta do? It looked like a pretty big set-up.'

'It is. They're not just into engine management. They produce all our on-car electronics.'

'All of them?'

'Pretty much.'

'Including radios?'

Backhouse's eyebrows raised as he realized the implications. 'Oh Christ. But that doesn't make sense, at all. Why would Trifecta be out to sabotage one of their own clients?'

Straker smiled, appearing to relish the conundrum.

'It can't be Trifecta on their own,' said Backhouse. 'It's much more likely to be another Grand Prix team behind this.'

'I agree. How many other teams would Trifecta be involved with?'

'Most, in some way, shape or form. They're more or less motor racing's in-house electronics firm.'

'No immediate leads there, then,' concluded Straker as he pulled out his iPhone and, flicking through his pictures to find the clearest shot, handed the device to Backhouse. 'Okay, what about this, then? Here's the guy Lyons met for breakfast. Any idea who *he* is?'

The race engineer looked down at the snatched portrait, before frowning. 'No.'

Backhouse studied the picture closely. He paused. 'Hang on, can you zoom in?'

Straker leant across and demonstrated a two-finger spread on the screen. Backhouse copied the action for himself, zoomed in to enlarge the picture, and then peered closely at the image. 'Well, looky there,' he said turning the screen round to show Straker. 'This guy's wearing a Benbecular lapel pin – logo and all. What's the betting he's a company man?'

'Where are Benbecular based, then?' asked Straker.

'Also in Leamington Spa.'

'And which teams do *they* supply?'

'Us, Lambourn and Massarella.'

Straker smiled resignedly. 'The Byzantine interconnectivity is utterly incestuous here.'

'Oh it is. You have to remember that pre-Bernie, Formula One was tiny – a set of cottage industries. Thanks to him, it's all grown proportionately: many of the firms originally involved in the sport are more or less still there – they've just got a lot bigger along the way.'

'Which is fascinating, charming, and impressive – but seriously reduces the chances of any one relationship indicating who might be behind the sabotage.'

TWENTY

Straker was given use of an office two doors down from Backhouse's within the Ptarmigan factory. He started writing on a whiteboard the sabotage-related entities he had discovered so far in his investigation. An electronic device. Jamming. An apartment in Monte-Carlo. Michael Lyons. A Warwickshire cottage. A Peugeot hatchback. Trifecta. He also wrote: FIA. Heavy fines. Motive?

Straker sat there and just stared at his board.

He tried to think out from – and beyond – each of the entities in front of him, his eyes darting between them.

After a few minutes, he was sure he *had* noticed something. It was subliminal at first.

But something was odd.

Inconsistent.

Yes, he thought. There's something there that isn't quite right.

He dwelt on a contrast – the significant contrast in affluence between Lyons's cottage and that apartment in Monaco. How much would a week's rental for a flat like that during the Grand Prix set one back? he wondered. He didn't know precisely, but he would bank on it being a tidy sum. Could Lyons really have afforded that, considering the modesty of the thatched cottage and two-door hatchback? Hardly. What was Lyons's *status*, then, while he had been in Monte-Carlo? Was he there privately, or on business? Because of the expense, it had to be business, didn't it? If so, was he there for Trifecta, or had Lyons been moonlighting – for somebody else?

If it *had* been his employer, would the company itself be behind his illicit radio jamming? Was that likely? Straker realized he needed to know more about Trifecta.

He rang Karen in London: 'Could you look into a company called Trifecta Systems for me? I need you to identify all their activities, key clients, directors, who their investors or shareholders are, and any news cuttings you can come up with – your usual magic!'

Leaving Karen to get on with that, Straker returned to staring at his whiteboard. Nothing came to him. For quite a while. Until, after his *n*th cup of coffee, he noticed something else. There was something missing. Something he knew, but which wasn't on his board. He realized he had no idea of its relevance, but had a feeling that he wanted to know more about the person Lyons had met for breakfast that morning in Leamington. Why was he suspicious of that meeting? he asked himself.

What was the significance of it? It was a meeting with someone wearing a Benbecular lapel pin. There was no significance at all, if those pins were widely available merchandize items. Except Benbecular was hardly a "designer" brand. Someone wearing one was, therefore, demonstrating a heavily esoteric interest in motor racing. And the meeting was intriguing, again because of a possible inconsistency. Lyons's office, which struck Straker as large and well-appointed, must have its own meeting rooms and hospitality facilities, surely? – *and* it was only a couple of miles away. Instead of meeting at Trifecta, then, Lyons had chosen neutral ground to meet this motor racing aficionado.

Why?

True, it was hardly clandestine – in a public restaurant, and in broad daylight – but Straker's interest was piqued. He wanted to find out more.

How?

After yet another cup of coffee Straker came up with a wheeze. Picking out his phone, he searched the web for two things. First, he wanted a barber's shop in the town; he found several, and picked one: Giorgio's. Then he searched for the number of the Regent Hotel and dialled it using the embedded link on the website's Contact Us page.

His call was answered promptly.

Straker asked to be put through to the dining room. A Black

Country-sounding voice soon answered and introduced herself as
Jill.

'Good morning,' he said. 'I have a strange request, and really
hope you can help me?'

Jill gave a nervous chuckle. 'Okay?'

'It's Giorgio's – the barbers – here, we're just around the corner
from the hotel,' said Straker. 'We had a client in this morning who
rang back asking whether he had left his glasses behind.'

'Oh.'

'At the time, we said no. But, would you believe it? – we've found them.'

'Err, okay?' said the girl, sounding a little unsure what this had to
do with her.

'I'm ringing because we don't know how to reach him. He did
mention he had just had breakfast with you, though.'

'Oh.'

'Do you, by any chance, have his name?'

'How would we know that?' she asked.

'He happened to say that he was breakfasting with another of our
clients, a Mr Lyons.'

There was a pause from the other end and Straker heard the
encouraging sound of a page being flipped over. 'Yes, you're in luck
– here it is. Mr Lyons ... and ... a Mr Jeremy Barnett,' she read out.

'Excellent. I suppose it's too much to hope that Mr Barnett left a
contact number when he booked?'

'I'm afraid you're right – he didn't.'

Straker thanked Jill profusely and rang off. Next, via his iPhone,
he looked up another telephone number on another website; he
found one for the main switchboard for the company in question.
He was going to take a punt.

Straker rang it. A few seconds later he was talking to an elderly
lady who answered the phone: 'Hello, Benbecular Engines?'

'I need to write to Mr Jeremy Barnett,' he explained, 'and am
anxious to get his title and address right, please.'

There was silence on the other end.

Oh shit, thought Straker. She doesn't even recognize the name. Jeremy Barnett doesn't mean anything to these people.

Suddenly he heard a sneeze.

'Sorry about that, love,' she said, still sounding distracted. 'Caught by a sneeze. Who was it you wanted, again?'

'Mr Barnett.'

'Jeremy?'

'Yes, that's him.'

Straker smiled and added: 'I've got him down as Engine Management Systems, is that right?'

'No, dear. He's in our Technology Development Division. His title is Management Engineer.'

'Many thanks,' he said. 'My letter to him will be in the post today,' and rang off.

Straker's wheeze had worked.

He walked across his temporary office and wrote: "Jeremy Barnett – Benbecular" on his whiteboard.

Straker stood back and studied this new piece of information in the context of the others. For uncounted minutes, his eyes flicked from one name to the next, deliberately, as if trying to spot the anagram from among the jumbled letters of a cryptic crossword.

Straker, after thirty minutes, realized he had drawn a blank.

But that conclusion wasn't completely useless. It did help confirm something for him: there *was* no apparent connectivity.

Straker's mind wandered back to his previous assignment for Quartech. What had been the breakthrough with that? he reflected. Links, he answered: the way things were linked together, sometimes without apparent reason.

With that, Straker had two thoughts at once.

What about Charlotte Grant?

Now that his investigation involved more names, could he test her connection with any of them? He suddenly thought of her phone, and the names he had seen on it in Monte-Carlo.

Turning it on, Straker looked into her directory. Spookily enough, Jeremy Barnett and Michael Lyons *were* there.

Both of the. n.

In the absence of any firmer leads, he wanted to examine everything her phone contained – including the call, text, and email logs. Maybe that data *could* now help him join up some of these dots. But there was a lot of it.

Extracting it all would clearly take some time.

Calling Backhouse's secretary, he arranged for Charlotte's phone to be couriered down to Cavendish Square in London. Then, ringing Karen in his office, he explained what was coming and what he needed the Quartech technicians to do when it arrived.

'Okay, Matt. I was about to ring you anyway. I've got some stuff for you on Trifecta. Do you want me to email it through?'

Five minutes later Straker was standing over the printer in Backhouse's office. 'Okay, Andy,' he said, as he lifted the sheets off the machine. 'What can you tell me about this list of Trifecta directors?' and read them out.

Backhouse replied: 'A former president of the FIA, a former chief executive of the BRDC and a former World Champion.'

'Not a group you'd expect to play fast and loose with the rules, then?' suggested Straker.

'Wouldn't have thought so, would you?'

'How do they square with Lyons's clandestine jamming, then?'

Backhouse shook his head.

'So Lyons *must* have been doing this as a sideline – a bit of moonlighting – mustn't he?'

Backhouse shrugged in part-support of the logic.

There was a moment of silence between them. Straker leafed through some of the other pages. 'There's a list of Trifecta investors here – and, hang on, that's interesting: There's been some recent corporate activity. Back in March, someone acquired fifty-one per cent of the company. Someone called Avel Obrenovich?'

Backhouse's face changed in an instant. 'I don't believe it?'

'What?'

'That's extraordinary.'

'Why?'

'He only happens to be Massarella's principal sponsor.'

TWENTY-ONE

Straker buzzed with this new intelligence, his mind swirling. What did it mean? Frustratingly, he was called away from his meditations before he could plan his next step.

Minutes after twelve noon, having had a pretty clear overnight run, the convoy of Ptarmigan lorries arrived back at the Shenington factory from Monte-Carlo. Backhouse led Straker down to the loading bay to see them arrive. Pulling in through the large hangar-like doors, their air brakes were applied and the engines cut. With only hours before the lorries would be away again, this time for Belgium, the team went to work immediately, unloading and processing all their kit and equipment. Most of the attention – including Backhouse's and Straker's – was paid to the lorry carrying the wreckage of Helli Cunzer's car. Fork-lift trucks, hand-pushed trolleys, and about twenty men converged round the tailgate as the segments, fragments and remains of the car were extracted and placed on the painted concrete floor of the bay.

'We'll be laying all the bits out on the floor in here,' Backhouse explained, 'and we'll subject every remnant to scrutiny and testing to try and determine the cause of the crash.'

Straker soon went back to his temporary office.

He was called by Backhouse ten minutes later. 'I've got Remy's helmet,' he said. 'Do you want to come and see us research the jamming device?'

They met up again as Backhouse was carrying the helmet into the electronics lab. He placed it on one of the work benches. Backhouse peered in through the visor and then ran his finger into the folds in the foam lining where the device had been put back.

His expression changed dramatically as he moved his fingers round the inside of the lining. 'I don't believe it.'

'What?' asked Straker.

'It's not there.'

'It's not there?'

'No.'

Carefully turning the helmet over, Backhouse unpopped some of the fastenings, pulled the foam inner out of the casing and laid it on the white workbench. Gently easing the foam panels apart, he opened up the groove where the jammer had been. 'It's definitely not here,' he repeated and looked up into the other's face. 'It's gone.'

Straker looked deeply concerned. 'I want the area around it on the lorry dismantled and checked. *Immediately*.'

Straker called Quartano an hour later from his temporary office.

'What do you mean it's gone?' asked the tycoon. 'You sure it hasn't just fallen out? Somewhere in the truck, or fallen out into its carrying case?'

'No, sir. I'm afraid not. We've stripped the compartment down completely.'

'Someone's taken it out for safe keeping?'

'No, sir. We've asked everyone if they've been near the helmet – not why, of course – and we've even made contact with absent members of staff who are away on a break for a few days.'

'Matt,' said Quartano with unexpected gravity. 'Are you sure? Are you *absolutely* sure?'

'As much as I can be.'

'Christ, you know what this means, of course,' said Quartano solemnly.

'It's been removed – to cover the saboteur's tracks. But worse, it means that even if Charlotte put it there, she clearly wasn't the person who took it out. Someone else did. And it must've been one of the team. It means we've got a serious problem. Our saboteurs *do* still have a collaborator … right here … on the inside.'

PART TWO

EAU ROUGE

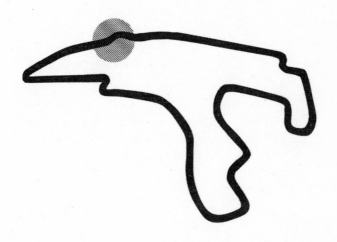

TWENTY-TWO

Straker returned home to Fulham early that evening, craving the comfort of familiar surroundings. But opening the door of his – their – empty flat, the hollowness hit him hard. Worse, among the backlog of post strewn across the mat, he saw an envelope franked with the name of his wife's solicitors. A pulse hissed through his ears. The grim reality of what that letter meant was all too obvious.

Dropping his bags inside the door, Straker placed the letter on the hall table, unable to bring himself to open it.

After running a bath, and pouring a hefty tumbler of whisky, he finally summoned himself.

Having read it, he sighed. And breathed deeply. He and Jo were, mercifully, not at war. They would clearly reach an agreement and looked like they would settle as fast as the process allowed. He had a flat. She had a flat. There were no children. But it was the *fact* of it that finally got to him. Six years, altogether, many of which had been happy and close.

Straker found himself swallowing hard.

His rendition and enhanced interrogation by the Americans, and resultant struggles to reconcile those ethics with everything he had believed in for twenty years, really did for them – well him, at any rate.

He hoped, now, that he was over the worst of his turbulent reaction to those experiences. The flashbacks had been becoming much less frequent. His recovery had been happening gradually, but – tragically – not fast enough to reassure his wife that his psyche was on the mend.

Straker spent his one day of leave moping around the flat. His curtains remained closed for the entire time. He sat slumped in a chair. His only distractions were a bottle of whisky and the track which best captured his mood – Miles Davis's 'Blue in Green' – which he played semi-hypnotically in a continuous loop on his B&O CD player. He didn't remember eating. He never felt hungry. Waking from another fitful sleep in the middle of the following night, he set out on a punishing run through the deserted streets of west London, trying to purge himself.

He was glad to be going away again.

Just before leaving their flat, breathing deeply, he signed the letter, slid it back into its envelope and posted it in a postbox at the end of his street.

This time it was Belgium.

He flew to Liège, timing his arrival to coincide with Remy Sabatino's flight in by private jet from Malta, she having asked for an update on his dealing with the sabotage threat. By the time they met up, Straker had just about forced himself to regain some equanimity.

They climbed aboard their chartered helicopter and flew in the Bell Jet Ranger up into the mountains of the Ardennes. Several silent minutes into the flight, Sabatino spoke to him over the intercom. 'You okay?' she asked provocatively.

Straker turned to face her. 'Sure.'

'You seem quiet?'

'No, no,' he said defensively, aware he was not being particularly convincing. 'I was … thinking about the investigation.'

'Right…'

Straker stepped straight back in before she could say anything else. 'We've made some progress,' he said.

'With Helli's car?'

Straker shook his head. 'No, not yet – they're still working on that. It'll be a few more days before we'll know any more there.'

'What then?'

'We've found some links with Michael Lyons – your radio jammer.'

Sabatino looked impressed. 'Wow – with who?'

'Trifecta Systems.'

'*No!*'

'We're pretty sure Lyons works there.'

'But they *supply* us, don't they? Why would they be sabotaging us at the same time?'

Straker's whole mood seemed to change with his subsequent smile.

Sabatino looked disapproving. 'What's so funny? How's that funny?'

'Don't you see?' he said searchingly. 'That's good news. It's a lead – a clue. Precisely because it *doesn't* make any sense.'

Sabatino looked blank.

'It's a clear invitation for us to look into this further,' he explained. 'If it did make sense, we wouldn't bother with it – we wouldn't give it a moment's thought. We'd move straight on.'

Sabatino's face registered a partial understanding of what Straker was getting at. 'Who are the other links with, then?'

'We've found a connection between Trifecta and Avel Obrenovich.'

'*No!* How?'

'Recently – very recently – Obrenovich became the majority shareholder in Trifecta.'

Sabatino looked impressed then somewhat concerned. 'That's *more* good detective work. Wow. Does that mean Massarella are behind this, then?'

'We've got no proof of any direct interaction between any of these people,' Straker went on. 'Elsewhere, we do have a different connection – this time one between Michael Lyons and Benbecular – through a man who works for them called Jeremy Barnett.'

Sabatino shook her head to indicate no recognition.

'At this stage, though, I can't see any reason to believe that's anything other than a routine relationship.'

Sabatino's expression showed a mix of intrigue and anxiousness.

'But,' continued Straker calmly, 'we do have *one* point of concern.'

Because of his tone, Sabatino looked at him intensely.

'I know you didn't approve of my putting the bug back in your helmet – after Qualifying in Monaco – to provide misinformation to the saboteurs?'

Sabatino nodded – and then shook her head, acknowledging that she now did.

'Well, when your kit was returned to the factory, I asked Andy to have the device taken out and examined, hoping we might learn something from it. But when he went to look for it … the bug was gone.'

'Fallen out?'

Straker shook his head. 'No, we're sure it was removed.'

'*Removed?*

'We searched everything.'

Sabatino fell silent for a moment. 'What does that *mean?*' she asked. 'Does it mean we *do* have a traitor – on the inside of the team?'

'I'm afraid it appears that way,' he said firmly.

Sabatino continued to look straight at Straker. Her dark brown eyes and tanned face suddenly looked less striking than they should have done. For all her brilliance as a driver, and her courage and toughness when racing wheel to wheel at breakneck speed, there was a glimmer of vulnerability. 'What are you doing about it, then?'

Straker smiled inwardly at the change in her attitude – how she would have so readily dismissed this before as spy games, as she first did in Monaco. Having expected this question, and knowing he had to sound convincing to retain her trust, he said: 'Several things,' and explained them confidently, without losing eye contact.

'And none of those will interfere with the workings of the team?'

'Minimally.'

'Who are you telling about this threat?'

Straker allowed himself to convey a little uncertainty at his point. 'I wanted to talk to you about that. This is a sport and you're the competitor. How would the guys around you react to the idea of a saboteur been in among them?'

Sabatino slowly rocked her head from side to side, as if weighing up the consequences.

'It's your call,' he went on, 'but making a big song and dance about it could just make people suspicious of each other – and so easily damage team spirit?'

Sabatino, far from looking vulnerable, now looked like she was ready to affect events rather than be prey to them. 'Given the other measures you've described, I'm happier not to advertize the existence of the insider. How many people know about this as of now?'

'That the bug was removed?'

She nodded.

'Only Backhouse, Quartano, you and me.'

TWENTY-THREE

The helicopter flew in over the extensive forests of the Ardennes. Sabatino looked out of the window. After cogitating Straker's news for a few minutes, she turned to face him – and smiled naturally. Then, moving her hand towards him, she laid it briefly on the clothed part of his sleeve, and said: 'What you've done so far with the investigation is impressive. If you do as much here as you did for me in Monaco, I know I'll be fine.'

Straker nodded his acknowledgment of her trust.

They began a sweeping banked turn. Straker was given a superb view of the magnificent Spa-Francorchamps race track spread out below. In contrast to Monaco, where the circuit was right in the thick of things, here the track was out in the wilds – in the middle of nowhere.

He could see the grey ribbon of road snaking its way through the dense dark green woodland as it rose and fell with the rolling topography of the mountains. The only vaguely similar aspect to Monaco was the short stretch of public highway that Spa – in this, its latest guise – incorporated into the circuit, complete with its everyday white lines and road markings.

'How does this track compare with the others?' asked Straker looking to lighten the conversation.

Sabatino's brown eyes flashed from behind her black-rimmed glasses. 'I've raced here only once, with a GP2 team, but it's easily my favourite.'

'Does it matter that you've not driven an F1 car round here before?'

'Yes and no – mainly no. I've spent a good deal of time in the simulator. The main difference for me, this time, will be Eau Rouge.'

'Eau Rouge?'

'*The* section of any race track in the world. When you drive it in the slower cars, you're not driving to the limit of the circuit – more to the limit of the cars. For me, this time, the test of nerve will be whether I lift off or not.'

Straker looked slightly puzzled.

'Whether I go through the compression and the S-shaped corners at full throttle,' she explained, 'or whether I chicken out and lift off – lift off the accelerator.'

'How fast will you be going through this Eau Rouge?'

'With any luck,' she said with a flash of a smile, 'at just over two hundred miles an hour.'

Soon after the helicopter put down Straker and Sabatino made their way to accreditation and were issued with their passes. As they parted company, there was a moment between them – an acknowledgement of the threat from an unknown source. Straker didn't want to be too upbeat and seem flippant, or too down, so as to be dispiriting. He ended up feeling pleased. He felt the overriding mood at their departure was one of stoicism.

Straker made straight for the pit lane, anxious to meet up with Backhouse and familiarize himself with the lie of the land.

The race engineer declared: 'I've got you a meeting with Spa's head of security just after lunch.'

'Good work. That'll help address our external threats. What happens, though, if we suffer another jamming signal?'

'Without the transmitting device? Is that likely?'

'Depends on whether that's all the saboteurs had,' replied Straker. 'We only found that one by chance. It's perfectly possible there's something else in the mix that we've missed or don't know about.'

Straker found the offices of the security manager behind the main grandstand. Maurice Beauregard was a middle-aged man with a paunch. But the man's alert blue eyes suggested to Straker that they didn't miss much.

Backhouse had done some useful homework and briefed Straker

accordingly. Beauregard had been with the Brussels police for ten years, ending up responsible for close protection of key personnel at SHAPE. A gunshot wound, sustained while fending off an attempt on the life of the Turkish Ambassador to NATO, had brought Beauregard's active service to an early close. His role at the Spa-Francorchamps circuit may have been a bit of a comedown in responsibility – and pay – by comparison, but, rather than be put out to grass, Beauregard preferred to keep active. Besides, it suited him spiritually as he was a fanatical motor racing fan.

Straker entered his office, shook hands, and asked whether he would mind if they held the meeting in private.

'Thank you for seeing me,' said Straker after shutting the door. 'We have a problem and we're keen to ask your advice. May I speak to you in the strictest confidence?'

Straker didn't mind sounding a little melodramatic. At least it was working. Beauregard lowered himself into his chair, his eyes fixed intensely on Straker's face. He had Beauregard's attention all right.

'In Monaco,' Straker went on, 'one of the radios we used to communicate with our drivers was jammed.'

'Jamm-ed?' repeated Beauregard. 'What is jamm-ed?'

'Blocked out by another signal. Deliberately interrupted.'

Beauregard looked unmoved.

Anticipating such scepticism, Straker had thought it wise to bring his recordings of the radio traffic in Monte-Carlo. He placed the digital recorder on Beauregard's desk and pressed play.

Even before he had run it all the way through, Straker was in no doubt he had Beauregard onside.

'We have removed the device that did this,' continued Straker not wanting to complicate the issue further, 'but we're concerned, of course, that there might be others that we haven't found.'

Beauregard looked suitably troubled hearing that his beloved sport might be sullied by this sort of thing. Hoping to reinforce the gravity of the situation, Straker said: 'We've made a representation to the FIA about this.'

Beauregard was clearly affected. 'This is terrible – but why are you telling me now?'

Straker, looking the security man straight in the eye, said: 'We also lost a car in Monaco – crashing unexpectedly, completely without warning. We are not sure, yet, whether that crash was linked to this sabotage. But with cars and drivers travelling at such high speeds – even faster, here, of course – this is serious. We don't want to put lives at risk, particularly your spectators.'

Straker ran his eye round the walls of Beauregard's office and saw the photographs of the security man standing with racing drivers, celebrities, film stars, Belgium's two famous Van Dam(me)s – José and Jean-Claude – and, in pride of place, was a picture of this former policeman standing with His Majesty Albert II, King of the Belgians. Straker added solemnly: 'I'd hate for a disaster to occur at the Belgian Grand Prix.'

An hour later Straker came away with the commitment of a doubled security detail on the Ptarmigan Team, a beefed-up screen around their trucks in the paddock, and a cordon round the garage in the pit lane.

At three o'clock that afternoon Remy Sabatino took her Ptarmigan Formula One car out onto the circuit during the first day of practice.

Apprehensively, Straker sat in the headquarters truck as before, listening out on the team radio between Backhouse in the pit lane and the car. On the screen in front of him Straker watched Sabatino via the on-board camera positioned above her helmet.

Day one of practice came to a close, though, with no visible sign of anything untoward.

Technically, the day had gone extremely well for the team. The car was performing well, giving Sabatino an excellent feel with outstanding pace.

Day two began, and Sabatino went out for a further series of practice laps.

With a few minor tweaks to the rear wing, and a couple of adjust-ments to the brake balance, Sabatino was thrilled with the Ptarmi-gan's performance. Everything about the set-up – hugely different from the one they had deployed in Monaco – was near perfect. The tyres were working well, getting quickly up to temperature. Aero-dynamically, the Fibonacci Blades were making a material contribu-tion through the slow corners without unduly damaging straight-line speed. All these elements came together, giving her a major confi-dence boost – indicated by her taking the double apex of Pouhon in seventh gear at full throttle, with no temptation to lift off.

The new aero package was clearly working superbly.

The balance of the car was exceptional.

Straker was pleased the car was performing so well. But he couldn't calm his mind. The next day was critical – Qualifying – and the ritual of timed laps to determine the places on the grid for the race. But he was getting concerned.

There had been no sign of the saboteur, anywhere.

He hoped to God he hadn't missed something.

TWENTY-FOUR

Straker had a restless night. Waking early, he left the hotel while it was still dark. He arrived at the track in the gloomy twilight of dawn. There was a crisp chill in the air, intensifying his senses – particularly smell. He became very aware of the forest, the earth, the rotting mulch of long-fallen leaves, and pine resin all around. Such smells brought back vivid memories of exercises during basic training, typically held in national parks and across wind-swept moors – periods of his life that had been hellish at the time but which he now looked back on with a degree of fondness. While they'd been times of great trial, he had ultimately excelled. He wondered if he would look back on this episode of the sabotage threat in the same way.

Arriving at the Ptarmigan garage in the pit lane he was confronted by a surprise. Three large security men were standing there in black overalls, each carrying a night stick and wearing a coiled wire from their right ear. Straker was encouraged, though. Beauregard was clearly delivering on his extra security screen. But was this really going to be any defence against such sophisticated saboteurs?

Qualifying One was now minutes away. Standing in the door of the garage, Straker waited to see Sabatino walking down the pit lane towards her car. Wearing her full turquoise racing suit and carrying her helmet under her arm – no longer prepared to leave it unattended – he was reminded of an astronaut heading for the launch pad.

Sabatino smiled as she approached. 'Keep them away from me,' she said, punching him on the arm as she walked into the Ptarmigan garage.

Straker, back in the headquarters truck and watching via her on-board camera, saw Sabatino head out of the pit lane and feed herself onto the circuit to start her first out-lap of Qualifying One.

She needed to post a fast time.

Sabatino found her Ptarmigan well and truly on song. She put in an early hot lap, and found the set-up to be as near right for this circuit as she could hope for. By way of confirmation, her time in Q1 was the fastest of all the cars by some margin.

'Fantastic, Remy,' said Backhouse shortly afterwards over the radio. 'You've taken it by point-*nine!* he shouted. 'Better still, you've pissed all over the Massarellas.'

Straker heard Sabatino's upbeat reply. He could sense the rising anticipation among the team for what lay ahead.

She prepared herself mentally for Q2. While only a stepping stone in the process, she could not afford to ease off. There was no carry-over of previous times. Her scorching lap in Q1 would be lost – reset to zero. Only by staying fast in the next session would she be assured of getting through to Q3 – *the* stage that mattered – the top-ten shootout. That was the clincher, when the competitive positions at the front of the grid were determined. The closer to the front at the start, the fewer the cars that would have to be overtaken under combative conditions during the race.

And to be sure of securing the biggest advantage, Sabatino was out for nothing less than pole. Not only would that be good for tomorrow, it would also help defend her six-point lead at the top of the Drivers' Championship.

Straker, once again, was sitting in the headquarters truck next to Oliver Treadwell – Ptarmigan's Australian Director of Strategy – monitoring the team's radio and CCTV coverage. Straker inhaled deeply and refocused, hoping they weren't going to have any trouble.

A number of cars went out onto the track immediately Q2 started.

Sabatino hung back in her garage, composing herself, psyching herself up for a peak effort. Presently, she fired up the engine and pulled out of her garage, turning sharp right into the pit lane. She ran on the limiter down to the end, and, crossing the line, powered up, feeding herself out onto the track. Several cars bombed past, trying to notch up their flying laps to secure good positions on the grid.

She put in a hot lap. But, running into traffic around Malmedy, she was four tenths off her best time. It put her only sixth fastest at that moment – and half the field had yet to post their best time. She would have to do better to be absolutely sure of getting through to the top-ten shootout.

She was ready, now, for a big one.

Building up speed, she felt good very quickly. Temperatures rose well in the Ptarmigan's oil and hydraulics, helped by some aggressive zig-zagging followed by a burst of top speed down to Turn Twelve. Sabatino saw all her metrics climb easily into their windows of operation.

The car felt ready.

She felt ready.

Heading down to the Chicane, sunlight flashed and flickered through the trees and across the track as she squinted to see the beginnings of the circuit's buildings, tents and infrastructure up ahead. Thirty seconds later and she was in the pit straight, building up the pace to start her flying lap.

Radioing the team, she declared: 'Here we go!'

In fifth gear and still accelerating as she crossed the start line, she focused on the run down to La Source, the famous three-twenty-degree Turn One. Pulling over to the left of the start/finish straight to open up the corner as much as possible, she braked as late as she dared and changed down four times to second gear before turning in hard right. Into the turn, she accelerated hard. Her right front clipped the inside kerb as she pumped power into the engine through the apex and then the exit, all the time feeling for any lightening of the back end as she turned the corner. The power was phenomenal, so much so she had to make two minor flicks with the steering wheel – of opposite lock – to correct her exit from La Source.

In a blink of an eye she was through and across to the other side of the circuit, clipping the red and white stones of the outside kerb, this time with her front left. She managed to straighten the car up while still on the black stuff, not flinching from feeding in as much power as the grip would take.

Changing up three gears and hitting eighteen thousand RPM each time, she pointed the car down the hill.

Now she was heading towards the most exhilarating section of any Grand Prix circuit. Anywhere.

Eau Rouge.

As she cleared the slight kink in the track, she could look down and see the famous part of the track stretched out below her. This was it. *The* corner combination of Formula One.

She was in sixth gear and still accelerating – up through one hundred and sixty miles an hour.

Sabatino's heart rate rose to a similar number as she breathed deeply, her eyes boring into the landscape ahead. She studied the topography as the road fell away to the bottom of the valley, with its left-hander and then right curve swooping away up the hill on the far side.

Sabatino was still accelerating. Seventh gear and two hundred miles an hour. Her eyes were flicking between various points of the road, trying to map out exactly where she needed to be to enter this roller-coaster of a complex and emerge the other side without losing line, speed – let alone contact with the surface of the track.

Hurtling on down the hill, she moved over to the right, still pushing the car as fast as it would physically go, beginning to hug the imposing white brick wall down the right-hand side. Then, as she seemed to be getting too close, almost brushing it with the wall of her right-rear tyre, she committed to slicing left. Darting across the circuit, she made for the first apex of Eau Rouge, her eye still focusing on the road ahead, already looking for the exit to get the best entry into Turn Three.

Her foot was absolutely flat to the floor.

She clipped the kerb on the apex, exactly where she intended, causing a jolt through the car, just as the massive downforce of bottoming out through the compression pushed her down heavily into her seat. Sabatino felt the air squeezed out of her lungs. Her line was spot on though, and, holding straight for a fraction of a second, found the perfect entry to Turn Three, slicing back across the track the other way, up through the apex of the right-hander – and on up the hill.

Eighteen thousand revs, seventh gear – reaching two hundred and five miles an hour – and Sabatino was completely committed.

Not once did she feel the slightest temptation to yield and lift off.

Screaming on up the hill in the sweeping right-hander, she saw the crest in the road where it began to level off. At that speed, even the slightest alteration in the attitude of the road could be severe. Cresting this would unweight the car and lighten the suspension, causing the aerodynamics to behave differently as the ride height rose, all of which would lighten the steering. Breathing deeply, Sabatino guided the car across the road to the left-hand side, straightened up to take the crest head-on and then, once over, reapplied the slight left lock.

She had to be immediately ready for the fast left-hander through Raidillon, Turn Four. In the blink of an eye she was through there, too.

Stretched out in front of her, now, was the awesome Kemmel Straight, a dead straight and deceptively rising section of the track, running five hundred yards up its narrow cavern between the trees.

Sabatino breathed deeply as, letting the car do the work in a straight line, she was able to savour the exhilaration of her run through Eau Rouge. A smile crossed her face at the thought. She had been through that legendary complex – absolutely flat out – faster than she'd ever done it before and with not a scintilla less than full commitment. And the car had been there for her every yard of the way.

In contrast, the Kemmel Straight was an inactive stretch of the circuit. It gave her the chance to assess the readouts on her steering wheel. Everything looked perfect. Her Ptarmigan screamed contently up to full-throttle, -power and -speed – touching two hundred and fifteen miles an hour. Up ahead she could see a car coasting home to the right of the racing line.

Sabatino breathed deeply again as she drifted to the left-hand side of the circuit ready for the sharp right-hander into Les Combes. She reached the beginning of the red and yellow kerbstones down the left-hand side of the track. She waited to brake – as late as she dared.

Wait…

She reached the latest possible point to decelerate. When, suddenly, everything went completely haywire.

From total stability – with the car running straight and true, and with the engine at its highest pitch – there was an instantaneous change in sound. Sabatino immediately thought the engine had blown.

There was a sudden – massive – drop-off in revs.

She was thrust violently forward against her straps.

The car's rear end started skidding.

In the shock, Sabatino's balance must have been thrown, her right hand collapsing downwards on that side of the wheel. As a result, the car's back end swung out immediately to the left. She reacted quickly, regripping the steering wheel with full force. Instinctively, she turned it hard left into the slew of the back end in that direction. Then, having prevented the spin, she found she had over-corrected. Consequently, the car slewed its rear hard to the right, the other way. Sabatino manhandled the lock hard right.

The car started to snake violently.

Nigel Mansell's high-speed rear-tyre burst in Adelaide suddenly flashed through her mind.

She was still doing over a hundred and fifty miles an hour.

How much longer could she hold this together?

She felt her rear wheels start to roll again.

The corner was looming.

There was no way she was going to make the sharp right-hander into Turn Five. With her full attention devoted simply to bringing the car under control, the racing line was no longer Sabatino's primary concern. Keeping the car out of the scenery was all she could think about.

From that blistering speed, it was taking what felt like an age to slow down. She could now only go straight on at Les Combes – leaving the track. Mercifully, there was an asphalt run-off straight ahead.

Sabatino felt a massive jolt up through her body as she banged over the red and yellow blocks marking the outside of the corner, which bounced the front wheels off the ground. She was still doing over one hundred miles an hour as she crossed the kerbstones. A section of carbon fibre from the right front wing broke off and rose up the nose, shooting straight at her head. Flinching, as the rear wheels then hit the kerb and bounced violently over the raised stones, she ducked as far as her limited movement would allow, but still couldn't avoid the broken component banging into the top of her helmet.

Once on the asphalt run-off she made several more attempts to brake. The surface was dirty. The fronts locked-up. She pumped the brakes repeatedly, until seventy metres later, and nearly onto the grass, she managed to bring the car to a halt.

Finally, the car was stationary.

Dust swirled up around it.

Sabatino's heart rate and breathing were stratospheric with the tsunami of adrenalin coursing round her body. She'd done it. *How* had she done it? How had she stopped the car safely? She couldn't think for relief. From the very top speed achieved on any Formula One circuit anywhere in the world, she had brought a stricken – practically out-of-control – car back from catastrophe to a halt without anyone getting hurt.

For a few moments she just sat in the cockpit while her whole body shook.

Two panicked-looking marshals came running over, clearly

dreading what they might find. Raising her hand, they were quickly reassured that everything was far better than feared.

Sabatino, looking to get out of the way of any car following suit behind her, sensed that the engine was still turning over. She paddled for first gear.

It engaged immediately.

What? How?

Pressing the throttle, the Ptarmigan responded immediately.

What?

As the car moved forward, she quickly realized she had not suffered any punctures. She kept moving, albeit slowly, still sensing for any other trouble with the car, particularly the suspension systems for each wheel.

Astonishingly, there didn't seem to be anything wrong. At all.

Could she get back to the pits?

She turned the car to the right so she could see back down the Kemmel Straight behind her – to check there was no one about to charge through the right and left of Turns Five and Six.

Seeing it was clear, she pulled gingerly out from the run-off area, onto the track, across to the inside of the racing line, still feeling for any damage to the car – from whatever had caused the rears to lock-up, or from her high-speed encounter with the kerbstones. The car was still responding. As far as she could tell, there was nothing wrong with it.

How could this be?

She accelerated a little, keeping a ready eye in her mirrors for anyone steaming through on a hot lap.

And ... still ... she sensed nothing wrong with the car.

Down the hill and into the straighter section approaching Turn Ten, she radioed in to Backhouse.

'What the hell happened there?' he asked – sounding, to Straker, pretty shaken up.

'Christ knows,' said Sabatino appearing remarkably composed. 'Took me completely by surprise. We were on the absolute straight and level. We were running beautifully. *Better* than perfect.'

'Bloody hell. How *did* you keep it under control? Any damage?'

'A bit. I've lost a chunk of the right front wing, and I've got major flat spots on both rears.'

'Nothing wrong with the engine or gearbox – suspension?'

'Not that I can tell.'

'Come in. We'd better check you over.'

'Where am I lying?'

There was a pause. 'Twelfth,' Backhouse said reluctantly.

'I've got to log a hot lap – I'm going to miss the shootout. How much longer have we got of the session?'

Straker was staggered. Moments from a death-defying disaster, and Sabatino was already thinking about her lap and grid position.

'It's going to be a struggle to get you in and out in time.'

'Fuck.'

An army of turquoise pit crew was ready waiting as Sabatino entered the pit lane. There was no time for congratulations or praise at her extraordinary handling of the incident. Swerving into her bay, more Ptarmigan mechanics than usual dived in around her to check the car. It was lifted straight up on its front and rear jacks. Off came all the wheels; the replacements were held back while the suspensions and brake assemblies were all checked. Off came the nosecone and front-wing. A replacement was quickly fixed into place, secured, and rapidly adjusted. At the rear, two mechanics dropped to the ground to look up underneath the car to check the undertray. Two more, one on either side, were checking the radiators for any damage sustained over the kerbstones, as well as the aerodynamic flourishes – bargeboards, wings and fins – to see if any of them were missing or broken and would affect performance. A "clear" signal was given: all the wheels were replaced, sporting a new set of tyres.

Backhouse, speaking with her over the radio, asked whether she was okay.

'Just get me out in time to complete a flying lap.'

A signal was soon given to the lollipop man. He raised his sign.

Sabatino shot forwards, swerving back out into the pit lane, charging down to the end on the limiter. She looked at the official clock. She only had ninety seconds to get right round the circuit to cross the start line before they closed the session.

It was going to be nip and tuck.

Particularly on cold tyres.

Feeding out of the pit lane exit, she passed Turn Four and headed up the Kemmel Straight to where the incident had just occurred. With such little time, she had no chance to coax the car gently up to speed and temperature. She had to cover the ground. And fast.

Q2's time was running out.

Hurtling round the circuit, her only chance was to hammer round every corner if she was to get to the start line in time.

One minute to go.

She rounded Rivage, getting a little ragged through the exit and rising up on the kerb. Down through Turn Nine and on to Pouhon, which she took with now typical verve.

Turn Twelve and on to Fagnes.

Thirty seconds to go.

She took Turn Fifteen, her back end slewing out through the apex and kicking up a cloud of dust as she scrambled over the patch of earth between the kerbstones and the grass.

Up to two hundred miles an hour down the bottom of the valley.

Fifteen seconds to go.

She had the Chicane and half the pit straight left. Was she going to make it?

A coasting car was in the middle of the Chicane, idling home. Sabatino had to swerve dramatically around it, thwarting her exit into the start/finish straight.

Five seconds to go.

She floored the accelerator.

The clock was counting down.

'No!' she screamed into the radio as she saw the ominous red lights and chequered flag before she could cross the line.

'No!' she screamed again.

Sabatino had missed the cut-off.

By one and a half seconds.

Straker heard a string of profanity over the radio at the failure to lodge a fast enough qualifying lap.

'She's outside the top ten. Hasn't made the cut for Q3,' said Oliver Treadwell in the headquarters truck beside him. 'She'll miss the shootout and will start only fourteenth on the grid. She's out of it.'

'What a waste, after all that speed,' said Straker. 'What the hell happened to her, though, down at Les Combes?'

Treadwell looked bemused. 'God knows. I've never seen anything like it. We'll rerun the telemetry and go through everything. We've *got* to try and find out what the hell went wrong out there.'

TWENTY-FIVE

Qualifying Three went ahead, to determine the ten places at the front of the grid, without her.

A dejected-looking Sabatino sat with Straker, Backhouse, Treadwell and several other team members at the meeting table in the Ptarmigan motor home. Laid out in front of them was a mass of printouts, charts, data sheets and other readouts.

'I just don't get it,' said Backhouse. 'Everything was optimal, right up to the moment it went. None of the components that could have caused the rears to lock-up like that show any sign of being anything other than perfect.' He ran a finger along some data. 'Absolutely fine. Then the trauma of the incident – and then absolutely fine again. Just like that.'

'What about mechanical failure?' asked one of the turquoise-uniformed team.

'If it were a major component, how come Remy could drive back in and sense nothing wrong?'

'What about an impact with something? A stone, an animal, a bird?'

'No sign of impact. The gyros show the car running unencumbered right up to and after the incident.'

'And again, any impact should have had a lasting effect,' added Sabatino. 'Except I found nothing wrong immediately afterwards.'

'What about fuel?' asked Treadwell.

'We're just running the data off the system now.' Leaning back, Backhouse called to one of the team for an update. A few seconds later a stack of paper was plonked down on the table between them.

'What's this?' asked Straker.

'The Fuel Injection trace.'

Straker looked at the landscape-formatted A4 sheets, with row upon row of graphs, extending left to right across each page. They put him in mind of a music score. 'What are these showing?'

'The injector pulse width – basically the workings of each fuel injection valve in the engine. These show how much fuel was going into each cylinder.'

'Why so many lines?'

'Eight cylinders, an injector each – eight traces.'

Straker studied just one row. As he did so, Backhouse offered more of an explanation: 'Each valve is opened and closed, electronically, by a solenoid at precise times in the combustion cycle, producing a square wave.'

Straker could see exactly what Backhouse meant: in each of the traces, he saw a line looking like a gappy row of squarish teeth.

'Each one of those columns – the up strokes – shows the injector opening,' Backhouse explained. 'The width of a column shows for how long – how much fuel – was injected. The down stroke is the injector closing.'

'Why so many pages of them?'

Sabatino smiled. 'Eighteen thousand RPM is three hundred-odd revs a second. In printout form, that takes up a lot of pages.'

'Okay,' said Straker, with a hint of apology, 'so which period does this lot cover?'

'Before and after the incident. As you can see, bizarrely, everything's okay after it.'

'What about at the very moment of the trauma?'

Backhouse leant forwards. He asked for the exact time code of the incident recorded in the telemetry. A few papers were shuffled before a readout was produced: '1.36.52.09.'

Backhouse found the corresponding page of the fuel injection report. 'Good God,' he breathed.

'What is it?' asked Sabatino.

Backhouse laid the sheet of paper in the middle of the table. 'Look there,' he said running his fingers vertically down through the rows of heart beats. 'At 1.36.52.09 the EFI effectively shut down – across all injectors.'

Running his finger along one of the rows left to right, Backhouse summarized: 'Full throttle – wide columns – fuel injection fully open. Then, for what looks like no more than a quarter of a second, the pulse width narrows significantly – is practically closed – to almost nothing. Then back up to fully open again.'

'What effect would that have?' Straker asked.

Treadwell looked up. 'For that short period of time the engine was all but switched off.'

'But only for a quarter of a second? What would that do to the car?' asked Straker.

'The revs would drop right off.'

'So it would seem like the engine had seized, I'm guessing?' Straker offered.

Backhouse indicated an appreciation of the thinking but with a gentle shake of his head. 'F1 engines have very little inertia, so it wouldn't feel like it had seized – not least as the engine appears to have been working normally less than a fraction of a second later. However,' Backhouse added with a more positive qualification of Straker's point, 'the shock – the jolt – of that momentary drop in revs could well, depending on the road surface, cause the rear wheels to lock-up. That *could* throw the car out of line – out of balance. An unexpected shock at that speed could affect anything. The loading. The aerodynamics. The weight distribution – on the road – between the front and back wheels. If all that happened, the driver – if they're lucky, or brilliant – would have to wrestle a car that's suddenly lost all stability and grip, particularly challenging if it was at over two hundred miles an hour.'

Straker nodded and looked at Sabatino, as if to acknowledge what had happened out on the circuit. There was a moment's silence.

He sensed a significant change in atmosphere. 'Does it look like we might have found the cause, then?' asked Straker studying all the faces for confirmation.

Treadwell turned to face him. 'It might do. It might give us an idea as to *what* happened, Matt, but it doesn't tell us anything about why.'

'Okay, let's see,' said Straker nodding slowly. 'You mentioned that each valve is opened and closed *electronically*? I'm assuming, being electrical, that it has something to do with the engine management computer?'

Backhouse nodded. 'It has. It's all controlled by the EMS.'

'So did anything happen on board to interrupt or interfere with that control?'

'Not that we can find anywhere in the telemetry.'

'Let me be sure I'm getting this right,' said Straker. 'You're saying this was definitely *not* an "organic" malfunction?'

Treadwell looked at Backhouse. 'Not caused by anything on the car, at any rate.'

Straker paused. 'If it wasn't tripped by anything that happened on board, how *did* it happen?'

Everyone looked blank.

Straker's mind, harping back to their experience in Monaco, was anxious not to jump to conclusions. Even so, he was concerned by possible sensitivities. Sounding generous, he suggested a break for the junior team members, leaving the senior Ptarmigan figures alone in the motor home. Then he said: 'What about some form of external interference?'

Backhouse looked at him, his expression almost accusing him of paranoia. 'I'm not sure that's likely.'

Straker sat back in his chair and looked Sabatino in the face, waiting for a similar reaction from her. This time, though, there wasn't one. Quite the opposite.

'It's not as if we don't have experience of such a thing, Andy,' she said flatly.

'Okay,' said Straker realizing the significance of that exchange, 'let's look at the timing of this. When, for instance, *could* this momentary shut-down have happened?'

Backhouse made a moue. 'Any time. It could have happened at any time.'

'Except it happened – when it did. At the end of that straight – right there. Is there any significance to *that*?'

Sabatino started nodding very slightly. 'It was in Q2, so critical to my getting through to the top-ten shootout.'

'And getting a competitive place on the grid, right?' added Straker.

'She was on a flying lap,' Treadwell chipped in.

'Having not clocked a fast enough one – to make the cut for the top ten – at that point?' confirmed Straker.

'Correct.'

'And with only a few minutes of the session left?'

Treadwell nodded.

Straker declared: 'Your Q2 lap time was critical to getting a competitive place on the grid, and, therefore, your chances of scoring well in the race?'

There were nods around the table.

'Because of this,' he said with a wave of his hand over the print-outs around the table, 'you've been baulked and will start in fourteenth. Anyone *wanting* to damage your chances in the race this weekend could – just about – have achieved what they wanted, no?'

There was silence in the motor home as the implications sunk in.

'Hang on,' said Backhouse with a hint of challenge. 'They did it at Les Combes? Why not at Eau Rouge?'

Treadwell looked Straker in the eye, then at Sabatino, and said solemnly: 'Because that would have killed her – without question.'

The faces round the table were aghast.

Sabatino said easily. 'A back-end lock-up in Eau Rouge, or in the middle of *any* corner for that matter, would have had me spin completely out of control – off the track, for sure. And at any kind of speed, that would have to have been fatal.'

'The very end of the Kemmel Straight makes perfect sense,' said Treadwell with an air of appreciative resignation. 'On the straight and relatively level. Plenty of run-off. It didn't do Remy any physical harm, and yet it's been blisteringly effective – easily costing her a place in the top-ten shootout, let alone a likely pole.'

'Also,' said Straker, 'the car exhibits no malfunctions or ill effects afterwards, as we've been struggling to prove.'

'*And*, any such incident gets written off as a freak – even blamed on driver error,' said Treadwell.

Almost involuntarily, Backhouse slammed his hand down on to the table. 'Who the fuck's doing this to us?' he bawled.

TWENTY-SIX

Straker was anxious to push on with the analysis. 'Let's suppose, for the sake of argument, that we're not wrong and that this *was* induced – that there *was* an external force. How could it have been brought about?'

After a pause, Treadwell offered: 'Some sort of timing device?'

'If we're convinced the time and place of the intervention are significant,' said Sabatino with a shake of her head, 'they'd have to be sure of hitting me at *exactly* the right moment. A pre-set timer could never ensure that.'

'How else could someone interfere with the running of a car, then?' asked Straker. 'What about remotely – by some sort of radio signal?'

Sabatino frowned. 'How could we even know whether that happened, this long after the incident?'

'By keeping our eyes open for clues,' replied Straker. 'Let's start by looking at all the radio traffic with the car – not just the intercom, but the telemetry and data channels as well?'

These reports were quickly printed off.

Treadwell laid them out on the table a few minutes later. Picking out the relevant time sheets, Backhouse said: 'Here's the data link carrier wave. Normal, up to 1.36.52.09.'

Straker took the page and studied the squiggly line – resembling the seismic measurement of an earthquake. He peered at the print-out for some time. 'There does seem to be some disturbance in the carrier wave,' he observed. 'Was that because of the incident, or was that disturbance the *cause* of it? Could interfering with the data carrier wave have thrown the engine management system?'

'Absolutely not,' said Treadwell firmly. 'Every F1 car would grind to a halt every time a local taxi firm radioed its base, or someone in a nearby town ordered a pizza. Our radio nets are protected using specialized frequency ranges and electronic filters. Any disturbance you've found,' he said pointing at the data sheet in front of Straker, 'would not have been enough to affect the EMS.'

Straker nodded his acceptance of Treadwell's answer, but somewhat half-heartedly, as he continued to peer closely at the graph. 'You know, there is *definitely* interference in that carrier wave – over and above the trauma – at the key moment. It's faint. But it *is* there,' and he spun the page round to show the engineers. 'Can we, at least, see if there were any other examples of radio interference like that at any other time today?'

Backhouse responded readily to the request. The pages, just produced, were split up and divvied out.

After several minutes thumbing through the printouts, each person in turn declared not. 'It appears, then, that the only interference we experienced all day was at 1.36.52.09,' Backhouse concluded.

'It cannot, then, be a coincidence,' declared Straker. 'It means that there was an unidentified radio transmission, of some kind, at the *very* moment the fuel injection system shut down and the car lost control.'

Sabatino said. 'What are you thinking?'

'That the disruption of your fuel system might have been triggered by a radio signal. If we could track down that unknown transmission – and find its source – we *might* find the cause of the intervention.'

'This is good, isn't it?' said Sabatino. 'You can do that – you did that, finding the guy using a radio in Monaco.'

'I did, but that was knowing the threat we faced in advance. Here, in Spa, we had no idea we'd be facing anything like this, so, obviously, we haven't deployed the relevant surveillance kit.'

'So you can't catch these people?'

'I didn't say that.'

'How do you do it, then?' she asked.

'We'll have to look for *other* clues.'

Sabatino pulled a face, indicating a lack of belief. 'Like what?'

Straker leant forward. 'Have we got a map of the circuit?'

Backhouse looked a little nonplussed by the apparent non sequitur. After consultation with another screen or two, and the whirring of a printer, a map was produced on a sheet of A3. Straker pored over it, looking at the topography around Les Combes.

'Something to help with our process of elimination,' Straker explained, 'is that all radio signals need line-of-sight to work. Unless they're rebroadcast – picked up and sent on through another transceiver – radio signals don't bend; they can't change direction or go round corners. They also don't work over a hill or well through buildings. That's helpful, here, in narrowing our search down, as there's chunky topography around Les Combes. It means that our unknown radio signal could not have come from the pit lane or paddock – there's far too much real estate in between. Not only that, the interference in the carrier wave is very faint – I'd say it could only have come from a low-power, local transmission.' Straker ran his finger round the contours; then, picking up a highlighter pen, he traced out a pink line across the map which ended up taking on the shape of a kidney. 'Because of the undulating ground, such a weak radio signal could only have come from somewhere within this boundary,' he said. 'The area does include plenty of woodland, up on the hillside above the track. Perfectly possible for someone to have secreted themselves and activated it from up there.'

'How big is the kit needed to do something like this?' asked Sabatino.

'For that weak a signal, not huge. Easily fit in a rucksack.'

'So it could even have come from someone among the spectators?'

'How many spectators would there have been inside this area?'

'Quite a few,' said Treadwell, 'on the outside of the Kemmel Straight before Les Combes, along here,' and pointed to the relevant section of the map with his finger.

'I'll check with Spa security and ask for their CCTV footage,' said Straker. 'Did *we* record any footage of the spectators on that bank, either from an on-board shot or from the main broadcaster?'

'We'll have a look,' said Treadwell.

'In the meantime,' said Straker looking at the faces around the table, 'we need to think this through. Could this kind of incident happen again? *Will* it happen again? Are we vulnerable to another attack in the race tomorrow?'

Sabatino's expression hardly faltered at the suggestions. 'Whoever did this is still out there. It *has* to be a possibility.'

Straker nodded. 'What do you normally do when you have a safety issue like this?'

Sabatino smiled lasciviously. 'We're all virgins, on this one, Colonel.'

Treadwell answered in clear Australian: 'We'd probably go to the Race Director.'

'Would you expect him to deal with it, or would he take it higher within the FIA?'

'Definitely higher.'

'But with our level of proof,' added Backhouse, 'if it did go any higher, it wouldn't help us much. You heard San Marino's response to the radio jamming in Monaco?'

'We've got to try – somehow – to corroborate our assertions, then. Okay,' said Straker, looking at his watch. 'It's three-thirty. Let's pull together any footage we have of that part of the circuit to suss out the lie of spectators near that corner. While you're getting on with that, I'll go and talk to my friend about the woodland area around Les Combes.'

Maurice Beauregard, the circuit's head of security, was troubled to hear of another possible sabotage incident, and immediately came up trumps. In double-quick time he recruited a sizeable search party of police sniffer dogs from two local stations. A dozen or so Belgian Malinois were soon deployed across the hillsides to scour the wooded areas Straker was concerned about – hoping to find spoor to indicate the earlier presence of or even the position used by a concealed radio operator.

Although buoyed by such substantial help to his investigation, Straker couldn't add much more once the search had started, so accepted a lift back to the security manager's office.

There, he asked Beauregard whether he was prepared to download all the circuit's CCTV recordings onto DVDs. Having seen Sabatino's high-speed incident, the security man was ready to help. He told Straker he would have them delivered round the moment they were ready.

Straker returned to the Ptarmigan headquarters truck. 'I've got the area around Les Combes being searched by police sniffer dogs,' he reported to the team.

Sabatino looked genuinely impressed.

'How have we got on with pulling together the footage around the corner – that we recorded?' he asked.

'Pretty well.'

'Let's start with that.'

Backhouse fired up a laptop to view what they had. 'This one,' he explained, 'is on-board with Remy – looking forward, approaching Les Combes.' As they played it, they were badly distracted from scanning the spectators – having to relive the horror of those fearful moments and seeing something of what Sabatino must have experienced as the picture violently swung about.

'How the hell did you hold that together?' said Treadwell. 'Also, it was really lucky you didn't hit that car alongside.'

'Hang on,' said Sabatino hitting the pause button. 'That's right. There *was* a car alongside, coasting home on the inside of the racing line.'

'A Massarella, by the looks of things,' said Straker, backing up the clip. 'Have we got anything to check the spectators from on-board that car?'

'Hang on. Yes, here we go – facing both backward and forward.'

They started with the rearward footage.

It showed a shot over and through the rear wing of the Massarella as it cruised slowly on an in-lap up the Kemmel Straight, along the channel-like passage through the trees. Looming in the distance, and closing up fast, came – head-on – the brilliant-turquoise shape of Sabatino's Ptarmigan as she hurtled up the hill towards the car-borne camera. In a matter of moments, it had shot past, out of the picture to the right.

'Okay, there were some spectators visible there, but they're too far in the distance to be studied properly. What about the *forward* view from the Massarella?' prompted Straker.

They found that segment on another disc, from further back along the Kemmel Straight.

This showed the front end of the black Massarella, as it slowly approached the corner on the inside of the circuit, with the back of Adi Barrantes's helmet – in the sky-blue and white of the Argentine flag – occupying the top right of the screen. One hand could be seen on the steering wheel.

A moment later the stricken Ptarmigan flashed into the left-hand side of the shot, already snaking violently as it hurtled past, off the track, heading to bounce over the kerbstones. Once again, spotting for spectators on the left-hand bank was not easy, given the distraction of the out-of-control car.

'Wow, it still doesn't lose any of its drama,' said Treadwell.

Straker frowned. 'We've got poor sight of the spectators before the incident – backwards from the Massarella – and very little after the incident – forward from the Massarella, let alone anything of the crowds *level* with Remy at the exact moment of the incident. Is there any shot that shows the crowd directly opposite the crash site?'

'Afraid not.'

A few minutes later there was a knock on the door of the motor home. One of Beauregard's people was standing there with a box of DVDs. Taking delivery, Straker immediately searched the collection to support their scan of the spectators. He found CCTV material that might work. It was shot from a gantry halfway down the Kemmel

Straight directly opposite the bank of spectators, pointing across the circuit from the inside, outwards and towards Les Combes.

'Okay, let's see if we can study the crowds from this angle,' said Straker.

They started to run it. 'This looks promising,' offered Sabatino.

But instead of studying the clear shot of the spectators on the bank overlooking the track, their eyes were, inextricably, drawn to the fishtailing Ptarmigan again, its violent changes of direction appearing even more disturbing when seen from above and behind.

Straker asked them to run through the clip again, this time in slow motion. As it ran, they stopped the video and zoomed in on a couple of potential suspects among the crowds, but it was clear they all looked completely disinterested in the drama on the circuit below them.

'There are several hundred people on the grass there, but none of them really sparks suspicion.'

'Agreed.'

To make sure, they ran through the footage a third time, this time frame by frame.

After a few minutes, two of the Ptarmigan team suddenly emitted grunts simultaneously. 'Hang on, wait a second! What was that?'

Treadwell tapped the space bar on the computer. 'We haven't seen that before.'

'Seen what?' asked Straker.

'Back it up, back it up!'

The footage was run again. Sabatino peered at the screen. 'There – stop!'

She clearly wasn't looking at the spectators.

The screen was frozen. It was a grainy image. Focus was poor, but the two cars could be seen – as blurs – side by side. Something eye-catching stood out against the grainy shapes in the image: a bright red light on the back of Sabatino's car.

'Well blow me!' said Treadwell. 'Blink and you'd miss that.'

'Miss what?' asked Straker.

'Her light's come on.'

Straker looked puzzled. 'Don't lights come on when you brake?'

Sabatino almost bawled: '*Hell* no! F1 cars don't even *have* brake lights. That's a high-intensity rain light – comes on when the visibility closes in.'

'A fog light?'

'Sort of – activated by a humidity and moisture sensor which … wait a second, that doesn't make any sense. It was sunny and dry all afternoon. *But*,' said Sabatino raising her voice – as if a realization was striking, 'our cars also activate that rain light automatically with *the engine limiter* when we're forced to slow down – to go slower than eighty kilometres an hour in the pit lane!'

Treadwell, Backhouse and Sabatino all looked at each other. 'Fuck, does that mean the engine limiter cut in?'

There was a buzz around the table.

Straker sensed they might be getting somewhere at last. Stepping back in to the discussion, he said: 'Okay, good, but we need to be robust here. Could that light have been activated by the jolt – would that have been enough to light it up? If not, were the light's sensors working properly? Can we see if the light came on at any other time today? Can we see whether the engine limiter was – or wasn't – working properly, and then can we see whether the limiter system was indeed activated at that critical moment?'

Treadwell nodded. 'That's logical, and disciplined, thinking, Matt. We'll get all the relevant data and check everything out.'

Production of the reports was delegated to different team members around the table, all of whom got up and went straight to work.

Straker was distracted from the bustling activity around the motor home by his ringing phone. It was Maurice Beauregard. He sounded disappointed. The sniffer dogs had completed their sweep of the area around Les Combes but had not found anything in the woods on the hillside above that part of the circuit. Although a dead end, Straker was far from disappointed. He was confident the dogs would have found something had there been a presence in the woods above the track. A sizeable area of ground could now reasonably be eliminated as the possible location of his unknown radio signal. He thanked the Belgian profusely – both for the police search and also for the CCTV footage.

Ten minutes later the findings of the research into the engine limiter were ready to be presented to the team.

'The engine sensors were fine,' confirmed Backhouse. 'Coolant, camshaft, oxygen. The rain light *didn't* come on because of faulty sensors.'

'I can confirm the light *didn't* come on because of the jolt or vibration of the incident,' reported Treadwell.

'Its illumination *was* linked directly to the engine limiter,' declared Sabatino. 'And, yes, the engine limiter *was* active for the duration of the incident – but had *not* been triggered by me.'

Straker sensed an agreement around the meeting room table. 'So we *are* confident to conclude, then, that the engine limiter was on, but not activated by us – either deliberately or by accident?'

'Absolutely,' stated Backhouse.

'And if the engine limiter was activated – out on the track – at that speed, we'd expect the effects to be as they occurred?'

Backhouse and Sabatino nodded repeatedly. 'Almost identical. Having found this,' he said, 'the incident now makes much more sense.'

'Okay,' said Straker, 'good. This is a clear step forward. But, if this was none of our doing, we need to establish *how* we think the engine limiter was activated.'

Straker was surprised by the ensuing silence in the room.

'We don't know?' he offered as rhetorical confirmation. He paused to be sure. 'In that case, does *when* the engine limiter was activated tell us anything? Can we identify the exact time, please?'

A page was consulted. '1.36.52.09.'

'And, just remind me, what was the time coding for the radio interference on the data link carrier wave?'

'1.36.52.09.'

'They're identical!' exclaimed Sabatino.

Straker, holding up his hand, said: 'Let's not jump to conclusions – correlation is not causation. Before we discovered this engine limiter dimension, we had been looking at interference in the carrier wave, possibly from an unknown radio signal,' he said. 'Let's try and close the circle, then: could the *engine limiter* have been activated by a radio signal?'

'Fuck a duck,' responded Treadwell. 'How can we not, now, see a link between the activation of the limiter and the unknown radio signal?'

Straker saw the same feeling reflected in the expressions around the motor home. 'Okay, if this logic is holding up,' he said, 'we're back to looking for that radio source. So far, though, we haven't got anywhere with it coming from the spectators – and we're pretty sure of that, having gone through some comprehensive footage from the CCTV camera. And, I've just heard from the Belgian police – who have drawn a blank with their sniffer dogs – that there was no sign of anything in the woodland above the circuit. Neither of these help directly, but they *are* reasonable eliminations. We need, then, to look for the next possibility for the source of that transmission.' Straker pointed at the image on the laptop. 'There's a car – bang next to the incident. Could the radio signal have come from that?'

There was further buzz around the table.

'Can we take another look at the on-board footage of the Massarella?' Straker asked.

The laptop was pulled back into position. Backhouse hit the play button. They saw the forward-looking view from above the driver's helmet again. The clip showed the turquoise Ptarmigan shooting past and swerving violently, heading towards the corner of Les Combes.

'Play it again, this time in as slow a motion as possible,' said Straker.

The footage was rerun.

The picture showed Barrantes, with his right hand on the wheel.

Then, with a tilt of the helmet to the left, the driver looked like he was checking the track behind him through his left-hand mirror.

'Bloody hell,' said Straker forcibly.

'What?' replied Backhouse.

'Didn't you see that?'

'See what?'

'Run it back.'

The footage jumped back by ten seconds and played again. It showed the familiar helmet tilt. A second later, the driver started raising his left hand, at which point Straker quickly leaned in and tapped the pause button with his finger.

'What?'

'*What?*'

'There,' said Straker, pointing at the exact spot on the screen. 'Barrantes has got something taped to his glove.'

'What – where?'

They all peered at the freeze-frame image.

'What the hell … well spotted, Matt! What *is* that?'

Treadwell prompted the computer to zoom in. 'Looks like some sort of fob – like a car alarm.'

The image was then nudged forward, one frame at a time.

'*And* it looks like he's squeezing it,' said Sabatino. 'With his thumb. Could that be some kind of zapper?'

'Mark the time code. What's the *exact* time he squeezes it?' asked Straker.

Treadwell read it out as he wrote it down: '1.36.51.99.'

Sabatino sighed audibly: 'Barrantes's action happened ten one hundredths of a second before my engine crashed. Matt, you've sussed it.'

Straker shook his head. 'Not yet. Let's be thorough,' and then said, in a way that acknowledged he was repeating himself: 'Let's not jump to any conclusions. We have no idea what that fob thing is for. All we have is the coincidence of two actions, but no proof of a connection. *Post hoc ergo propter hoc.*'

Sabatino pulled a what-the-fuck-does-that-mean smile. 'Matt, the right word here is *coincidence*,' she countered. 'That's cause and effect, right there. We have proof of a button being actively pressed, on what looks like a fob – an item that has no place on an F1 car. We have proof of a radio signal – which you called the unknown radio – and which you spotted from a burst of interference in the data carrier wave. We've discovered an indication that my rain light was activated, which we have verified was not because of any fault in the sensors – but because it's linked to my pit lane engine limiter which, at the critical moment, *had been* activated, but not by a malfunction or by me.'

'I agree,' said Treadwell, emphatically. 'There's a line of best fit, here; these discoveries clearly point to some kind of remote activation of Remy's engine limiter.'

Straker was anxious that he – they – be sure. A lot of credibility would be riding on this.

'Oh come on, Matt,' said Sabatino, 'it's *far* too coincidental to be dismissed.'

Straker finally nodded. He really could not dismiss their deductions.

'Holy shit,' said Backhouse.

'It's Massarella, then. It's Massarella doing this. The *sons of fucking bitches*.'

TWENTY-SEVEN

Within the hour, the President of the FIA – Bo San Marino – received Matt Straker and Andy Backhouse in his hospitality suite within the Spa-Francorchamps complex.

Straker, having been at the last meeting to reveal the discovery of sabotage in Monte-Carlo, made contact through official channels and offered this meeting to the President as an update and follow on. San Marino agreed to see Ptarmigan immediately.

As Straker and Backhouse walked in through the President's doors, though, they were taken by surprise. Joss MacRae, the head of the F1 commercial rights holder, was there too. In response to Backhouse's expression, San Marino said: 'I hope you don't mind Joss being in on this,' but offered no chance for them to demur.

They were invited to sit. Straker looked over at Joss MacRae who, already sitting and working on some papers in his lap, seemed far from ready to engage.

'What's happened to prompt another meeting?' asked the President.

'Sir,' replied Straker, 'when we met before in Monaco, we presented you with evidence of interference with Ptarmigan's radio communication.' Straker glanced across at MacRae who still seemed distracted. 'We regret that we've had another case of intervention here this afternoon. We had an incident during Q2 when Remy Sabatino's car went unexpectedly out of control approaching Les Combes. We have findings to indicate that this was induced by another team.'

Joss MacRae suddenly looked up and glared at Straker. 'How convenient that one of the overpaid chauffeurs should cite a third party to excuse lousy driving.'

Straker felt his hackles instantly rise, but fought to freeze his face to prevent giving away the strength of his reaction. He determinedly maintained eye contact and, judging the moment to reply, did so in a slow, soft voice: 'Do facts not have a bearing in assessing such things?'

'The stuff you produced for the President in Monaco – some crackle on a radio – hardly warrants serious consideration. And, as for this afternoon, when a driver makes a clear error – dropping their car under braking – what facts are needed? If you don't have any proof, shut the fuck up.'

Straker turned to look at Backhouse, who appeared fit to burst.

'Is that it?' asked the race engineer. 'You're not prepared even to listen to our findings?'

MacRae leant forwards and looked Backhouse straight in the eye. It was an intimidating stare, one that MacRae was known to have used to devastating effect during his career. 'This is what I know, Mr Backhouse. This is a *business*. Billions of dollars are at stake, as are many thousands of jobs. The last thing Formula One needs, right now, is another scandal. You make a sanctimonious song and dance, based on unsubstantiated allegations, about an obvious rival of yours for the Championship – and you know what sponsors will say? Sour grapes. No thanks. And how would that look to your new benefactors and the vastly inflated sum of money you're hoping to fleece them for? I say grow up, and grow a pair,' he said, which, after a few moments, seemed to amuse him.

Backhouse's face changed colour several times while MacRae had been speaking.

Straker looked across at San Marino, trying to judge *his* reaction to this unexpected line. Straker was disappointed to discern no real reaction from him to MacRae's comments. But San Marino was a dignified man, and might be being old-fashioned, Straker hoped. Wasn't he remaining silent for the sake of presenting a collective front from the leadership of F1?

'Can I ask you a question, Joss?' said Straker.

MacRae, slightly surprised by such a reasonable response to

his provocative tirade and Straker's tutoiement, looked a little off balance.

'Just suppo. e that there *is* some validity to our findings?' said Straker. 'And what if,' Straker went on deliberately ignoring Mac-Rae's grunts, 'someone were to be killed, because of this – which could so easily have happened this afternoon. Your first death since 1994. What would that do to your *business*?'

MacRae shook his head in a particularly dismissive way. 'It would make for great spectacle, great TV, and great news coverage. Cunzer's spectacular balls-up in Monaco – shown in countless news bulletins around the world – easily added ten points to our ratings.'

Straker weighed up the situation and reached a clear conclusion. This exchange was getting them nowhere. Rising slowly to his feet, he said: 'I can only thank you both for your time,' and looked across at Backhouse, inviting him to follow his lead out of the room.

'Fuck me,' said the race engineer as they exited the President's suite onto the corridor. 'What the *hell* was that?'

Straker, suffering the after-effects of suppressing his own reaction, felt his heart rate and body temperature rise. 'We may not have a cast-iron case, but any reasonable mind would remain curious, surely – at least until it had been completely disproven.'

Stomping down through the grandstand complex they reached the Ptarmigan garage in the pit lane. Once ensured of some privacy, Straker pulled out his iPhone and rang Quartano in London. He invited Backhouse to lean in to hear the conversation.

'He said *that*?' replied Quartano. '"*Ten points to our ratings*"?'

'Verbatim.'

'"Don't rock the boat". Don't upset this multi-billion-dollars-a-year business. MacRae's attitude – complacency, let alone callousness – is staggering.'

Quartano was enraged but realized quickly he had to rationalize the situation. 'What's your response to all this, Matt?' he asked, restoring his equilibrium.

'We need to get over the offence of this and try to understand MacRae's response. The man's behaviour was completely disproportionate. My starting point, whenever faced with someone behaving so unreasonably – in any circumstance – is to try and identify their emotional starting point.'

Quartano grunted. 'Sorry? Don't know what that means.'

'That there is clearly more to this than meets the eye. I'll wager something's going on between the people involved in this – or is happening behind the scenes – for MacRae to have had such an exaggerated and unreasonable reaction.'

'Like what?'

'I've no idea. But, *some*how – inadvertently – we must have touched an already-open sore. If I could find any indication as to what that is, we might understand this a little better.'

'I like that.'

'Good, but obviously it isn't going to happen this afternoon. For now, we've got to focus on protecting Remy.'

'What can you do?'

'A fair amount. We're already reconfiguring the engine limiter system – changing its frequencies and computer code. Nobody will be able to interfere with that anymore. Also, we're adding second frequencies to the data links now – as we did, before, to the radio net. That means we'll be transmitting over parallel channels – so we can be sure of maintaining contact, even if there are further attempts to disrupt any one of our communications.'

'Matt, that's good work. But don't let up on exposing these people. I want us to bring Massarella to book for what they did there this afternoon.'

'Right, sir. Further accusations without proof, though, *will* simply look like sour grapes. We'd have to build a cast-iron case, if we're to have any hope of nailing them properly.'

'Do whatever you have to do, Matt. And, now, of course, for the added satisfaction of exposing that odious little arsehole MacRae.'

That evening, just before midnight, Straker found Backhouse in the bar at Ptarmigan's hotel in Malmedy. The room was fairly dark, lit by spotlights here and there, but with most of the illumination coming from behind the display of bottles against the back wall. Backhouse was sitting on a bar stool on his own, and had clearly been there for some time, his mood unimproved since their distressing meeting with San Marino and MacRae earlier that day.

'How can they behave like that?' he asked Straker. 'They were *no* help – and we need help against Massarella's ... devi-*us*-ness.'

Straker could only nod his agreement. He caught the eye of the barman and ordered a drink for them both.

Backhouse swayed slightly as Straker climbed onto a bar stool beside him: 'But can you be sure, Matt, that you can stop them?'

'We need evidence, Andy, particularly if they go on being as *devious* as they have been.'

'And they *will* be – they *will*. It's the FIA penalties that are forcing them to be so underhand. If they got caught, they'd be fined tens of millions of dollars.'

The barman reappeared with their drinks, placing Straker's whisky down on a napkin in front of him. 'Indeed, Andy. Worse, they could end up killing someone.'

A hint of panic flashed across Backhouse's face. 'That could be *catastrophic*,' he said. 'I dread sending Remy out again – after today – knowing she might be hurt.'

Straker took a sip of his whisky and looked at Backhouse over the rim of his glass.

'It's wrong, Matt, it's *wrong*. They shouldn't be getting away with this. How *do* we show the world what they're doing,' Backhouse asked almost forlornly. '*How?*'

'Without being proactive,' Straker replied, 'and I mean invasive – I really don't know. We have no power to interview them, nor any power to eavesdrop. We have no intercept rights – no entitlement to search premises.'

'So there's nothing more you can do to prove it's them – or be sure of stopping them?' said Backhouse almost with a catch in his voice. 'We've just got to sit back and *take* this?'

Straker saw the race engineer's face say it all. He suddenly felt the man's anguish.

Was now the time? Straker asked himself. He thought of Sabatino – of Cunzer – of Ptarmigan – even the $750 million sponsorship that was at stake. Straker seemed to come to a decision. Leaning in, he whispered close to the man's ear – for several seconds.

Straker pulled back to study Backhouse's expression.

He was baffled.

Backhouse's face was suddenly impossible to read.

Straker turned in shortly afterwards, his mind in turmoil. Knowing he was so preoccupied, he was anxious about falling asleep in case he suffered an episode. Every time he felt he might be dropping off, he jolted himself awake in anticipation of suffering one of his flashbacks. It began to be wearying. The only thing keeping him sane was the thought of being responsible for keeping someone else safe.

Finally overcome by tiredness – towards two o'clock in the morning – he eventually succumbed to sleep. Even so, he woke at four, starting himself awake again to find every light in his room still burning brightly. With a heart-felt growl of frustration he took solace in the only way he knew how while in this frame of mind. Climbing into his running kit, he let himself out of the family-run hotel, setting off on a purging run through the darkness. A chill in the air was welcome. Its edge served as a refreshing distraction.

Running straight up a long drag from the valley bottom, Straker used the pain and exertion to try and clear his head. Only after a prolonged stint of anaerobic respiration, and the resultant muscle burn searing his concentration, did he start to calm himself down. As he ran along the dirt track of a long woodland ride, he began to turn the sabotage incidents over in his mind, along with that monstrous reaction from MacRae.

What the hell was going on there?

Straker quickly realized that trying to fathom all that out would have to come later. For now, he had to focus on the more immediate issue: how to protect Ptarmigan and Sabatino from further sabotage of their performance – let alone safety – here in Spa. Clearly, the FIA or MacRae weren't going to be of any help. He had to think of something else.

Straker ran on. Dawn broke and the first sunlight struck the tops of the mountains.

After a long uphill drag of a solid mile through the forest, he reached a bend in the road. There, a gap in the trees gave him a superb view out over Malmedy and the valley below. Breathing deeply to aid his recovery, he thought through the sabotage again and made a decision. There *might* be a way of buying some protection – for today, at least.

Monza, in two weeks' time, would be another bridge to be crossed at a later date.

Race day of the Belgian Grand Prix rolled on. The sun was shining, and there was a light breeze. Track temperatures were around twenty degrees Celsius.

In spite of the clear danger of sabotage, and her fury at MacRae's bizarre outburst, Sabatino was adamant she was going to race.

By half-past one the cars were on the grid and the pit straight was chock-a-block with mechanics, the ubiquitous pit lizards holding the drivers' name boards, other team members, hoards of media, and showboating celebrities inauthentically professing years of interest in Formula One.

Straker escorted Sabatino from the garage in her turquoise suit, he carrying her fire-retardant balaclava and helmet. Immaculately turned out – her short nut-brown hair was freshly clean, in place, and shining – she didn't need to wear make-up to show that she'd made an effort, not least as her mood had changed. Her brown eyes behind the black-rimmed glasses were sparkling. Straker inferred she'd managed to harness her anger at the FIA reaction into positive energy and self-belief, once again.

Or was it the idea Straker had put to her?

They ducked through the pit wall onto the track. Her car, in P14, was way down to their left. Instead, she turned right, along the start/finish straight towards the front of the grid. Straker struggled to keep up as she strode between the mass of bodies, cars, mechanics and trolleys. Sabatino made her way up to the leading Massarella car, driven by Simi Luciano, in P3.

'Hey, Eugene,' Straker heard her say as she barged into the Massarella clique standing in front of their car and caught the team boss by surprise.

Van Der Vaal glowered at the interruption.

'I know what you're up to,' she said with a smile. Slowly, and entirely at her own pace, she pulled three pieces of paper from inside her turquoise racing suit, unfolded them and held them up against her chest so he could see them. 'This page shows my data link carrier wave and telemetry up to my incident at Les Combes yesterday,' she said pointing with a finger. 'This is a photograph of Barrantes activating some form of zapper at exactly the same time. And this picture shows my rain light coming on – indicating the engine limiter being activated – at over two hundred miles an hour. Look at the time code on all the pictures, Eugene.' Then with throwaway levity she added: 'I know *exactly* what you're up to.'

Despite his irritation at the interruption, Eugene Van Der Vaal couldn't help looking down at the images. But then he pulled an amused but dismissive expression. 'More of your fantasies – to make up for being only a woman, my dear?' he said, clearly softening his Afrikaans accent. 'You know, male drivers don't need these sorts of excuses when they make such a rookie mistake.'

Straker saw her smile in return, completely unfazed by the patronizing tone. Her face then hardened. 'I know that you, Eugene, and Massarella, limited my engine.'

'I have no idea what you're talking about, young lady.'

A mechanic tried to squeeze past two TV crews doing an interview with Luciano and inadvertently bumped into Straker, knocking him slightly off balance. Holding Sabatino's helmet didn't help his centre of gravity. Stepping quickly out to the side to steady himself, he tried desperately not to put his foot down on the Massarella's front wing. As Straker looked down to place his feet, though, he saw something that took him completely by surprise.

On either side of the Massarella's black nosecone, he saw a shape he recognized almost instantly – identical to the distinctive airflow surfaces he had been shown by Ptarmigan's aerodynamicist and seen tested in the wind tunnel in Shenington, and which were now on Sabatino's car. Weren't they *their* Fibonacci Blades? How the hell had they got there? Straker couldn't believe it. He almost shivered at the breach of trust by their infernal traitor. Regaining his balance, he turned back to the exchange.

'I heard you went running off to San Marino,' Van Der Vaal was saying. '*He* threw your whingeing out as inconclusive.'

Sabatino, stretching herself up, moved in just a little closer to the Afrikaner, which induced a look of awkwardness on the South African's face for the first time. 'You've put me down to fourteenth place. I've got nothing to lose today. So, Eugene,' she said as she folded up her pages, and put them back in a pocket, 'how many cars do you want to lose in this race, eh? One? … Both?'

For a fleeting moment there was a glimmer of hesitation. Straker sensed that Van Der Vaal didn't quite know whether she was being serious.

'Any trouble from you, Eugene, and I take your cars off. *Capiche*?'

Straker was engrossed; he even forgot the work of the rogue insider for a moment. He watched this electric encounter, his eyes flicking from one to the other. Then he saw Sabatino attempt to throw Van Der Vaal off balance again. Slowly, gently, she stretched up and leant in even closer to the Massarella team boss. Equally slowly, she raised a hand and placed it on his arm. Van Der Vaal's look of hesitation returned. Sabatino, well aware of the effect her closeness and touch was having on him, deliberately held her position and stance well within his personal space.

'What the hell are you talking about?' growled the Afrikaner, but with less commitment as he ever so slightly tried to lean back away from her.

'If you can make something look like driver error, my friend, so can I,' she said and, in a surprisingly sensual way, started stroking Van Der Vaal's wrist with the backs of her fingers. 'Have a good race, Eugene,' she said, and, turning round, walked calmly away.

Straker could hardly keep the smile off his face. 'That was superb,' he breathed.

'Felt good,' she said returning his smile. 'You're sure throwing this at them won't blow your spy game – won't damage your chances of catching them next time?'

'For future races, maybe. But not today. With no help from MacRae, or spine from San Marino, there's not much more we can do. It has its risks, and it's not what we would've done for choice. But what else is left to us? Shocking Massarella – even half as well as that – must surely throw them off balance.'

As they walked back down the grid, Sabatino turned her head to look up at him. Straker met her eye. For perhaps a minute or two, all the baggage he was cursed to carry around with him was banished from his thoughts. The spunk of this woman was a real distraction. For a moment he had a feeling of liberation. Straker could not help but smile thinking about her tour de force. 'You've got balls, Miss Sabatino, I'll give you that.'

Reaching her car in their disappointing P14 on the grid, his mind was returned to the here and now. Straker wanted to throw a second punch at their suspected saboteurs. In the light of the high-speed incident the day before, he had been considering the Trifecta, Benbecular, Michael Lyons connection – particularly that man's meeting over breakfast, which Straker had witnessed, in Leamington Spa. He thought: how could that, now, not be connected? Handing over to Sabatino her helmet and balaclava, Straker pulled his phone out of his pocket and made a point of drawing her attention to it. In her earshot, he dialled the number Treadwell had found for him. It rang.

'Hello?' said Straker. 'Is that Mr Barnett?'

'Yes,' came the voice on the other end.

'Mr Jeremy Barnett?'

'Yes,' came a terse confirmation.

'Mr Jeremy Barnett from Benbecular Engines?'

'Yes,' but this time with a hint of irritation.

'Glad to have got you, Mr Barnett. Olly Wragg, here – I'm calling you from *Sabotage Digest*…'

Straker let his words sink in for a few seconds.

'Who? What?'

'Olly Wragg … *Sabotage Digest*? We're doing a feature on the sabotage you've masterminded against Ptarmigan for the Massarella Formula One team. We loved what you did for them in Spa. That whole remote engine limiter disruption thing – it's brilliant. We're wondering whether you'd be prepared to do an interview with us.'

'Who the hell *is* this?'

'We're doing a double-page spread,' Straker went on. 'We've got all the telemetry, and a photo of Adi Barrantes at the very moment he activated your system. It's all quite ingenious on your part. We're very impressed … we want to give you full credit. Would you care to give us a quote at all?'

Straker moved the phone slightly away from his ear and smiled at Sabatino. 'D'you know what? He swore … and rang off.'

'No kidding,' she smiled mischievously back. 'That ought to have put the wind up him.'

'I'd love to be on the call, now, between Barnett and whoever he talks to at Massarella.'

Sabatino, once again, took Straker by surprise. Walking up to him, she reached up on tiptoe and kissed him on the cheek. 'It feels good to be hitting back at last. Now, piss off. I've got a Grand Prix to win.'

TWENTY-EIGHT

Sabatino sat in the cockpit of her Ptarmigan, fully six rows back from the front of the grid, and tried to shut out all thoughts of missed opportunities, missed positions, and what might have been. It could have been galling to think about where her performance should have put her that weekend. But for the intervention by Adi Barrantes, she could so easily have been on pole. By quite a margin.

Her altercation with Van Der Vaal, though, was proving to be cathartic. She found herself able to focus on what was coming. Instead of jobbing backwards, she focused on the machine immediately around her, the track, and the cars in front of her. She focused on what she saw. A race. Forty-four laps of motor racing round her favourite circuit in a car that she knew to be point-nine faster than any of the others on the grid.

Psyching herself up, she blipped the engine several times, breathed deeply, and checked in with Backhouse.

She was ready – she was in the zone.

Straker heard that short exchange through his headsets in the motor home headquarters truck. He was now also able to "see" it.

In front of him, this time, Straker had numerous screens set up. He had a split TV shot of the forward on-board views from the two Massarellas – showing both drivers' hands and their steering wheels.

Another screen was segmented into four boxes, each a separate display, resembling an oscilloscope. These four showed the carrier wave of their different radio frequencies. The top one was Sabatino's original voice radio. The next one down showed her second radio. The next box indicated the Ptarmigan's original data link frequency, while the last box at the bottom of the screen showed the new parallel channel also carrying the engine data.

On any transmission, now, the display for the frequency in question would change colour from black to orange, helping to catch his eye. Through this form of monitoring, Straker could instantly "see" any traffic across their radio networks, particularly on the carrier wave. He was pleased. Even that brief radio exchange between Backhouse and Sabatino showed the system to be working. If the saboteurs tried to hit any of their frequencies, now, Straker would know immediately they were active and presenting a threat, allowing him instantly to trigger preventative measures.

The view of the grid changed from chaos to regimented order in a matter of seconds. All extraneous personnel hurried off, leaving only the neat pair of parallel lines – the cars – out on the track.

Their roar began.

Moments later, the two Ferraris on the front row moved off on the formation lap round the 4.4 mile circuit. The slighted lower-placed cars followed on, growling their readiness to challenge those up at the front.

Within minutes, the parade lap complete, the grid re-formed.

Behind the two Ferraris on the front row was Simi Luciano in the Massarella. Against Sabatino's 50 points for the Championship, Luciano was lying third on 40. Paddy Aston, lying second overall with 44 points, held P5 in the Lambourn.

One red light came on.

The engines' roar increased.

The second, third and fourth lights lit up.

Sabatino checked her steering wheel one last time. She steadied her breathing.

The roar crescendoed.

Five lights burned. They were all on. They stayed burning. Then, suddenly, they were out.

GO!

The noise was deafening. All twenty-one cars screamed off the line. All that energy and testosterone headed down to the entry of Turn One, the famous La Source.

Simi Luciano got away well on the clean side of the track from the second row. Ahead of him were both Ferraris. They had pulled level with each other and were racing side by side as they hurtled into the braking zone. No team orders could have been at work between these two drivers. Both Ferraris dived for the racing line into the first corner. The second place man aimed for a tight line on the inside, while the pole sitter tried to come in, claiming the line for himself. A massive test of nerve. The two Ferraris banged wheels, momentarily throwing themselves off pace and rhythm. Both decelerated as a consequence. The whole field was suddenly bunching up behind them.

Remy Sabatino, in P14, was a long way back from all this. But the field concertinaed quickly. She was able to see the convergence of the front runners – one of the few consolations of being further back. It afforded her more time to try and read what was going on.

Up at the front the mêlée continued. Compression of speed and space into such a bottleneck gave the drivers little room fore and aft, let alone amidships, to move. A hair's breadth soon separated the cars, meaning the only protection against bumping the car in front was to lift off.

The pack as a whole more or less ground to a halt.

Remy Sabatino, resigned to be patient – because of her unrepresentative grid position – had been ready to play a waiting game in this race. But all that was abandoned in the blink of an eye.

She spotted Simi Luciano flinch to the outside – an act of evasion, desperate to miss running into the Ferrari squabble directly in front of him. Sabatino saw immediately where he'd been forced to go. With the rest of the pack still to his inside – all fighting for the racing line – she extrapolated the possibilities of Luciano's move. She thought she saw a chance. And went for it.

The Ptarmigan Team looked on, their hearts in their mouths. Was this the move of a champion or an outlandish punt from someone so frustrated that they might have reached the end of their tether?

Immediately swinging wide herself, Sabatino made to go

completely right round the outside of La Source, out to the left. She was going to take herself deliberately off line.

The moment she started this move, her car struggled for grip. Sabatino's gamble became all too apparent. The rear end got away from her – twice. Badly. The Ptarmigan then yawed dramatically as she tried to slow and turn in round the outside of the corner on the dirty surface.

Out on the marbles, she was wrestling frenetically with the wheel.

Over to her front and right, at the apex of the reflex bend, the leaders were still trying to unravel themselves. There was a collision between Paddy Aston in the Lambourn and a Lotus – the Lotus losing its front wing in the process. Shards of carbon fibre – as it shattered into pieces – were bounced like pins across the surface of the track. La Source was now littered with razor-sharp splinters.

Sabatino was still going wide. She soon found herself bouncing along the red and white stones on the outside of the corner.

A car to her inside nearly hit her as it, too, swerved outwards, taking evasive action. Sabatino was forced to go even wider – to start straddling the kerb. There was a soul-wrenching grunt as her under-tray hit and scraped along the ground. Was this now a mistake? Had she really gone too far – taken too much of a risk? Sabatino kept pushing, knowing she was well past the point of no return.

Somehow, though, she managed to hold it together, even while rallying, her left wheels well and truly on the ungrippy artificial grass.

Still Sabatino fed in the power, fighting all the way to maintain the balance of the car. She started veering back – back towards the black stuff. Moments later she was fully on the circuit again, with all four wheels, and quickly accelerating aggressively through the exit of the turn.

She breathed deeply as the car found stability. Sabatino took in her surroundings – and position. The leaders, breaking away down the hill in front of her, were picking up speed heading towards Eau Rouge, while the chaos through Turn One was slowly starting to unwind behind her.

'Amazing, Remy,' said Backhouse over the radio. 'You've jumped ten places to fourth – quite superb.'

But to Sabatino's frustration, that was nearly all the excitement for the Belgian Grand Prix. The race order remained unchanged for a number of laps: Ferrari, Ferrari, Luciano, Sabatino, Red Bull, Aston. There seemed little available to the two Ferraris in front to pull away from Luciano's Massarella, while Sabatino got more and more frustrated every time she closed in on Luciano. Her Ptarmigan was performing brilliantly and was able to make up ground. But, under braking, any dirty air killed the effectiveness of her front wing. She couldn't pass, because she never managed to get close enough to mount a serious challenge.

Sabatino had to settle for a waiting game for twenty laps.

Then the race-leading Ferrari dived in to the pits. Changing tyres, the crew worked extraordinarily fast, but the fuel rig jammed at a critical moment, taking a full twenty seconds to be disengaged. By the time the Ferrari had regained the track, he'd dropped back down to seventh.

By default, Sabatino had gained a place.

Luciano in the Massarella passed the other, front-running, Ferrari two laps from the end and, as a consequence, took the chequered flag.

Sabatino was confirmed in P3, so even making it onto the podium.

Paddy Aston, after fending off the rebounding Ferrari, prevailed and retained fourth.

Straker heard and saw Backhouse's radio message to Sabatino on her in-lap: 'Not the cleanest weekend. But third, from fourteenth on the grid, Remy? *Much* better than we might have feared.'

'Yeah, but without Massarella's sabotaging of my qualifying, we should've been on pole. This race should've been mine.'

Sabatino made it back to the headquarters truck after the TV interview. She took a shower to rid herself of the sticky champagne – a hazard of the spray on the podium – and emerged wearing a large baggy jersey and jeans. She was rubbing down her hair with a towel.

'A great drive, Remy,' said Treadwell. 'A disappointing weekend but a great save, considering. After yesterday, six points are far better than we hoped. It keeps us just ahead, by one, in the Constructors' Championship. While your six points to Luciano's ten still keeps you at the top of the Drivers' by six.'

Sabatino clearly wasn't warming to any attempt to be philosophical. Trying further, Treadwell said: 'Also, confronting Van Der Vaal and the guy from Benbecular must have frightened Massarella off today.'

She slumped down onto the bench in the motor home. 'Who cares – I should have been on pole. This should have been mine.'

Suddenly she looked distracted.

Sabatino had just caught sight of an image on one of the plasma screens. Jumping up, she crossed the floor of the motor home to take a closer look. A live CCTV shot showed the front of the Ptarmigan garage in the pit lane and – and beyond it – Massarella's. 'What the hell?' exhaled Sabatino to the others in the motor home. 'What the fuck's *he* doing?'

They all moved over to see the same screen. On it they saw Sabatino's race engineer chatting on the pit wall.

Andy Backhouse was engaged in conversation with Eugene Van Der Vaal.

She asked: 'What the hell's Andy doing talking to *that* bastard?'

An hour later, Straker kicked himself. With all the other distractions, the showdown with Van Der Vaal, setting up and monitoring the new countermeasures, and the race itself, he'd completely forgotten to tell Backhouse about his surprising discovery, earlier, on the grid: he'd seen an exact copy of Ptarmigan's Fibonacci Blades – on the front wing of the Massarella.

And when he finally did remember, it was too late.

By the time Straker tried to catch up with Remy Sabatino's race engineer, he was out of reach.

Not just from Spa.

Andy Backhouse had had enough.

He had resigned from the team.

PART THREE

LA PARABOLICA

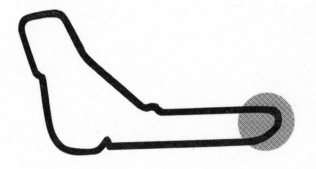

TWENTY-NINE

'What do you mean he's defected?' barked Quartano over the phone. 'I knew he'd resigned. How's he defected?'

'You won't believe it,' replied Straker. 'He's gone over to Massarella.'

Quartano exploded. '*What?* How could that even be *possible?* What on earth would've possessed him to do that? The Judas, the fucking *Judas*. Makes him as big a bastard as they are. Hang on, doesn't that prove once and for all that he *was* the insider saboteur?'

Straker stayed silent.

'He's under contract, for Christ's sake,' bawled Quartano. 'Non-compete. Matt, get onto legal and have them nail this.' Quartano just seemed to grunt for a moment. 'Damnit, this *has* to make him the bastard insider,' he repeated. 'All the more reason to slap an injunction on him,' he little-less-than bellowed. 'Straker, I want you to stop that arsehole getting anywhere near Massarella!'

Straker decided to stay on in Spa, over Sunday night – after the rest of the team had left – to try to handle the fallout from Backhouse's departure. Taking a walk through the race complex as the place started to empty, he looked out over the valleys of the Ardennes in the last of the evening sun, trying to visualize and rationalize the whole sabotage situation.

He thought through each of the elements he had encountered so far: Michael Lyons. Radio jamming. Jeremy Barnett. Benbecular engines. Adi Barrantes. Massarella. The strange fob-like device. Trifecta. The engine management system.

Every time he thought of a new incident or person to add to the web of influences in his mind's eye, he realized an association of some kind could be made straight back to a common denominator: Trifecta Systems. Visualizing all these elements together helped make the circumstances all the clearer.

But why were these people all involved? It didn't seem to make any sense.

How could he set about rationalizing this? Then he thought of something else. Could there not be something – or some*one* – behind it all? A controlling mind? That got him thinking.

What about this Avel Obrenovich?

Wasn't he something of a connection between these parties? He was majority shareholder of Trifecta *and* the principal sponsor of Massarella. Might *he* be the one empowering all this?

What on earth, though, was the motivation to launch these malicious assaults on Ptarmigan and Remy Sabatino? This was "just" a competitive sport. It was completely beyond Straker's comprehension that anyone should go to such lengths – particularly being so invasive, let alone demonstrating contempt for rules, law, fair play, even to the point of risking human life.

Such malicious intent had to be about more than just winning a few races.

The following morning Straker was ready to act on his theories. Standing on the platform under Calatrava's magnificent canopy at Liège-Guillemins station, he called Karen in London. Looking round him on the platform to make sure he couldn't be overheard, he asked: 'How's the research on Charlotte Grant's iPhone going?'

'Not bad, Matt, but it *has* been the weekend since you asked.'

Straker smiled, having lost track of time. 'Sure, sorry. Any idea how long it's all going to take, though?'

'I.T. said it should be done by close of business today.'

'Okay, Karen,' he conceded, and checked the privacy around him again. In slightly hushed tones, he said: 'I need something else. Can you do me an all-sources search on those involved with Avel Obrenovich: Obrenovich Oil & Gas, the Massarella Formula One team, and its boss Eugene Van Der Vaal? Could you print off the top fifty stories for each, and put them into one of your binders for me?'

'You want cuttings too?'

'You're one step ahead of me, as always. International, as well as domestic, please.'

'No problem.'

Straker felt that his research into the other side's emotional starting point was now under way. His immediate priority, though, was protection. 'Karen, who's our head of legal?'

'Stacey Krall,' she replied.

'Can you put me through?'

'Sure, hang on.'

A deep voice soon said: 'Stacey Krall.'

'Hello Stacey, Matt Straker. We've not met. I'm a director of Quartech's Competition Intelligence and Security – CIS. I'm on assignment with Ptarmigan.'

'Yes, hello. I've just been processing your directorship papers with Companies House.'

'Sorry I can't come and see you – I'm on my way back from Belgium.' Once again Straker looked around him to be sure no one was in earshot. 'We've got an issue with a member of staff. Mr Quartano's asked me to take out an injunction on him.'

'Mr Backhouse – yes, I know – Mr Quartano's already been on to me.'

'That was quick.'

'He doesn't hang around on many things, least of all with breaches of trust.'

'And?'

'I've been through the Backhouse file. Unfortunately – and this *didn't* go down well with Mr Quartano – his contract with Ptarmigan isn't one of ours.'

'What do you mean?'

'It's an original – a pre-Quartech one. It's not as robust as ours would be.'

'Does that mean we can serve him or not?'

'Afraid not.'

Straker found himself smiling. 'So we've no way of stopping him going to Massarella?'

'Not legitimately, no. We can threaten him with legal action – and put the frighteners on him.'

'But in the meantime, we can't stop him working for Massarella?'

'No.'

Straker could only pull a face at his luck.

Once back in Britain, Straker went directly to the Ptarmigan factory in Oxfordshire. On arrival, he met Tahm Nazar who led him straight to the loading bay, serving as the examination space for the crash investigation of Helli Cunzer's car.

Right across the polished white-painted floor were the recovered components of the wreckage, placed more or less in the same relational position to each other as on the original chassis. It reminded Straker of a technical illustration where bits of an object are expanded out and cut away to show its innards and workings. 'To think there was a human being right in the middle of all this as it disintegrated,' said Straker almost dreading the thought.

'Amazing, yes,' said the professorial-looking Nazar. 'It's a testament to modern design and safety standards that he lived. He suffered a serious wound to his thigh, and a couple of broken ribs – but that's about it. He's already back in part-time training.'

'That's extraordinary,' breathed Straker.

'He's been up here on the simulator a couple of times – he'll be fit to race again soon.'

The two men walked in among parts of the wreckage, and Straker looked at the twisted remains. 'How much of the car do you think you've recovered?' he asked, as he watched five men working intensely across the floor, measuring, scraping and weighing components, while a colleague was busy recording their findings into a computer to one side.

'About eighty per cent.'

'Will that be enough? What if we're missing key bits?'

'We won't get an answer,' replied Nazar flatly.

'And there's no indication, so far, of what caused the crash?'

The team boss shook his head. 'Not yet, but these things take time, and they really only come together once the initial – time-consuming – recording is completed. We're still in the assimilation phase.'

Nazar led Straker away, and up to his office. Treadwell was waiting for them there.

'How's Remy taken the news of Backhouse's defection?' Straker asked.

'She's mighty pissed off,' replied Treadwell in surprisingly soft Australian. 'She and Andy were incredibly close.'

'How will you handle his departure?'

'Ollie used to be one of our race engineers,' offered Nazar.

'Yeah, I'm going to work with her.'

'Will she be okay with the disruption?'

'Hope so.'

'Good,' said Straker sounding a little relieved.

'How the hell did this happen?' Nazar asked. 'How did Backhouse crack – then defect?'

'Maybe he never *left* Massarella,' offered Treadwell suspiciously. 'You know he was with them for ten years before he came here.'

Straker shrugged. 'I do know he was pretty cut up about the threat to safety from the saboteur.'

'That doesn't wash,' replied Nazar dismissively. 'It might explain the resignation – but is completely inconsistent with his going to the team that we think're behind the sabotage.'

'Unless he only left Massarella in the first place to infiltrate us as part of some long-term deception?'

Straker shook his head. 'It could just be more prosaic than that. When I came up here before and stayed with him, Backhouse was pretty open about his domestic affairs. He's recently divorced. His wife cleaned him out financially as well as emotionally, taking the children. He lives in a pokey little terraced house in Tysoe. Drives an ancient Ford Focus. I can imagine Massarella would have offered him an appealing solution to his money troubles.'

'We'll only know for sure when we get to ask him, and that's not going to happen anytime soon.'

'Right,' said Straker, taking the comment as a welcome cue to change the subject. 'Can we talk about protecting ourselves, from now on, against Backhouse's defection – and against Trifecta?'

'I thought the Big Man was serving him with an injunction, even if it was only a phoney one?' replied Treadwell.

'What Backhouse knows about our cars – now – is going to be out of date pretty quickly,' said Nazar. 'I'm not that fussed.'

'Really?' said Straker a little surprised. 'Remind me to talk to you about our Fibonacci Blades when we're done.'

'I thought you said on the phone that you wanted to talk about Trifecta?'

Straker nodded. 'I do. Our sabotage experience is becoming extensive. We've uncovered a number of people who seem to be involved in this. But I believe there is a clear common denominator. Somehow every incident we've suffered links back to Trifecta. Every one. It strikes me that we've either got to stop them, which would not be straightforward – or we have to remove them, completely, as any form of future threat.'

'Couldn't we just confront the senior management?' suggested Treadwell. 'Do we really believe the board are behind all this – even aware of, let alone sanction, these incidents? It's a grown-up firm – with grown-up directors. Surely a word with any of them would cleanse the firm of any roguish activity?'

'Fair point,' Straker replied. 'How big's the company – how many staff?'

'About a thousand.'

'A security nightmare,' observed Straker with conviction. 'Far too big for us to be sure they've flushed out every rogue employee. And we'd still have the influence of Obrenovich, as a shareholder. I was thinking – can we not be more surgical? Can we not switch everything to another provider? That way, we would cut Trifecta out as a risk – once and for all.'

Treadwell scoffed. 'Okay for things like our radios and data links, but Trifecta are integral to our engine management system. Starting again – in the middle of the season – could set our performance back months.'

Straker had already considered this difficulty. 'Aren't there other ECM contractors in the swim? Don't other Benbecular runners use different firms?'

'Yes,' said Nazar. 'Valentines would be the biggest. Cohens are probably the more specialized.'

'Can we not at least ask them some questions about their capabilities and discuss a possible switch to them?'

Treadwell looked decidedly unhappy.

'We'll look into it,' said Nazar, with a hint of an overruling.

'Good,' said Straker. 'I think that's it, then, for now.'

'Thanks for your help, Matt,' said Nazar. Then, sounding slightly intrigued, he said: 'Hang on. You asked us to remind you about our Fibonacci Blades?'

'Oh yes,' replied Straker, 'should I be surprised to see precisely the same design on the front wing of the Massarella in Spa?'

'*What?*' asked Nazar, sounding genuinely taken aback. 'Are you serious?'

'Completely.'

'How the hell did they get there?'

'What about Andy fucking Backhouse?' offered Treadwell, slumping back in his chair. 'If he was only ever with us as a Massarella plant, why *wouldn't* he have leaked our modifications and ideas back to them as well?'

THIRTY

Straker returned to Fulham.

But the empty flat didn't do it for him. His sense of loss nearly prompted him to move out and stay in one of the shockingly retro bedrooms in his beloved Brooks's.

In the end, though, his tiredness prevailed, and he fell asleep. But the talk of treachery and betrayal had clearly triggered Straker's subconscious.

During the night, his psyche harked back to the last time he felt betrayal – his last encounter with Charlie Grant. He relived every moment of the night he had spent with her, in this flat, in London.

His mind swirled back to the morning after. It was all so vivid still. Leaving her sleeping, Straker had gone through to the kitchen to make breakfast for them both. He was wallowing in the afterglow of intimacy and first sex with this amazing new woman in his life.

But that feeling didn't last.

Heart-stoppingly, he came across, entirely by accident, the woman's ID card, lying on the floor, having fallen from her bag – collateral damage from their frenzied passion of the night before. He realized immediately that this serene beauty was *not* with him by accident. It was clear that she had deliberately targeted him, aiming to exploit information about his assignment – so as to thwart Quartech's defence contract with Buhran and Quartano's relationship with that regime. She turned out to be nothing less than an – as-yet-unmet – colleague in Quartech's Competition Intelligence, his own department. Charlie Grant, he had discovered through her own proximity to him, turned out to be the traitor he had been tasked to uncover. *She* had been the one leaking highly secret and commercially sensitive data to outsiders. She was the reason the weapons contract with Buhran needed salvaging. *She* had been the one betraying the company.

Straker felt embarrassed and angry with himself. Angry he had been so clearly taken in, angry at his own sense of feeling betrayed and hugely embarrassed that he had failed to anticipate such tactics. All this hit him hard and taught him a serious lesson about the secretive and cutthroat competitiveness of the arms business. That episode with Charlie Grant also did something else. It stripped away any lingering naïveté he might have had about the likely practices he should expect from exponents of industrial espionage. That first assignment for Quartech saw him well and truly bloodied, in numerous senses of the word.

Now, in the immediate present, Straker couldn't help but wonder what other havoc Charlie Grant might have wreaked against Ptarmigan? Such thoughts were alarmingly significant: throughout the period she had been so damagingly engaged in industrial espionage against Quartech's weapons contract with Buhran, Charlie Grant had been officially on secondment to the company's Formula One team.

The following morning, Straker made it in to Quartech's London global headquarters in Cavendish Square. Having not spent any proper time in his department office since his previous assignment, it was strangely comforting. With his domestic difficulties, and the hollowness of being on his own in their marital flat, this felt more like home than home did.

Walking into the Competition Intelligence and Security offices on the ninth floor, he saw the cityscape of London through the ceiling-to-floor plate-glass windows. In the morning sun, which had now burned off all the earlier mist, the capital appeared warm and inviting to Straker – something he never thought possible after leaving his outdoor life in the Marines.

Karen was already at her desk. They caught up, particularly given the dramatic goings-on in Belgium.

Straker slipped off his coat and hung it over the back of his chair. 'Have you managed to get anywhere with Charlie's phone?'

'A bit. It's really weird prying into her affairs.'

Straker nodded his sympathy. 'I appreciate that. Sadly, Karen, she was up to things that did us a fair amount of harm. Now, her phone can help us.'

'There are loads of numbers in there, and I.T. have said that most of them are entered as nicknames or some sort of code name.'

'I saw that. Okay, we need to do something about it. Let's try this. Can you rope in some of the research team and get them to call each of the entries that aren't fully named? But they're only to call using a Caller ID Withheld number – so there's no way we can be identified.'

'Okay? And what do you want them to say?'

'Let's think ... What about that they've found the phone – as lost property, or something – and are trying to identify its owner by ringing some of the numbers in its directory?'

'Okay, Matt. I'll get on to it.'

'Good. How did the all-sources search go?'

Karen pointed to a lever arch file placed in the middle of his desk.

Straker opened it to find a contents page, dividers and comprehensive index references. 'Immaculate,' he said looking up to meet her eye.

She smiled coyly and returned to her screen.

Straker offered to get her a cup of coffee, which she accepted. Having put it on her desk, he went back and poured one for himself which he then carried along with the folder into a quiet room in the corner of their floor. This room had its own eye-catching views of the City of London and Canary Wharf in one direction, and the Victoria Tower of the Palace of Westminster and the London Eye Ferris wheel through the other.

The whole Formula One scene and the extraordinary sabotage incidents were about to become a whole lot murkier.

He started with the earlier press cuttings which referenced Massarella and Van Der Vaal.

MASSARELLA'S VAN DER VAAL SAYS OPPORTUNITIES BEING LOST, read one headline from two years before.

VAN DER VAAL ATTACKS GRIP OF F1 POWER, read another.

TOO MUCH POWER IN TOO FEW HANDS was published at the end of the previous season but one.

Van Der Vaal, it seemed, had been constantly criticizing and sniping at the governance of Formula One.

Then, in the middle of last season, Straker noticed the angle of Van Der Vaal's comments began to change. This seemed predicated on the story headlined: **MASSARELLA LANDS OBRENOVICH MILLIONS.**

There were dozens more like this. Among them: **VAN DER VAAL + F1 + OBRENOVICH = THE MIDAS TOUCH.**

A few months after that, Straker picked up a new theme which Van Der Vaal was clearly encouraging – or at least doing little to discourage. One article summed it up:

VAN DER VAAL: THE FUTURE TSAR OF F1?

""F1 is only successful – turning over billions of pounds a year – because of the teams," says an emphatic Van Der Vaal, 54, Massarella's burly South African team boss. "The teams put up the money. We take all the risks. For too long the commercial rights holder has been taking commercial advantage of the spectacle and sport we provide."

Mr Van Der Vaal seems well qualified to talk about the sport's finances, having recently landed substantial investment in his Massarella team from billionaire Russian oligarch Avel Obrenovich. "Formula One could grow so much more quickly – and equitably – if only it showed itself to be more modern and professional."

When asked whether these comments meant he saw himself in a future leadership role of F1, Mr Van Der Vaal declined to answer."

'Bloody hell,' said Straker out loud.

HOW I WOULD RUN F1, SAYS VAN DER VAAL, was the headline above an interview in which Van Der Vaal launched his strongest diatribe yet against Motor Racing Promotions Limited and the commercial interests of the sport. The quote that caught his eye was: "I'm the man to run Formula One."

Talk about a blatant challenge. Van Der Vaal's chutzpah was amazing.

Straker read on.

MASSARELLA WELCOMES QUARTECH TO F1

"Eugene Van Der Vaal, 54, the boerish (sic) team boss of Massarella Formula One, today welcomed Ptarmigan's new owner, Quartech International, to the ranks of the sport. "If there's anything I can do to help them get started," said Van Der Vaal, "I'll be delighted to do so. As I'm sure's the case with the other teams, I'm ready to help Quartech find their feet.""

Big of him, thought Straker. The ego which gave Van Der Vaal the status of self-elected leader of the group was quite remarkable.

And then everything changed.

Literally overnight.

Remy Sabatino came on the scene.

The moment Quartano signed her to Ptarmigan, the press coverage exploded. Most of the subsequent references were unreservedly positive – praising the excitement of adding a female driver to the Formula One grid. They applauded the huge increase in public interest this was creating. Quartech was hailed for its imagination, innovation, and ability to advance the sport.

There was at the same time, though, some fierce opposition.

While Straker accepted this snapshot of press cuttings was filtered, it did seem clear that the detractors of a woman driver had found themselves an emphatic front man.

Karen had played a blinder in unearthing all this. She had not limited her search to one medium, either. She had even found a YouTube clip, and identified the relevant link in the folder. Firing up his laptop, Straker clicked on the two minute video entitled: **F1 IN DANGER OF DAMAGING STATUS OF SPORT.**

As far as he could tell, this was from a local news programme in France – recorded in English but carrying French subtitles. Despite the poor quality of the clip, Van Der Vaal's gruff personality came through loud and clear:

"Formula One is unashamedly a masculine sport," he was heard to say. *"It's all about speed, machines, danger, courage and raw competitiveness. Any softening of these elements can only damage the sport's appeal."*

In another article, headed: **SPONSORSHIP REVENUES TO BE DAMAGED BY EFFEMINACY,** Van Der Vaal attacked the presence of Sabatino on the grounds that male and masculine brands were being diminished by a woman driver.

His attacks intensified after Sabatino first made it onto the podium.

Then there seemed to be a dramatic key change.

The first major counter to Van Der Vaal's attacks came from within the sport and from a highly respected source:

VAN DER VAAL TOLD TO BUTTON IT BY F1

""Mr Van Der Vaal's repeated outbursts and attacks on the presence of a female driver are unwarranted and unsporting," says Lord Lambourn, 61, the dashing aristocratic boss of the Lambourn Grand Prix Team. "Remy Sabatino's appointment, and Ptarmigan's brilliance in marketing her and the team's new-found competitiveness, are what this sport should be celebrating. Eugene is not speaking for the mainstream of this sport with his out-of-date gender politics. Prideaux Champagnes, Lambourn's superb sponsors, have reported a twenty per cent increase in sales this year – which they attribute entirely to their female consumers. Women – since Remy Sabatino started driving for Ptarmigan – are finding a whole new reason to watch, follow, and get excited by Formula One.""

Straker found the following headlines and supporting articles:

QUARTECH SHOWS F1 HOW TO MARKET ITSELF.

PTARMIGAN TEACHES VAN DER VAAL A LESSON.

THE TSAR-ELECT IS DEAD – LONG LIVE QUARTANO.

One thing was becoming abundantly clear. While Straker believed he had been accurate in deducing Massarella's involvement in the sabotage incidents on the track, he was now convinced he had unearthed a clear motivation for causing Ptarmigan harm.

An emotional starting point.

Van Der Vaal's vaulting ego had clearly got the better of him. He had raised the stakes – having held himself out as the next Bernie Ecclestone – and clearly overreached himself. He'd been completely outshone by Quartech. Van Der Vaal, it seemed, had been humbled – even humiliated, some might have said. That meant Avel Obrenovich might not be the prime mover behind the sabotage attacks on Ptarmigan.

With this re-evaluation, another related thought came to him.

What about that bizarre reaction from Joss MacRae in Spa? Was that MacRae just being MacRae, or was there something else behind his behaviour, too? MacRae's total dismissal of Massarella's alleged wrongdoing had been mighty peculiar. Straker was prompted to check him out.

Walking back into the office, Straker said to Karen: 'What you've found is superb,' he said. 'Thank you. Could you have a further look and see if you can find any connection, this time, between Van Der Vaal and Joss MacRae?'

'Just those two?'

'Good point, the other names involved might be Massarella, Avel Obrenovich, Obrenovich Oil & Gas and Motor Racing Promotions.'

Karen wrote down the names and an outline of the task. 'Righto.'

'How's Charlie's phone coming?'

'I've just heard. Should be finished soon after lunch.'

Having spent three hours cocooned in the quiet room, Straker left the office for some fresh air. He bought a sandwich, walked up to

Regent's Park, and sat down on the grass to eat his lunch. The park's trees, planting and manicured lawns helped calm his thoughts. Even so, it didn't stop his mind eventually drifting back to his divorce, the causes of it – and the other stresses stemming from the effects of his rendition and torture by the Americans. Not even the tranquillity of Regent's Park could save him from those thoughts.

Straker walked back to the office, desperate to be distracted again.

'Oh, Matt,' said Karen. 'I've just got the research back on Charlie's phone – the directory numbers and some of the names.'

Glad to be occupied again so quickly, Straker took the latest batch of research and returned to the quiet room to sift through what they had found.

Now with a fuller name attributed to each number, he hoped to cross-reference these with the itemized phone log. It might enable him to build a picture of the people and organizations with whom Charlie Grant had been in contact. Straker set to work. From the list of calls in and out he found high volumes between her and Adi Barrantes, Lord Lambourn and Andy Backhouse.

Straker ran his eye down the length of the call logs.

What leapt out from the whole list was the extraordinary volume of traffic Charlie had engaged in with one particular number. She had been in contact with it at least twenty times a week over the last two months. This had obviously attracted the attention of the research team, too.

A detailed note – in with the bundle of findings – declared they had been unable to identify its owner, though. It was clearly an Italian mobile phone. They had made numerous calls to it, but none of them had been picked up. They had found no voicemail, either – except on several occasions the ring had been cut short, as if the call was being actively rejected.

This number sparked Straker's curiosity.

Then something else – from that same Italian mobile – also grabbed his attention. Charlie Grant had received an SMS from it which used an unrecognized term and, intriguingly, did so in an active voice. It read:

Hope the ASD idea is going over well...

What on earth did that – let alone "going over well" – mean? Straker had become familiar with a number of the terms the team used, or had learned to work them out from their context. But he was sure he hadn't heard of ASD. Picking up his own phone, he rang Oliver Treadwell at the Ptarmigan factory. 'Ollie, what does ASD mean?'

'*ASD?*' repeated the Strategy Director quizzically. 'No idea. Never heard of it.'

'Not a racing term, then?'

'Not one of ours, at any rate.'

'Very strange.'

Discovering the frequency of Charlie's contact with that Italian mobile number, the anonymity surrounding it – and its mysterious use of an unfamiliar term – all served to pique Straker's interest. He had no idea whether any of this was important, but immediately felt he was unable to ignore it.

THIRTY-ONE

At the end of the day, heading home, Straker was walking down Regent Street – still mulling his inconclusive findings – when his phone went.

It was someone he wasn't expecting to hear from at all.

'Remy? How are you? I'm really sorry about the whole Backhouse defection thing.'

'I'm sad, more than annoyed. I'm fond of Andy. He's been amazing to get me this far. But I like Oliver. The rest of my team's still there. So I'm okay. I have faith in them all.'

'Good,' said Straker genuinely. 'I was worried this might've knocked us all off our game.'

'I think Massarella's far more likely to do that,' she said without levity. 'Talking of which, can you update me on the sabotage issues?'

'Sure.'

'Where are you at the moment?' Sabatino asked.

'London.'

'Can we meet up this evening? Did you have any plans for dinner?'

Just before seven that evening Straker was waiting for Sabatino at a table in the London institution of Rules in Maiden Lane. She walked in on the dot of their appointed time. Several heads turned as she walked through the restaurant. She was wearing a stripy baggy shirt, skinny jeans, and close-fitting knee-length boots. No make-up. Straker was taken with her presence and suddenly hit by a phrase whose significance just dawned on him – that of someone being comfortable in their own skin. She seemed completely that. There was no invitation to "look at me", but, at the same time, no self-consciousness either. Here was someone who lived at two hundred miles an hour – and was breaking new ground in a male-dominated sport. Having seen her dish it out to Van Der Vaal on the grid in Spa, Straker was engrossed, here, by how at ease and unassuming she was. Wasn't this, he had to think, one of the best examples of someone leaving it all at the office?

He stood as she approached. Unexpectedly, she reached up and kissed him on both cheeks.

'That was a fair bit of recognition,' he offered indicating the attention she had attracted from parts of the room as they settled into a corner table.

She shrugged and grunted dismissively. 'I dread becoming any kind of celebrity,' she said. 'No privacy. Cameras picking you off wherever you go. Still, I'll have to win the Championship for that to be a real problem. I've got a long way to go – further still if Massarella keeps trying to trip me up.'

Despite Straker's unease at not yet ridding the team of saboteur interference, he was glad the subject had come up so soon. It would allow him to clear the air. 'Let me bring you up to date with where we are, then?'

'Why don't we order first?'

Straker was brought a glass of wine, while Sabatino took half a Guinness. With their privacy restored, Straker described the conclusions he'd drawn from the press coverage of Eugene Van Der Vaal, the problems with the injunction on Backhouse, the move away from Trifecta and, finally, the issue of the Fibonacci Blades.

'That's impressive work – particularly the decision to move away from Trifecta. Are we going with Valentines or Cohens?'

'Treadwell's not happy with any move, but would accept Cohens – at a push.'

Sabatino nodded her agreement. 'Okay. And when do we get enough evidence to nail Van Der Vaal and Massarella?'

'I'm working on a plan to do that right now.'

Yet again, Sabatino took Straker completely by surprise, particularly given her initial dismissal of his spy games. Moving her hand forward across the table, she placed it gently on his. She looked him in the eye and said: 'An F1 team doesn't have the ability to deal with this kind of sabotage bullshit. Without your efforts, I don't know where I'd be – not on top of the Championship, that's for sure. I'd more likely have been withdrawn – or suspended from driving – because of the danger. I want you to know I'm grateful, even if I seem impatient with our progress from time to time.'

Straker suddenly felt conflicted. He found himself relishing the physical contact with her, but he also wanted to pull back, for the sake of maintaining the professionalism of their relationship. He had responsibilities here, and did not want them to be any more complicated than they might already be.

THIRTY-TWO

In the gloriously old-fashioned surroundings of Rules – the cluttered walls with political caricatures by Gillray, prints from *Vanity Fair*, portraits of West End stars, naval vessels, mounted antlers – and its unashamedly English food, with dishes from seasonal game to bread-and-butter pudding, Straker and Sabatino talked on into the evening.

He felt there had been a mood change during their dinner – and their level of communication – undoubtedly triggered by the unexpected physical contact and personal gratitude earlier. Their new level of connection almost overwhelmed him.

Straker found himself drawn to her self-confidence. For all Sabatino's shunning of the public recognition of her F1 achievements, her success was having an effect on her. It showed in her face. There was an energy there. A radiance. It was powerful. Her dark hair, dark eyes, olive-coloured skin, and her soft but worldly-sounding accent all seemed to sparkle. Was this effect on him, Straker wondered, some equivalence to the aphrodisiac of power?

Straker kept feeling his self-awareness pull him back – questioning how these developments would affect their working relationship. But as he listened to her talk – animatedly, with passion – her magnetism overrode it. He couldn't prevent himself wallowing in the uninhibited moment with this striking and fascinating woman.

'There's something utterly spiritual about Monza,' she told Straker as the conversation swung round to the next race on the calendar.

'Why spiritual?'

'A number of things. The heritage? There's the no-longer-used *Pista di Alta Velocità* – the High Speed Circuit – the one with the old style banking. There are the inimitable Italian fans – the Tifosi

– who create a unique atmosphere, except I'm really nervous about them. And then, of course, there's the rawness of the speed?'

Straker frowned. 'Hang on a minute, the Tifosi? Why are you nervous about the Tifosi?'

'Because of these,' she said cupping her breasts with her hands.

'*What?*'

'Italian motor racing is so male. I can only pollute their sport.'

Straker said without levity: 'Speak to them like you talked to Van Der Vaal. You'd soon put them right.'

Sabatino laughed.

'They like bravado,' Straker went on. 'If that's a male thing, then you've got the female equivalent – what would that be, bravada? You'll be hailed. That's completely a non-issue. And what's this you said about the rawness of the speed at Monza? Isn't that the case at every circuit?'

'Pretty much,' she said taking another sip of Guinness, 'but seventy per cent of Monza's taken at full throttle – the highest proportion of any track, by a long way. Aerodynamically, we have to run a very low downforce set-up, to reduce the drag, but that decimates the grip. It makes the speed much more difficult to control – makes it very raw.'

'And overtaking?'

'Limited. Only real chance is into Turn One and the chicane – the *Variante Della Roggia* – Turns Four and Five.'

Straker smiled. 'It does help that you're Maltese to pronounce these fabulously Mediterranean names.'

'*Variante Della Roggia*,' she said again extravagantly, as if to make the point.

'That definitely proves you're sophisticated,' said Straker with a nod. 'But … the question is … are you *as* sophisticated with your music?'

Sabatino raised her eyebrows at the hefty change of direction. 'If you mean Mediterranean music – opera – I'm afraid not.'

'No, no – I was thinking more about music to feed your soul.'

'Hip hop?'

'What? *No!* Jazz!'

Sabatino pouted. 'No, but then I've never been properly introduced.'

'Excellent. There's not a moment to lose.' Straker caught the eye of a waiter and signalled for the bill. 'Let me take you straight to the high altar.'

Sabatino made a face. 'You want to take me to *church*?'

'Almost. It'll be my honour to introduce you to the hallowed ground that is … Ronnie Scott's.'

Jazz clearly took to Remy Sabatino – as she did to the club.

Although still early – the second house only just settling in – there was already a buzz about the place, with its usual diversity of people drawn by great music – *the* music for atmosphere.

Sabatino was captivated by its immediate sense of intimacy. Mood, though, also oozed from walls, awash with striking black and white photographs of jazz legends. Low ambient lighting was broken by the brighter pools coming from the shaded ceiling and wall lights. Red velvet benches were trimmed with chunky brass railings – and, topping off the atmosphere, were the numerous red glowing table lamps set among the tiers of table bench seats rising back up from the stage.

Shown to a table in the corner of the pit, Straker and Sabatino ordered drinks and sat together for an hour, listening to a set by a young quartet from New Orleans – playing an unusual mix of trad and lounge jazz with an occasional hint of Cajun.

Straker glanced at Sabatino's face from time to time, to make sure she was enjoying all this. He quickly realized he should have no concerns on that score – her expression showed her to be fully immersed, soaking up the scene. He still kept checking, though – but soon realized he was doing it specifically to enjoy her enjoyment.

Although there was no dancing, one beat got Sabatino moving rhythmically while sitting at their table. Without even moving her whole body, Straker was taken with her superb sense of rhythm. She turned to make deliberate eye contact with him. She kept moving without inhibition. It could so easily have induced awkwardness – self-consciousness – but there was none on her part. Why should there be any, then, on his? She continued to move. Her movement was suggestive – without being lewd – but her message seemed clear.

At the end of the number she leaned across the corner table, close enough that he would be able to hear her – even over the noise of the applause. 'I'm sorry to hear about your divorce.'

Straker almost flinched. Her personal directness hit him hard. It wasn't the starkness of it, blunt though it was, it was more the sense of a crystallization. This was the first time he had heard the D word spoken out loud by somebody else.

'It's complicated,' he replied defensively, pulling back slightly.

Her expression showed a similar thought or memory crossing her mind.

Sabatino smiled sympathetically, and turned back towards the stage to enjoy the resumption of the set. Nothing was said between them for nearly ten minutes. Straker was intrigued. He got the sense that something was brewing. Suddenly she turned to face him. He was struck by the mischievous – voracious, even – expression on Sabatino's face. 'You've got to tell me something,' she said.

Straker breathed in. 'Tell you what?'

'How *did* Charlie Grant die?'

The look in her eye was not hesitant – it was demanding. It was quite clear she wasn't going to let this go as she had during their dinner in Monte-Carlo.

Whether it was the sense of well-being from digesting Rules's jugged hare, the treacle pudding, or the three glasses of a half-decent Malbec – their better familiarity with each other, or even the increased sense of closeness between them that evening – Straker didn't react as sharply as he had before.

'You won't believe it,' was the most dismissive defence he could mount.

'*Try* me.'

'It'll repulse you.'

Her expression, if anything, became more anticipatory than ever. 'I doubt that.'

Even with this momentary focus on Charlie Grant, Straker found it impossible to stop his imagination summoning up – all too clearly – their final scene.

Sounding defensive, he said: 'We were in the Middle East, in the wake of the Arab spring. Quartano had finally – and successfully – negotiated a billion-dollar weapons contract with the Buhrani Defence Minister. A signing ceremony was arranged out on a desert firing range, within what should have been a secure area – a Buhrani military garrison. Except that Charlie Grant, I uncovered through my investigation, had been leaking details of that weapons contract – as well as the blueprints for a top secret Quartech rifle.'

'Leaked to whom?' Sabatino asked, now turned fully to face Straker across the corner of their table.

'A German rival – which was also involved with an Al-Qaeda-aligned terrorist cell in Buhran, a group determined to overthrow the monarchy there and declare an Islamic state.'

'Heavy, heavy. Why was Charlie *doing* all this?'

Straker tilted his head as an invitation to be patient. 'The signing ceremony was ambushed – by the Al-Qaeda cell. Numerous dignitaries were killed. The Defence Minister, who was also an heir to the throne, and several Quartech staff were taken hostage.'

'No!'

'Quartano and I arrived at the ceremony – from Germany – half an hour too late. There was carnage. Bodies everywhere. Through binoculars, I was fortunate to catch a distant sight of the hostages – being driven off across the desert on the back of open army trucks.' Straker took a long drag of his wine.

'How were they released, then?' she asked. 'Quartech pay a ransom?'

Straker shook his head as if to say how-could-you-suggest-such-a-thing. 'I flew a tactical helicopter recce of the desert behind the firing range. I managed to locate the terrorists' camp – the place where they had taken the hostages. It turned out to be a lost city among the dunes of the hinterland. I pulled together a team of soldiers, from what was left in the garrison. I put together an operation, briefed them, and led a company attack at dawn the following morning. We took out all the terrorists in a raid, and succeeded in releasing the hostages.'

'Wow. And you led *all* that?'

'Was the company commander.'

'How many soldiers made up this attack group?'

'Eighty-odd.'

Sabatino clearly looked impressed. 'Then what?'

Straker's mind's eye suddenly took over. 'Dawn was just coming up over the Buhrani desert. I was releasing the hostages – when I heard a click.'

'What does that mean? What kind of click?'

'A safety catch.'

'Meaning?'

'Someone had a rifle and was preparing to fire.'

Sabatino's eyes widened. 'Who?'

'Charlie Grant.'

'At whom?' she asked hurriedly.

'Dominic Quartano.'

'No!'

Straker, looking down, could bring it all back. So painfully. Charlie was standing there, the low early morning sun gleaming off her perfect skin, her hair flowing in the gentle desert breeze, her white diaphanous robe wafting in the wind – standing there with the rifle at the aim, trained on Quartano, her brilliant dark grey eyes flashing with anticipated triumph. Straker inhaled deeply. That image would haunt him always: the incongruity of a beautiful woman confidently handling and aiming a weapon with lethal intent.

'Why? Why did she *do* all that – why did she want to harm Quartano?'

'Revenge,' Straker said matter-of-factly. 'It was all about revenge.'

Sabatino pulled a face that showed this was hard for her to comprehend. 'For what?'

'The death of her father,' Straker explained: 'Quartano had mounted a hostile takeover – taking over the Grant family company. Its entire board was fired and replaced, including Charlie's father. Apparently, the man never got over it. Killed himself six months later.'

'And Charlie blamed Quartano?'

Straker nodded.

'How did the standoff in the desert end?'

'Quartano, very coolly, started trying to reason with her. But Charlie being Charlie – that wasn't going to work. However, while she was directing her anger at him, I managed … to … intervene.'

Sabatino's face was suddenly a picture – clearly drawing her own conclusions. 'So you … you…?' she said, oddly unable to complete the sentence.

Straker lowered his gaze.

'Wow,' said Sabatino.

Straker lifted his eyes. He looked at her through the moody cabaret-style lighting of Ronnie Scott's, her face partly in shadow. 'I told you that you wouldn't believe it.'

He looked her in the eye. Her response was strange.

Hard to read.

Straker tried to discern her reaction. But couldn't do it. Didn't know what to make of her expression.

Then Straker was completely taken by surprise. Sabatino, very suddenly, half rose, leant forward across the L-shaped bench, and kissed him forcefully but sensuously square on the mouth. For several seconds. Then, pulling back – but only by a fraction – she held intensive eye contact with him, her eyes flicking backwards and forwards between his.

Straker was utterly floored.

'You like sex, right?' she said slowly, taking him by surprise yet again.

He nodded, shrugged – and then smiled into her face apologetically at the lameness of his reaction.

'Why don't we keep it that *un*complicated. Let's go and atone – purge – ourselves for our deeds, right now, through raw physical release.'

Straker's reservations, voluntary or involuntary, professional or social, suddenly vanished. Her reaction to his deeply private revelation was extraordinary. He would have expected most people – he didn't know for sure, having never actually told anyone – to be repulsed by such a barbaric secret. To Straker's way of thinking, Sabatino's reaction was counter-intuitive. What triggered her to react *this* way? Was it the danger? Was it something more primeval – a moth-to-the-flame attraction to the killer instinct?

'We shouldn't go back to your place,' she said, 'you'll have too many vibes from your wife, and will feel awkward. We'll go to my hotel.'

Straker, abandoning any earlier reservation about complicating their professional relationship – the intrusion into his divorce – the revelation about Charlie, smiled uninhibitedly and said: 'Sure, I get that. Where are you staying?'

'The Dorchester.'

'Stylish.'

'I'm paid an indecent amount of money. The least I can do is spend it in decent places.' She looked at him intently as she smiled. 'You coming?'

'Very nearly.'

'Don't you dare. Not yet, at any rate.'

Reaching her hotel room in Park Lane, she turned on the light, kicked the door shut behind them and approached him directly, kissing him firmly on the mouth. Her body, pushed in hard against his, was already inducing a strong response. Straker found her predatory approach erotic and intoxicating.

Kissing him, Sabatino started unbuttoning his shirt and, within a few moments, was at his belt and trouser buttons. With a hand into his fly, and a gentle cupping and circling of her hand and fingers, Straker felt a shock wave run through him. She was electrifying.

Pushing him back on the bed, and kneeling astride him, she finished removing his clothes and then lifted her top over her head, revealing her slim taut figure. Unclipping her bra – passing both hands behind her back which served to project her chest – Straker was treated to the sight of her round, hand-sized breasts. No effects of gravity or the surgeon's knife were anywhere to be seen.

Leaning down, she kissed him hard on the mouth and, without lifting herself off him, deftly removed her jeans and knickers. This was amazing. Straker had never been so passive and yet so aroused.

Sabatino grabbed both Straker's wrists, and pinned his arms above his head. He was lying spread eagled with this writhing, spirited, energetic and beautiful woman on top of him.

She continued to pleasure them both with the rhythmic action of her hips. That continued for a time, her knowing exactly how far to excite him before slowing up and letting him subside. She came three times in the process.

Starting again, she felt Straker's movements intensify. Very quickly, she lifted herself up and off him – and took him further by surprise. She grabbed the end of him between thumb and forefinger and squeezed him hard. 'Oh no, you don't,' she said firmly. 'The Colonel hasn't finished his duty ... not by a long shot.'

It worked.

He laughed out loud, at her directness, her control – and the clear knowledge of what she wanted, and how.

What a woman. Not then, but afterwards, he was given to mulling whether she was this confident and direct because she lived the high-octane life of a racing driver, or whether she was a racing driver because she was naturally this self-assured.

In the end he concluded he didn't give a stuff.

Thankfully, she was what she was and was magnificent for it.

THIRTY-THREE

The next morning, following an even more energetic "round four", Straker shared an expansive breakfast with Sabatino, served off a crisp white linen tablecloth in her room in the Dorchester. Just after eight, he left her to walk to the office.

There was suddenly a different feel to his world. Halfway across Mayfair, Straker felt himself to be better. It wasn't simply the endorphins of last night, powerful though they were – nor was it just the intimacy with another human being, which he had been without for so long. Straker felt his buoyancy was more profound than that. Several strands of his new life seemed to be helping distance him from his troubles. There was the role at Quartech. His status with Quartano, particularly after the Buhran assignment. His involvement in the spectacular world of Formula One. And now, after last night, a closeness to one of the most fascinating women he could imagine. What might this closeness to Sabatino end up meaning? he wondered. Straker's mind only knew positive thoughts that morning – a sensation he had not experienced for a very long time.

Irritating him – as it broke his reverie – was the ring of his phone. But seeing who it was, he relaxed – feeling this incursion to be a part of his new-found optimism. 'Karen? How's it going?'

'Pretty well, I think, Matt. I've got something for you.'

'Oh yes?'

'You asked me to look for any connections between Van Der Vaal … Massarella … Obrenovich and Joss MacRae?'

'Yes…'

'Were you aware that in March – just gone – MacRae sold a thirty-three per cent stake in Motor Racing Promotions Limited – for a mix of cash, equity and convertible prefs?'

'Interesting,' said Straker recovering some of his buoyancy. 'No. I didn't know that. For what sort of money?'

'Around £500 million.'

'Christ. To who? Hang on, if that's the case why doesn't everybody know about this?'

'Because,' said Karen knowingly, 'nobody does. I couldn't find a single article on it. I talked to our bank in Zurich. It's all been done completely hush-hush. The stake was bought by a Lichtenstein Anstalt.'

Straker exhaled audibly. 'That's, surely, why nobody knows about it, then – but, by the same token, neither can we. A corporate shield'll stop *us* from knowing who's behind it, too. Sod it – that's a tantalizing dead end.'

Karen chuckled teasingly. 'There are no shareholders listed, no. But I *have* done some digging.'

She paused for effect.

'There *was* a director named … just one.'

Straker stayed silent.

'I assumed he would be one of those professional company secretary – trustee – director – types?' Karen went on. 'I made some further enquiries around Vaduz. And that's when I struck gold.'

'How?'

'This guy's only ever named with the interests of one other client.'

'*Who?*'

'A Swiss oil company … Helveticoil.'

'Never heard of it.'

'You probably won't have. But you *will* have heard of its owner.'

'Who's that?'

She paused again. 'None other than … Avel … Obrenovich!'

'Shit – no!'

There was silence on the phone.

'Matt?'

'Karen, that's brilliant work. You might just have blown this whole thing wide open.'

Straker continued his march to the office, buoyed up once more. Before he had the chance to think through the ramifications of Karen's discoveries, his phone went again. This time it was Oliver Treadwell.

'How soon can you get up to the Ptarmigan factory?' he asked.

Straker heard an edge to the Strategy Director's voice. 'As soon as you like. Why? What's happened?'

'We've found the cause of Helli's crash.'

Straker sensed the answer was sinister. 'What was it?'

'It would be better to show you – in person. I should warn you, though … it's not good news.'

THIRTY-FOUR

Just under two hours later, having hammered his Honda Civic up the M40, Straker was standing in the loading bay of the Ptarmigan factory. Treadwell led him over to a temporary workbench, set up for the purposes of the investigation. Straker still had no inkling of what was coming.

Treadwell had laid out two component fragments from Cunzer's car on the work surface. 'This is what we've found,' he said gravely.

On the table were two things. Straker understood one of them to be a wishbone – a V-shaped boomerang-looking component made of carbon fibre, part of the car's suspension. The other, he would hazard a guess, was a section of exhaust.

'This is what we believe caused Helli's crash,' said Treadwell seriously, lifting up the V-shaped component. 'These wishbones are made of carbon fibre – a lightweight, strong material. But it has a drawback…'

'… it won't take the thread of a screw,' offered Straker, remembering his tour with Andy Backhouse.

'Precisely – the stuff just crumbles. The only way to fix it to other components and materials, therefore, is glue.'

'Okay.'

'So on the wishbones – to fix the V-shaped spars at either end – we fit metal lugs, or flexures. These flexures are then used to bolt the wishbone to the wheel assembly at one end, and to the chassis mount on the other.'

'And the flexures are held to the spars by the glue?'

'Except that here, on Helli's car, the glue on the chassis flexure of the wishbone has failed.'

'Does it do that?'

Treadwell's face looked even blacker. 'Not normally, no. In any case, this was no wear-and-tear failure.'

It was Straker's turn to look grave. 'Why? What's happened to it?'

'It's been melted.'

'What do you mean – *been* – melted?'

Treadwell placed the wishbone back down on the table top and picked up the other component lying on the workbench. 'On our cars,' he said, 'the exhaust system runs very close to the chassis-mounting of the lower rear wishbones. We can do that because we heavily insulate the exhaust with a special silicon-based polymer – as you see, here,' he said pointing to the lagging around the pipe.

Straker leaned in and studied the casing. But then he spotted something else. And leant in closer.

There seemed to be a tiny, ragged-edged hole through the metal tubing and insulation. 'What's that?' he asked. 'That's not machine made?'

Treadwell's face told him he had hit the mark. 'It isn't,' said the Strategy Director. 'It's not meant to be there.'

Straker frowned. 'What're the consequences of that hole? You talked about the wishbone first – I'm guessing there's some kind of cause and effect here?'

Treadwell nodded at Straker's quick thinking. 'That hole, even that small, could have, over time, released heat – enough heat, given its precise location, to melt the carbon fibre glue. Hot gas had been escaping from the exhaust – straight onto the metal flexure on the end of the wishbone.'

Straker ducked his head down to look at the hole in the exhaust pipe again, and even rubbed a finger over it. His mind was already whirring with the inevitable question: 'Okay, Ollie,' he said. 'How did that hole come about?'

Treadwell now looked like he was in mourning. 'We've never had a failure in that exhaust system. Not one. That's not to say we couldn't – but we haven't yet. In any case, a natural failure wouldn't happen right there – it's not subjected to that much heat- or pressure loading.'

'So you're saying it didn't just give out – you're saying it was *made?*'

Treadwell nodded.

'Deliberately?'

Treadwell nodded again.

'We're working on determining how it was made – but that hole, in that exact location, is utterly suspicious.'

Straker straightened up. 'Let's suppose someone *did* make this hole. What could they have expected to happen because of it?'

'One thing – and one thing only. Suspension failure. Melting that glue would inevitably degrade the wishbone. That wishbone giving out would completely degrade the rear axle. Any rear axle failure would collapse the back end, rendering the car undriveable.'

'And what would be the consequences?'

'Depends on the speed the car was going at the moment it failed. At high speed – as in Monaco – we saw the results all too clearly.'

'You think that's what the saboteurs were going for?'

Treadwell shook his head. 'Possibly, if they're psychotic. To do us straightforward competitive harm, they didn't need it to fail quite so spectacularly. Even at a slow speed, suspension failure would still degrade the car completely. We'd have been significantly inconvenienced – because of the time and work it would take to replace it. It would have *easily* disrupted Qualifying or our race, had the car survived that long. So – no – I don't think they minded, really, when it gave out. Any amount of use – even over several sessions – would have taken its toll on the glue, and, certainly over the course of a race weekend, would have provided enough cumulative heat to degrade it to the point of failure at some point.'

Both men fell silent as the malice behind all this sunk in.

'These bastards are up to more than just interfering with our electronics,' said Straker almost to himself.

'And, again, it's clever, Matt,' said Treadwell. 'This interference was so small and hidden we'd be unlikely to see it – as, indeed, we didn't during Andy's checks in Monaco. And, a broken suspension could be so easily dismissed as mechanical failure or driver error – especially with the unforgiving bumps, barriers and kerbstones in

Monte-Carlo. Who wouldn't suspect a young driver like Helli of hitting something around that circuit over the course of a weekend? As a way of attacking us – without immediately arousing suspicion – this sabotage, along with the radio jamming, is fiendishly clever.'

'We should be in no doubt, then,' said Straker as a conclusion. 'These people are deadly serious about wanting to do us harm.'

THIRTY-FIVE

Straker felt this new evidence intensely. He had to get outside, to take some fresh air. Needing to be alone, he stood on the terrace to the north of the factory, and looked out over the rolling Oxfordshire countryside – trying to calm himself down. Even the soothing breeze and hazy summer sunshine had little effect on him.

Straker was motivated, anyway, by his professional duty to complete this assignment – and honour the responsibility he had been given to counter the sabotage risk to Ptarmigan. But now, he clearly had to defend the team against a very real life-threatening danger. And that, in the light of his intimacy with Sabatino, prompted a powerful urge in him to defend her personally. How dare these people be out to threaten the life of anyone, let alone someone he was close to.

Straker wanted to fight back – to retaliate in some way. He was angry that these people, whoever they were, were able to do all that they were doing with impunity. Even so, he fought to rationalize his response, very aware that it was largely driven by emotion, which he fought to control. That emotional tussle, though, ended up helping him. It prompted him to think of ways to fire a shot back at these arseholes, even if it might be indirectly.

An idea he had been toying with finally took hold.

Going back inside, he found the Strategy Director in his office. 'Ollie, have you and Tahm thought any more about the switch away from Trifecta?'

'Yes,' replied Treadwell, clearly not happy with the idea.

'I take it, then, we're transferring to Cohens,' Straker concluded. 'Have we told Trifecta?'

'Not yet.'

Straker offered him a sideways smile. 'Let me, would you?' he said with a clear edge to his voice.

Treadwell looked a little surprised. 'Why, who are you going to tell?'

'Someone whose resultant discomfort might do us some good.'

An hour later Straker had managed to photograph the wishbone, the hole in the exhaust system, and download his pictures to a Ptarmigan iPad – along with a sequence of photographs of Helli Cunzer's spectacular crash in Monaco, including the horrific moment when his car was completely engulfed in flame. Driving away from the factory in his Honda, Straker headed for Leamington Spa.

He drove onto the now-familiar industrial estate and pulled up a discreet distance away from, but with a clear view of, the main entrance of Trifecta Systems. He was instantly relieved. The Peugeot he hoped to see was parked out front. His quarry, therefore, ought to be inside. Straker killed the engine.

He readied himself to wait.

He willed his quarry to emerge.

Nothing happened for quite a while. A stream of people came and went from the office building, more exiting it with the onset of lunchtime. None of them, though – as far as Straker could tell – was his man.

Suddenly Straker sat up.

There he was.

Michael Lyons – balding, middle-aged, and slightly overweight, wearing an ill-fitting suit – appeared through the glass front doors of the Trifecta building. Straker immediately felt relieved again – not only that he had spotted his man, but also that Lyons was alone and didn't seem to be walking with any degree of urgency or purpose. Nor was he carrying anything – briefcase, laptop, files – so it didn't look like he was heading off to an appointment.

He watched Michael Lyons walk through the business park. Straker climbed out of his car and, after a considered interval, started to follow him on foot.

Straker was able to keep up.

From a distance, he kept Lyons in view.

The man ambled down a narrow footpath out of the complex, and turned left at the far end. Straker needed to jog briefly to maintain visual contact. Lyons – and then Straker – soon emerged onto a street with shops, bustling with shoppers. Looking left, Straker caught sight of his man – some way along the pavement – as he disappeared into a watering hole.

Straker quickened down the street to follow him inside.

It turned out to be a chichi bar occupying a redundant branch office, hived off by a high street bank. Straker entered in time to see Lyons make his way across the crowded room, between groups of chattering people, towards a free table and set of chairs against the back wall.

Straker picked his moment to pounce.

Moving swiftly across the room himself, he headed towards Lyons's table. In one movement, Straker pulled out the opposite chair, dropped himself onto it, and said: 'Michael, you should take a look at this,' swinging the iPad round to face him. 'After you jammed Sabatino's radio in Monte-Carlo, and that psychotic crash you caused in Spa, this is the latest evidence of your sabotage – damage to Helli Cunzer's exhaust and wishbone, and the cause of *his* crash in Monaco.'

Such an invasion of space was so unexpected – and so rapid. Moreover, a stranger had addressed Lyons directly by name. Then he was confronted with the series of images, the latter ones showing Cunzer's horrific crash, the wreckage of his car, and an arresting one of the fireball that engulfed him. Lyons was completely thrown. The man looked up, an expression of concerned bemusement on his face. 'Who the fuck *are* you?' he spluttered.

'Someone who knows precisely what you and your scumbag friends are up to. You don't have to be part of this, you know, Michael. Jamming may just be a bit of technical fun, even if it is still a violation of decency. But threatening lives is something very different. Always remember this,' he said tapping the frame of the iPad on the table, 'we can prove, now, that you've all got form. If you and your *friends* do go on to cause a death,' said Straker with considerable menace, 'it … will … be … murder. You will be named as an accessory. Do you understand? Do the right thing, man – shop these arseholes, before it's too late … too late – for you.'

Lyons's equilibrium started to return, fuelled by a growing sense of intrusion at this confrontation. He tried to smile, but did so lamely. 'You quite clearly don't have the faintest idea of who you're dealing with.'

Straker paused, saying nothing – deliberately for effect; he simply looked the other man straight in the eye. 'The real question, Michael,' he said, his voice quietening significantly, 'is: do you?'

Straker paused again.

'Do you *trust* them, Michael? Have you thought about that? Have you thought about what they might do – the moment they think you know too much? Have you ever thought they might even be setting you up as the fall guy?'

Straker was pleased.

The unexpected angle of this last comment clearly threw Lyons anew. 'Here's what I'm going to do, Michael: I'm going to give you a week – to do the decent thing and expose these people. If I've not heard from you by then, Ptarmigan is going to sack Trifecta – and we are going to cite your unethical conduct as the reason. You know, Apartment 5 at 25 Rue des Princes?'

Lyons suddenly looked genuinely startled.

'We will make it perfectly clear that it was you – Michael – that lost Trifecta its business with us. You will then have to tell your scumbag friends that you lost *them* their opportunity to do Ptarmigan any more harm.'

Straker stared intently into the man's face. 'You've got a week to put this right,' he said, placing a business card with his contact details down on the table. Standing up, Straker retrieved his iPad, and walked out of the bar.

Making his way back to the Ptarmigan factory, Straker turned this ploy over in his mind. Had he even gone far enough? Should he not have terminated the link with Trifecta, then and there? Straker was soon smiling, though, pleased with what he had done. His gambit – and deadline – had to put Lyons under some sort of pressure.

Straker was thinking all this through as he rounded the corner at the bottom of the Edgehill escarpment, when his attention was jolted away. Dropping a gear to start up the long climb, he heard a soul-wrenching growl of protest from his Honda engine. It got worse – before the thing packed up completely, and ground to a halt. Straker tried to restart the engine, but it wouldn't even turn over. Nothing.

On a blind corner, he was stranded on a slope – fully in the road. Twisting quickly round, concerned about traffic hitting him from behind, he flicked the car out of gear, let it start rolling backwards down the hill and, once freewheeling under gravity, applied a little left-hand-down. With enough momentum, the car soon bumped up off the road, and completely onto the grass verge. There, close in against the hedge, Straker applied the handbrake.

Half an hour later Treadwell arrived to pick him up. There was a blast of Australian piss-taking over the state of Straker's car. 'I'll get Morgans of Kineton to recover it. Probably far more humane to take it straight to the crusher – save everybody's time.'

They abandoned the Honda on the side of the road, and drove back to the factory. 'How did you get on with Trifecta?' Treadwell asked.

Straker explained his tactics and relayed the conversation.

'Oh to be a fly on the wall when Lyons has to fess up to that lot.'

Straker, though, wasn't smiling. 'We will have tweaked the tail of the tiger, all right. And they *won't* like it. They're bound to lash out. We have to be ready, Ollie, for whatever they throw at us next.'

THIRTY-SIX

Straker returned to London by train that same afternoon. Most of the way down through the Chilterns he was smiling to himself – savouring his first obvious move in striking back – and the protection it might afford Sabatino. His thoughts then turned to her in the context of their night together. He spent considerable time on his iPhone, drafting a text. It took him numerous iterations to get the tone and balance exactly right. Finally, as the train pulled out of High Wycombe, he pressed Send.

While waiting for a reply, Straker rang the factory. He pushed Nazar hard for a meeting with the drivers – to discuss Cunzer's sabotaged suspension, and its implications in light of the other sabotage the team had endured. Although keen, the team principal was concerned about timing – the challenge of arranging a get-together before Monza, given everyone's commitments elsewhere: he declared he could only give it a try.

Before arriving back in London, Straker got a reply from his text to Sabatino.

It wasn't what he was expecting. At all.

All it said was: *Me too, RS.*

And that was it.

How could that be it? What was he meant to make of so little?

Tahm Nazar managed to come up with a clever solution for a meeting with the drivers. A forum was found – on common ground for the key players – surprisingly soon.

Within forty-eight hours Straker was able to meet them and Treadwell in Sussex, at the foot of the South Downs. Both Sabatino and Cunzer had long been scheduled to appear at the Goodwood

Festival of Speed. To ensure comfort and privacy for their meeting, Nazar even sent down one of the Ptarmigan motor homes.

The Goodwood estate was bathed in summer sun. A gentle breeze blew across the English countryside. Thousands of people had come to enjoy the day out, and to celebrate the *car*. All kinds and marques were there – all treasured, cared for, and adored by their owners.

In among the automotive stars were plenty of human ones too. Rally drivers, MotoGP riders, and, in large number, Formula One stars – past and present. All were celebrated by the public – fans just looking for a glimpse of, a moment of interaction with, an autograph from, even a photograph standing beside one of their heroes. Age didn't matter. Enthusiasm for the stars seemed to be the same from small boys, right up to pensionable men.

Straker was on site and in the motor home ahead of time. There, he waited for the drivers to appear. How was Sabatino going to react? he wondered. To his disappointment, he had heard nothing more from her since that brief text the day after their night together.

Now, waiting for Sabatino, Straker had to admit that he was apprehensive. He became agitated, and then even angry with himself. Why was he feeling this unsure of himself? Disconcerted by his troubles? Certainly they had undermined his confidence in other areas. Was it his divorce? He had never been awkward around women. Was there something else going on? Or was it *this* woman?

Shortly after eleven, the door of the motor home hissed open and Sabatino climbed up the stairs. Straker waited anxiously to see how she would behave.

She greeted Treadwell, and then him – exactly the same. This was functional – professional to professional. Sabatino was clearly being cool.

That was good, wasn't it? thought Straker. Put on an indifferent front – not give anything away to the rest of the team. Much better to pretend.

But then there came no breach in the façade from Sabatino. No discreet "Hey you" wink, no hidden-from-other-people's-view nudge, no accidental physical contact. She was cold. Completely cold. Straker was knocked back. He hadn't expected anything like such a clinical reception.

After a few minutes, he realized – starkly – that this was to be the shape of it.

Thrown by her coolness, he kept his distance, leaving Treadwell and Sabatino to catch up between themselves – this being the first time the two of them had been face to face since Treadwell's appointment as Sabatino's race engineer.

Straker's reaction to this was far worse than he had expected or feared.

He suddenly felt raw. Trying to rationalize things, he tried to persuade himself it would be easier this way. An intimate relationship – even an emotional one – would *have* to be complicated in such a high-pressured workplace, wouldn't it? Mess things up. It had to be better to keep this professional.

Straker worked hard to convince himself that this was the better outcome.

Every time he came close, though, he found himself falling short – coinciding, more or less, with each time he looked at her. Why couldn't he accept that line? His disappointment increased, almost to the point of distraction. He realized he was going to have to deal with this somehow. He was going to have to go on working with Sabatino. Even letting his feelings show would complicate things. He felt he was in a jam.

Bizarrely, Straker found himself an immediate and powerful cure.

A truly perverse one.

His antidote to all this was to summon up his troubles with the Americans and his flashbacks – which very quickly and all-too effectively distracted him from thoughts of what might have been with Sabatino. Despite the pain that that induced, Straker soon had to smile at his twisted fate. It seemed ironic that the very thing he was trying to escape from had become the antidote to his failing recovery from it.

Around Goodwood, Helli Cunzer, back up and about again after his terrifying Monaco crash – albeit on crutches – was a crowd favourite. Everywhere he went or tried to go he was fêted by fans and admirers. It took him much longer to get anywhere around the showground.

Later than planned, Cunzer climbed up into the Ptarmigan motor home. Sabatino, who hadn't seen him since her hospital visit in Monte-Carlo, jumped straight up, flung her arms round him and hugged him closely. The contrast of her interaction with Cunzer hit Straker like a train.

The pint-sized German with his fine boyish features and close-cropped blond hair manoeuvred himself deftly onto one of the turquoise leather benches and stacked his crutches on the floor beside him.

Sabatino looked into her teammate's face with genuine interest and feeling. 'I still can't believe you didn't break anything major.'

'Amazing, isn't it? Several cuts – one big gash from a piece of carbon fibre through my thigh. But otherwise, no. I was extremely fortunate. What a car … What safety!'

'When will you be able to drive again?' Sabatino asked.

'Monza,' he said with a confident grin.

'Wow! That soon?'

Straker felt he needed to step in. Time was tight. Both drivers were expected to appear at the Festival at lunchtime. 'I've got us all together,' he said severely, 'because I'm anxious you're made fully aware of the sabotage threat we still face. It's more serious than we thought.' Bending down, Straker reached into a holdall and lifted the two key components from Cunzer's car – the wishbone and the exhaust section – which he placed on the table between them. This was Treadwell's cue to give an account of the conclusions drawn from the crash investigation.

Cunzer and Sabatino looked increasingly shattered.

They ended up studying the flexure on the wishbone, and inevitably rubbed a finger over the hole in the exhaust.

'Someone *did* this to me,' said Cunzer, the shock of the realization all too clear in his face and voice. 'Someone *made* me crash.' Looking directly at Straker, he said: '*Who* did this? Who could *possibly* do this – who could be putting my life in danger?'

Straker realized he needed to sound authoritative and yet remain genuine, knowing all too well that he didn't have enough of the answers. 'This *had* to have been done by someone in the team – an insider,' he stated.

The drivers fell silent.

The mood was eerie.

'It must be the same person who planted the bug in my helmet,' offered Sabatino to the room rather than to Straker directly.

'Highly likely, but not known for sure,' he replied. 'Both interventions – the bug and this,' said Straker with a sweep of his hand over the damaged components, 'were done some time ago – in the build-up to Monaco – and nothing like this has happened since. They could simply be historic acts, nothing more than a legacy from Charlie Grant.'

'What about my engine limiter in Spa – and, particularly, the *removal* of the bug from my helmet after Monaco?' Sabatino asked. 'Don't they indicate more recent evidence of an insider?'

Treadwell stepped in: 'Possibly, Remy. Certainly Andy Backhouse handled your helmet, and he's since defected. He, too, is a suspect. With Charlie and Backhouse now both out of the picture, though, we're clearly hoping the saboteurs have lost their insider, if it was in fact either of them.'

Sabatino looked far from convinced or settled. She picked up one of the components, and drew attention to the wishbone by waving it. 'This shows real intent to do Helli and the team harm. My high-speed loss of control at Spa, and now knowing about this from Monaco, means that Helli and I have been at serious risk.'

Straker made himself meet her eye, despite the awkwardness he felt – anxious to maintain his professional credibility. 'I wish I could say that wasn't the case.'

Cunzer looked back and forth between the others around the table. 'Do you think we are *still* at risk from an insider, Colonel?'

This time Straker looked Cunzer in the eye: 'I can't guarantee that you aren't.'

THIRTY-SEVEN

Water. Cold water, smashing down into his face. And the panic of not being able to move. He was struggling – violently struggling, straining against the straps. But he couldn't breathe. The contraction of his diaphragm – as he fought *not* to breathe – was unbearable. How much longer could he hold out? Now the cramp. The pain. The pain in his leg was agony. Bastards! These people were allies. *Allies*, for fuck's sake! Straker fought on against the straps, thrashing from left to right. Something warm: he felt something warm. That wasn't right! It didn't fit.

Straker's brain began to compute. Why was it warm?

He struggled again and then, finally, broke from his sleep. Dripping with sweat – his head spinning – he regained consciousness. The bedroom light in Fulham was still on. Angrily, he ripped away the duvet.

Straker pulled himself up, swung his legs over the side of the bed, and sat there, his chest heaving and heart racing, trying to calm down. It took several minutes for him to register his immediate surroundings. Looking at his alarm clock he recognized all too clearly the return of his affliction. It was three-forty a.m.

What the hell had triggered such a relapse? He thought through recent events, but didn't have to for long. His meeting with Sabatino loomed large. His disappointment with her behaviour. That was undoubtedly the cause of this disturbance. That – and the intensity with which he had conjured up memories of his troubles to get him through that meeting with her.

Oh Christ, Straker thought. Now setbacks in parts of his new life were pulling him straight back – down – even deeper into the dark.

Knowing the rest of the night was now lost for sleep, he climbed into his running kit. He pounded the streets of Fulham, through the darkness, until the sun came up.

All manner of thoughts swirled around Straker's head for several days. He would have to shut Sabatino out of his mind, at least in the way that might have been. He decided to fill the days before Monza with activity and distractions.

He resolved to throw himself into anything, however small, to take his mind off her. An early necessity was his car. He rang Treadwell for the number of the recovery shop, but learned he was away – and that his office didn't have it. Straker tried to remember what Treadwell had said: Morgan of Kineton – or something – wasn't it?

To get a contact number, Straker threw some guesses into Google. Scores of results were displayed – including the one he was after. Attracting his attention, though, were several to do with a different Morgan altogether – the Morgan of Morgan sports cars.

Out of curiosity he clicked on their website. He was captivated. Their latest design was prominently displayed, which didn't do it for Straker at all. Much to his delight, though, the British design icon – the Morgan Roadster – was still there, portrayed in an eye-catching and fresh electronic brochure. Evidently, the classic Morgan was still very much in production.

Forcing himself to concentrate on the job in hand, he returned to his search for the intended Morgans and found the name of the recovery shop in Kineton. When he got through, the news on his Honda was not good. It was terminal. It had basically had it. Little more than scrap. Straker cursed. He couldn't do without a car.

Then he had a flippant thought.

After the downer of his divorce, and the unwanted complexity of his involvement with Sabatino, didn't he deserve to give himself a lift? Following Quartano's offer on the completion of his last assignment – which included a directorship on the Quartech main board and a substantial bump in salary – wasn't he in a position to indulge himself? If so – why the hell not?

He could only resist the idea for so long.

Logging back on to the earlier Google pages he looked up a list of local Morgan dealers and emailed a showroom in Henley-on-Thames.

Forty-eight hours later Straker had plenty else to think about and keep him occupied – activity triggered by the passing of the deadline he had issued to Michael Lyons. Straker requested a conference call with Nazar and Treadwell.

'I take it we've heard nothing from him?' Treadwell asked.

'Of course not,' Straker replied.

'Hardly surprising,' said Nazar. 'Even so, your ploy was probably worth a shot – to try and unnerve the other side.'

'It may still happen, Tahm,' offered Straker casually, 'if, when you inform them, you make a point of citing Michael Lyons as the reason for terminating our business with Trifecta. The ploy could still have caused unseen – or delayed – consequences.'

'I'll send the termination notice today,' said Nazar, 'mentioning Apartment 5 at 25 Rue des Princes, yes? – and stating that this takes immediate effect.'

'Spot on,' said Straker.

'Okay, fine. But Matt, if this *is* going to have unseen consequences, I trust you to be ready for whatever they might be.'

Straker grunted positively. 'I have a week to work with our new electronics firm, Cohens, to prepare our defences.'

THIRTY-EIGHT

Ptarmigan F1 pitched tent in Monza, twelve miles north-east of Milan. In the lead-up to the Italian Grand Prix, there was a frenzy of media speculation. Many commentators were building up expectations for a dramatic reaction to a female driver's incursion into this most masculine of environments. The anticipation was electric. How would all this play out in the spiritual heart of macho Italian motor racing? How would the Tifosi react to a woman driver?

In the end, Sabatino's apprehension of the Tifosi was completely unfounded. Italian men, for all their love of cars and motor racing, proved themselves to be first and foremost lovers of women. The Tifosi took Sabatino instantly to heart. There was even a hint of mania.

Being Monza, the circuit was crowded – even for the first day of practice. Sunny and warm weather helped. In every direction, the packed stands appeared like seas of fluttering scarlet, rippling in the breeze. Scarlet flag upon scarlet T shirt showed the black prancing horse on its famous yellow shield. Ferrari devotees were there in force. But this time, there was a surprise. Another colour was prevalent. Ptarmigan's brand of turquoise.

The Tifosi were hailing Sabatino.

This welcome may have eased Sabatino's own apprehension, but it created – if anything – a bigger irritation for Massarella. Even more so than usual. Massarella may have had the Italian heritage, but they always found themselves playing second fiddle to Ferrari – especially in Italy. Under normal circumstances that may have been galling enough. But this time Massarella seemed to be demoted even further – because of the Tifosi's excitement for Sabatino and her Ptarmigan.

Van Der Vaal's expression conveyed more and more of his angry chippiness. To counter his irritations, he projected his recruitment of Andy Backhouse as a major coup – revelling in having won over a key member of a rival team. The Massarella boss paraded Sabatino's former race engineer up and down the pit lane, through the paddock – and had Backhouse stand next to him during every TV interview Van Der Vaal gave in the build-up to the race.

Just before a practice session, Van Der Vaal even walked Andy Backhouse across the front of the Ptarmigan garage – with an arm across his shoulders – in full view of Nazar, Treadwell, Cunzer and Sabatino.

Sabatino tried to distract herself from all that pettiness by throwing herself into practice. Taking herself out onto the famous circuit for the first time in a Formula One car, she set about doing her job.

Even on her first out-lap, as she worked temperature into the car, she found it was understeering far more than on any circuit to date. With the very low downforce set-up, the Ptarmigan was seriously struggling to hold the line through the slower corners. Before completing half a lap she was on the radio to Treadwell, her new race engineer. 'The car's all over the place. Completely out of balance. I'm getting hideous understeer going in, and a fishtail coming out. Everything's changed.'

Straker, listening in, fully expected this drop-off in stability to be blamed on his instigating the change of engine management system.

Sabatino drove on. She reached the approach to the faster corners of the legendary Lesmos. Only when the Ptarmigan was cranked up did the aerodynamics start to kick in and give her any confidence.

Because of the understeer, the Ptarmigan team worked without a break over the following two days, dissecting all the telemetry – running endless simulations through their models back in Shenington. They tried everything to mitigate the lively handling of the car. Only by increasing the angle of the front wing could they make any difference – and that seemed to cost her badly in straight-line speed.

Extraordinarily – despite all her difficulties – Sabatino took everyone by surprise. She managed to qualify in P2, having learnt over the two days of practice to work with – rather than fight – the vagaries of the car. Simi Luciano, in his Massarella, was only just able to beat her, putting himself on pole.

Straker remained apprehensive. If the saboteurs were still out to do Ptarmigan down, surely this challenging pace was a renewed invitation for them to try again. He tried to convince himself that, with the help of the new electronics firm, he had done enough since Spa to reduce Ptarmigan's risk from sabotage.

But he couldn't relax.

He set up all his usual surveillance systems in the motor home headquarters – just in case.

THIRTY-NINE

The day itself started as a perfect morning for the Italian Grand Prix. The sun shone. The air temperature was in the late twenties. And there was the gentlest of breezes. Nothing less than deserved for the spiritual home of motor racing.

Nevertheless, Van Der Vaal was spitting. What more did he have to do here? He had put an Italian – in a Massarella – on pole, and yet the Tifosi were celebrating one of their beloved Ferraris on the second row.

But that was Van Der Vaal's problem. To everyone else, the stands were in magnificent voice, creating the classic Monza atmosphere in the build-up to the race.

Straker hoped he was ready. Now with Cohens supporting them, he had been able to set up even more sophisticated surveillance and feedback systems. He hoped he was not being complacent in having the BBC coverage on one of his three screens and their commentary in one ear of his headphones. As the start of the race approached, he began to listen in. The grid walk had just finished, and the show was being thrown up to the commentary box, ready for the race:

'Thank you, David, and welcome, everybody, to the Italian Grand Prix, staged on the hallowed circuit of Monza. Conditions are looking good. No sign of rain, and the temperatures are forecast to peak out in the low thirties. Twenty-two runners, and a tight Drivers' Championship – all promise an exciting afternoon of motor racing. Currently leading – and really beginning to attract attention – is the history-making Remy Sabatino, Formula One's first female driver to mount a serious challenge on the Championship. Seven races in, and she is six points ahead of her nearest rival – Italy's own Simi Luciano. The excitement looks like continuing here today – Luciano is one place in front of her on the grid. If

the grid positions were held to the end, though, Remy would stay on top of the Championship table, albeit with her lead reduced.'

'Indeed, Ben, it really is all extremely *tight,'* chipped in the other commentator. *'And it's* because *it is that tight that Sabatino's had such a strong reception. Even in her rookie year, she's taking her fight straight to the big dogs. And that's not been lost on the knowledgeable Tifosi.* Look *at the stands – here in Italy – here at Monza. I can't remember the last time I saw the scarlet of the Scuderia so diluted like this. See that Ptarmigan turquoise – it's* everywhere,' he said as the producer quickly backed the commentator up with several different wide shots of the stands, showing a mass of flags and banners fluttering in the gentle Lombardy breeze. *'It's amazing.'*

'Certainly is, Mike. Sabatino and the whole of Ptarmigan have shaken things up this season. And we mustn't forget, of course, that the team was on its uppers – as recently as the back end of last year. And yet, here they are – less than twelve months on – with a superb car and a woman driver – both as serious contenders for both *Championships. Don't let anyone say that Formula One is boring.'*

'Absolutely not, and, of course, the drama doesn't end there. The pit lane, paddock, and stands are all pleased, today, to welcome back Remy's teammate, Helli Cunzer – making his first return to the car after that heart-in-the-mouth crash in Monaco a few weeks ago.'

The TV picture cut away from scenes around Monza to a slow-motion replay of Cunzer's death-defying high-speed crash in Monte-Carlo, the drama of it losing none of its potency despite the countless times it had been shown. At the end of the clip, which showed Cunzer being airlifted off the Monaco circuit and flown out over the harbour in an emergency helicopter, there was a happier shot of the youthful good-looking blond German walking down the pit lane in Monza that weekend, waving at the crowds, acknowledging his reception from so many well-wishers.

'Well said, Mike, and his return's all the more impressive with him qualifying P6 on the grid. That result shows, formidably, that his confidence and speed have been restored so quickly – further tribute to driver and car.'

'Indeed, and we shouldn't overlook the competitive significance of that, either. If the Ptarmigan drivers hold their starting positions to the end of today's race, Ptarmigan's one-point lead would be preserved as the mid-season leaders of the Constructors' Championship.'

Action was soon visible along the crowded pit straight as the team bosses, mechanics, and array of celebrities started scurrying off the grid.

'Okay, we're getting close to the start. The engines are running. We're ready for the parade lap, round this three-and-a-half-mile circuit.'

Straker used the time during the slow procession to check all his screens and frequency settings at his console in the motor home. A couple of messages, between the pit wall and the Ptarmigan drivers, were helpful testers. They showed all his new Cohens systems to be working perfectly.

'The cars are retaking their places on the grid. The backmarkers are in position. A green flag is being waved by a marshal from the back. Race Control has confirmation to start.

'Yes, here we go. We have one red light.

'Two, three, four – and now five.

'Just listen to that roar – that crescendo – of power.'

'Wait!'

'Wait…

'And the lights are … OFF!

'GO! Monza is GO. Luciano's away well. He's on the clean side of the circuit. Sabatino's got a good start, too – if anything a better one. She's clearly found grip, even down that dirty side of the track. And look, she's moving up on Luciano, moving up on the Massarella – down the inside of the run into Turn One.'

'She certainly is, Ben, she's had a great start. And, so far, everyone's got away okay – no apparent incidents.'

'Luciano's moving … sorry, Mike … over to the right – aggressively across Sabatino's front. He's trying to shut her out, well before the corner. But look, there – look, look, look – she's not having any of it – she's not yielding – she's holding her nerve – holding her position.'

To bring home the drama, the TV shot zoomed in on the extraordinary bottleneck of cars, power and noise into the impossibly narrow first corner.

'Sabatino's being squeezed over to the right. She's going in at a sharp angle. She's going in deep. And, whoa! – watch that Ptarmigan's understeer. She's been suffering from it all weekend – practice and Qualifying – particularly in the slower corners. I don't think it's ever been quite as bad as that, though.'

'It's the low downforce set-up, Mike – that's what's doing it.'

'She's having to seriously wrestle that car into Turn One. And look out for that Ferrari – off the second row – looking to pounce on her from behind. Heh, heh! Sabatino's managed to fend him off – but, oh, watch that Ptarmigan fishtail through the exit. She so nearly lost it there.'

'Sabatino cannot have enjoyed that – the Ptarmigan's, clearly, a real handful with that low-downforce set-up.'

The leaders were are all quickly through the first four corners, and soon approaching the Lesmos.

'And that's interesting, Ben – Sabatino seems to be finding some stability, now – at last.'

'Yeah, Ptarmigan's aero package showed, all through practice, that it works much better at the higher speeds.'

'Well, she's managing to use it, now, to hold her gap behind Luciano to point-seven of a second. Simi would've wanted to get away further – with a clear track in front of him – but Sabatino's not letting him go that easily.'

'And, Ben, she's holding her lead over the Ferrari just behind her, too.'

Suddenly, Straker's eyes and ears were caught. His surveillance screens flashed and, over the headphones, he heard Treadwell speaking with Sabatino. It turned out to be simply routine – a message that her temperatures were all showing comfortably in their respective windows.

'Now the front runners are coming round to the end of the circuit – to La Parabolica. The whole field seems to be running well – no major upsets.'

'Certainly not yet, anyway, Ben. And now, let's see how they run round this hairpin, and enter the Rettifilo. This, if anywhere, is where we're likely to see some action on the overtaking front. Who, though, is going to have the straight-line speed advantage. This is where all of that starts – right here, going into La Parabolica.'

Luciano braked late and hard.

'Sabatino's braked even later than the Massarella. She's closed right in.'

'Now it's all about the corner and the exit – which car's giving its driver the better balance and control.'

The Massarella turned in tight. Sabatino's Ptarmigan was right up behind.

'Through the apex – and, now, down goes the power.'

'Both drivers were pretty tight through there.'

'Luciano seems to be accelerating hard – third, fourth, fifth – right up to eighteen thousand revs.'

'But Sabatino's keeping pace out of the hairpin, Ben. She's right there with him.'

The camera switched to the far end of the half-mile-long Rettifilo, to look back, offering a long, head-on shot of the approaching cars. Through the heat shimmer, the Massarella's black and business-like profile was all that could be seen, as Sabatino was tucked so closely in behind. Travelling at that speed, the Massarella seemed to bobble over a silvery-watery mirage on the surface of the track. Then the TV picture switched to a helicopter shot, directly overhead, giving the commentators something much more obvious to talk about.

'There they go – nose to tail. Sabatino's right up behind the Massarella. She's getting a good tow, using the hole punched through the air by the car in front, to reduce the drag. But, of course, its turbulence will disturb the airflow over the Ptarmigan, reducing her downforce. But, here – at this very moment – on this straight – that's okay. There're no lateral forces on the Ptarmigan right now.'

Sabatino's car was now almost bumping the rear end of the Massarella. Seemingly in an instant, the turquoise Ptarmigan dived out to the left.

'Here she goes! She's having a go down the left-hand side.'

'Yes, but look at that – Luciano's seen her in his mirrors – and is moving straight across – to the left – to try and block her.'

Sabatino, being aggressively squeezed over to the dirty side of the track, suddenly lifted off for a fraction of a second before changing direction, darting back the other way – back behind the Massarella – to try a dive again, this time down the right-hand side.

'That's clever, Ben – Sabatino knows Luciano can only make one defensive move, under the rules – and that he's just made it. Now going down the right-hand side, she's still got three-quarters of the Rettifilo left to mount her challenge – without legitimate influence from Luciano.'

The overhead camera followed the two flat-out cars down the start/finish straight. It showed all too clearly how close the cars were – almost touching – as Sabatino's Ptarmigan started inching its way alongside.

'Aargh, this is sensational. Two Formula One cars – absolutely at full throttle – throwing themselves down the pit straight at two hundred miles an hour – and we're only interested in the tiny relative speed between them.'

'Which is, what, Mike – no more than two or three miles an hour?'

The TV picture switched again – to the forward-looking camera mounted on the front wing of Sabatino's Ptarmigan – only inches off the ground. The surface of the track swept by, below, in a hypnotic blur. Filling the left of the picture was the black wall of the Massarella's rear-right tyre, spinning in another blur – while the car's black radiator pods and front wing tapered away down to the blurred surface of the road ahead.

'Wheel to wheel – inch by inch – they couldn't be any closer.'

'Is she going to do enough – do enough before the corner?'

'Who knows, Ben,' said the other commentator with a chuckle clearly delighting in the drama. The shot changed yet again, this time from behind. Viewers could see the rears of both cars – appearing, from that angle with the compressing of perspective, to be absolutely side by side. Beyond them, hazily in the distance, was the looming braking zone of Turn One.

'I don't think Sabatino's going to do it – she's not done enough. Her engine hasn't quite got the grunt.'

'No, and here comes the end of the straight. Luciano, surely, has the right to retake the line.'

'I'd say so. And if Sabatino's going to hold her current line, she'll be in the dirt very soon, and on a very tight line into that corner.'

Sabatino finally had to yield.

'Wow, what a shame, Ben – but what a charge! What a charge!'

'Absolutely. What an effort. It shows one thing really clearly, though, Mike – Luciano's going to have to be on his guard. Any mistake he makes out of the Parabolica, and Sabatino will surely have him.'

'Provided that understeer of hers doesn't let Luciano get away round the rest of the circuit. She's got to be right up behind him into and out of the hairpin to stand a chance.'

Round they raced for another lap.

Their high-speed joust was repeated seven more times, with Sabatino harrying Luciano all the way down the majestic start/finish straight into the first corner, only to find she never quite got the shot she needed.

Then something happened.

'Look, Ben, Sabatino's trying a different entry into the hairpin this time.'

'Let's see if it works? Sabatino's hanging left and braking slightly earlier. She's turning in slower – but – but – she's faster out. Look at that! She's got a much better exit this time. She's definitely closer as they straighten up.'

'It's looking good – she's tucked right up behind, in Luciano's slipstream. Can she do it?'

Sabatino darted out, this time to the right.

'Here they go again. Look – look at them run.'

'It's a drag race!'

The two cars pelted down the full length of the magnificent long straight, inches apart. All the way.

'*Two hundred miles an hour, and we're still only interested in the relative speed between the Ptarmigan and the Massarella. It looks like it'd probably be measured in* feet *per hour, this time.*'

The two cars were hurtling down towards the end of the Rettifilo. The crowds started roaring. They had come for excitement – the excitement of Monza – the home of Italian motor sport. Expectations were not being disappointed.

'*Aargh – it's all too much. She's got enough time, hasn't she, Mike?*'

'*The Ptarmigan is giving its all – but where's that extra handful of horsepower she so desperately needs?*'

'*She* is *still gaining.*'

'*Side by side. Wheel to wheel.*'

'*At over two hundred miles an hour. Sabatino's still* pulling forward. *She's edging further forward.*'

'*But will she do enough?*'

Both cars hit their respective rev limiters. Straker willed Sabatino's car on, almost unable to breathe as he watched the titanic struggle play out over nearly ten seconds.

'*That Ptarmigan Benbecular is giving its all. She's gaining … gaining – so slowly. It does look, though, that she could just about draw level and take him.*'

'*But can she do it in time?*'

'*She hasn't yet. It all depends on who blinks first. It's all about braking, now – into Turn One.*'

'*Wait, Luciano's been spooked – he knows this is threatening his lead of the race. He's starting to move – moving across towards her. He's already staking a claim on the line – does he still have the right?*'

'*It might just be to try and intimidate her. They're getting closer and closer. Who's got the nerve to face the other down? Does Sabatino have the nerve to hold her ground?*'

The other commentator laughed dismissively. '*Oh, I shouldn't worry about her nerve, Ben. Our rookie woman has definitely got the anatomy for this game.*'

The other commentator – and Straker – chuckled. '*Indeed, and *neither's giving way.* Neither's *giving way. But they're going to have to brake soon – one of them's going to have to back off.'*

Straker suddenly saw a puff of blue smoke off one of the front tyres between the cars, but they were so close and it was all so fast that he couldn't tell whose tyre had locked-up. The commentators were none the wiser.

'Who was that braking?'

'Who knows – but Luciano's pouncing. He's now definitely staking a claim on the line. He's moving over – moving across.'

'Luciano's going to shut the door – going to hold her off.'

Then Sabatino very clearly hit the brakes.

'Yeah, there he goes – taking the chance to cut right across in front of her. He's got it – he's secured the line.'

'But he's cutting right across her path. What about Sabatino's under-steer? Is she going to be able to slow down fast enough?'

'Hang on – hang on. Oh no, look at that!'

'That's understeer. Sabatino's got the mother of all understeers.'

'The front end's going away from her. She's going to end up T-boning him – isn't she?'

'She might, she might…'

'She's almost on full right lock – but its having no effect. She can't avoid him. She's going to ram him, smack in the ribs.'

The TV picture switched to the camera on Sabatino's front wing. The shot put the viewer right in the middle of the action. There was dramatic convergence. An almighty crunch. Bits flew off both cars. The Ptarmigan's front left bashed into the Massarella's radiator pod. The cars juddered on the impact. Both cars' back wheels interlocked – and bumped – momentarily bouncing the Massarella off the ground. It fell back down – heavily. The two cars intertwined, and slid ignominiously off the circuit onto the run-off on the outside of the corner, grinding to a halt. A cloud of dust enveloped the scene.

Both sets of suspension were degraded, and Luciano had very obviously suffered a punctured front right.

The Massarella and the Ptarmigan were well and truly out of the race.

Sabatino made her way back to the pit lane on foot, still wearing her helmet to conceal her fury at being forced to drop out of the race. Keeping her helmet on was also the clearest possible sign that she did not want anybody to talk to her.

Once safely inside the Ptarmigan garage, she took it off. Clearly agitated.

Ten minutes later her mood exploded. The stewards announced a formal investigation of her crash with Simi Luciano.

FORTY

Massarella, they soon learned, had lodged an official protest, accusing Sabatino of unsportsmanlike behaviour – deliberately taking out her principal rival for the Drivers' Championship. Ptarmigan was summoned to Race Control.

Sabatino was incandescent at the slur. Without even smartening herself up, she strode out of the motor home, straight off to see the FIA steward with Treadwell jogging behind, anxious to catch her up.

Mario Pinolla, a tall, thin, elderly Italian with an aquiline nose and angular face, called them into a meeting room and asked Sabatino to explain herself at Turn One. Peering over his half-moon glasses, Pinolla made her and Treadwell feel like a couple of naughty school boys in front of the headmaster.

'It was a racing incident. I went for the inside of Luciano. He closed the door on me. I tried to brake. Locked-up, and just slid into him.'

Pinolla looked at her with a completely sceptical expression on his face. 'What about the threat you made to Mr Van Der Vaal, then? At Spa. That you would run his cars off the road?'

Sabatino bristled but remained silent.

She happened to glance at Treadwell. He closed his eyes and shook his head – as if to dissuade her from raising the whole sabotage story – before quickly stepping in himself: 'Mr Pinolla, please look at the course of the whole race. For eight laps, Remy exited the Parabolica, ready to mount a challenge. Both cars were very evenly matched in straight-line speed. Remy had a legitimate shot at holding the inside line into Turn One. Our telemetry – all weekend – shows the Ptarmigan's downforce is severely affected when any lock's applied to the front wheels. Every time Remy went to turn in, the downforce fell away. Into that corner, where the surface on the inside is still dirty, a combination of low downforce and dirty track caused a complication in a justified racing manoeuvre.'

Pinolla removed his half-moon glasses.

Before the steward could respond, Treadwell went on: 'I would ask you, please, to point to any action on Ms Sabatino's part that you think was deliberately intended to destabilize her car?'

Pinolla's expression hardened. He looked Sabatino in the eye. 'What about this threat you made in Spa?'

Yet again Treadwell stepped in before Sabatino could speak: 'Mario, you know Eugene Van Der Vaal – he dishes out this sort of stuff all the time. Remy was indulging in nothing more than a bit of a psych-out.'

'What is sick out?'

'*Psych*-out – *psycho*logical playfulness. Words, Mario. They're just *words*.'

Five minutes later Sabatino and Treadwell re-emerged into the brilliant Italian sunshine as the noise of the race continued all around them. Walking back to the paddock they had to fight their way through the inevitable media scrum.

'Did you mean to crash?'

'Did you deliberately take Luciano out?'

'Are you going to apologize to Massarella?'

They had to wrestle their way through a jostling press pack all the way to the Ptarmigan motor home.

'How did it go?' asked Straker as Sabatino and Treadwell climbed the stairs and shut the door on the rabble behind them.

'Those bastards at Massarella never let up, do they?' she growled.

Treadwell tried to be philosophical: 'We were cleared by the stewards. The system worked properly,' he said calmly.

'Massarella's little game didn't work,' offered Straker. 'We were exonerated.'

'We can't brush all this off so easily. It's fucking up my Championship.' She turned to face Straker. 'None of this would be happening

– *at all*,' she snapped at him, 'if you had succeeded in getting rid of the sabotage bollocks from Massarella. We're always on the fucking defensive. Why aren't we exposing their sabotage incidents and chewing *their* arse?'

Straker reacted viscerally to her outburst. It hit him like a body blow; he felt her accusation even constrict his chest. How could she lash out at him, let alone in public like this – not to mention after their night together? Straker fought hard to retain his professionalism. He looked her straight in the eye. 'We don't have the evidence, yet.'

Sabatino made for the cabin at the end of the motor home. 'Well for fuck's sake, *get* some. I'm tired of being the victim,' after which she stormed inside and slammed the door behind her.

PART FOUR

SINGAPORE SLING

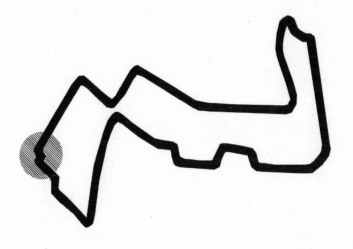

FORTY-ONE

After a respectable pause, Straker got up and left the motor home. He had to get away from the humiliation. To walk off his anger. "How *dare* you?" he screamed – to himself, marching out of the paddock and into the crowds. He knew Sabatino was under stress; they all were. Interference from Massarella must have been taking its toll on her nerves, but so it was on everyone else's. He was damned if he was going to be spoken to like that – let alone in front of other people.

Straker fumed.

His dealing with this and her conduct, though, was going to have to wait. His phone was ringing. It was Dominic Quartano.

Acting as a distraction to Straker's uncalmed mood, the tycoon was flying into Milan that evening. Straker was asked to get himself and Nazar airside and ready to board the Quartech Falcon the moment it came to a standstill.

Straker spent some time arranging things, able to put the Sabatino issue out of his mind – at least for the time being.

Later that day, on board the company jet, Straker and Nazar were greeted by Quartano and Bernie Callom, Quartech's Marketing and PR Director.

'Welcome,' said Quartano. 'This trip to Shanghai should be momentous. Get it right and we should be on for signing Mandarin Telecom and landing the biggest sponsorship deal Formula One has ever seen. Let's get you all a drink. Then, Tahm, you can tell me what went wrong for Remy this weekend.'

Straker sat silently in the cabin, not engaging with any of the subsequent conversation.

Quartano accepted the racing incident explanation. 'Where does that leave us?' he asked.

'Still okay in the Constructors' Championship,' reported Nazar. 'Remy and Luciano didn't score here in Monza, even so Helli's spirited second place to Barrantes's seventh actually extended our Constructors' lead. We're on 94 as against Massarella – in second – on 87 points.'

'So not a total disaster. And in the Drivers' Championship?'

'Tighter as a result of the weekend. Remy *is* still on top – with 56 – ahead of Aston, now in second, on 54.'

'So just two points in it. And Luciano? Where's he now?'

'Still on 50, but back down to third.'

Quartano smiled and exhaled. 'Three drivers covered by six points. Pretty close. We're going to have to find some extra performance or consistency, soon, for us to break away.'

Following a refuelling stop in Dubai, the Quartech Falcon landed in Shanghai early the following evening. Monday. A limousine met the Ptarmigan party at the airport and drove them straight to the Four Seasons Hotel in Weihai Road.

Two hours later another car took them, through the dusk, from the hotel to their dinner engagement on the Bund. Driving through the city, the bustling energy of Shanghai and the Chinese people was clear to see. Streets were thronged. Neon signs were glowing in every direction. In the midst of all this bustle were striking juxtapositions of the ultra-modern with the traditional – the most obvious being the frequent sights of curved wooden Chinese rooftops in between huge expanses of glass and concrete.

Their car reached the Huangpu River as an orange sun set behind them. They turned north onto the Bund, the city's western frontage along the river. Before them was a fantastic sight – full of diametric contrasts.

'Here, on the left,' Callom offered, 'is the colonial city – I've been doing some reading for our promotional material. You'll see the buildings are all pretty grand – baroque – from the time of Shanghai's trading heyday. Most of the big European powers were here from the eighteenth century on – the British, French and Russians. This place boomed in the 1930s. With its style and buzz, Shanghai was even dubbed the Paris of the East. Over to the right,' he said pointing through the opposite window, 'look at the contrast! That's Pudong.'

Straker looked across the river to the east. The architecture could not have been more different. A skyline as futuristic as he had seen anywhere in the world. Adding to the impact, most of the buildings carried vast neon signs stating the names of their occupants. Prominent among them was Mandarin Telecom's sign and logo.

'No carved columns or verdigris domes over here,' Callom went on. 'All the same, the buildings are pretty distinctive. The one with the ball top and bottom – that's the Oriental Pearl Tower. And the tallest building is nothing less than the tallest building in the world – the Shanghai World Financial Centre. Welcome, gents,' said Callom with a flourish, 'to the world's economic superpower. Twenty-five years ago all that area on the other side of the river was a paddy field.'

'Is that all it took?' asked Nazar. 'You'd hardly see that kind of energy and drive in Europe,' he added with a hint of provocation.

Straker thought of Canary Wharf, smiled – but didn't take the bait. The car pulled up in front of M on the Bund.

Alighting in front of the restaurant, they made their way up through the historic Nissin Shipping Building. Mandarin Telecom had reserved exclusive use of the roof terrace. Their table was outstanding – laid up for just eight of them – on its own in the centre of the outdoor space. In the balmy evening breeze they were treated to views of sparkling lights – across the skyline of Pudong, among the boats plying the Huangpu River, and down the curved sweep of elegant colonial buildings fronting the Bund.

There to greet them was Dr Chen, flanked by some of his directors.

Quartano turned and gestured to Pudong. 'The economic

sensation continues,' he said. 'I'm impressed to see Mandarin Telecom's name as the most prominent of the lights across the river.'

Dr Chen bowed his acceptance of the compliment. 'Thank you, sir, we are pleased with our progress – domestically. With the prospective association between our two companies, we hope to develop just as fast internationally, going forward. We are looking to Ptarmigan and Formula One to accelerate our brand awareness around the world.'

'An excellent thought on which to begin our evening.'

In deference to the Chinese culture of doing business, Quartano was careful only to react to topics of conversation and not initiate them. The protocols were keenly observed.

During dinner, the Quartech and Ptarmigan visitors were treated to multiple courses – Straker lost count of how many. Each one, it was explained, being a tribute to the culinary style distinctive of a different region of China.

Straker, returning to the Four Seasons quite late, found himself brooding – brooding over his unresolved tension with Sabatino back in Monza. Why the hell was this weighing on him so heavily?

As if he didn't know the answer.

Straker couldn't relax with all that occupying his mind. His hotel room felt like a prison. He had to get out. Setting out on a long run through the early hours, he only made it back to the Four Seasons as the first pinkish-orange light of dawn was breaking to the east.

A Mandarin Telecom car arrived at nine to take the Ptarmigan party across town – and across the river – to the headquarters building in Pudong.

Arriving at the foot of the forty-eight-storey glass tower, there was a sign welcoming the visitors flanked by two enormous arrangements of orchids.

'That's very symbolic,' whispered Callom. 'Orchids mean fertility – implying abundance, growth and prosperity.'

'Did you learn that through your research, Bernie, or did you just happen to know that anyway?' asked Nazar mischievously.

An elegant thirty-something Chinese woman appeared wearing an immaculate dark suit, a Mandarin Telecom logo tastefully embroidered into the lapel of her coat. She introduced herself as Dr Chen's assistant and asked the visitors to follow her to the lifts.

Crossing the atrium of the building, they were struck by its size. Stretching up over five floors, it hosted three full-sized palm trees, a large rock display, and copious amounts of running water – including a thirty-foot fountain. Bypassing the reception desk and elegant waiting area, they were led straight to the lift marked Guests Only.

With a slight popping of their ears, the lift rocketed up through forty-seven floors in a matter of seconds. The Ptarmigan team was soon ushered gracefully into a vast open office occupying half the floor. Over by the large continuous plate-glass window Dr Chen and his directors were sitting at a long conference table. They rose and greeted their visitors once more. Before the formal meeting began, the visitors were invited to make the most of their platform in the sky – being introduced to the aerial views of Shanghai. An astonishing sight. All the shapes on the far side of the river were shrouded in a mist as the sun was only just beginning to burn through the cloud. Several landmarks were pointed out. The M on the Bund, where they had dined the night before. The Old HSBC building. The extent of the International Settlement. And the area of the French Concession.

The CEO of Mandarin Telecom soon invited the visitors to sit at the long table. 'Gentlemen,' said Dr Chen as he took his seat. 'We are pleased to have reached a satisfactory point in our negotiations.' Looking up he nodded to his female assistant who promptly walked forward carrying a number of leather folders. Each person, starting with the visitors, had one placed before them.

'We have, here,' Dr Chen explained, 'the Memorandum of Understanding covering the sponsorship of the Ptarmigan Formula One Team for the next three years.'

Straker waited until it was evidently okay to open his folder. As he did so, he saw the agreement was beautifully laid out, typeset in English alongside Chinese characters.

'This is indeed exciting,' said Quartano addressing Dr Chen and then looking into the faces of the Chinese directors in turn. 'We are all inspired by the potential of this association between our two companies.'

'Thank you, Mr Quartano. Likewise. As we have agreed, and is set out formally in here,' continued Dr Chen laying an open hand deferentially over his leather folder, 'we will move to full contracts as soon as we can. We have agreed with your Mr Callom that news of this will be embargoed until the Singapore Grand Prix in two weeks' time. There, we will make a preliminary announcement, looking to sign the contract itself at the Chinese Grand Prix, here in Shanghai, two weeks after that.'

'That would be most fitting, Dr Chen.'

At which point the Chinese CEO was handed a Montblanc fountain pen by his female assistant. Through his thick black-rimmed spectacles Dr Chen looked down and signed the Memorandum of Understanding on the largest sponsorship deal in Formula One history.

Seven hundred and fifty million dollars over three years.

The deal was done.

Almost.

FORTY-TWO

Quartano flew the team back with him from Shanghai to London in the Quartech Falcon later the same day. There was an exuberant mood on the plane as they toasted and revelled in the prospect of the Mandarin Telecom sponsorship.

For Ptarmigan, there was the excitement of knowing the team had secured an unprecedented budget and the wherewithal to challenge unhindered for the two Championships in Formula One over the next three years – providing an opportunity, with a level of financial predictability, none of the staff would have known in their motor racing careers.

For Quartano, there was the satisfaction of having done it again – even in his seventies: of spotting an opportunity, of committing to a distressed commercial situation, of providing leadership and business expertise, of appointing the right people, of building the right team, and of then seeing his judgement bear fruit. Rarely, though, had such a turnaround yielded such a quantifiable – and sizeable – benefit quite so quickly. Ptarmigan, bought for a symbolic £1 when the team was on its uppers nine months before, was now attracting third-party funding worth three-quarters of a billion dollars.

Straker, still thinking about the tension in Monza, was so buoyed by the mood on board he decided to take some initiative. Firing off a text to Sabatino while they were in the air, he wrote:

I think we need to talk about things. Can we grab some time in Singapore? Matt.

He felt it was unemotive, short – to the point.

He felt better just with the sending of it.

Two days later, though, he had not had a reply.

This did not do his frame of mind any good. Unresolved tension threatened to drag his psyche down. He craved a distraction, but the bank holiday weekend was long and empty. Straker found solace occupying the part of his mind he always felt energized when playing bridge – except the last thing he wanted was to be sociable. Instead, he played – alone in his flat – against his Pro Bridge Professor. He played the machine for hours on end, making, among other contracts: two small slams, a dozen game calls, and managing on one occasion to get the machine four down in three no trumps. For Straker, an electronic game didn't come anywhere close to playing the game for real, particularly the feeling of being on a wavelength – when bidding tightly – with a partner. And, he was well aware how sad playing this game – alone – truly was. But, at the same time, he also knew that, currently, he was not himself.

Whatever the stigma of such a solitary occupation might be, he didn't care. Its mental stimulation – made possible in delicious isolation – served a therapeutic purpose, and worked for him. It managed to tide him over psychologically, until he was ready to leave for Singapore.

As Straker left for the Far East, though, there had still been no reply of any kind from Sabatino.

The press conference announcing Mandarin Telecom's sponsorship of Ptarmigan was to be held in the Ballroom of Raffles Hotel on the morning of Qualifying for the Singapore Grand Prix.

Quartano flew out to join the Ptarmigan team – to present this coup to the sport and to the world.

The ballroom was heaving with journalists and TV cameras.

Everyone was there.

At the appointed time, the lights were dimmed and a video was run. Dramatic music and a stirring voice-over announced the tie-up between China's largest telecommunications business and the glamorous world of Formula One racing.

The imagery was spectacular, but so was the message.

A substantial business from an Eastern communist country was ready to break out globally and embrace the consumer markets of the West – through the medium of the world's most exciting sport. Formula One was showing itself to be significant enough to begin breaking down geopolitical barriers.

At the end of the video, Quartano took to the stage accompanied by Dr Chen, the CEO of Mandarin Telecom, and Tahm Nazar, Ptarmigan's Team Principal.

The room fell silent.

Quartano's rounded baritone voice commanded complete attention as he declared the partnership with Mandarin and introduced Dr Chen.

The Chinese tycoon, ironically a card-carrying member of the China Communist Party, declared his company's delight in the sponsorship of the team and stated that their aim was to enjoy the exposure of motor racing around the world to build the most successful telecoms company on the planet.

Having made their statements, there were questions from the journalists. Their recurring theme was clear: 'How much is this sponsorship worth?'

Quartano, with unwavering control of the floor, replied: 'We still have some discussions ongoing. In any event, we consider this is an issue of confidentiality, and the final amount will not be disclosed.'

There was a considerable clamouring to ask related follow-ups, all of which Quartano batted away. One journalist launched an oblique attempt to elicit the magnitude of this number.

'In light of this sponsorship,' he asked, 'will Ptarmigan still need financial help from other sponsors, or even Quartech, anymore?'

Quartano's face remained neutral, even though he appreciated the subtlety invested in the question. 'Need and want are two very different things.'

The journalist came back with: 'You haven't answered the question.'

'How about that?' Quartano replied and smiled broadly. 'Ladies and gentlemen, we thank you all for coming. We'd like to thank the Singapore government for hosting this spectacular Grand Prix, and look forward to an exciting weekend of motor racing.'

It was to be an exciting weekend, all right.

At lunchtime on Saturday the heavens opened.

The rains, substantial even by Singaporean standards, were torrential – likened by everyone to an out-of-season monsoon.

Driving conditions were little short of treacherous.

Straker, although taking comfort from their switch away from the troublemaking Trifecta Systems to Cohens, and having been sabotage-free in Monza, was still vigilant – set up as usual in the headquarters motor home.

Being a night race, Qualifying One started at the same time of day as the race proper – therefore after dark. Singapore looked all the more impressive at night. Lights burned across the towering skyline – not for cleaning or weekend servicing – but because, in all probability, the Lion City was still working, even on a Saturday evening. Industriousness, not birthright, earned this entrepôt its respected status as an economic powerhouse

Five minutes into Q1 there were six cars out on the track. All were on full wets. And while the treads and sipes on each tyre may have been designed to displace sixty litres of water a second, they were as near-useless against the standing water around half the circuit, some of which was over an inch deep. Driving an F1 car through this was like walking in leather-soled shoes on sheet ice. Cars were sliding about all over the place.

Against the lap record of one minute forty-five, no one had completed a lap in under two and half minutes.

Six minutes into Q1 a backmarker lost control under braking into the Singapore Sling, Turn Ten. First the front left locked-up. Then it started aquaplaning, there being virtually no help from the aero-dynamics at such slow speed. The car simply headed on in a straight line. Going deep into the corner, it showed no response to the direction set by the steering wheel. Then, suddenly, with full left lock on, the car hit a dryer patch of road, caught some grip, and started to turn. But the back wheels, still on the surface water, kicked out to the right. The driver steered aggressively into the slew, but in vain. The water had made the track like ice. The car started to spin.

Going at only fifty miles an hour, the driver was merely a passenger. The car spun, slammed into a section of the circuit's unforgiving barriers, ripped off its right-front wheel, the whole of its front wing, and shattered the nosecone. Debris, from the splintered carbon fibre, skidded out across the chicane like ducks and drakes across the water.

Race Control immediately red-flagged the session. The remaining cars teetered back to the pits, the drivers soaked to the skin in their open cockpits.

Marshals were able to clear the wreckage away fairly quickly. But the rain would not abate. Down it came.

Race Control really had little choice. They called a halt to Q1 and declared that Q2 would only start when the rainfall diminished.

For two hours nothing happened.

Finally, well into the evening, the weather began to ease. Q2 was started and all teams were able to try and post a time.

In Qualifying Three, the track even started to dry out. The key decision – gamble – each team had to make was whether to run on full wets or intermediate tyres. In the current conditions, the time difference in lap times between the two types could easily be up to ten seconds. Be on the wrong tyre, and a competitive position on the grid would be lost.

Sabatino took a massive gamble.

She and Treadwell waited until the last possible moment. They opted for intermediates. Only Paddy Aston had done the same thing – managing to clock up the best time so far by six seconds, but his lap was absolutely heart-stopping. Twice he came within a whisker of colliding with the barriers.

His punt, though, had paid off.

Driving into his garage, Aston could subsequently sit back and watch the rest of the field fight for second place, no closer than three or four seconds behind him. Tyres were clearly critical.

On her hot lap, Sabatino started well. Sheares Corner was dry. Turns Three and Four were okay too. Into Turn Five, though, the car became a boat. Sabatino surfed on the top of the water for fifty yards in a dead straight – no-control – line. Miraculously, the tyres found some grip somewhere – somehow – before it was too late. With a massive yaw and twitch, she regained control, kept the car pointing down the course, and accelerated on hard down the straight to the kink at Turn Six.

Round she went. At the end of Sector One she was nearly a second up on Aston. Then there were the treacherous bends – particularly in the wet – around Memorial Corner, Turn Seven, and the one-hundred-degree rights of Turns Eight and Nine. With everyone holding their breath, she powered on, barely lifting off at all.

Another scary moment at Turn Thirteen.

At the end of Sector Two Sabatino was a full three seconds up.

Then came the extraordinarily unforgiving sharp turns of Sixteen through Twenty-one. The car was barely on two tracks throughout these bends. Only Sabatino's feel, ability to anticipate, and her lightning reactions kept the car on the road. Water was flying off all the tyres – spray hurtling into the air, creating the classic cock's tail in the night behind her.

Round the relatively slight bends of Turns Twenty-two and Twenty-three she brought the car into the end of the start/finish straight and hammered the Ptarmigan, as hard as she dared.

Crossing the line, she chalked up an extraordinary time of one minute fifty-five seconds. Although much slower than the lap record in the dry, her drive – in these conditions – was quite astonishing. Moreover, she was a full four seconds clear of Paddy Aston in the Lambourn.

It took Sabatino most of the following in-lap to steady her breathing and nerves as the waves of adrenalin slowly ebbed out of her system.

But the endorphins soon flowed in their place. Pole position, particularly fought so hard for in the wet, had a rush all of its own.

And for the Championship this was a good – and a very necessary – result. She needed to keep Aston at bay. Currently, she only enjoyed a two-point margin for the title. Any mistake by her over the weekend could easily see that lead slip through her fingers.

FORTY-THREE

Next day, Sunday, the weather if anything worsened. Unbroken rain fell all morning. Being a night race, everyone was hoping the change in temperature around nightfall would reduce the intensity of the rain.

That didn't happen.

Umbrellas were everywhere, particularly on the grid; under the floodlights, the teams put the final touches to their cars.

Rainfall did nothing to dampen the usual anticipation and turnout of all and sundry – and certainly not among the fans. If anything, the crowds were bigger, everyone coming for the added excitement of seeing a race in such hazardous conditions.

The red lights came on, and the formation lap started round the 3.2 mile circuit.

From pole, Sabatino led the field slowly away. As pole sitter, she should have a major advantage. So long as she was in the lead, she would have clear air in front of her. All the others behind would have the misery of trying to see and drive through everyone else's spray. And two, three rows back – in the dark, to boot – it would be almost impossible to see more than fifty feet ahead. These conditions would dilute the commitment of some drivers. To capitalize on this significant advantage, all Sabatino needed to do – really – was keep ahead of Paddy Aston into Turn One. If she came through that unscathed, she would have the unique advantage of clear vision for the rest of the circuit. Her anxiety rested on the speed with which the car would reach all its operating windows and the ability of the tyres to grip through the surface water.

Round they went on the parade lap, all feeling for just how far they could push their cars – and themselves – in these conditions.

Even with the usual short sprints and swerves to raise the temperatures, the cars were frequently losing control, prompting the drivers to back right off.

Forming up again, the race was soon ready to start. Still the rain fell. Every wet surface was given a diamond-like sheen and sparkled in the intensity of the arc- and floodlights.

The first red light came on.

Then the second.

Fifteen thousand horsepower screamed into the night, as the sound of the engines bounced off Singapore's high-rise buildings.

Three lights. Four.

All five lights were now lit.

Then … they all went out.

GO!

Sabatino released the car and started accelerating, feeling every nanosecond for any loss of traction through the rear wheels. She shot forward. Changing up, she applied more power. God bless the Ptarmigan. It was accepting the monstrous power without complaint. On she accelerated.

In the mirror, she snatched a glance behind. Her spray ballooned up into the air. Let's hope Aston's getting a visor-full, she thought to herself as she refocused on the corner ahead. The car was up to eighty miles an hour. Water was still lying on the surface of the track.

She claimed the racing line into Turn One.

After the first corner, Sabatino grabbed another rearward glance. She saw exactly what she had hoped for. The rich purple livery of the Lambourn was very clearly confined to her wake.

She'd done it!

Gingerly, Sabatino opened up out of Turn Three – feeling for both the grip behind and the responsiveness of the steering in front. So far, she was comfortable. Marginally up on qualifying speed from yesterday, she was a long way down on the lap record.

Even with the significant advantage of clear air, she still had the disadvantage of a sodden track.

On the fourth lap came the very faintest hint of a drying racing line – just about visible on the surface of the road. By lap eight, it was becoming more pronounced. By lap twelve, the dry line was pretty much permanent, despite the continuing fall of rain.

While good news from a grip point of view, this triggered a new dilemma. Sabatino's intermediate tyres, on the dry line, were starting to degrade fast – they were getting far too hot and blistering badly. She took the precaution of moving off the dry line while on the straights, to drive through wetter parts of the track to keep her tyres cool.

'When do we switch to drys?' Straker heard her ask Treadwell over the radio.

'It'll cost us in strategy – if we stop so soon.'

'Sure. But these tyres are dying. What if we fuel for a longer middle stint?'

'We'll run the numbers.'

Over the air Straker heard the team talking to each other. Those in the headquarters truck were immediately talking through the trade-offs between being faster on dry tyres, heavier with extra fuel on board, as well as estimating the position Sabatino would feed back into after a stop to change the tyres.

Suddenly everything changed.

There was commotion and lots of radio traffic.

Aston had dived into the pits – throwing down the gauntlet.

He was clearly making an early dash for drys and taking a chance on the racing line staying dry.

'Remy? Paddy's in – Paddy's in – we'll bring you in next lap. We need to try and estimate his fuel level.'

All the Ptarmigan team members in the headquarters truck and on the prat perch followed Aston's purple car into the pit box. Stop watches were triggered the moment the Lambourn came to a halt. Aston's mechanics removed the intermediates, replaced them with drys. In the artificial light, the crew seemed to move as a blur.

'Drys – definitely drys,' shouted Treadwell over the radio. 'How long?'

The Lambourn rigger was still pumping fuel into the car. He heaved the ring around the nozzle up and lifted the hose away. The lollipop man swivelled the paddle. And then lifted it clear. Aston powered out of his box, slewing the back end as he made for the exit of the pit lane.

'Nine seconds. He's going for a long middle session – long – around thirty laps.'

'Right,' called Sabatino. 'I'm coming in next lap. Drys, and let's fuel for thirty-five.'

Treadwell acknowledged her shortly afterwards.

'Okay. Where would that put me back in?'

Treadwell paused as he studied the electronic plot of the cars around the circuit, and used the touch screen commands to run some "what ifs" through the computer. 'It would put you in behind Aston. He's already lapping at one forty nine, three seconds faster.'

'Okay, let's do it now, and let's do it quickly.'

Less than a minute later Sabatino was into the pits. Her crew executed a perfect stop. She was out in a matter of seconds on drys, fuelled for thirty-five laps. She regained the race in tenth position, three places behind Aston on the circuit.

Within half a lap, as the new tyres bedded in, she was significantly faster than the intermediate runners around her. On the next lap she overtook three cars, without breaking a sweat. The difference between the two tyres in these conditions was huge.

But Paddy Aston, of course, was benefiting equally up ahead of her – slicing through what were the soon-to-be backmarkers.

In response to the leaders' clearly successful switch to drys, the other cars started peeling away, each one coming into the pits to do the same. Within three laps, the race order had shaken down – all the front runners having switched to the faster tyre. The order ran: Aston, Sabatino, Luciano, Mercedes, Ferrari, Cunzer and Barrantes.

The race continued. Aston should have been able to make ground on Sabatino by virtue of being five laps' lighter in fuel. Sabatino was able to keep in touch, though – still holding on to P2.

Twenty laps later, everything changed.

Again – dramatically.

Treadwell had been asking – just about every minute of the race – for updates from the weather guys in the headquarters truck. They were now ready to make a significant call. 'Remy, we're forecasting heavy rain – imminently.'

'How heavy?'

'Heavy.'

Straker was able to switch one of his screens over to the same one as Treadwell.

'Let's go intermediates, now,' she ordered. 'I'm beginning to lose out to Paddy anyway. Let's take a punt on the rain. I'm coming in.'

A lap later Sabatino had pitted, switching back to intermediates, and fuelled to the end of the race.

Within three-quarters of a lap on the new cold tyres, she pushed the car back up to race pace.

Except, very soon, she was desperately questioning whether this was the right thing to have done. In no time at all, her tyres started getting hot.

Worse, they were making her slow.

For two painful laps, she stayed off the dry line for most of the way round the circuit – keeping on the wetter and dirtier parts of the track. Even doing that the tyres weren't cooling down. Much longer at these temperatures and they would start to blister – degrade – badly. They were not going to last any length of time.

Unfortunately, it soon looked likely that she would *have* to make another pit stop, which would seriously cost her in time, position, and points.

Over the next three minutes Sabatino lost ten seconds to Aston.

And there was no sign of the rain.

What the hell had they done?

'Where's the damn rain?' she bawled.

This switch of tyres was *killing* her performance.

Three minutes after the predicted arrival, there was still no rain.

Another eleven seconds lost to Aston.

Four minutes and twenty seconds after the time predicted, the rain did start to fall. And when it came – it *came*. Water smothered the track in a matter of seconds.

All those still on drys were completely baulked – right back on the ice again.

In no time, Sabatino was running fully on the racing line – the line itself soon wet enough to keep her intermediates cool. Her tyres were no longer overheating.

By contrast, the pace of the dry runners fell away immediately, all of them tottering round the rest of whatever lap they were on – at less than a fraction of the pace they had just been setting. From laps in the one minute forties, they were now lapping at well over two minutes – and slowing all the time. One of the Ferraris lost control on Turn Twenty-two, slamming into the wall.

Before any of the front runners had made it back to the pits to change tyres, the safety car was deployed.

Suddenly, Sabatino was laughing. The field was completely bunched up, thus reducing the gap between her and Aston in P1. Not only that, she was the only runner on intermediates – while none of the other cars were permitted to switch their tyres until Race Control reopened the pit lane.

Two laps later the lights on the safety car went out – meaning they were racing again.

Less than three after that, Sabatino was twenty-five seconds clear of the field, Aston having pitted the moment he could but still losing out to Luciano, who had managed to get in and out again in front of him.

Sabatino romped home at the end of the Singapore Grand Prix by over thirty seconds clear of Luciano in second. Aston was third with Cunzer putting in a late surge to finish in the points, in P5. Adi Barrantes made it to P8.

This was encouraging news for Sabatino in the Drivers' Championship. Enhanced by the points being tapered, her lead was now extended from two points to six – her 66 to Aston's 60. Luciano's eight points for second kept him in third, but in closer touch with 58.

People dismissive of Sabatino's Monaco success as a rookie fluke had to credit her, now, with true all-round motor racing skill – evidenced by her phenomenal equanimity under the pressure, her tactical opportunism, and her brilliance of racing in the rain.

The Sabatino band wagon was rolling once again.

But not for long.

FORTY-FOUR

It all happened an hour after the chequered flag.

'I've been summoned to Race Control,' said Nazar sounding surprised. 'Are we concerned about anything to do with the race?' he asked his two race engineers.

'Not that we're aware of,' replied Treadwell.

Nazar made his way to Race Control. As well as the rain, which showed no sign of letting up, the humidity was oppressive. The sensation of all-over dampness was impossible to shake off.

When Nazar arrived through the dark he was met by one of the stewards and shown into a side room harshly lit by the bluish glare of fluorescent light. Someone he wasn't expecting to see was there waiting: Bo San Marino.

'Mr President? What a surprise.'

San Marino, far from radiating his 1950s movie star contentment and charm, looked concerned and uncomfortable. 'Come in, Tahm. Please take a seat.'

There was a period of silence from the FIA President. Finally, he said: 'I'm afraid we have a problem,' and slowly placed an envelope bearing the FIA logo on the glass and chrome coffee table between them. 'Massarella have lodged an official complaint. We have to take the issue seriously, not least because of the precedent to their allegations.'

Nazar was surprised and deeply troubled by *any* accusation. He was equally distracted by how ill at ease San Marino appeared to be. 'What are they alleging?' he asked calmly without picking up the letter.

'Unauthorized use of their intellectual property.'

'What?'

'It's all in there,' said San Marino, laying his hand on the envelope.

Nazar, in his precise Indian lilt, said calmly: 'But that's absurd. You can't be taking their bullshit seriously.'

'We are – we have to – given the supporting testimony we've received.'

'From whom?'

'Andy Backhouse.'

Nazar pulled a face of resigned exasperation.

'He, now, represents an authoritative whistle-blower – a credible source. You can see why we would *have* to take Massarella's allegation seriously?'

Hunch-shouldered against the rain, Nazar scuttled back through the dark to the Ptarmigan headquarters. Inside the motor home his team members were already there, two of them equally soaked by the continuing downpour.

'We've been served,' declared Nazar.

'*What?*' blasted Treadwell incredulously.

'Massarella have lodged a formal complaint against us.'

'For what?' asked Sabatino heatedly.

'Don't know yet – I'll read it to you,' with which he opened the envelope and extracted the letter.

Mr Tahm Nazar
Ptarmigan Formula One

Dear Mr Nazar

Summons: Hearing before the World Motor Sport Council

The FIA has received a complaint against Ptarmigan F1 from the Massarella Formula One Team. They assert that Ptarmigan has received confidential designs developed by Massarella and that Ptarmigan has used these to its own advantage. The design in question relates to the spiral surfaces on the front wing first recorded on Ptarmigan cars at the Belgian Grand Prix in Spa-Francorchamps this season.

If confirmed, such conduct would be in direct contravention of the International Sporting Code. The FIA is suitably concerned by these assertions that it is demanding Ptarmigan account for its actions.

Your team is called to an Extraordinary Meeting of the WMSC to be held on 25th July at the FIA headquarters, 8 Place de la Concorde, Paris, to answer the allegations. We would ask you to submit a Statement of Facts and responses to the following points no later than two weeks before the hearing:

1. When did Ptarmigan conceive of the spiral surfaces for their front wing?
2. Please submit all the design, development and testing records relating to the spiral surfaces.
3. Please identify all your members of staff who were involved in the design, development and testing of the spiral surfaces.
4. Please confirm, in written statements from anyone concerned, what contact took place between Ptarmigan members of staff and Massarella this season. Where Ptarmigan personnel did make contact with Massarella, please list all the occasions, venues and the nature of such meetings.

Yours sincerely

San Marino

President
Fédération Internationale de l'Automobile

'What the fuck are they talking about? How can they be serious about those *spiral surfaces*?' yelled Treadwell. 'Those are *our* Fibonacci Blades.'

'This is bloody ridiculous,' said an incandescent Sabatino. 'How the hell does Massarella get away with this bullshit with the FIA – when the FIA flatly refused to take our evidence of sabotage any further?'

'I quite agree, Remy,' answered Nazar. 'But San Marino *has* taken these allegations seriously – because of the testimony on which they're based.'

'Whose?'

Nazar paused, almost bracing himself. 'Andy Backhouse's.'

Sabatino looked like she was fit to burst. 'The *bastard*,' she yelled. 'The *bastard*.'

'When's the hearing again?' asked Treadwell.

'25th July.'

'A month's time.'

'Three days after the Chinese Grand Prix.'

'Christ, what do you suppose the topic of conversation will be in Shanghai?' offered Treadwell rhetorically. 'What the hell's this going to do to the Mandarin Telecom deal?'

Matt Straker chose this moment to rejoin the discussion. 'At the risk of getting my head bitten off,' he said, looking Sabatino directly in the eye, 'I believe a hearing with the FIA should be welcomed by us as good news.'

The team in the motor home fell silent, almost in shock. His pre-emptive caveat seemed to have worked, at least with Sabatino. Her reaction to his counter-intuitive comment was a semi-apologetic smile. 'How could this *possibly* be good news?' she asked more calmly than he expected, but still conveying considerable disbelief.

Straker smiled back. He had wanted to clear their air, and had made a previous offer to do so – which Sabatino had not taken up. Now, alluding to the tension between them – light-heartedly in a public forum – was addressing their issues without seeming to make things worse.

'Tell me,' he asked her directly, 'do we steal things as a rule?'

Sabatino frowned. 'Of course not!'

'So a public hearing with the FIA would allow us to vindicate ourselves, right out in the open. Massarella will look ridiculous when they are unable to prove anything. This hearing will have another big advantage. It will allow us to bring up all the sabotage bollocks

Massarella have been levelling at us. It could, actually, be the only viable way to end Massarella's interventions – once and for all.'

Sabatino's complex expression suggested that she had registered some strands of Straker's thinking.

Treadwell, on the other hand, wasn't convinced. 'That doesn't make any sense,' he said. 'Why would they be doing this – why would they make this claim without any proof? Massarella *must* have a case!'

Straker shook his head. 'Van Der Vaal is motivated by vanity and hurt pride. This is all about the media attention on commercial and financial success shifting – from him – to Ptarmigan. Which means part of it's about Mandarin Telecom. Van Der Vaal's ego is so big he'd do this simply to rubbish Ptarmigan's name and image. It's a spoiling tactic. If he can fling enough shit, he'll damage us – by frightening off the Chinese.'

'Whatever,' said Treadwell. 'It's pretty obvious the Chinese will be frightened off by this anyway, so Van Der Vaal's plan of shit-flinging is going to work.'

'Not if I can help it, Ollie,' said Straker, but was immediately distracted from elaborating: his phone was ringing. Looking down at the caller ID, he lifted the phone up and announced to the room: 'Quartano.'

Everyone's expression changed in an instant.

Straker stood up, moved to leave the meeting, and, trotting down the stairs, let himself out of the motor home into the night.

'Jesus Christ,' blasted Quartano, 'I've just seen your text about the FIA hearing. What the fuck's going on? Are these people at Massarella barking mad?'

To Straker's relief Quartano started to laugh. 'Yes, sir – and I'd like to say to our advantage. I am actually thrilled they're doing this. If we play this correctly, we could encourage them to seriously over-reach themselves. We could use a public hearing to expose them – and draw everyone's attention to their bullshit tactics.'

'I'm glad you see it that way, too, Matt.'

'But, sir, if Massarella are *not* to win by shit-flinging, we've got to keep Mandarin onside. We've got to move fast.'

'Agreed – where are you now?'

'Still in Singapore.'

'Hold on.' Quartano pressed a button on his phone and then another. Straker could hear a pre-stored number being dialled out. It was answered.

'Jean?'

'Mr Quartano. What can I do for you?'

'Sorry to disturb your weekend, but I need us to go to work. First, can you get the plane crewed, fuelled, and ready to fly in an hour?'

'Certainly, sir,' replied his PA without hesitation. 'Where are you going?'

'Singapore then Shanghai.'

'Okay.'

'Second, can you get hold of Stacey Krall?'

While Straker was still on the line, Jean also contacted Dr Chen at Mandarin Telecom and managed to arrange a meeting for 6 p.m. the following day.

'Right, Matt, here's what we're going to do,' concluded Quartano. 'Stay in Singapore overnight. Stacey and I will fly in and pick you up tomorrow morning. We'll all go on to Shanghai together, and break the news to the Chinese face to face. While we're en route, I want us to come up with a plan to deal with these bastards at Massarella. I'm buggered if they're going to cost me $750 million. Between us, I want a bash-it-out-of-the-ground defence and, specifically, I want to give those fuckers at Massarella cause for regret.'

FORTY-FIVE

Despite the negative developments of the evening, Straker was feeling buoyed by the all-round reaction to them. His instinct to welcome a public hearing had thrown Sabatino, but had clearly found favour with Quartano. He had left the team meeting some-what dramatically – to take the call from the Big Man – which no one there would have envied taking. And soon, he had another reason to be pleased.

Straker's value to the team had clearly not been lost on Sabatino.

She made the next move.

Straker had just hung up on arranging the emergency flight to China, when he saw her text message on his phone.

Sorry not to have been in touch sooner. Happy to speak now, if you've got time. R.

Ten minutes later Straker climbed back up the steps into the motor home and found her already sitting, on her own, at the meeting table.

'How did Quartano take the news?' she asked with a hint of sym-pathy in her voice, 'can't have been an easy conversation ... with so much at stake.'

Straker sat at the table across the corner from her. 'He's annoyed, but we've got a plan. He's flying from Heathrow within the hour – to come here. We're going straight on to Shanghai to explain to Man-darin – face to face – what all this means.'

Sabatino smiled supportively before she appeared to stiffen slightly. 'I am aware we've had an issue since Monza,' she said neutrally.

Straker waited for more. He wanted more. He paused, looking to see if she was prepared to say anything substantial.

After nearly fifteen seconds of silence, she relented. 'We were under pressure. The car wasn't performing. I'd just had a rough ride with the stewards. Massarella were coming at us again, with no sign of any retaliation from us. I was tired of it all.'

He remained impassive. Finally, Straker said: 'I was – and still am – gutted at not being able to see them off. It remains a matter of professional discomfort to me. Even so, there was no call for your outburst.'

Sabatino's face conveyed a hint of mocking condescension. 'You're offended by being treated like that by a woman.'

Straker's tone was commanding: 'No, Remy – none of your chauvinism crap this time. This has nothing to do with gender. It has everything to do with acting as professionals.'

'Or,' countered Sabatino, still mockingly, 'as one-time lovers?'

Straker smiled and looked down.

Dismissively, she added: 'Intimacy would *have* to make things difficult. I *knew* the Ronnie Scott's night was going to be a mistake.'

Straker looked back up. His mood seemed to change in an instant. 'It might have been a mistake for you,' he said, 'but unforgettable for me,' and found himself smiling. He felt exposed and vulnerable the very moment he did so, but knew immediately that he didn't care.

Sabatino frowned, looking him directly in the eye. Was she gauging him? Reading him?

Within a second or two, her expression changed – markedly. She seemed unable to hold back a vulnerable smile of her own.

The Quartech Falcon flew into Singapore Changi Airport. Straker boarded immediately. Quartano's private jet was on the ground for less than an hour. Refuelled and recrewed, it streaked down the runway and was soon climbing into the eastern sky, heading for China.

On board, Straker was introduced to Stacey Krall, Quartech's Head of Legal Services.

She was nothing like Straker imagined, having spoken to her on the phone. Then, on his return from Spa – talking with her about serving Andy Backhouse with an injunction – he had been struck by her deep voice and seriousness. In person, she was in her thirties, petite, with a roundish face, red-haired, severely dressed but, despite the intense appearance, had a mischievous smile and a wicked sense of humour. For all the grown-up things she had to deal with for the firm, and the unimaginable pressure Quartano must put her under from time to time, Straker was impressed by her calmness.

Quartano wasted no time. 'Right, where are we?'

'Here's the letter from the FIA,' said Straker.

Krall took it and read it intently.

When she'd finished she asked Straker: 'What are your thoughts?'

He replied: 'First, the team is adamant this is completely ground-less. For some reason, Massarella's allegations get traction with the FIA while ours don't.'

Straker then asked: 'What must Massarella prove – to make this allegation stick?'

'They've pretty much got to prove a physical handover or transfer of the design. If they only reference an *idea* for the blades, they'd have a job to prove it in law. That should be the principle part of our case. Anyway, let me illustrate this more fully by setting up the framework for the statement of facts we've been asked for.'

Krall spent an hour on her laptop sitting at the small desk in the sumptuous cabin. At the end of that time she printed off a couple of copies of her draft.

'Excellent,' replied Straker.

'I take it you'll be organizing all this, Matt?' Krall asked. 'How long before you'll have collated this stuff?'

'I'll get on to the team and have them start each element of it immediately. Will you also be drafting the statement our people should sign to confirm no contact with Massarella?'

'Sure. Mr Q?' she asked, addressing him as he worked at his own desk in the cabin. 'The sabotage by Massarella – are we planning to launch a counter-claim against them? The forum of the World Council would be an appropriate place to hit back.'

Quartano seemed to ponder this. 'Let's pull together the work to do so, but I can't make that call until we've seen Mandarin tomorrow. If we've clearly blown it with the Chinese, we'll hit Massarella with everything we can think of. If Mandarin Telecom are still talking to us after this, though, then probably not; counter-claiming might just stir everything up and appear undignified.'

'Fine, but I'll draft a framework for that too – just in case it's needed.'

Quartano nodded in affirmation.

'Matt,' she said, 'once it's all together, we'll take these responses and go to see Oscar Brogan.'

'And he is?'

'Quartech's QC. We'll be briefing him to represent us in Paris at the hearing.'

'Good,' said Quartano hearing how the response was taking shape. 'Now you've heard all about it, Stacey, what's your take on this case?'

'We need to take it seriously, however bogus we believe this allegation might be. The FIA has a range of surprisingly punitive powers, and can levy some pretty hefty fines.'

'How hefty?'

'I've been through the Statutes and, for an incident like this, anything up to $100 million.'

Straker was surprised at his own reaction to the conversation with Sabatino before leaving Singapore. Relief was the main sensation – that the air might have been cleared. Except that that didn't seem to be all.

During the flight, though, he was too busy to think about much more than their hearing at the FIA. He spent the following hour on the jet's dedicated email link, sending instructions to various members of the Ptarmigan team – delegating the compilation of material to populate Stacey Krall's statement of facts.

Just before the Quartech Falcon began its descent into Shanghai, the three of them had lunch together.

'Have you decided how to play this with the Chinese?' Straker asked.

Quartano inhaled. 'More or less. Above all, we've got to prevent Mandarin Telecom from losing face over any embarrassment our hearing might cause them.'

'How do you do that? Do we apologize? Do we withdraw unilaterally from the negotiations? Do we give *them* the opportunity to withdraw?'

'There are, I expect, two levels to this,' replied Quartano. 'There's the personal level – between Dr Chen and myself. I need to demonstrate my readiness to shoulder responsibility and honour his exposure to Quartech. And then there's the public level – of how Quartech takes responsibility, so as to protect Mandarin from any embarrassment.'

'Doesn't this kind of boxing and coxing tire you?' asked the lawyer.

Quartano smiled. 'Not in the slightest. Quartech may be a vast multinational conglomerate, but whatever institution or government we do business with, the decision to buy from us is always made by a human being. Unless we remember, that – above everything else – we will miss out. Badly. Understanding how people think – how they make their decisions – is critical to making a sale and keeping them as a client in future. The Chinese may formalize these considerations more than other cultures, but we all know that nobody, wherever they come from, likes to *lose face*. Nobody likes to be embarrassed. Other people might call it something else, or not have a name for it at all, but the dynamic of human interaction is exactly the same the world over. I love dealing with the Chinese for this simple reason: their protocols for doing things are far, far clearer than anybody else's. Those who adopt an informal approach to negotiations, and profess to a free and easy attitude, are very often the people who are the most difficult to deal with.'

'So what's your game plan for the two levels?' asked Straker with a curious smile.

'Very simple. I'm going to imagine I am Dr Chen. How would I want this to be handled if I were him?'

Quartano, Straker and Krall made it through Shanghai to Pudong and pulled up in front of the headquarters of Mandarin Telecom. Registering at reception, the Quartech party was escorted to the lifts and up to the office of Dr Chen, the CEO. On the forty-eighth floor, his office was as remarkable as the first time they had seen it, with its astonishing views out over Shanghai. There was another haze hanging over the city, this time in the early evening sun.

'Dr Chen,' said Quartano deferentially, as he was shown into his office. 'Thank you for seeing me. I was anxious to inform you personally, and immediately, of a development with Ptarmigan and to apologize for the embarrassment this may cause you.'

Dr Chen, retaking his seat behind his desk, held his expression more inscrutably than usual.

'Ptarmigan has been accused of something – of which we are not guilty – and we have been asked to account for ourselves in a public hearing. I am here to offer you our unconditional withdrawal from our negotiations and to make a public apology to you, your board, and employees for the difficulties we might cause you.'

Dr Chen, very quietly, asked what the allegations involved.

Quartano asked Straker to explain.

At the end, Dr Chen said: 'And you believe that Ptarmigan is blameless?'

'Yes, sir,' replied Quartano.

'And that you can successfully defend this?'

'Yes, sir,' said Krall.

Dr Chen sat still and mulled this for a moment. 'Who is the party making the allegation?'

'The Massarella Formula One Team, sir.'

'That's Mr Van Der Vaal, isn't it – the man from South Africa?' asked Dr Chen.

'Yes sir.'

'I believe you introduced me to him in Monaco.'

Quartano nodded.

For the first time Dr Chen smiled. It transformed his face. 'I remember him well. A charming man, as I recall.'

Dominic Quartano was relieved by Dr Chen's philosophical and pragmatic approach to the FIA hearing, and that everything with Mandarin could still be on track. But he wanted to make one final gesture.

'Dr Chen,' said Quartano, 'I am concerned – for you, sir – about the PR consequences of our timing. If we announce our contract, immediately ahead of a key public hearing, it could prompt adverse and damaging press coverage for Mandarin Telecom.'

Dr Chen acknowledged Quartano's sensitivity with a small inclination of his head. 'What do you propose?'

'I would feel happier, for you and your team, if we postponed the signing ceremony, previously scheduled to be held here in Shanghai during the weekend of the Chinese Grand Prix.'

Quartano was well aware that this gesture, which he intended to be magnanimous, was also a huge gamble.

If the deal was postponed once, how much easier would it be to postpone it again – if not then permanently – should the FIA hearing go the wrong way?

FORTY-SIX

Straker made it home midway through the following day. He was glad to be back, despite the emptiness of his flat. Collapsing into the bath, he put on 'Blue Rondo à la Turk'. The dissonant energy of the 9/8 signature was hardly restful. But that's what he wanted – to help stimulate him. To help him stir up all that was going on.

His mind was soon whirring.

It was buzzing with the FIA letter, the hearing, the effect of all that on Sabatino, Dr Chen, Quartano's brilliant handling of the meeting with Mandarin, Sabatino, the work needed to prepare for the hearing, what Massarella was playing at, Remy Sabatino – and all the work he still had to do.

Not long afterwards, tiredness got the better of him. He managed to sink into a sleep – deep enough to save him from his troubles. Indeed, he didn't wake *himself* up the next morning – the first time that had happened in he couldn't remember how long. Straker slept right through, woken instead by an external factor: the bleep of an incoming text.

And it made an instant difference to his day.

His Morgan had arrived – and would he ring to arrange collection? Needing to be up at the Ptarmigan factory that morning anyway, and Henley being en route, Straker dressed as quickly as he could and left the flat. He took the train, and made it to the showroom by mid-morning.

Straker revelled in the car the moment he saw it – and felt immediately fulfilled in his choice. Connaught Green. Bonnet louvres. Wire wheels. Walnut dash. Pale leather seats and trim. Even the new-car smell inside exceeded his expectations.

On a near-perfect summer morning – with blue skies, no cloud and virtually no wind – Straker drove his brand-new Morgan

Roadster up and out of Henley and headed off through the beech woods of Nettlebed. With the top down, he could not imagine a more engaging way to enjoy The Road. Changing down, he accelerated off a long sweeping left-hander towards Huntercombe, and congratulated himself on the power and torque of his car's 3.7 litre V6. He popped his Dave Brubeck CD into the player and wallowed in the saxophone of 'Take Five' – on repeat – all the way to Shenington. Straker delighted in the temporary escape of his car.

But the effects didn't last long.

Reaching the Ptarmigan factory just before lunch, he met Nazar and Treadwell in the team principal's office immediately upon arrival.

'I've discussed the hearing and our submission to the FIA with Quartech's counsel,' Straker explained. 'I'm sorry about the prospective workload and timeframe we need to follow to prepare for the hearing.'

'You're sorry,' said Treadwell. 'What a ball-aching amount of work.'

'It is,' admitted Straker. 'What material have you been able to dig out on the development of the Fibonacci Blades?'

'A fair amount,' replied Nazar. 'A design history, and a full log of work in the design studio.'

'Excellent. I'm going to need several more things. We'd like every member of staff to sign a statement saying they have had no contact with Massarella people. Also, I'm going to need to see all our employees' email records – particularly any contact with Massarella – and everything sent to us from outside with an attachment.'

'We can do that.'

'Thanks, Tahm. Can you send it all down to me in London?'

'What happens if people have been receiving stuff on home or private emails or numbers?' asked Treadwell.

'Quite,' said Straker. 'We've no guarantee of finding every piece of communication. If we were the police, it'd be different – we'd have investigative powers and the authority to search premises.'

'Why wouldn't we *want* to bring the police in?' asked Treadwell impatiently. 'Wouldn't that show we had nothing to hide?'

Straker smiled and shook his head. 'The feeling is that doing so would be far too media-worthy. It'd kick off a Spygate-all-over-again media circus. There'd be a press feeding frenzy. I should tell you we've been out to Shanghai to see Mandarin Telecom – to try and keep them onside. Any full-blown media attention around this would see our $750 million down the pan.'

'Why not counter it, now – *with* the power of the law?' asked Treadwell. 'It's going to come out anyway, isn't it – this thing's going to a hearing?'

'Not necessarily. Stacey Krall believes that, if we put together a strong enough case, we could apply to the governing body to strike it out before it ever got to a hearing. So long as there's a chance of handling all this quietly, we should play it straight – for as long as possible.'

'Okay, Matt. You're wearing the stress of this,' said Nazar. 'You've also seen the Chinese reaction first-hand and discussed it all with the lawyers. How long before we'll have pulled together the first draft of the statement of facts?'

'About a week.'

Straker enjoyed his new car all the way back to London. By the time he reached the office in Cavendish Square Karen had pulled off the records of all electronic communication into and out of Ptarmigan during the life of the Fibonacci Blades. Being in spreadsheet form, Straker was able to sort and sift the entries pretty easily. What he found surprised him.

Via email, there were no instances of any electronic communication between Ptarmigan and Massarella. And, by phone, he found exactly the same outcome. Straker challenged and double-checked his findings, even asking for a rerun of all the data. The result – the second time – was exactly the same.

Straker was as sure as he could be. There had been no electronic communication between Ptarmigan and Massarella.

None.

It was baffling. What the hell was Massarella playing at?

They didn't have a case.

Or did they really *have* something – and he'd just missed it?

FORTY-SEVEN

First thing on Monday morning Straker and Krall rode in a London taxi east along the north bank of the Thames towards the City. Stopping before Blackfriars Bridge, they alighted on the Victoria Embankment and made their way through the park and across the cobbles to King's Bench Walk. There, in one of the townhouse-style offices, they climbed the steps under a wrought-iron arch and entered the Temple chambers of Oscar Brogan QC.

As they approached, Krall whispered: 'For the scale of the cases he does, and their contemporary nature – nearly all about Intellectual Property and I.T. – it's hilarious his chambers are so antiquated.'

Straker saw exactly what she meant. It was years since the set had spent any money on the building. Its paintwork looked tired, while the carpets and curtains looked decidedly threadbare. It even smelled fusty. An elegant Persian runner led them along the corridor from the front door, but the wooden floor was showing through it in some places. Within the so-called reception area Straker and Krall were asked to take a seat. The upholstery had seen better days, the springs in Straker's chair giving way substantially as he sat down. Only the pictures and books seemed to have been favoured. There were several attractive landscapes, in oil, while a floor-to-ceiling bookcase was jam-packed with apparently brand-new leather-bound legal volumes.

Brogan's clerk apologized for the delay and offered them some coffee.

'So sorry to keep you waiting,' said Brogan in his powerful, well-enunciated voice as they were shown into his rooms half an hour later. Brogan was six feet two tall – the same as Straker – slim, longish swept-back grey hair, with an upright bearing. Brogan had presence. On a break from a trial in the Royal Courts of Justice, he was still wearing bands, the two white tabs hanging down from the collar.

'Now Stacey, this is an encouraging piece of work,' said Brogan as he referred to their statement of facts. 'Very comprehensive.'

'Good to hear. Any thoughts at this stage?'

'Yes,' he said, his voice sounding ready to reach the back of a courtroom at any moment. 'With a case like this, the judge – I know this is going to be heard at the World Motor Sports Council, but you know what I mean – has to be sure there was physical contact and that documents were exchanged. With the statements you've collated, and the records for telephone and email traffic, there seems to have been no such contact. Your defence, therefore, leaves little to be desired.'

Brogan closed the cover of the document. 'However,' he went on with a tone that instantly dampened the mood, 'in any adversarial hearing, I always advise my clients that, even with a cast-iron case, things can happen in court. There can always be surprises – peripheral issues or evidence can turn a case completely on its head. As a result, I never give the chances of success – in a trial – higher than seventy per cent.' Brogan paused to look both his visitors in the eye. 'Please be realistic. Something unexpected could happen.' Another pause. 'That said, I do believe your defence is strong.'

Straker absorbed the caveat. 'If that's your *realistic* view,' he said, 'have we at least strengthened any application we might make to the governing body to strike out the case – before it gets to a hearing?'

Brogan nodded. 'On the back of these findings and assertions, I'd say, certainly. I'd be happy to draft an application?'

Straker nodded Quartech's instruction to proceed.

'While on the subject of next steps,' said the barrister, 'can we talk for a moment about the counter-claim?'

'Mr Quartano is not pursuing this pro tem,' Straker explained. 'Ptarmigan has a very promising sponsorship deal with Mandarin Telecom. We've just signed an MOU. We have already felt it necessary to postpone signing the contract, because of the FIA hearing. We'd rather not stir things up by complicating this legal distraction – so long as that deal's still viable.'

'That's clearly a business consideration,' replied Brogan with reluctant understanding. 'I would be keen to mount the counter-claim, though – given the evidence you've amassed. I mean, let's just think about Mr Backhouse, for a moment – and about going after him. That whole incident with Ms Sabatino's helmet – the jamming bug mysteriously disappearing as he walked it from the truck to the workshop – is all pretty odd, not to mention his defection to Massarella? I'd love the chance to cross-examine Mr Backhouse.'

'That's good to know,' said Straker, 'except – for the time being – we're content to play a straight bat.'

'We'll keep the counter-claim in the drawer for now, then,' said the barrister resignedly.

Before even the close of business that day, Oscar Brogan QC sent Straker and Krall his draft application to the FIA to strike out Massarella's claim of industrial espionage against Ptarmigan. Given its clarity, the affidavit required no amendment. It was readily signed off by Quartech's in-house counsel.

The application was officially filed by the barrister with the governing body first thing the following morning.

There was no indication, though, of how long the FIA would take to decide and respond.

PART FIVE

JIADING

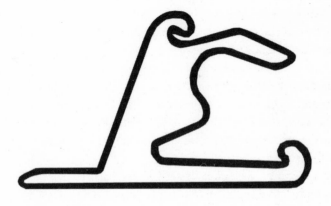

FORTY-EIGHT

After Singapore, the Formula One world moved east – to Shanghai.

At the Chinese Grand Prix, Ptarmigan's mood was soured by the threat to their sponsorship deal. All around Shanghai, and the circuit, Mandarin Telecom hoardings were visible in nearly every direction – a constant reminder of just what was at stake for them. But that opportunity with the Chinese company seemed completely dependent, now, on the case overhanging them with the FIA, its shadow having already caused the signing of the contract to be postponed. There was no escape from the apprehension felt by every member of the team.

Making things worse was Van Der Vaal's overt gloating in the media. He gave countless interviews, savaging Ptarmigan's misconduct. His allegations *had* to be valid, he claimed, otherwise why else would the FIA have taken them up and called for a public hearing?

Straker hoped Ptarmigan would find solace out on the track. But that, too, could invite more trouble. If Sabatino and Cunzer showed themselves to be competitive this weekend, wouldn't that prompt further action from Massarella or Van Der Vaal, given the bullshit they had already had thrown their way? For all these reasons, Straker remained vigilant.

Coming as an added blow, Lambourn had truly hit top form in China. Their upgraded aero package absolutely found its forte on the Jiading circuit. Paddy Aston was eight tenths up in Qualifying Two and, in the top-ten shootout, notched up a lead of nine tenths.

Remy Sabatino found her Ptarmigan hard to fault, and was on song, too. Which made the frustration worse. The Ptarmigan was simply outclassed by Lambourn. There seemed to be nothing more Sabatino could do, however hard she pushed.

Her one consolation was that Massarella were struggling with tyres. Every time a Massarella came into the pits, the Ptarmigan team focused their CCTV shots on the graining – even blistering – of Massarella's rubber, and took some comfort from seeing the extent of their problems.

Whatever comfort Ptarmigan might have drawn from that, though, everything changed at the start of the race.

Sabatino's plans went awry on the very first lap.

Starting second on the grid behind Aston, she seemed to get away well, but still found Luciano's Massarella, Helli Cunzer, and a Mercedes all over her gearbox approaching Turn One. Into that bottleneck, an aggressive move by the Massarella forced Sabatino to take evasive action at the last minute. She jabbed at the brakes to avoid a collision. Was she overreacting – anxious not to repeat her bump with him in Monza? A puff of blue smoke rose from under her front right. Sabatino swore loudly inside her helmet. She held her nerve, position, and onto – she thought – her eight points.

Having set themselves up for a one-stop strategy, she was relieved to have held her position. The plan had been for her to keep up with Aston and, when his two-stop strategy forced him to pit for the second time, she could then hope to take the lead and bring it home.

Except that exiting Turn Four on that first lap, and accelerating into the following long straight, she felt quickly what she dreaded. Having locked-up the front right – and skidded it along the surface of the track into Turn One – she had scrubbed a bad flat spot into the rubber. As she built up speed, that wheel started to vibrate – feeling like a fifty-pence piece – the flat spot juddering with every rotation.

She hoped – desperately – that this abnormality would wear itself out as the race went on.

But it only got worse.

Sabatino found her vision blurring, even at the lower speeds – and that, on the immaculate surface of the Jiading circuit, hardly ever happened.

Ten laps on, she radioed Treadwell in the pit lane: 'It's no good,' she said, her voice clearly sounding vibrato. 'I'm going to have to pit and change tyres. I can hardly see.'

Sabatino pitted, changed boots. Even though she took on fuel for an additional ten laps, she wasn't going to be able to complete the remaining three-quarters of the race without stopping again. She would have to stop for a second time – which was going to cost her badly.

Feeding herself back in, down in P10, she built up the car's temperatures to their optima and then, coming as some consolation, she found her mojo – even managing to keep up with the Lambourn in lap times. Five laps later, as the fuel load lightened and the tyres bedded in, she started recording successive fastest laps.

Into the last fifteen, the cars completed their final pit stops. Sabatino found that, little by little, she had worked her way back into contention. Amazingly, there was a chance, now, even of a podium. Except that to take it, she would have to overtake her teammate, Helli Cunzer, in P3. There were no team orders to have him move over. And the last thing she wanted was to go head-to-head with him and run the risk of having a bump, taking each other off.

Even though her Ptarmigan was running like it was on rails, Sabatino had to settle for fourth. With those five points, though, she would still keep her lead of the Championship on 71. Aston, winning Shanghai and picking up ten points, was now only one point behind her on 70. Luciano, making P2 here and picking up eight points, was up to 66.

All nerve-rackingly tight.

Any one of Sabatino, Aston or Luciano could – mathematically – still win the title. They were all so closely bunched it wasn't going to be decided at the inaugural London Grand Prix in two weeks' time, either. This season, as nearly every year, was going to see the Formula One drama played out to the very end. Brazil, as so often before, looked like it would be the final showdown.

But that was on the track.

There was a significant amount going on – off it – which could still ruin everything.

Not least as Ptarmigan's faith in their defence in the case was about to take a serious knock.

Oscar Brogan's application to the FIA to strike out the claim against them was denied, almost by return.

Straker was now deeply concerned.

How was their evidence and argument not strong enough to succeed?

What *was* Massarella asserting that Ptarmigan didn't know about?

FORTY-NINE

The FIA hearing was upon them.

The night before, the Ptarmigan team travelled to Paris and checked into the Hotel Splendid Etoile, looking directly out on the Arc de Triomphe. Were it not for the spectre that hung over them all, they might have enjoyed the majesty of where they were – the setting, the location, the views.

Straker remained agitated. Unnerved. He – they, Ptarmigan – had been able to demonstrate to the FIA that they had not been able to find any evidence of wrongdoing to substantiate Massarella's claim of industrial espionage. At all.

On the face of it they were clean.

And yet their affidavit to that effect had achieved no traction: the FIA still held that Ptarmigan had a case to answer.

Didn't that mean, then, that Massarella *had* presented substantial evidence of their own?

What was it?

The Ptarmigan party met for breakfast.

'As discussed on the train coming over,' said the Team's silk, Oscar Brogan QC, 'I'll act as our chairman in the hearing. This is not a courtroom – so none of us should feel under that kind of pressure.'

'No,' said Nazar, 'but we are, to coin a phrase, in the courtroom of public opinion. The charge shouts louder than the verdict.'

'We're as certain as we can be that we're in the clear,' said Straker. 'There's a lot we can gain by making ourselves look reasonable and measured – rising above the bullshit.'

'Precisely,' said Brogan. 'Talking of public opinion, a key part of today is how we handle the inevitable media onslaught. The press loves this kind of bun-fight. Remy's involvement will make it all the more intense. There will no doubt be an unedifying media scrum outside the FIA building.'

'We shouldn't scurry in,' offered Straker. 'We should wait for the right moment for Remy and Tahm to turn and face the bank of cameras – looking as calm as possible. The press are going to want to publish pictures, whatever they manage to shoot. Much better to give them some with body language that indicates a little dignity and poise, and that we've got nothing to hide.'

The party, to settle itself and freshen up for the hearing, walked down the Champs-Élysées. On any other occasion they would have savoured the experience – the view down the length of the boulevard and avenue of clipped horse chestnut trees towards the Louvre – and enjoyed the sunshine that was already hinting at a perfect summer's morning.

Reaching the edge of Place de la Concorde, they saw what they were in for – even at some distance away. Already parked, two or three deep around the northern edge of the square, were media and TV vans with enormous satellite dishes on their roofs pointing to the heavens. There was a police cordon, holding back a public throng – all trying to snatch a glimpse of some of the world's best known and glamorous sports personalities. Inside the police cordon was a jostling pack of journalists, TV cameras and sound recordists, with a copse of furry microphones held aloft on the end of long poles.

Hyenas. The media pack looked and sounded like a bunch of hyenas.

The Ptarmigan team began their approach towards the mêlée gathered in front of 8 Place de la Concorde. The headquarters of the International Automobile Federation was in an imposing building. Above them stretched the magnificent Palladian Trouard façade, its honey-coloured stone catching the early morning sun. It radiated grandeur: two portico-like ends were each supported by four columns. Twelve Corinthian columns were ranged in between. Eye-catching pilasters, ballustrading and baroque detail rose above a plinth-like, street-level arcade. Sabatino's face registered heightened unease, almost induced by the building alone.

Approaching the media-surrounded entrance, the noise began in earnest. Straker stood to the outside of Sabatino, shielding – but not hiding – her from the throng.

'REMY! REMY! REMY!'

Flash guns were fired off like a fusillade. The noise seemed to become a roar as everyone shouted – demanding that she look their way.

At the appropriate moment, Straker looked over to Sabatino, asked if she was ready, and, seeing her nod, turned her and Nazar round slowly to face the wall of media.

Their senses were almost overwhelmed – virtually blinded by the flashes, and nearly deafened by the crescendo of shouting.

Sabatino took a couple of deep breaths. Then, as planned, she smiled broadly, waved, and began slowly panning through the arc of three hundred-odd journalists, giving each one of them a head-on shot for their still cameras and B-roll VT. Extraordinarily, it seemed to work. The frenzied yelling seemed to abate. Giving the journalists something of what they wanted just about turned the mood.

It might be an altogether different story on the way out.

Sabatino, facing such a wall of people, cameras and noise, would have been forgiven for looking concerned or defensive. Calmly, without cockiness, she managed to convey a powerful sense of dignified composure.

After thirty or forty seconds, which seemed an age, Sabatino turned away and walked towards the entrance of the FIA. Once through the blue doors with their elegant panels of leaded lights, they found relative privacy inside the building.

'Well played,' Straker said. 'That was utterly composed. Don't know how you do it,' he added reassuringly.

Without saying anything she merely touched him on the arm in thanks.

The Ptarmigan party was greeted by an FIA official. They were soon led through to a waiting room. 'You'll be called in at around ten o'clock,' the member of staff declared. 'Please help yourself to refreshments.'

The waiting proved agony, despite the considerable calm provided from time to time by Brogan.

Ten o'clock came and went.

Ten-thirty.

Eleven.

When the hell were they going to be called in?

Finally, at a quarter to twelve, the door opened and another official asked them politely to come through.

As they walked into the Council Chamber their level of apprehension and stress increased markedly. Entering midway down the long wall of the long thin room, they were confronted by a sea of faces around the huge rectangular table arrangement. While there was a sizeable hollow area in the middle of the tables, there was very little space around the outside, reduced further by a row of people sitting on chairs against one of the long walls.

Directly opposite them as they entered was Bo San Marino, the President of the FIA, flanked by the Deputy President on one side and the former President of the FIA, currently President of the Senate, on the other.

Further away from the President, on either side, were five of the seven Vice-Presidents and thirteen of the seventeen other members of the Council.

At the right-hand end of the table Straker spotted Joss MacRae, head of the commercial rights holder.

San Marino, at least, had the courtesy to stand as the Ptarmigan party entered the room. He welcomed them and indicated three seats at the table directly opposite him. These, it was explained, were for the team boss, a driver, and their counsel. He asked that other members of the contingent take a seat behind them, against the back wall.

Straker was amazed there was still chatter around the room. It came as no surprise that MacRae was in full voice.

Now sitting with Treadwell beside him, Straker looked over to his left and down the length of the stark unadorned room to one of the short ends. There, he could see a plate-glass partition. Through its greenish tint Straker observed a small room beyond, packed full of what he supposed were journalists. The press gallery? More like *les tricoteuses*, he thought.

Straker took in the rest of the room.

It was austere. There were no pictures hanging anywhere. The only objects to break the large expanse of white wall were two plasma screens, one mounted opposite him, above San Marino's head, and the second above his own. These appeared to be hooked up to some form of video-conferencing facility. Several grainy faces appeared jerkily in their own little windows.

Straker could not help but wonder who all these people were around the table. They were all of a fairly obvious stamp – elderly, portly and male. Indeed, he could only see one woman among them. In his sweep of the Chamber, Straker spotted the backs of the Massarella contingent, already seated at the table; they were over to Straker's left, down towards the press gallery: Eugene Van Der Vaal was flanked by one of the team's drivers, Simi Luciano, and an Italian-looking man in a suit.

San Marino quietly called for order. 'Gentlemen, and lady member of the Council. We are now ready to begin this Extraordinary Meeting of the World Motor Sport Council. Can I ask you, Tahm, to introduce your companions here today?'

'Certainly, Mr President. I am joined by Ms Remy Sabatino, Ptarmigan's number one driver, and Mr Oscar Brogan QC, Ptarmigan's legal counsel. Behind me we have Mr Oliver Treadwell, Strategy Director for the racing team and currently Ms Sabatino's race engineer, and Colonel Matt Straker, a representative from Quartech International, Ptarmigan's owner.'

'Thank you, Tahm. You have had our letter and you understand our reasons for calling this meeting? May I start by stating this Council's jurisdiction in these matters? This hearing is conducted under

Article 27 of the FIA Statutes which empowers the World Motor Sport Council to assess and, where appropriate, directly impose sanctions provided for under the International Sporting Code.'

San Marino paused and looked up at Tahm Nazar over his half-moon spectacles, as if to invite a response.

'Mr President, Ptarmigan accepts the jurisdiction of this hearing.'

'Thank you, Tahm. On to our business. This hearing relates to the allegation levelled at Ptarmigan by the Massarella Formula One Team that Ptarmigan benefited, unlawfully, from Massarella's intellectual property.'

'We are aware of these allegations, Mr President,' replied Brogan, taking over as the front man for Ptarmigan. 'My client is of course here to deny vigorously – and refute – any such assertion. I trust that you, sir, and the Council have received our statement of facts?'

'Indeed.'

'We have also prepared a counter-claim, here,' said Brogan holding up a document.

San Marino looked a little surprised. 'Mr Brogan,' he said slowly and courteously, 'we have had no prior warning or submission of such a response from your client. I regret the Council cannot receive or acknowledge such a document without due notice.'

Brogan didn't sound surprised by the response. 'I understand, Mr President. I will, nevertheless, draw from elements of my client's counter-claim in our repudiation of Massarella's gratuitous allegations.'

'I am sure you will…'

'…at the very least, Mr President,' said Brogan quickly before San Marino was able to cut him off, 'it should be declared to the Council that my client has approached yourself on two separate occasions so far this season, sir, with concerns of sabotage they believe to have been perpetrated by the Massarella team. The Ptarmigan team, including Mr Straker, who is here today, presented you with their concerns in both Monaco and Spa.'

This was clearly new news to most of the Council members around the table.

'At the Spa meeting,' Brogan went on, 'those assertions were presented to you in the presence of Mr Joss MacRae.'

Again there were murmurings around the table at this disclosure.

Straker recognized the canny game their barrister was playing. Brogan wasn't answering the charges, yet – but was trying to throw up enough dust to show that this was not a clear-cut, one-sided situation.

San Marino levelled his attention at Brogan. 'I thank you for bringing that to the attention of the meeting,' he said. 'Can we revert to the business of our agreed agenda – your client's statement of facts and the answers to the FIA's questions?' This time, it was San Marino who kept talking – to retain control of the floor: 'In addressing Massarella's allegations, I would like to refer to your client's answer to Question 1: that Ptarmigan first came up with the design for the spiral surfaces – or the Fibonacci Blades, as I believe your client calls them, on the Monday after the Bahrain Grand Prix, May 25th?'

'That is correct, Mr President. We have, in the statement of facts under Tab 1, set out a schedule of our development of this device from inception to its presence on the car in Belgium.'

There was a theatrical grunt from Van Der Vaal. Without an invitation to speak, the Massarella boss growled: 'We have proof of development of this device as long ago as March 12th.'

There were mutterings around the table – both at the intervention and the information imparted.

San Marino looked mildly irritated. 'Eugene, please, let us conduct this meeting with some order. I will call for comments at the appropriate time.' He paused, looked at Van Der Vaal, and waited – as if to receive some form of acknowledgement of his point. None came.

'Mr President,' said Brogan very quietly. 'May we see some evidence to this claim by Mr Van Der Vaal of 12th March?'

There was a flurry of papers from the Massarella section of the table before a document was passed all the way round – between the council members – to reach San Marino. Repositioning his half-moon glasses, the patrician-looking President read the page indicated by Massarella.

For the first time the room remained quiet while this evidence was assessed. San Marino looked up. 'Mr Brogan, it would appear that Massarella are correct. They do seem to have an earlier start date for their development of these spiral surfaces than Ptarmigan's. Would you like to comment?'

Straker watched Brogan intently to see how he would react to this.

'Certainly, Mr President. The surfaces, we admit, look vaguely similar. However, is it not possible for two people or two organizations to come up with the same idea concurrently but independently? Let us remember that *all* cars are faced with the exact same challenges. The exact same Formula, no less. Are not the exact same problems likely to inspire hugely similar solutions? After all, the way the teams deal with their braking, cooling, aerodynamics, etc., are all remarkably similar, are they not?'

'We accept that, of course, Mr Brogan. But we are considering, today, the possibility that ideas were not developed independently, but that they were actually *transferred.*'

'Indeed, Mr President. Thank you for raising my very next point. Transference. For an idea to be transferred, it needs to have someone to give it and someone to receive it. Can I ask Mr Van Der Vaal who it was in his own organization that supposedly made this idea available in the first place, and presumably breached Massarella's own security systems – and trust – to do so?'

San Marino's face clearly registered the point. 'An interesting observation, Mr Brogan. Eugene, would you like to comment?'

'That's irrelevant, Mr President,' snapped Van Der Vaal. 'In any case that would be a Massarella problem and concern. It has no bearing on the benefits Ptarmigan have derived from our work on the ASD. Can we please focus on that and the violation of Massarella's intellectual property rights?'

'Sorry, Eugene, what did you say? A .. S .. D?'

'Yeah, ASD – *A* .. *S* .. *D*,' repeated Van Der Vaal impatiently. 'Massarella call this the Aero-Spiral Device. You've referred to our innovation as "spiral surfaces". Ptarmigan refer to our idea as Fibonacci Blades.'

'Thank you.' San Marino refocused on the Ptarmigan contingent: 'Mr Brogan, you've made an interesting point about the source of information inside Massarella – one we will put to them later. Can we turn to the evidence that a transfer took place?'

'Certainly, Mr President,' said Brogan. 'To help with this, we were grateful to the FIA for asking Question 4 in your letter, in which you asked my client for details of all contact with Massarella by any of my client's team. If you turn to page 25 of our statement of facts you will see that my client identifies a handful of face-to-face contacts, but they categorically deny any transfer of data, ideas, or intellectual property. Ptarmigan have produced for you comprehensive schedules showing the telephone and email traffic of all other members of staff. There are no records to indicate that there has been *any* electronic communication between Massarella and Ptarmigan.'

'Thank you for the confirmation, Mr Brogan. Eugene,' said San Marino turning to Van Der Vaal. 'Do you wish to comment?'

'Indeed I do,' came a growled reply.

Being behind and to one side of him, Straker only had an oblique view of Van Der Vaal's face. He saw enough to gauge the expression of self-satisfaction as the gruff Afrikaner addressed the President. 'We know that the design for the ASD – this crucial performance-enhancing development – was transferred to Ptarmigan after Bahrain.'

ASD! A memory went off in Straker's head like a thunderclap. Hang on a minute! he screamed to himself: A – S – D!

That was it! He suddenly remembered where he'd seen that acronym before. Hurriedly he pulled Charlotte Grant's iPhone out of his pocket, turned it on and waited impatiently for it to power up. When it finally did, he scrolled through the texts in her inbox.

There!

Yes – there – there it was!

He found the message to Charlie Grant from that mysterious – unidentified – Italian mobile number, which, just as he remembered, referred to this ASD acronym.

No wonder Treadwell had been unable to recognize it when Straker had asked him what this term meant – ASD was clearly one of Massarella's own. Whatever this coincidence meant, Straker had found a connection between proprietary Massarella terminology and Charlie Grant.

Didn't this channel of communication *have* to be the basis of the allegation?

He had to find out more, fast, to have any chance of countering it.

The other end of this text message was that Italian mobile phone number which the researchers in London had tried multiple ways, unsuccessfully, to identify.

How, though, could he identify the other end of this "connection"? And quickly? Being in the very hearing to pass judgment on this matter, they were quite obviously running out of time.

Suddenly Straker had a mischievous thought. Was this really the time to try it?

What the hell! They had little else to go on to defend themselves. And nothing to lose.

Opening up the text message on Charlie's iPhone that referred to ASD, Straker hit Reply. In the space below he typed in his message:

I'M RIGHT BEHIND YOU!

He read it several times as if to make sure he should be doing this.

Four seconds later he pressed Send.

The phone did its thing, pulsing several times before reluctantly dispatching the message.

Straker could now only wait.

His mind whirred. What if the Italian mobile was switched off? Or not manned? Or what if his assumptions were wrong – and this had come from somebody else?

Any of these outcomes would leave Straker none the wiser.

But he hoped for something more.

If the message did "get home", it would have a double effect. The recipient would see a completely unexpected Caller ID, which, under the circumstances, would be a shock – and the message itself might carry a metaphorical meaning all of its own.

Straker waited.

How long would this take?

Then he sensed rather than watched the room intently. Nothing happened. Damn! This wasn't going how he thought it would.

But then – Bingo!

In the row along the table, one of the figures – to the left – suddenly started fidgeting and moving awkwardly in his chair – clearly looking for something in his pocket. After a short wrestle with the layers of his clothing, the figure pulled out his mobile phone.

The Massarella team boss looked down.

Straker, from the side, saw something to behold. Van Der Vaal's eyes widened dramatically.

And then, in almost cartoon-like panic, Van Der Vaal spun round to look down the row of chairs behind him along the back wall. The brutish South African panned along the faces. Straker, holding the phone out of sight below the level of his thigh, was quick enough to have looked away towards the centre of the room before he felt Van Der Vaal's stare wash over him. Through his peripheral vision, Straker soon saw the Massarella boss return his attention to his mobile phone.

Straker had made a connection. A *solid* connection. Not just from Massarella – but from Van Der Vaal *himself* – to Charlie Grant. What now, though? What the hell could this mean? This completely unexpected revelation showed that there *had* been electronic communication between the teams. Didn't that blow their whole defence wide open?

Straker was beside himself.

Grabbing a piece of paper, he leant across and whispered a request to borrow Treadwell's pen. Straker soon started scribbling out a note.

Van Der Vaal, refocusing on the room, was soon back in full flow: 'Mr President, I have a claim – a good claim against Ptarmigan. Our technology, which we have proved we started developing before Ptarmigan, has ended up on their car. Their components aren't just similar to ours,' he said. Then, dripping with Afrikaans pronunciation, he grunted: 'They ... are ... *identical*. How did this happen without Ptarmigan stealing our ideas? That's what this Council should be asking. We are one hundred per cent the victims here. It is un*conscion*able to think that Ptarmigan should not be held to account for this blatant infringement.'

Straker finished scribbling his note. He folded the piece of paper, leant forward, and tapped Brogan on the shoulder. Somewhat taken by surprise, the barrister turned round. He saw Straker offering up the folded paper. Brogan took it. Opening it up the legal counsel read:

Oscar, I've JUST worked out who the Massarella and Ptarmigan contacts were.

Brogan looked round to meet Straker's eye. His face registered surprise, then seemed to search Straker's – as if to verify that he was sure.

Straker nodded and held up Charlie Grant's iPhone as if to provide some form of physical proof.

Turning back round to face the room, Brogan said commandingly: 'Mr President? I am sorry to interrupt. May I ask Council's indulgence to confer with my client for a moment?'

'This is highly irregular, Mr Brogan.'

'I accept that, sir. But a five-minute conversation, in private, might help us all to speed this process along.'

San Marino seemed to sigh. 'Very well. Let us all take a ten-minute recess.'

In the noise of the meeting being adjourned, Brogan stood up and left the table, indicating that the Ptarmigan contingent should follow Straker out of the chamber. They made it back to their waiting room, filed in, and Straker closed the door behind them.

FIFTY

Fifteen minutes later Oscar Brogan was ready to address the hearing of the World Motor Sport Council once again. San Marino called the meeting to order and asked him whether, in the light of his conference with colleagues, Brogan had anything to say.

'Thank you, Mr President, I do. I am not sure how to explain this, sir, but as bizarre as it may sound my client has, during the course of this very hearing, come into new information.'

Oscar Brogan QC, ever the master of controlling a room's attention after thirty years of practice in court, was sure he had the FIA hanging on every word. 'Without prejudicing my client's position, I am prepared to acknowledge a contact within Ptarmigan *who might* – I say again *who might* – have been in contact with someone at Massarella. But only,' he said quickly and loudly to pre-empt the expected hubbub from the Council members, 'if, Mr President, the Council will accept a request to grant my client extra time to re-examine its submission to this Council and prepare to account for itself more fully at a follow-up hearing.'

Brogan conspicuously stopped talking to yield the floor. He had fired his shot – his conditional shot – and believed his statement and request were complex enough to avoid a reflex or snap answer from the governing body.

The room was in uproar. None of this was expected. Few Council meetings – if any – had ever had such a googly bowled at them.

Only one person seemed unfazed by the commotion and complexity of the moment. The 7th Marquis of San Marino retained his gravitas and composure throughout. Calling the meeting to order, the President waited for quiet before he spoke directly to Oscar Brogan.

'I dare say all of us are a little bemused by a claim that your client has come by evidence – if we might call it that – *during this very meeting*. Whatever the trigger, though, your acknowledgement – I'm sorry, your *provisional* acknowledgement – of a Ptarmigan name in contact with Massarella would certainly move this case along and, from the sound of it, give us some much-needed fact on which to base any judgment or action.'

'Thank you, Mr President,' said Brogan in response to the states-man-like summing up. 'So, would the Council be prepared to grant my client additional time to re-present its submission to the FIA under the current allegations?'

San Marino had clearly made up his mind on this but, to ensure collective responsibility, he cast a quick glance around the room as a form of consultation. Facing forward again San Marino said: 'I believe in the interests of equity, the Council would be so moved – but I would add one proviso. That a grant of more time depends entirely on our knowing the name or names in question.'

Straker, sitting against the long wall as before, climbed quickly to his feet and leant forwards to whisper into Brogan's ear. The bar-rister's head could soon be seen nodding.

'Mr President,' said Brogan as Straker sat down, 'my client would like to do so by asking for confirmation from someone here in this meeting.'

San Marino's expression conveyed some surprise. 'Very well, Mr Brogan, but through me – through the Chair – if you please.'

The room fell silent.

'Thank you, Mr President. If Mr Van Der Vaal is not prepared to identify and reveal the source of the leak inside Massarella, will he at least confirm the person who my client now believes was the contact point at Ptarmigan?'

Straker looked straight at Van Der Vaal, who seemed momentar-ily thrown.

'Well, Eugene?' asked San Marino over the continuing noise. 'Will you?'

Van Der Vaal remained looking uneasy. Leaning to his left, he conferred quickly with the rather stiff Italian-looking fellow beside him. The Massarella boss soon straightened up, looked at San Marino, and nodded hesitantly.

Brogan addressed the chair. 'Very well, Mr President. Was the Ptarmigan contact … a Ms Charlotte Grant?'

The room burbled again, but sounded like it wasn't quite sure why. No one present was likely to have heard the name before. But at least a name sounded a little more specific. In search of the next instalment of this story, all eyes around the table soon turned to Eugene Van Der Vaal.

'Well, Eugene,' said San Marino. 'Are you prepared to answer?'

The Massarella boss looked stunned, as if he was trying to weigh up the consequences to him of any possible response.

'Well?' asked the President again. 'Will you give the Council an answer?'

Van Der Vaal conferred again with the thin man beside him.

'Eugene, a Yes or No will do.'

Van Der Vaal sat up straight and looked at San Marino. Finally, after a long pause, the Massarella boss gave the shortest and sharpest of nods.

Chatter broke out around the table. At last, they thought – this might be information that could move things on.

'Mr President,' stated Brogan loudly over the chatter filling the room. 'Thank you. I hardly need point out that this has changed almost everything to do with this case. Mr Van Der Vaal's confirmation has provided genuinely new information to my client. Furthermore, this throws up endless questions,' he said, increasing his volume to emphasize the point. 'How is it that Mr Van Der Vaal, personally, knows the name of the Ptarmigan contact? How *does* he know? *When* did he know? *If* Mr Van Der Vaal knew, why did he not notify Ptarmigan immediately that his team's IP might be being divulged to another team? Indeed, why is this the first time *we*,' he said with a sweep of his hand round the room, 'know anything about it? Most obviously, though, why did Mr Van Der Vaal not do anything to stop it? More particularly, *if* Mr Van Der Vaal knew all about this, and *didn't* do anything to stop it, what was *his* role in the leaks? Mr President, I could go on – these are only the questions I have come up with off the top of my head. We now request, as mentioned before, the opportunity for Ptarmigan to reassess its response and reposition its entire defence to the charges made against it by Massarella.'

'Hang on a minute – not so fast, Mr Brogan,' said Joss MacRae, sniping in from the end of the table. 'This identification of a Ptarmigan employee involved as a contact with Massarella proves that there *is* a case to answer. Moreover, your acceptance of Mr Van Der Vaal's confirmation of this name shows your client's submission to this hearing to have been wholly incomplete – inaccurate – if not misleading.'

There was a new burst of mutterings around the table.

'Not so, sir. Not so,' said Brogan firmly over the noise. 'Mr President, there's an exceptionally good reason why my client could not have been expected to identify Ms Grant as the contact point with Massarella.'

MacRae's face showed a sneer. 'And what is that, Mr Brogan?'

'Because, Mr President, Ms Charlotte Grant … is dead.'

The noise became tumultuous.

Chat and exclamation was coming from every part of the room, even from the assistants and juniors on the chairs against the back wall of the Chamber. No one had expected anything like this.

'I hasten to add, Mr President,' said Brogan over the noise, 'that Charlotte Grant died in circumstances completely unrelated to Formula One.'

San Marino held up his hand to try and calm the chatter.

'That's as maybe, Mr Brogan,' he said loudly. 'However … *however* … thank you … However, we cannot escape the fact that we seem to have confirmed this afternoon – at least – that a member of Ptarmigan staff *was* in contact with Massarella. Her being deceased in no way removes the allegation or the responsibility, Mr Brogan.'

'My client accepts that completely – in principle – Mr President. But I respectfully submit that Ptarmigan could not have been aware of this fact and so my client has not – and could not have – prepared a defence with this individual in mind. As a result, I respectfully submit that no decision that you or this Council might make on this discussion – today – could possibly be regarded as fully-informed, equitable, or just.'

San Marino squinted in one eye as he considered the situation. 'I, as President of this body, am anxious above all to ensure fairness and equity. I am prepared to acknowledge your request on behalf of your client, Mr Brogan. But – *but* – I must ask you to re-present to this Council at the earliest possible opportunity. How long do you believe your client will need to reorganize its defence?'

Brogan conferred with Nazar.

'Sir, when is the FIA Council next due to meet?'

'We have a meeting at the RAC Club in Pall Mall, London, on the Monday after the London Grand Prix. In two weeks' time.'

'In that case, Mr President, might I suggest we have the opportunity of re-presenting to you then?'

'Agreed. We will continue with the enquiry into the allegations of Ptarmigan's industrial espionage on August 9th. This hearing is adjourned until then.'

FIFTY-ONE

Confused and dismayed were the only ways to describe the Ptarmigan delegation as they returned to their room in the FIA headquarters.

'Holy crap,' said Sabatino the moment they had shut the door behind them and were alone. 'How the fuck has this – whatever this is – happened?' she blasted in a more agitated state than Straker had ever seen her before. 'This is going to cost me the Championship, for fuck's sake.' Straker thought she was about to fly at him as she had in Monza.

'Indeed, what the hell is going on here?' asked Nazar accusatorily of Brogan and Straker. 'Where the hell did this Charlie Grant stuff come from? Are we completely out of control?'

Straker spoke calmly, trying to diffuse the tension in the room: 'Not at all,' he said with more conviction than he probably felt. 'Tahm, you've seen the work that's been done. We had no idea there was any contact between Massarella and Ptarmigan. We do *now*. Moreover, we have a name – a name around which to build a proper rebuttal of these ludicrous charges.'

'But that's just it,' Sabatino retorted loudly. 'We have … a *name*. We have just admitted – and had it confirmed by the claimant – in an FIA hearing – that we *did* have someone in contact with Massarella. How can that do anything for us but scream: "We're guilty!"?'

Brogan answered calmly. 'I know it's not going to seem so, but this is a beneficial development for us.'

Sabatino looked completely incredulous.

'For there to be a Ptarmigan contact,' the barrister stated, 'there had to have been someone who leaked the designs from Massarella. Van Der Vaal, personally, confirmed Charlotte Grant's identity. That admission, alone, opens up a whole new line of enquiry and defence.'

'But that's just it, isn't it. *Defence*,' said Sabatino. 'We're always on the damn defensive. And Quartano doesn't want us to attack – for fear of upsetting Mandarin Telecom.'

Straker looked at Nazar then at Brogan. 'After this morning, Remy, the sponsorship deal will be long gone. Having looked the Chinese in the eye and said that we were clean, we've completely lost face as well as our credibility with them. Quartano's going to be mad, but at least this'll remove any reticence about fighting back. We may have lost the sponsors, but we *will* protect your position in the Championship.'

Straker let that comment hang. Its significance was not lost on Sabatino; she began to calm slightly, even before Brogan backed Straker up.

'The legal argument has been complicated today, but I strongly believe it's been so in our favour. It's thrown significant doubt on Massarella's claims. Matt and I will conduct a wholesale reassessment of our approach to fight this case.'

'That's all for another time,' barked Treadwell. 'Let's get the hell out of here.'

The room finally quietened down.

Sabatino still looked far from happy. 'Christ, the press are going to kill us on the way out.'

'How are we going to deal with them?' asked Treadwell with unresolved tension in his voice.

Straker stepped straight in: 'We should make a short statement.'

'Like what? How the hell do you spin this?' said Sabatino in exasperation.

Straker, looking and sounding like he was making it up on the hoof, said: 'How about: "We have received new information only today, confirmed by Massarella … The FIA has granted us time to consider this … and has invited us to re-present it at the next Council meeting in London … We are more confident than ever of clearing our name"?'

Brogan nodded. 'That works.'

Nazar followed with: 'What do we say to: "Doesn't this make you guilty?"'

'"Innocent until proven otherwise",' responded Straker. '"No one's proved anything, yet"?'

'Again, that's good,' said Brogan.

Sabatino asked testily, intoning as if she were a journalist: '"Who is this Ptarmigan person who received the information?"'

'"That's under review",' suggested Straker. '"Our case will be presented formally to the FIA in London".'

She came back with: '"Now that a contact name *has* been confirmed, doesn't that make it more likely that Ptarmigan *did* use Massarella's ideas?"'

'"First, we haven't. And, second, not proven",' answered Straker.

'Good,' said Brogan. 'All those lines work. I think those are the most obvious questions. Who's going to do the talking?'

There was a moment's silence.

'Shouldn't it be Oscar?' suggested Treadwell.

'Wouldn't that make it look legal and defensive?' countered Nazar.

'I think it would,' offered Straker.

Nazar said: 'It should be me.'

There was agreement around the room until Sabatino said quietly: 'I should do it.'

Straker looked genuinely impressed by the gesture. 'Remy, that would make a strong impression, but it *would* tie you into the incident – and you had nothing to do with this.'

'True,' said Nazar. 'Remy, it's big of you: Matt's right.'

'He is,' replied Sabatino. 'But either I'm in this business, or I'm not. I don't want to be precious and seem like I need protecting from the manly stuff.'

Five minutes later Sabatino and Nazar emerged from 8 Place de la Concorde and faced the music. The moment they exited the FIA headquarters the noise from the hundreds of journalists and camera crews was literally deafening. Far louder than before.

It was immediately obvious that Massarella had already departed from the hearing and briefed the press. The journalists' questions were informed, accusatory and hostile.

'How do you feel about Ptarmigan cheating?'

'Are you only able to win using other people's ideas?'

'Are you going to give up some of your points in the Constructors' or Drivers' Championships?'

'Is Ptarmigan going to apologize to Massarella?'

The barrage was relentless.

Sabatino remained extremely calm. She stood there – in front of this baying rabble – without saying anything but looking like she would be ready when they were. Slowly, the pack quietened down.

Without notes, Sabatino began to speak over the still-jostling mêlée, reciting from memory the gist of the statement they had prepared indoors.

'We were asked to account for the actions of a deceased member of staff,' she said clearly and firmly. 'It's easy to see why we asked for – and were granted – an adjournment. We are more confident, now, than we were before all this started, of clearing our name.'

The hyenas yelled and screamed once again.

Sabatino parried each of their assaults:

'Nothing's been proven…'

'We have faith in the FIA…'

'*Yes*,' she said with genuine emphasis, 'if there has been wrongdoing, we expect there to be punishment … *whichever* side's found guilty.'

'No, I want to win the Championship fair and square…'

Finally, she got to: 'Thank you, gentlemen. I look forward to seeing you all in London,' with which she tried to break from the press towards a taxi Treadwell had already flagged down, waiting at the kerbside. As she moved, though, the media surged forward as a mob, continuing to shout questions. Sabatino was surrounded – badly jostled. Nazar tried to hold them back. Straker, too, opened his arms to try and give her space to move in the direction of the waiting taxi. The press completely crowded around her. Sabatino could hardly get through the door. Nazar shepherded her into the back seat. Straker was there too, so Nazar shouted at him to get in – and to get her away.

The car door was shut. The taxi started to move off, still sur-rounded by running paparazzi, firing off shots through the windows on the move.

Finally they were clear.

Rounding the Place de la Concorde, Straker said quietly: 'Well handled, Remy. That was skilfully done.'

Sabatino didn't acknowledge the compliment. Dismissively, she said: 'It won't have made the slightest fucking difference to tomor-row's catastrophic headlines.'

PART SIX

HYDE PARK CORNER

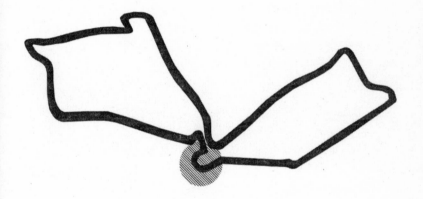

FIFTY–TWO

Sabatino remained slumped back in the seat of the cab as the collapse of the hearing started to sink in. Her chances of winning the Championship had been completely derailed. Any adverse judgment from the FIA, and all her achievements this year would be for nought.

Straker, not knowing her exact thoughts but having a fair idea of their direction, did not disturb her stare out through the window. Instead, he had to brace himself to call Quartano.

The industrialist was incandescent at the news. '$750 million, this is going to cost me. $750 fucking million. That bitch Charlotte Grant,' he bellowed to Straker over the phone. 'Didn't I tell you it was her? How weren't Ptarmigan able to *stop* her doing this kind of thing?'

Sabatino interrupted her stare as she heard the boom of Quartano's voice through the phone. Straker tried to keep his voice calm. 'That's what I've got to find out before the resumption of the hearing in London, sir. First, though, I have to try and find *how* she fed any of Massarella's ideas into the design process at the factory. That's the only way to unravel this.'

'Godamnit,' said Quartano. 'Let's, for once, get some good news out of this fucking team.'

Quartano rang off.

For the first time since leaving the hearing, Sabatino smiled – at the look of obvious relief on Straker's face. The taxi made its way up the Champs-Élysées. Before he could respond, Straker's phone started ringing. Looking at the display, he saw: "Unknown Caller". He was cautious about who this might be: given the scale of the fallout from the hearing, Straker could only think it would be a journalist. Pressing the green bar, he answered it with a degree of care.

'Hello – Matt Straker,' he said formally.

There was a silence on the phone and what sounded like the background hum of a crowded place.

'Hello?' repeated Straker.

'...I have information that you would want to know regarding Van Der Vaal and Trifecta,' said a very – almost deliberately – muffled voice.

Straker paused, his mind already beginning to whir. He looked at Sabatino. Her face quickly registered his distracted expression. She tried to lean in to hear the voice on the other end. Straker pressed the phone hard against his head and indicated to Sabatino that the signal was poor, pulling a face in apology for her not being able to listen in.

'Are you interested, or not?' came the voice.

'I don't think we should even be talking,' answered Straker still not quite sure what he should be doing with this call. He didn't want to embroil himself – or this case – in any further transfer of illegal information, if indeed that had happened already.

'Do you want the info, or not?'

Straker tried to think how he should best handle this. 'Could I ring you back?' he asked.

'No way. Do you have any idea how much of a risk I'm taking?'

'Could you call me back, then? In about half an hour?'

There was a grunt from the other end of the line.

The line went dead.

Straker breathed deeply several times.

'Who was *that*?' asked Sabatino, sitting up.

Straker looked at her quizzically, as if trying to think it through; then half-smiling, he said: 'Erm, I suppose you'd call them some kind of whistle-blower?'

'Wow, can he help us? What did he say?'

'Nothing, yet.'

Straker raised his phone. He immediately dialled Quartano's London office. 'Jean? It's Matt here. We have an urgent situation. Is Mr Q available?'

Without missing a beat she said: 'Yes, I believe he can be.'

'Excellent. First, can you try and reach Stacey Krall and get her on this call as well – and then patch us both through to Mr Q?'

Jean could hear the genuine urgency in Straker's voice. 'Hang on.'

Buttons were pressed.

A number was pulsed out.

'Stacey Krall,' came the deep voice.

'Stacey, Jean here. I have Matt Straker on the line. Are you okay to be put through to Mr Quartano?'

'Sure.'

'Hold on, please.'

More buttons were pressed. There was a period of silence.

Quartano's rich baritone came through. 'Matt, Stacey, what's going on?'

Straker breathed deeply. 'A significant development,' he said. 'I've just been rung by some kind of whistle-blower.'

'Good God,' said Quartano. 'What the hell did he – she – say?'

'Says he's got some information on Van Der Vaal and Trifecta that he thinks we'd like.'

'What did *you* say?' asked Krall sharply.

'Nothing. I asked him to ring back in half an hour.'

'Good.'

'Did he demand anything for it?'

'No.'

'Good.'

'Stacey, how do I play this?'

'First, let me say, I'm not happy about Matt even talking to this guy again. We've no idea whether this is a put-up job by Massarella, a set-up, being recorded, or even some sort of sting operation mounted by a tabloid newspaper. For the sake of the returned call, you must play a straight bat. We do *not* want anything to come to us. Any information that might be offered should only go directly to the President of the FIA.'

'Good, that'll work,' acknowledged Quartano. 'Much better to go through the neutrality of the governing body.'

'Okay. Do I ask him to send us a copy of anything?'

'Absolutely not. The FIA, I am sure, will inform us anyway. Let anything he offers go through official channels. Only.'

'Do we know who this guy is?' asked Quartano.

'What if he *does* ask for something?' responded Straker over the top of his boss's question.

Krall jumped in. 'Refuse it … outright. Offer him nothing. Tell him he's going out on a limb entirely for reasons of his own conscience.'

'Fine. Do I make a note of the exchange, or this call?'

'No, I'll make a file record of both from here.'

'Okay, thanks. I think I'm clear about what I've got to do.'

Quartano's tone seemed to lighten with curiosity. 'Do you have any idea *what* this information might be?'

'No, sir. But it must be considered helpful to us, otherwise why would this guy run such a huge risk of breaching whatever confidence to make an approach?'

Straker, still sitting next to Sabatino in the back of the now-static cab, rang off as they alighted opposite the Arc de Triomphe.

'Bloody hell,' she said, manifesting a clear change in her mood at the prospect of supportive information. 'What on earth do you think's going on?'

Straker smiled broadly. 'No idea. But it's edgy stuff.'

Thirty minutes later, and there was no sign of the whistle-blower. He hadn't rung back.

A quarter of an hour after that and there was still nothing.

Had he been frightened off?

Had they lost the opportunity?

It was an agonizing hour before Straker's phone rang again. He and Sabatino were still waiting – outside the Hotel Splendid – in the privacy of a public space for the follow-up call. Once again, Straker had to force the phone in hard against his ear, pulling another face at Sabatino by way of apology for the poor quality of the line and her not being able to listen in.

'Well?' asked the mysterious voice.

'First,' said Straker, 'thank you for making contact,' adding rather stiltedly, as if he was being recorded: 'We cannot accept anything that might be someone else's property.'

'Fine,' said the reply resignedly and dismissively.

'…but,' jumped in Straker fearing he might ring off, 'if you are prepared to do something, whatever you've got should be sent directly to San Marino.'

There was a pause on the phone.

'Hello?' said Straker hesitantly.

'It's not a document,' said the voice.

'What is it then?' Straker asked.

There was silence on the line.

Straker wasn't sure the man was still there. 'Hello?'

'Trifecta have fired Michael Lyons,' said the informant. 'Lyons is pissed off. It's thought he's taken copies of all kinds of documents and emails.'

The phone went dead.

Straker immediately rang Krall in London. 'I tried to pass on your advice,' he reported.

'But?'

'He didn't offer any documents. It was more of a tip-off.'

Krall listened attentively. 'Okay. I'll add that to my note. If your phone has stored the number, please do not feel tempted to ring him back.'

'It hasn't.'

'Who else knows about your calls with this guy?'

'Only Remy, who's with me now.'

'Let's keep it that way, okay?'

Straker's buzz, though, faded quickly that afternoon.

As a pre-emptive strike, Quartano issued a press release declaring Ptarmigan's regret at the embarrassment it had caused Mandarin

Telecom – apologizing unreservedly – and confirming the team would be withdrawing from any further sponsorship negotiations with the Chinese company.

Straker felt the news of this badly.

Having deduced Van Der Vaal's motivations from the press cuttings – that the Massarella boss sought to remove Ptarmigan as a threat to his ambitions of being the commercial Big Dog of Formula One – Quartano's withdrawal meant that Van Der Vaal had succeeded in exactly what he had set out to do all along: to sabotage or even destroy Ptarmigan's commercial standing and reputation – simply through unsubstantiated insinuation.

In not being able to stop it, Straker took this as a failure in his own assignment. His disappointment was severe.

What crushed his soul was the injustice of it all – that Van Der Vaal had got away with this using such twisted assertions, such despicable tactics – and, worst of all, by lying.

Straker felt his mood turn dark. His mental recovery was stalling. From somewhere deep, though, another emotion grew. Anger.

If only he could find a way to harness it.

FIFTY-THREE

The next day, Human Resources circulated another email around Ptarmigan personnel – this time asking members of staff about their involvement with Charlotte Grant earlier in the year. From the responses, it was clear that she had been in contact with almost every part of the factory. Narrowing the investigation down was not going to be easy. Straker began with those people Charlie had interacted with in Design and Aerodynamics – logically the most obvious areas connected with the Fibonacci Blades, or ASDs, as they now knew Massarella called them.

Straker and Nazar set up a temporary interview room in the Ptarmigan factory. He and Nazar started questioning all members of these two departments in turn.

'Jason, we're in trouble with the FIA,' Straker explained to his twentieth interviewee that day. 'We've been accused of using Massarella's proprietary technology. Can we talk about your involvement in the Fibonacci Blades, and where this idea came from? And, secondly, whether or not you had any contact with Charlie Grant over it.'

Jason, a somewhat shy thirty-year-old designer with glasses and carrying a couple more stone than he should, looked and sounded rather defensive.

Hesitantly, he explained: 'I was brought a basic idea for these things by Charlie.'

Straker fought to control his reaction to this admission. He sat up and leant into the conversation. 'She came to you?'

'Yes.'

'And you didn't think it strange that she did this – when she had nothing to do with Design?'

'Kind of,' replied Jason, 'but she said that she was working for us as an industrial spy, and she'd come back with this from the grid.'

'Did she say which team she'd got it from?' asked Nazar.

'No.'

'Did you discuss drawing this up and developing it with your boss?'

'Charlie told me not to. She could be very persuasive,' he said coyly as his voice began to break.

'Okay. Did you talk about this with *any*one else?'

Jason nodded. 'Only one other.'

'Who?'

'Andy Backhouse.'

'Oh my God,' hissed Nazar, as he slumped back in his chair.

Straker dismissed the exclamation, trying to keep Jason calm. 'When did you talk to *him* about it?'

'When we were testing it in the wind tunnel.'

'That far into development? Can you remember what he said?'

'He asked me how we'd come up with the idea.'

'And what did you say?'

'That the idea had come from Charlie.'

'How did Andy react?' asked Straker.

Jason looked unsure of himself. 'He seemed relaxed about it all. I didn't get the feeling there was anything wrong. He said it was important for us to get the best ideas – wherever they came from – to see our cars go as fast as we could possibly make them.'

'Okay, Jason, thank you – and for being so open with us. You've been very helpful,' said Straker with a reassuring smile. 'I'm going to need more of your help, though.'

'Anything,' said Jason with an air of relief, sensing the tension might have abated somewhat with Straker's investigation.

'I need you to write down everything you can remember about this design – how you talked it all through with Charlie, how she gave you the idea, in what form, and what happened afterwards.'

FIFTY-FOUR

Oscar Brogan QC came to lunch in Quartech's London headquarters two days later. Hosted by Quartano in his private dining room on the top floor of 20 Cavendish Square, they were joined by Straker and Krall. Nazar was away.

'I wanted to talk through the possibilities mentioned by the whistle-blower,' said Quartano.

Brogan was helped to a fillet of beef by one of the stewards. 'Sure,' he said. 'But there's little point, Dominic, if you're not interested in mounting a counter-claim.'

Quartano was served last, with his main course and vegetables of red cabbage, spinach and roasted sweet potatoes. 'My reservation about launching a counter-claim was before we lost Mandarin, Oscar. Now Massarella have cost me $750 million from that sponsorship deal, I want to hit them with everything we've got.'

Straker saw that Krall was fighting to contain herself.

'Stacey, what's your take on the substance of the counter-claim?' Quartano asked.

'We need hard proof of their acts of sabotage,' she replied. 'Oscar and I have been discussing some possible courses of action.'

When Krall finished, the lunch seemed to fall silent as the full possibilities sank in. Straker, aware he was breaking the silence, then said: 'Andy Backhouse seems to have been involved in different aspects of this. Are we able to cross-examine *him* as a witness – if we needed to?'

Brogan nodded, looking slightly surprised. 'If you think that would help? The World Council is keen to give people a fair hearing. If a witness is required – even a hostile one – they'll sanction their being called.'

With brusque scepticism Quartano asked: 'And you think that would be helpful, do you, Matt?'

'If we can put the man under oath, sir, yes.'

For the following few days Straker watched Stacey Krall work frenetically. After Quartano's go-ahead for filing a counter-claim, she was completely pumped up with preparing to take the fight to Massarella.

Straker helped Krall work up a supporting application to the High Court. In it, she set out Ptarmigan's charges of sabotage against Massarella F1.

Once filed with the Court, Straker saw Krall's stress levels go stratospheric – as she waited anxiously for the judgment.

Straker had been involved in many intelligence-gathering operations in the Royal Marines, but these had typically involved concealment and stealth. This was to be his first civilian, up-front, and intrusive experience.

Moving out of London to base themselves at the Ptarmigan factory, Straker helped Krall pull together the finishing touches and details of their plan.

At three o'clock in the afternoon, Straker and Krall drove into Gaydon, behind a police car and a civilian saloon. Parking the three cars on the verge outside Flax Cottage, there was a moment's huddle in the single-track country lane before Ptarmigan's court-appointed solicitor turned with two colleagues and, accompanied by a uniformed policeman, walked through the gate and across the gravel to Michael Lyons's front door.

The doorbell was rung.

Straker and Krall stood back in the driveway.

The door was answered.

Hesitantly, and looking more than a little alarmed, Michael Lyons peered out and saw three men in suits standing in front of him, along with the uniformed policeman.

'Mr Lyons?'

'Yes?'

'I am Arnold Close, a solicitor with Grumman & Phipps. I have here a Search Order issued by the High Court under the Civil Procedure Act 1997. This order states that as the Supervising Solicitor I have been given the power to search your house for intellectual property, technical documents, and any postal, email, or SMS correspondence relating to the Ptarmigan and Massarella Formula One teams.'

Michael Lyons suddenly looked like he had seen a ghost.

'Do you understand the situation, Mr Lyons?'

The man stared at the solicitor. Then he looked at the policeman, then at Krall and Straker, whom he seemed to recognize, standing at a distance. Finally, he looked back to the solicitor again.

Lyons seemed to be processing this information. 'What's all this about?'

The solicitor handed him the Search Order. 'It's all set out in here, Mr Lyons. Ptarmigan and Massarella are accusing each other of industrial espionage. Ptarmigan assert that their cars have suffered from certain acts of sabotage on the race track, while Massarella allege that some of their secrets have been stolen. Ptarmigan believe you have documents or information that could clarify the situation.'

Lyons looked down at the order. His face registered shock.

Straker could see the man's eyes flit across the document, but Lyon's stare indicated that he was soon deep in thought. Was he weighing up his adjusted loyalties – now that he'd been sacked? Straker wondered. Somehow, though, the man looked resigned.

After a pregnant pause, Lyons looked back at the policeman as if for confirmation and reassurance.

'Okay,' he said flatly. 'Maybe the truth should come out,' with which he stood back and let the Supervising Solicitor and his colleagues into his house.

An hour later a computer, a laptop, several boxes of files, a small credenza, and a handful of rolled-up tubes of paper from Lyons's house were loaded into the back of the solicitor's car.

As Straker and Krall walked out of the drive, Straker snatched a glance back at Michael Lyons standing on the doorstep of his quintessential English cottage.

He was bemused by the man's expression.

If he had to describe it, Straker would have said Lyons showed, of all things, relief – an odd emotion given that his privacy and possessions had just been so unceremoniously violated.

An hour later Straker and Krall were in a similar convoy, this time pulling up outside the entrance of Trifecta Systems on an industrial estate on the outskirts of Leamington Spa. They alighted and walked as a group up to the glass front doors, and through them into the main reception area. Arnold Close approached the reception desk and addressed the elder of the two women sitting behind it.

'I'd like to see Justin Greening, the legal officer of the company,' he said firmly. 'Please explain that I have a Search Order from the High Court – please make sure you say that: a Search Order.'

The receptionist looked at the solicitor, and then across at the uniformed police officer standing a few feet back. Straker could see the woman was taking the request seriously. Sheepishly, she picked up her phone. When it was answered, she equally sheepishly passed the message on to the legal officer.

It was just as well the police officer was with them this time.

A few moments later a man burst through a pair of inner doors and strode aggressively into the reception area.

'What the hell is this?' he shouted as he cast his eyes across the six strangers. 'What the hell are you people doing here?'

Arnold Close turned to face him. 'Are you Trifecta's legal officer?' he asked.

'What if I am – what the hell's it got to do with you?' the man bawled and moved uncomfortably close to the visitor asking the question.

'Mr Greening – I'm assuming that's who you are – I have a Search

Order, here, issued by the High Court on behalf of the Ptarmigan Formula One Team. We have the authority to search your premises,' and offered the order up for inspection.

Greening flicked the document away with the back of his hand.

Sensing trouble, the policeman stepped forward – extending an arm out in front of him, as if to separate the two men: 'Excuse me, sir, if you'd like to take a step back.'

'No, I fucking well *don't* like – not in my *own* fucking offices.'

Arnold Close realized this wasn't going to get anywhere. Turning to the policeman, he said: 'Perhaps Mr Greening would like to call Trifecta's own solicitors – in case he's not familiar with the Search Order process?'

That could so easily have been taken as a professional insult by Greening. Looking at the policeman as Arnold Close said it, though – and, with the policeman nodding his agreement to the idea, Greening seemed to calm a fraction. Turning to the receptionist, he barked: 'Get me Rafe Cushing at Cushing & Partners.'

There were several moments of silent standoff, until, cowing slightly, the receptionist declared curtly: 'I have Mr Cushing for you,' and tentatively offered up the handset.

Greening grabbed the phone and conducted a conversation in hushed tones, shielding himself from the visitors. Handing back the receiver he said defiantly: 'Mr Cushing will be here within five minutes. Then we'll kick you all off these premises. In the meantime, you are prohibited from setting foot beyond this area,' and stormed away, back through the inner doors of the reception hall.

Five minutes later, through the glass windows of the entrance hall, Straker could see a car swing wildly into the Trifecta parking area, and, sweeping round at some speed, screech to a halt on the neat asphalt surface. A short man with red hair and brown-rimmed glasses jumped out. Leaving the car – with its door open and engine running – the man ran towards the glass doors and barged through them into the reception area. At the same time, Greening reappeared from inside the building. The two men converged in the middle of the hall, with Greening saying – and pointing: 'These are the people, Rafe, to be thrown off the premises.'

Arnold Close turned and, calmly addressing the new arrival, said: 'This is a High Court Search Order, and I am the Supervising Solicitor – here to enforce it on behalf of the Ptarmigan Formula One Team,' and handed the document over.

The solicitor raised his glasses and started to read. He flicked the pages over several times, backwards and forwards, seemingly to check and recheck the document.

Having finished he looked up at Justin Greening. 'This is a valid High Court Search Order, Justin,' he said gently, 'I can't advise you to do anything but comply with it.'

Justin Greening looked fit to burst. Grabbing Cushing by the arm, he wheeled him away from the visitors into a corner of the reception area. Strong words were clearly exchanged. After nearly five minutes, Justin Greening stormed off, barging back through the inner doors of the office, and disappeared.

Walking slowly over to the reception counter, the recent arrival said: 'I am Rafe Cushing, Trifecta's solicitor. I *will* accompany you to the documents identified in the Search Order. They are not in an accessible state at the moment. Please wait here until they are, and then I will *personally* escort you through the building to get them.'

It was over an hour and half before Cushing accompanied them into the Trifecta office building to access the files and email traffic identified in Ptarmigan's High Court Order.

Straker shared his concerns with Krall. With such a long delay, Justin Greening had had plenty of time for all kinds of deleting and shredding.

FIFTY-FIVE

The Ptarmigan raiding party returned to the Supervising Solicitor's offices in Leamington Spa where Stacey Krall and Straker set themselves up in Grumman & Phipps's conference room. There, the two of them with some Grade C help from the local practice started going through the documents they had seized – arranging and indexing every item methodically into different piles, right across the expanse of the large table.

They ordered takeaway food and set about working into the night. Come two o'clock in the morning, Straker and Krall were the only people still there. Both were beginning to feel the effects of sustained concentration, and decided to call it a day.

Only on exiting the conference room, did they become aware of how late it was. The building was empty. Darkened meeting rooms haunted them from either side of the corridor on their way back to reception. It was also quiet. Nothing more than a background hum from the sleeping building. Krall turned off the remaining lights on the meeting rooms floor, before they walked down the stairs to the main entrance. A night watchman sat behind the reception counter, reading a copy of the *Racing Post*. Handing over their day passes, Straker and Krall walked towards the main doors. The guard pressed a button to let them out.

The night air was surprisingly warm – even balmy. There didn't seem to be a breath of wind. It was particularly dark – a star- and moonless sky, encased by a high blanket of cloud. At street level, lamps bathed isolated patches of the road in pools of orange light.

It was deathly quiet. Two o'clock in the morning – and a school night – Leamington Spa was quite deserted. There was no sound, only an occasional bark from a lone dog somewhere off in the distance.

Straker and Krall emerged from the Regency stucco-fronted office in Newbold Terrace, and walked across the narrow strip of private parking – separated from the road by an elegant low balustraded wall – and out on to the street. On the far side was a long row of public pay-and-display parking bays, at right angles to the road facing onto the far pavement, a set of iron railings, and then a high wall-like overhang of dense foliage.

It was dark under the trees.

Only a handful of cars were still parked in the street, with dozens of empty spaces strung out in between, their white lines showing in the dim and patchy orange street light.

Turning half-left, Straker and Krall walked out into the middle of the road, towards their own cars – past a parked saloon.

Straker's pulse started to quicken.

What was it? What was wrong?

Something wasn't quite right.

He immediately put a hand on Krall's arm, instructing her – silently – to halt and be alert at the same time. Straker scanned further down the street. It was not easy to see. There were plenty of shadows.

Straker sensed it again.

Wasn't it a shape? The wrong shape? In the wrong place?

Krall's Audi R8 was parked a short distance ahead. But the line of the car seemed wrong. Was one of its doors open?

That wasn't all.

Straker was immediately on guard.

He became aware of movement. Fleeting movement. In any kind of breeze, he'd probably have missed it – easily confusable and lost against the background movement of leaves and branches. But in this stillness, he was absolutely sure.

Turning to Krall, he breathed: 'Go back to Grumman & Phipps office,' and hissed: 'RIGHT NOW!'

Krall looked even affronted at the tone, not used to following such direct instructions – and certainly not blind. She hissed back: 'Why?'

'Someone's breaking into your car,' he said. 'Now GO!'

Krall's face registered instant alarm. Her attention was held. '*Breaking?*' she repeated emphatically.

'Sitting inside it.'

Krall cringed. Stepping back, she made to turn away. But doing so, she let out a squawk.

Out of the shadows from the other side of the road between two of the Regency office buildings, three dark figures came running at them – fast and purposefully.

Running straight at them.

Unexpected dark figures at night would alarm most people. Sinister thoughts of muggers immediately crossed their minds. Adrenalin surged. Whoever these people were, Straker's hope of Krall getting back to the Grumman & Phipps building had gone.

Instinctively, Straker put himself between her and the rapidly approaching figures. Looking over his shoulder, he saw the rear end of the largish saloon, and tried to manoeuvre her in behind it – as some kind of cover or protection. Straker noticed the flashing red light on the dashboard of the car.

His attention was soon back on the group of approaching figures. There was nothing ambiguous about their intent; they were still closing in, striding menacingly – across the road – still coming straight towards them.

Krall squawked again.

Straker broke his gaze to look round to see what had alarmed her this time. Another figure had emerged, standing up from inside Krall's Audi, a little further up the street.

That figure was now closing in on them too.

Then there was something else.

They heard an engine start – down to their left – back towards the Grumman & Phipps office building. A large black car pulled out. Even in the gloom it was very obviously a Range Rover. Ominously, it had no lights on – and was moving at little more than a walking pace. It, too, was closing in on them.

The dog, barking in the distance, seemed to up its frequency – perhaps even sensing the higher level of tension in the air.

Straker tried to do an immediate assessment – anxious to rationalize this scene. Whichever way he saw it, it wasn't good.

What the hell did these people want?

It was all too clear that his tactical position was poor. Straker had three men in front of him, and both his flanks were covered – by a man on one side, and a car on the other.

This was nothing less than an ambush.

Straker cursed his vulnerability.

He had to go on the offensive – at least cause a distraction. Throw them off their stride.

But how?

Straker edged into the street, passing the end of the largish saloon. Raising his knee, he horse-kicked backwards, square onto the saloon's boot, just above the bumper. The impact did exactly what he wanted. Against the silence of the night, the car alarm started screaming – blaring out its earpiercing screech along the street, reverberating off the white Regency buildings.

Straker was pleased. The noise immediately affected the three figures coming towards him. They seemed to hesitate at the alarm's intensity, looking around as if to gauge what effect it might have on the neighbourhood.

Straker immediately exploited their hesitation.

Tipping forwards, to maximize acceleration, he sprinted, running straight at the smallest of the three figures – the one to his right. Suddenly dropping his head and shoulders, he aimed a punch at the man's chest. His act of pre-emptive self-defence caught all three of them off guard, particularly his target. Before the latter could do anything, Straker had made solid impact. He heard breath forcibly exhaled as he caught him right in the solar plexus – the force of collision strong enough to knock the man backwards off his feet. Quickly disengaging, Straker watched the man buckle – doubling up – and collapse down onto the ground, wheezing for breath.

Straker rebalanced himself – straightening up – and tried to read the new situation. He was effectively through the line of the "triplets" – on the other side of the road – now with his back to the row of offices. He had the remaining two assailants between him and Stacey Krall. As far as he could see, there was no sign of the other figure over to his left – approaching from the area around Krall's parked car – and in the other direction the darkened Range Rover seemed to have stopped – waiting? – watching? – some distance away, over to his right.

Straker wanted to act quickly, to keep the initiative – to maintain the element of surprise.

Still the shriek from the car alarm was blaring out into the night, its four yellow flashers keeping time with the noise. No one seemed to have been drawn by it – to come and check the car was all right. It didn't look like it was going to attract any intervention or third-party help.

Their new positions in the street relative to each other changed the angle of lighting and shadow. Straker suddenly saw the bigger of the two men brandish something level with his chest. Shit – was that a weapon?

The figure started to move towards Straker. Not a weapon – not a firearm, at any rate. It was some form of bar – bat – or handle.

Straker took guard, ready to defend himself.

The figure started to rush him.

Straker had no idea how agile this guy would be.

As the handle – or whatever it was – was raised, Straker saw the man wield it with two hands from his right shoulder – to give it a double-handed swing across his front, aiming to hit Straker from the left.

Again taking the attackers by surprise, Straker charged *into* the attack. It seemed to work. It threw the attacker's rhythm – forcing the man to hurry his stroke.

At the last minute Straker stopped and ducked.

That worked too.

The swing missed him – going straight by, clean above his head. But its momentum – undiminished by contact with the target – meant the assailant's swipe continued round on its arc. Straker then, jumping up, landed a full-bodied kick in the assailant's genitals.

Straker's impact was well-timed. It caught the assailant completely by surprise. Testicular pain disabled him instantaneously, buckling him up, causing him to let go of the handle – still continuing round on its swing – which went clattering off across the road. The man fell into a heap on the ground clutching himself.

With two attackers down, Straker turned his attention on the third. But as he did so, he missed the fourth figure – the one over by Krall's car. Out of the dark, this man smashed into Straker's side, sending him twisting to the ground. Straker fell badly and rolled on the rough tarmac. He wasn't badly hurt, but was momentarily disorientated.

Straker could still hear the infernal screech of the saloon's car alarm.

He was scrambling up as quickly as he could to his feet, ready to face his new assailant, when a colossal thump crashed into his chest. A heavy-booted kick had been landed – solidly – in his ribs from the last of the triplets. It knocked the wind out of him.

Suddenly – over the commotion – and even through the noise of the car alarm Straker thought he heard a voice. A female's voice. Straker panicked – was that Krall's? He heard it was hers, but it didn't sound distressed. It sounded deep and commanding. She was talking forcefully. He tried to look up to see that she was okay, but couldn't see her. It sounded like her voice was coming from the far side of the saloon car.

Straker suffered another crippling blow to his side as the other assailant landed a powerful kick to his flank. The blow was fierce. Straker tried to roll away, desperate to regain his feet. But his problems were compounded. Not only was he winded – and his ribs burning in pain – but there were now two sets of kicks coming at him from two different directions.

Straker couldn't regroup, not out in the open like this.

Alternating rhythmic blows soon thwarted any effort he made to get to his feet.

Kick followed kick.

Krall watched on in horror as Straker suffered blow after blow. She didn't think she could do any more to help.

In what seemed like an agonizingly long three minutes, Straker was hammered by the thugs. All he could manage, having been overwhelmed, was to protect his face and neck.

Then, as if by wishful thinking, Straker heard a noise.

An alarm – but not the saloon car. No, not an alarm – a siren. He definitely heard a siren.

Krall heard it too. Coming from her left, down the street from behind the Range Rover.

She was not the only one to hear it. One of the assailants raised his head from the kicking. Then the other did the same.

The Range Rover honked its horn – urgently – several times, and revved its engine.

The assailants finally broke away from Straker.

The car roared some more, and Krall watched it accelerate towards the attack scene. All four of the thugs ran to converge with the Range Rover, two of them still partly doubled-up. The car braked heavily, dipping its bonnet. It stopped. The assailants pulled open the doors and dived inside.

Krall suddenly realized the danger Straker was in. She ran out into the road – towards his immobile form – and stood over him, facing the Range Rover down. All she could do was give the driver a dilemma. Would he have the balls to run them both over?

Krall stood there, behind Straker's body, staring at the approaching car, bracing herself for the worst.

Blue flashing lights were now strafing the white stucco down the line of Regency buildings. Those in the Range Rover could see and hear that the police were closing in fast. Their sirens were deafening.

The Range Rover roared towards Krall.

She held her breath. At the last minute, the bulky black car swerved violently, brushing past. She even had to jump to the side to miss being struck by its wing mirror as it sped away.

The police car screeched to a stop. Its headlights illuminated the foetal form lying in the middle of the road. An officer jumped out carrying a holdall and ran straight to Straker.

'The attackers have just gone down there,' shouted Krall to the driver, as she pointed down Newbold Terrace. 'A black Range Rover,' and rattled off the registration.

Without delay, the patrol car backed up, circled round them, and sped off in pursuit of the attackers – its siren blaring, and lights flashing angrily.

The policeman attending Straker was now kneeling down and shining a torch over his stricken form. Bending right down, he said: 'Are you able to move at all, sir?'

Straker groaned negatively, tasting iron on his tongue. Blood was dribbling from the corner of his mouth. His nose, teeth, cheekbones, back, guts, ribs, and knees all hurt like hell. The policeman grabbed his radio and called an ambulance to Newbold Terrace, immediately.

Within ten minutes it arrived. Two paramedics, exercising great care, lifted the still-horizontal and foetal Straker onto a stretcher and then into the back of the ambulance. Accompanied by Krall, he was driven to A&E at Warwick Hospital in Lakin Road. For the next four hours Straker was put through extensive tests, scans and X-rays. He barely recovered his demeanour and lucidity.

Krall's anxiety showed in her face – amplified by her tiredness. 'What kind of mugging *was* that?' she asked.

Straker inhaled through his mouth, the pain still keenly felt around his nose. 'That was no mugging,' he said with a light coughing fit. 'Muggings don't involve five people and a getaway car. That was a deliberate attack.'

Krall's face registered even more concern. 'Who'd want to attack *us*?'

Straker groaned, clearly not comfortable in the A&E bed. 'Someone involved in the case? Someone looking to intimidate us – to frighten us off?'

'You *think* so?'

'Why not? It's the most obvious possibility.'

'But why now?'

'Because of the raids,' he said quietly, trying not to exert his chest. 'Those Search Order raids will have changed,' he said pausing to inhale, 'the whole dynamic of Massarella's spat,' another shallow breath, 'or whatever the hell this is.'

Krall looked up from a plastic cup of coffee bought from one of the hospital vending machines. 'Massarella took us to a hearing at the FIA. How much more could the dynamic change beyond that?'

'Quite a way,' replied Straker with a half-pant of discomfort. 'Until then, we've only been the reactor to their bullshit.' He paused to breathe. 'Your invoking the High Court has shown our readiness to take the fight *to* Massarella. Those Search Order raids were proactive – they were an invasive act.'

'But they were done in self-defence.'

'To us,' replied Straker. 'To the other side – they're an act of war.'

'I don't get it. How's this *worth* all that?'

'Very easily,' groaned Straker again, now trying to shift his position in the bed. Krall put down her coffee cup and helped him rearrange the pillows behind his back. 'Control of billions of Formula One dollars – let alone our $750 million from Mandarin Telecom – are at stake here,' Straker half-whispered. 'Whoever's behind this: Van Der Vaal? MacRae? Obrenovich? God knows who else,' he breathed, 'might just fear our raids could expose what they're already doing – or stop them from getting their hands on it all by unlawful activity.' Straker had to breathe deeply, but slowly. 'I *had* expected them to react, in some way. I'm pissed off I hadn't anticipated them do so this quickly.' He inhaled. 'Even then, I'd never've expected *that* level of violence.'

Straker settled back against the pillows with another groan and a grimace. 'The only consolation I can take,' he said, with a smile-through-the-pain, 'is that we've quite obviously got them rattled.'

FIFTY-SIX

Straker was not discharged from hospital until late the following morning. While he had only broken a couple of ribs, they were still painfully sore – as were his black eye, fat lip, and the other bruises across his face. Taking him by surprise was the party that came to pick him up. Accompanying Krall was Remy Sabatino. Up at the Ptarmigan factory to work on the simulator, she had been distressed by news of the attack, and insisted on coming with Krall to pick up Straker and his car.

Sabatino was clearly disconcerted to see the state of Straker's face and his general condition. She even felt moved to offer him an arm as the six-foot-two figure tried to shuffle from the main entrance of the hospital towards the waiting Ptarmigan courtesy car.

Driven back to Grumman & Phipps's office in Leamington, Krall, clearly fired up by the events of the night, was motivated to fight back – ready to go straight to work on the documents seized from Michael Lyons and Trifecta Systems the day before. Straker – finding it hard not to lisp – gave her a series of firm instructions: 'Do not touch your car – I will arrange for the police to check it over, and then for it to be collected – and repaired – if necessary. Do not leave Grumman's offices unaccompanied – I will have you picked up later by a Ptarmigan car, when you are ready. Also, I will arrange for you to be put up locally in private accommodation, instead of in the hotel you've been at.' Straker, this time, was not asked why these precautions were needed. Krall nodded her acquiescence to them without objection.

Straker, too, was keen to get back into the assignment – to return to the factory and push on with the next stage of their FIA defence. Sabatino, though, having seen him heave himself so awkwardly out of the Ptarmigan car, and grimace as he pulled himself to his feet alongside the Morgan, declared he was not fit to do anything, let alone drive – stating that she would instead.

'I've seen the way you drive,' he retorted. 'The difference is that I don't have a team of mechanics to take out the dents – when it all goes tits.'

Sabatino just smiled, letting the taunt to go by. She simply walked to the passenger's door, ready to hold it open. But then Straker, very suddenly, took her by surprise. He lunged forwards and grabbed her forcibly – staying her arm – stopping her touching the car door. He almost lost his balance doing so. She looked startled by the ferocity of his action. Gently, he let her go. Then, instead of making to get in, Straker, inelegantly – and with much groaning – lowered himself down onto the surface of the road, to look up under the chassis of the Morgan.

'What the hell are you doing?' she asked.

'Taking heed of last night's attack,' he hissed as, in a contorted press-up position, he crawled awkwardly across the tarmac to the next wheel arch.

Sabatino, seeing how seriously Straker was taking all this, didn't find herself laughing at or mocking his unusual actions – particularly having heard from Krall about the viciousness of the attack.

Straker crawled awkwardly round the whole of the car, checking its entire underside. Having finished, and groaning back to his feet, he then fiddled with the external release catches, and looked under the engine covers, particularly around the electronics. He finished his security check, and closed the car back up.

'Right, go and crouch down behind that wall,' he wheezed, pointing her across the street to the low balustrade. Sabatino looked concerned, but didn't argue.

Checking she was a good distance away, Straker gingerly opened the car door manually. Without getting in, he checked the car was in neutral – before inserting the key. He turned the ignition. The V6 fired. There was nothing untoward – it fired cleanly first time.

Sabatino walked back across the road. Straker limped round to the passenger side. She suddenly found herself looking at him, almost asking permission to open the door. With her help, he lowered himself gingerly down into the low-slung sports car.

Sabatino, trying to lighten the mood, asked: 'Can we drop the top?'

He explained how, and the roof was stowed away. She climbed in behind the wheel. 'British Racing Green, bonnet louvres, wire wheels, cream leather seats, walnut trim – very nice,' she said musically in genuine appreciation of the car.

'Look after it, then,' he said as he tried to pull on his seat belt. Hearing the stifled groan that it induced, Sabatino leant over and helped him buckle up.

Sabatino reversed out of the parking bay. 'I heard Stacey's description of the attack. You took some beating. Is this where it all happened?'

Straker nodded.

'Talk about taking one for the team,' said Sabatino. 'The least I can do is buy you lunch.'

They found their way out of Leamington and onto the southbound stretch of the A429. Straker may have felt less than comfortable, and while the open-top Morgan on such a glorious sunny day should have cheered him up, his mind was still working – and concerned. His senses were sharp.

The A429 was a straight, fast and busy road. He used its openness to check behind in the passenger-door mirror. On such an open road, he was confident he would have spotted any unwanted company, had there been any. As they reached the Fosse Way, he checked again.

So far, at least, he was sure they were not being followed.

Twenty minutes later they passed through the market town of Shipston-on-Stour, and were soon heading east on the B4035 towards Banbury.

Just after one o'clock, Sabatino pulled the Morgan Roadster into Brailes and onto the elegant sweep in front of the lychgate of St George's church. Appropriately, a St George's flag flew lazily in the gentle breeze from the top of the stone tower.

Parked in front of the Old Parsonage, Straker awkwardly climbed out and stretched himself up. He was still in significant discomfort. Sabatino offered him an arm again. They walked side by side down to the edge of the main drag through the village. Crossing over towards the pub, Straker looked discreetly left and right. As far as he could see, there was no one there.

It would be a very different story on the way out.

Inside the George at Brailes, Sabatino scouted a table in the garden before leading Straker – walking unsteadily – out into the sunshine at the back. Having ordered, and got themselves settled with a drink, Sabatino said: 'Stacey told me you reckon the attack was related to the case,' and took a sip of her Guinness.

Straker nodded. 'It was far too well organized – particularly at two o'clock in the morning – to be a random crime,' he said firmly. 'It was too carefully co-ordinated.'

'God, and Stacey said you think they'll have another go?'

Straker shrugged. 'We'd be daft not to think they'll try something else. That attack shows we've put them on the defensive, now.'

Sabatino looked worried by the implications of this violence. The contrast between the mood of their conversation and the serenity of the English garden all around them – bathed in sunshine – was stark. Their food arrived, but a cloud hung over their lunch while they ate. Straker had to eat carefully and hesitantly, his fat lip making chewing particularly uncomfortable.

After an hour, they left the pub. Emerging onto the main road out the front, they looked both ways, and made to cross over.

Straker was instantly aware of something. Over to his left.

Looking that way again – as if being extra careful while he crossed the road – he made a mental picture of everything in view. Some way down was a car, parked among others on the opposite side. He was sure there was something about it. Under his breath he said: 'That black Range Rover – two hundred yards down there on the left – is trouble … *don't* look round!'

Her face registered concern.

Straker walked them back up the side road to his car.

'How? How do you know?' she asked, her voice also indicating concern.

Straker's 14 Int Company experience and his two tours with the Hereford Gun Club were not really for public discussion. 'A bit of military training and hard experience in Iraq.'

'What does that car being there mean, though?'

'That we need to be on our guard going back to the factory.'

Sabatino nodded. 'Just as well I'm doing the driving, then,' she said in a nervous attempt to lighten her mood.

Straker checked under the car again before they got in.

Sabatino fired up the engine, swung the Morgan round the rest of the elegant sweep in front of the Old Parsonage, and headed back down towards the war memorial to rejoin the B4035, the Shipston to Banbury road.

As she pulled up to the junction, Straker said: 'See if you can clock the Range Rover when you check both ways – but *don't* make it obvious.'

She looked left and lingered slightly to the right. 'Yep. It's still there. What now?'

'See if it's going to follow us,' said Straker without taking a look himself.

Sabatino turned left and accelerated gently away up to the speed limit. Reaching the end of the village, she accelerated a little more as they headed up Holloway Hill, out into the countryside. The Morgan's 3.7 litre V6 purred effortlessly up through the revs and gears, comfortably reaching fourth towards the top of the hill.

Despite the aches in his side, Straker leant forward to take a look in the wing mirror of the passenger door. As the car crested the rise – emerging through the tree line on the upper side of the spinney – his field of view improved, enabling him to see further back down the road behind them. 'It's definitely there.'

Sabatino had a discreet look for herself.

'Okay, keep going,' said Straker. 'Let's get some distance between us, but don't make it look like you're trying to get away. Don't want them to know *we* know they're there.'

Sabatino accelerated on, the car responding well on the smooth tarmac surface as they headed for the foot of the next hill by Coombe Slade.

With the road still level, Straker took another look in the passenger-door mirror.

The Range Rover was there all right, hanging back about a quarter of a mile.

They started climbing the hill, the ribbon of grey road leading off into the distance – its neat dashed white line running up the middle – standing out against the fields of crops on either side. The Morgan gave more without protest. At the top of that hill, Sabatino eased off at around the sixty-mile-an-hour mark. Here, the road straightened out, with good visibility for at least half a mile. She looked back in her mirrors. Drifting to the left-hand side of the road, she said: 'What if we gently invite them to overtake?' and allowed the Morgan to drop its speed.

'Worth a shot. This'd be the perfect place for them to get by.'

Straker watched in the mirror to see the reaction. He saw the Range Rover emerge round the last corner behind them as it joined them on the straight. Now the Morgan had slowed, the size of the vehicle's image in the mirror started to grow larger.

Sabatino's sedate pace on such a straight road with good visibility was a clear prompt for the car behind to overtake.

The Range Rover continued to close in.

Straker watched in the passenger-door mirror.

The Range Rover was approaching – as it continued to accelerate.

It looked like it was building up speed to overtake.

It was closing in.

Still on their side of the road.

It *stayed* on their side of the road.

It wasn't showing *any* sign, though, of pulling out.

It was still getting faster.

Getting closer and closer.

Now heading straight for the back of the Morgan.

Sabatino looked on disbelievingly. Then swore ferociously.

Urgently, she revved the engine, double declutched, dropped two gears, and started accelerating hard – racing the V6 up to a straining growl. Sabatino hammered the engine, desperate to build up speed to get away.

But it wasn't enough.

They could hear the sound of the bulky Range Rover closing in behind them.

Sabatino screamed the Morgan's engine.

The Range Rover slammed into the back of the Morgan.

Sabatino wrestled violently with the wheel – the downward impact of the bull bars momentarily lifting the Morgan's front wheels off the ground. She fought vigorously to keep the car straight and on the road after the collision.

'Holy shit, what the fuck are these people doing?'

FIFTY-SEVEN

With a heavily revving engine, Sabatino accelerated hard, trying to get out of trouble. She had just enough torque to pull away.

Straker turned round and saw the huge intimidating front of the Range Rover looming above them. He tried to look up at the faces in the Range Rover behind, but the windows were smoked and reflecting the sun's bright glare. He couldn't see inside.

This was insane. How far were these people prepared to go?

Straker heard and felt the Morgan's 3.7 litre engine continue to roar in earnest as Sabatino tried to get away.

They pounded along the straight section of road – the favourable power-to-weight of the Morgan starting to kick in. The road rose up a hill. Even with considerable performance disadvantage, though, the Range Rover was still powering along, just as hard – disconcertingly even seeming to match the pace of the Morgan. How was that even possible?

Sabatino gunned the engine and headed towards the crest in the road. She looked in her rear-view mirror. The Range Rover was still there, and not far behind. She realized any unnecessary slowing down on their part would have the Range Rover right back up their arses in no time.

'That's one powerful tank,' she shouted, as the wind started rushing over the top of the Morgan.

The road began to rise again, in a gentle left-hander – now the neat ribbon of grey tarmac had solid white lines painted down either side of the tarmac, along the kerbs. Two hundred yards ahead was a sharper turn, round to the left. Sabatino continued to increase their speed. They were keenly aware of the persistence and speed of the Range Rover behind them.

Straker looked across the open-top sports car at Sabatino.

Amazingly, her expression of concern – manifest during lunch, and after he'd spotted the Range Rover in Brailes – had completely gone. Her face was radiant. He could see her eyes flashing as she flicked them around her environment – to the front – to the rear through the mirror – down at the dashboard – back on to the road ahead.

'Better hold on,' she said as she drifted the car over to the right – fully across into the oncoming lane. Sabatino downshifted with another fluid, heavily revved double declutch. Still on the wrong side of the road, she held her position until Straker thought it impossible to recover. Then, with a flick of the wheel, she threw the Morgan across the road to the left, straight at the grass verge on the inside apex of the bend, kissing it with their front left.

Rather than look at the death-defying angle of attack, Straker looked across at the speedometer. He couldn't believe it. They were doing over ninety miles an hour through the corners on this bendy country road. The wind was now roaring over the top of the Morgan.

The car, though, was handling beautifully. It took the full force of the turn, slicing through the corner, despite the significant G-force.

Because of the twists in the road, Straker's view back through the passenger-door mirror was swinging here and there. Only at the last minute, just before their lurch through the next right-hander, did he catch a fleeting glimpse of the menacing bull bars on the front of the chasing Range Rover, rounding the bend behind them. Despite its size and weight, the 4×4 was following an amazingly similar line to the much lighter, nimbler sports car. The Range Rover might have been listing more obviously on its softer suspension, but it wasn't letting up. At all.

Sabatino drifted the Morgan fully over to the left of the road. Then, looking up and over the hedge to the right, she saw there was nothing coming the other way. Double declutching down, she dropped a gear, and, at the last minute, almost at the point where Straker thought the car was going to go tangential to the road – and off down a track – swung the car over to the right, cutting across the oncoming lane and clipping the grass verge at the apex – this time on the opposite side of the road.

Sabatino looked behind – and saw something ominous. Not only was the Range Rover still large in their mirrors, it even seemed to be gaining on them.

Sabatino kept accelerating

The B4035 wafted left and right between its high hedges on either side, the sun dappling through the leaves onto different parts of the road. In the warm summer air – and the smells from the surrounding countryside – this should have been an idyllic, even spiritual drive. Catching a glimpse out to the right – through breaks in the hedge – Straker saw the rolling Oxfordshire landscape as it stretched off towards the Cotswolds away in the distance. What had been a roar over the open-top car soon turned into a thundering gale. The car was really travelling now. Straker had to take another look at the speedometer: it was showing one hundred and ten miles an hour. At that pace – on a road normally driven at a third of this speed – the Morgan was giving off every sensation of speed imaginable.

Two cars came at them from the other direction, preventing Sabatino using the wrong side of the road to set up for the next corner. Those cars whooshed past.

The corner ahead had an overhang of branches, concealing its apex as the road fell away to the left behind its leaves. Revving hard, Sabatino double declutched – gaining a lower gear without slowing the car's speed over the ground – and, using the torque from the higher revs, accelerated down into the slope.

One hundred and twenty miles an hour. Along a *B road*.

Straker was growing increasingly uneasy. This was astonishingly fast.

They were soon in a dip – the road could be seen rising ahead and above them, up the other side of the narrow valley.

Bottoming out in this compression, Straker was pushed down heavily into the seat with significant centripetal force. His ribs screamed as the force took hold; he gritted his teeth to stifle the pain.

Up and out from the dip, the road rose up for a hundred yards before looking to swing right-handed, round and over a crest. A junction was visible off to the left – to Epwell – on the outside of the bend, which they should have been taking to go back to the factory in Shenington. But they were going far too fast to make that now.

Sabatino was lining up for this next apex at high speed. A car suddenly appeared – side-on – up ahead of them. And pulled straight out from that side road. It didn't stop to look – it pulled straight out from the junction – onto the main road – heading in their direction. Another big 4×4.

Straker instinctively pulled upwards on the shoulder strap of his seat belt, tightening the strap across his waist, forcing him further down into his seat. They were closing in incredibly fast on the back of that car, which clearly hadn't seen them.

It turned out to be another Range Rover.

The Morgan's momentum was bowling them on. Sabatino sliced through the right-hand corner. The Range Rover hadn't picked up much speed yet – meaning they were still closing in fast on the back of it.

Sabatino further swerved to the right – to overtake it immediately – looking to make an urgent avoiding sweep past the slower-moving vehicle.

She checked the road ahead. It was clear – no oncoming traffic.

The Morgan darted out decisively from behind this Range Rover, crossing the white line down the middle of the road

They were now pulling out into the oncoming – overtaking – lane. They were set to pass easily, maintaining their speed. When, with absolutely no warning, the Range Rover in front of them shot violently to the right – straight across the Morgan's path.

Sabatino, in nothing more than a reflex, swerved fiercely enough to the right, and jammed on the brakes, somehow preventing the Range Rover from smashing into them.

Instinctively, Sabatino had avoided a collision. But the bulking rear end of the Range Rover was now slap-bang in their way.

'Fuck!' screamed Sabatino at the top of her voice, wrestling the car back onto the proper side of the road, and changing down again. Then, the Range Rover, itself, swerved back over onto the correct side.

'What the fuck's going on here?'

Straker looked forwards and then backwards in his passenger-door mirror. 'Holy shit. This is a tag team,' he yelled. 'It's another of the scumbags.'

Looking backwards, he saw the first Range Rover rounding the corner and closing in fast behind them. 'The other one's coming right up behind us,' Straker yelled. 'We're about to be in a Range Rover sandwich.'

'Holy crap,' Sabatino shouted. 'This isn't good.'

Straker looked ahead, trying to see beyond the back of the now-slowing car in front of them. 'What about that turn – up ahead on the right,' he shouted. 'Can you cut down there?'

Sabatino clocked the turning, and then swore. 'There's something coming the other way.'

Sure enough, a second or two later, an oncoming car whooshed past – hemming them in – denying them the chance to peel off down that side road.

The Range Rover behind was taking advantage of their containment.

Sabatino looked in the mirror and yelled: 'Holy Mother of God – brace yourself,' when there was another deafening crunch. The Range Rover slammed into them again from the rear. Sabatino fought the wheel, double declutched, and tried to accelerate away, but there was nowhere to go. The second Range Rover was still completely blocking their way in front.

She made another attempt to overtake it.

Exactly as before, the Range Rover in front swung violently – straight across their path – blocking them in.

Sabatino was forced to tuck back into her side of the road again.

Seconds later, there was another almighty crunch from behind

– as they suffered another ramming. This time, after the jolt of the impact, there came a sound of crunching – then straining, tearing – metal. Straker's spare wheel had been caught in the bull bars. As the Range Rover disengaged, the tyre and the boot of the Morgan were brutally ripped away. Straker, despite the pain in his ribs, swung round, just in time to see the damage being wrought to his beautiful new car. Seconds later, the spare tyre and boot fell from the bars at the front of the Range Rover, and disappeared underneath it – its bulk only juddering slightly as it drove over and crushed the wheel and boot panel beneath its fat tyres.

'Fucking hell,' said Sabatino over the noise and the wind. 'We've got to get out of here!'

Straker looked across at her. He was staggered. Despite the urgency in her voice, her face was calm – albeit completely in the moment. Her eyes flicked between the road in front and the view in her mirror behind.

'How are we going to do that?'

The three vehicles, line astern – Range Rover, Morgan, Range Rover – rounded the next right-hander.

The road ahead meandered gently left and right for the next half a mile or so. Sabatino looked behind, and winced as the Range Rover behind accelerated at them once again, clearly looking to slam them in the rear.

Suddenly Sabatino shouted: 'Hold the fuck on!'

Straker didn't know what she had in mind, but automatically found himself pulling upwards on that seat belt strap once more.

He heard Sabatino rev the engine, change down, and accelerate – heading straight for the back of the Range Rover in front. Straker braced himself against the door, the transmission tunnel – anything he could find.

Without warning, Sabatino jerked the steering wheel over the right – as if to overtake. The Morgan darted out into the oncoming lane.

Up ahead, at the end of the long left-hander, Straker suddenly saw the looming front of a lorry – coming the other way – heading straight at them.

'Holy *fuck!*' he shouted.

They and the lorry were less than two hundred yards apart, with a staggeringly high closing speed.

The inevitable was going to happen.

How could it not?

A head-on smash.

The startled lorry driver clearly thought the same – as he frantically blared his horn and flashed his lights.

'What the *fuck* are you *doing*?' screamed Straker.

Sabatino, still accelerating, tried to build up speed.

They were drawing alongside the front Range Rover, now to their left, but were only about a quarter of the way up its length. The lorry was still coming the other way – straight at the Morgan.

And closing in fast.

But at least, this time, the front Range Rover *wasn't* pulling out to block them. It certainly wasn't going to try and head off the sports car with that lorry bearing down.

'*F U C K !!*' shouted Straker, bracing himself, despite his pain, against everything on the inside of the car. He couldn't believe it – what *was* she doing? They were never going to get past. The "window" was closing – the lorry was closing in far too quickly.

The Morgan clearly wasn't going to get past the Range Rover in time.

Then – without warning – Sabatino heaved the steering wheel. Again to the right. Straker was flung over to the left, against the passenger door, as she drove the hurtling Morgan off the road altogether – pulling up onto the grass verge – on the opposite side of the road.

Travelling at such speed over the grassy surface, the sports car started bouncing and bucking violently over the bumps. Sabatino rapidly worked the wheel this way and that, fighting to keep the fast-moving car straight on the uneven and much slippier ground.

'Hope we don't hit a culvert or a ditch,' she shouted with a laugh in her voice. 'We might really take off.'

Straker couldn't believe it.

They were travelling at over sixty miles an hour – along a grassy verge – on the wrong side of the road.

He was suddenly distracted – almost flinched – as, to his immediate left, the lorry, its horn still blaring, shot by – with a pronounced Doppler effect – right between them and the Range Rover.

Straker looked back across the road.

The Morgan, he suddenly realized, had got ahead of the Range Rover. More importantly, and spectacularly, the Range Rover, out of sheer self-preservation, had stayed – resolutely – on its own side of the road.

Sabatino swung the wheel to the left, dropped the Morgan back on to the tarmac, pumped power through the V6 – the revs of the engine screaming – before changing up and heading back over to the correct side of the road.

Quite astonishingly, they had passed the road-blocking Range Rover. Sabatino had done it – she'd got them in front of their tormenters.

Straker immediately examined the road behind via the passenger-door mirror. Because of their speed and the vibration, though, it was virtually impossible to see anything clearly in it, save the black foreboding shapes of the two Range Rovers still behind, still giving chase.

The Morgan was bowling on.

The road surface here was somewhat bumpy anyway but, at that speed, even the undulations were keenly felt as they sped along. The road started snaking here – left and right but also up and down – to form a succession of three-dimensional "S" bends.

Turning back to look at Sabatino, Straker was soon in a mild state of awe. She was now something to see. Behind the wheel of this car, her demeanour, expression and body language all looked supremely relaxed – with her left hand loosely on the gearstick, her right hand – palm up – on the bottom right part of the steering wheel, and with her legs gently apart, her right knee resting against the door, while her left was hovering – poised – immediately ready to work the clutch. Straker saw Sabatino in a completely unhurried and relaxed state, apparently without a tense muscle in her body, gently but quickly working the wheel as the car bucked and careered at full pelt through this rapidly varying topography.

But there was no let-up possible.

Straker was about to see more of Sabatino's exceptional confidence and car control.

'They're still there – and coming after us,' she declared.

Straker looked across at her. He could see that she was thinking. 'I don't know how far we go till we get to a village,' Sabatino yelled. 'But we're back to square one if we do. We'd *have* to slow down – and that would have those bastards ramming us up the arse again. We've got to get some distance between us. Hold on!'

Straker was all too well aware that if she said 'hold on' something hairy was likely to happen.

Up ahead, it was clear the road was about to head sharply left and up a steepish hill. The entry looked to be a tight ninety-degree left-hander at the foot of the slope – which also had a crossroads – the left-hand junction being on the very inside apex of the bend. As the Morgan shot past an earlier turning to Burdrop and Sibford Gower, and didn't seem to be slowing down, Straker instinctively breathed in and braced himself.

The speed they we were going at – for the upcoming corner – seemed far too fast for a public road. Straker switched his attention between the direction of travel and Sabatino, trying to convince himself he should stay calm, have confidence – and enjoy the ride.

Sabatino, still with the Morgan travelling at over a hundred miles an hour, offered the merest adjustment to the steering wheel. Wafting the car across to the opposite – oncoming – side of the road again, she changed down with a high-rev double declutch. A moment or two later, she threw the car back across her side of the road – to kiss the apex on the inside with the front left.

This turn was going to be tighter than anything they had taken so far.

In – round – and up – they ran.

This time, Straker felt the back end of the Morgan step out, the force of the cornering proving too much for the grip of the rear tyres. Despite feeling the significant effects of the various G-forces, he was able to watch Sabatino as it happened.

At over ninety miles an hour round this corner, and into the hill, the Morgan slewed onto three tracks. Sabatino – all seamlessly in one continuous movement – unhurriedly turned the wheel into the slide, corrected it, feathered the power, changed down with another extraordinarily fluid double declutch, and, containing the car's stability into a controlled power slide, accelerated away on up the hill, changing up again as the revs hit their upper limit.

He was utterly absorbed – fascinated – by her calmness, confidence and apparently effortless car control. It then hit him why this moment and experience was so special. No one ever got to see how a Formula One driver drives: they were only ever cocooned – and hidden – by their cramped monocoques, while the on-board cameras could film only their helmets and hands. There was never any portrayal of their bodies, demeanour, expressions, or attitude while they were driving. No one was ever given that insight – not even passengers in the handful of F1 two-seaters.

Straker's Morgan may not have been an F1 car, but it was giving him an extraordinary understanding of how a driver handled a car right up to the very limit of its capacity and environment. Sabatino suddenly reminded him of a jazz musician: she was jamming with the car like a virtuoso – a complete master of her instrument, environment, and performance – making it sing, move and dance with the smallest apparent effort – anticipating, reacting to, and playing off the moment. Above and beyond that, her demeanour and confidence finally served to relax him – convincing him that he *should* have full confidence in this woman's extraordinary ability and car control.

As they straightened up, climbing the hill, Straker snatched a rearward glance. The corner they had just rounded below and behind them was now partially obscured from this angle, with cow parsley and long grass overhanging the inside of the bend.

But then he saw something back there.

An altogether different car had approached the crossroads from the inside of the bend, and the very front of its bonnet could be seen side-on, insinuating into the main road. Around the end of that car's bumper, Straker suddenly saw the large shape of the lead Range Rover flash into view. Despite his aches and pains, he couldn't stop himself twisting round to watch, looking down the inside length of the Morgan and over what was left of its boot. The Range Rover was clearly trying to keep up with their nimble sports car – hoofing it into that corner. But its line was all wrong. Instead of hugging the apex on the bend, it seemed to be going too wide. Maybe the approach of the car to the inside of the crossroads had thwarted its set up for the corner? Now, though, the Range Rover was fighting to turn on a line that seemed too wide – looking very much like understeer. Straker saw the front wheels flicker, as the driver was clearly fighting the force of the corner, trying to hold the car to the line.

But the bulky weight of the Range Rover wasn't having it. It had far too much forward momentum. It wasn't able to turn anything like sharply enough.

Straker watched the 4×4 run even wider, right across the road to the outside of the corner, well over into the oncoming lane. There was a puff of smoke from the front wheels – the driver panicking, as he jammed on the anchors. But the Range Rover kept going.

At considerable speed it slammed into the grassy bank on the far side, and bounced violently upwards. Once flicked up, it started rolling over, Straker catching a glimpse of its underside as the bulking 4×4 smashed through the hedge, and careened out of sight. That was all he saw.

Their own bit of road levelled off.

Straker strained to keep watching behind, waiting to see the second Range Rover. Had it followed the first into the field?

He waited.

The Morgan charged on down the B4035 towards Swalcliffe.

But there was no sign of either pursuer.

A turning appeared, off to the right.

Without warning, Sabatino hammered the brakes, almost standing the Morgan on its nose. Straker, still looking backwards, was caught completely unawares, and was hurled forwards against his seat belt. Involuntarily, he groaned with the pain.

Sabatino, swinging the car to the left, then heaved the wheel over to the right, giving the handbrake a determined upward yank. As the back end swung out immediately to the left, she dropped into a low gear and fed in power, feathering the clutch and throttle, encouraging the car to rotate. Using only the heel of her right hand, she balanced their rotation and direction by variously steering into and out of the slide.

Straightening up, Sabatino accelerated hard and changed up, heading off down the side road – to get themselves out of sight from the road behind them as quickly as possible. She took another random turning a few hundred yards later, to Wiggington, to start an unpredictable route back to the factory.

Two minutes later – after Straker had composed himself again, and checked the road behind them several times – he confirmed that they had surely lost their pursuers.

Turning his head back towards the front, Straker had to smile as he looked at the mischievous expression on Sabatino's face. 'That was quite extraordinary,' he said, with admiration and disbelief clear in his voice.

'Yeah,' she said unenthusiastically, 'but what the hell are these people doing? What the fuck is going on here?'

Despite Straker's aching ribs, the moment they got back to the Ptarmigan factory – he called a meeting with Sabatino, Nazar and Treadwell.

'We cannot ignore the new level of threat we're facing,' Straker declared.

After being told by Krall of the beating Straker had taken in Leamington Spa the night before – let alone its effects being all too clear in the contusions and broken skin across his face – not to mention the damage inflicted to the back of his brand-new Morgan starkly visible out in the car park, there was no disagreement from the Ptarmigan bosses.

'Most significantly,' Straker went on, 'these scumbags have moved beyond trying to screw us on the field of play. It means we're all now potentially at risk. At any time.'

'What do you think we should do?' asked Sabatino.

Straker handed them each a single sheet of paper. 'Here are some thoughts I've drawn up to enhance the security and safety of the team.'

The two men read their sheets in silence.

Sabatino didn't: 'You want to remove any predictability from my discussed or published timetable?' she stated half mockingly. 'You want a complete change of all my plans – travel, accommodation, and timings, including moving me out of the Dorchester to another hotel decided on at the last minute before the London Grand Prix? You want me to cancel all public appearances – in order that I keep a low profile?'

Tahm Nazar endorsed Straker's entire package of measures, and strongly encouraged Sabatino to comply.

Surprisingly, she sort of agreed to do all of it.

Straker's sense of injustice hit new levels of intensity. After their disastrous press coverage from the Paris hearing, and Quartano's announcement of Ptarmigan's withdrawal from the massive Mandarin sponsorship deal – not to mention Straker's personal violations from the assault in Leamington and the violence to his car as they were chased through Warwickshire – Straker was about to be pushed to the edge.

A tweet started trending – with the hashtag "#closetoJoss".

It boasted that Massarella had made an approach to Mandarin Telecom. The tweeter crowed that Formula One was still capable of benefiting from this phenomenal endorsement of its sport, even if some teams appeared to be no longer worthy of it.

"Our sport is bigger than any one team," said the tweeter.

Straker was incensed by this news.

He lived through the next forty-eight hours over the following weekend not knowing which way this blow to his psyche would take him.

FIFTY-EIGHT

Somehow Straker survived. Holding it together.

Anticipation of the next race might have played a part.

The first London Grand Prix loomed. This idea had been a long time in the making, seemingly thwarted by decades of bureaucracy and nimbyism. To its advocates, it made perfect sense. London, over the centuries, had pioneered major public sporting events – the Boat Race, the Festival of the Empire, two previous Olympic Games, a World Cup Final, and, more recently, phenomena like the London Marathon, and, spectacularly, the London 2012 Olympics. The London Grand Prix seemed to be from the very same stable. Furthermore, how could this not be a fitting legacy to 2012 – and be yet another opportunity for Britain to show off her organizational flair and sporting heritage?

In the media build-up to the race, Sabatino was fêted – celebrated for her status not only as the first serious female Formula One driver but also as the current leader of the Drivers' Championship. Luckily, editors chose to focus on that, rather than the pall overhanging the Ptarmigan Team of their prospective follow-up hearing in front of the FIA, to be held the following Monday.

Despite the distractions, Sabatino was mentally focused. During the practice sessions, she had taken several laps, but none of them yet at full speed. She was now ready for her first all-out flying lap.

For the London Grand Prix, the grid was laid out in front of the Dorchester Hotel, in the southbound carriageway of Park Lane – while the pit lane was made up by temporary structures along the northbound lanes, on the other side of the central reservation.

Rounding Marble Arch, Sabatino headed down the eastern side of Park Lane and built up speed into what, that weekend, was the start/finish straight. Down past some of the most expensive real estate in London, she sped the car up through the gearbox to eighteen thousand revs on each change before hitting one hundred and eighty miles an hour as she passed the Grosvenor House Hotel. Seventh gear, and the car was running well.

Now!

She crossed the start line outside the Dorchester and hurtled southwards, on past the massive grandstand in front of the Hilton.

Sabatino swept the car gently to the right, holding the inside line of the gentle curve, as she headed down towards Hyde Park Corner.

Keeping over to the right, she could see the Wellington Arch loom into view in the middle of the roundabout. Pulsing the revs while dropping down three gears, she readied to slice left onto the Hyde Park Corner roundabout.

Rounding Turn One – almost reaching the wall by the Machine Gun Memorial – she applied a little more left lock through the second apex, putting her into the end of Piccadilly. Grandstands had been erected on the roundabout, which now gave their occupants a superb back view of the Championship leader as she roared – hurtling directly – away from them down Piccadilly.

Sabatino reached one hundred and ninety miles an hour as she sped down the slight incline, alongside Green Park to her right. This section of the circuit was dead straight for nearly three-quarters of a mile. A slight dip in the road to cross the Tyburn – at the normal intersection with Brick Street – had her slightly compressed in the cockpit, but she was soon rising up the other side towards the Ritz. Cresting the rise opposite the hotel, she entered the more built-up part of Piccadilly – down past Fortnum & Mason. Still dead straight, her Ptarmigan screamed between the narrow confines of the street at over two hundred and ten miles an hour. Banks of seats, along either side and in very close proximity to the track, gave the spectators a vivid sense of the speed these cars could do – and a clear understanding of the noise they made, as the sound reverberated off the buildings down the narrowish street.

After another five hundred yards, Turn Two was ahead, a

left-right-left into Piccadilly Circus, round Eros and past the Trocadero. Drifting over to the right towards the end of Piccadilly in preparation, she waited to judge her braking zone – as discussed with Treadwell on their walk round. Passing Waterstone's, she breathed deeply and started to brake. Again, with the engine management system pulsing the revs to prevent any rear-wheel lock-up on any downshift, she shaved one hundred miles an hour from her speed before judging the moment to slice left into Turn Two. Eros was blocked out by more grandstands which were giving spectators a magnificent view of the track.

Into Piccadilly Circus.

A forty-five-degree left-hander. Sabatino ran straight for no more than fifty yards before applying opposite lock and turning right, over the slight mound in the road at the end of Shaftesbury Avenue, before straightening up, pulling left in front of the Trocadero and then swinging right through Turn Four, into the top of the Haymarket.

She smiled to herself as the car performed beautifully. It was balanced – the downforce being spot on – and the grip, even on the places where the road surface had been heavily touched up, was as much as she could have wanted.

Sabatino thundered down the Haymarket. The noise from the engine bouncing off the high buildings on either side was deafening – even through her helmet. She had three hundred yards to run straight down the hill. Passing the Haymarket Theatre, and the end of Sector One, fifth gear was all she could reach before running to the right and dropping two gears before a forty-five-degree left turn at the bottom of the hill. Turn Five. This took the circuit across Pall Mall. Sabatino accelerated hard through the apex and on down the slope of Cockspur Street towards Trafalgar Square.

Next up was Turn Six, and a novelty for Formula One.

This corner could be very different, depending on the exit. Round to the right, drivers had to shoot under Admiralty Arch, but were presented with a choice of two arches – the middle or the left-hand one – each being only one-car wide. Depending on which arch a driver was aiming to use, they would have to vary their entry to the preceding corner in Trafalgar Square. Sabatino, in practice, had opted for the left-hand one each time, making the corner more open and, therefore, faster.

Holding herself over to the left of the entry at the foot of Nelson's Column, she changed down and cut right, rounding the corner. Admiralty Arch loomed over her head as she shot under the left-hand arch. Emerging the far side, she had an amazing view down The Mall – the pink surface of the wide, dead-straight- and tree-lined road – stretching for half a mile to the façade of Buckingham Palace at the far end. Opening right up, she felt the awesome power of the Ptarmigan propel her up to top speed.

To the spectators on the grandstands to her left, the view was enthralling. They watched her brilliant turquoise car emerge through the splendour of Admiralty Arch, accelerate at an awesome rate from right to left in front of them – against the backdrop of Nash's Regency masterpieces – and disappear at breakneck speed down between the trees towards the Palace.

Three-quarters of the way down The Mall, about level with Clarence House, Sabatino, running at two hundred and ten miles an hour, drifted left – onto the St James's Park side of the road. She was setting herself up for Turns Seven and Eight: a contrived chicane beside the Victoria Monument.

Through this tight right-left-right the car was completely balanced. There was no understeer – no hint of the back end trying to step out. This felt as good as it had in Spa. She powered easily through the chicane to reach the bottom of Constitution Hill. Sabatino now had the four hundred yards run up that rise along the wall of Buckingham Palace, all under the canopy of the spectacular avenue of trees.

She heard Treadwell over the radio, telling her she was fastest by point-five in Sector One.

Towards the top of Constitution Hill, she prepared to shoot the

Memorial Gates on the right-hand side, readying her entry for Turn Nine, which led onto the roundabout at Hyde Park Corner. At that speed, she felt some lightening of the car as she crested that rise, but was soon back on the power as she headed down the short straight towards Grosvenor Place. The next corner, on the roundabout, Turn Ten, was a ninety-degree right-hander with a scoop-like camber. She hoped its banking effect would act as slingshot round the Australia Memorial, sending her quickly up the hill towards Hyde Park. In third gear, the Ptarmigan did precisely that, digging in round the bend and offering total solidity as she pushed the car hard. G-force, at around three-point-nine, was the highest anywhere on the circuit.

Up the short straight.

She accelerated hard. Hanging left, she set the car up for one flowing S-shaped motion. Cutting in right, Sabatino drove the combination of the right-handed Turn Eleven, by the Lanesborough Hotel – the short straight along the top of the roundabout – and then the left-hand Turn Twelve, circling round Apsley House, heading north up Park Lane. Once again, the car responded to everything she asked of it.

After rounding Turn Twelve, Sabatino was back in Park Lane but only for seventy-five yards. Almost immediately she had to prepare to turn again.

Holding her line to the right, she needed to shoot the Queen Elizabeth Gate to the left.

She was through there. No sooner than she was, did she need to slice right, through Turn Fourteen, into the long straight of Serpentine Road, cutting through the middle of Hyde Park.

Sabatino blasted along under the maple trees, below the Cavalry Memorial – past the open space at the southern end of the Parade Ground of Hyde Park – and on towards the boathouses.

Serpentine Road was wide, straight and level – and, running along the northern shore of London's most famous lake, the Serpentine, was for Formula One fans wholly evocative of the scene around Albert Park in Melbourne. Four hundred yards further on, and hitting her top speed, she drew level with the lido on the far side. A flock of geese, moorhens and ducks took flight as the noise of the Ptarmigan's Benbecular engine screamed by.

End of Sector Two.

Sabatino felt she was flying.

Preparing for the next corner, a right-hander, she first hugged the inside kerb of the right-hand kink and set herself up for the thirty-degree right of Turn Fifteen, by Magazine Gate. There was a huge bank of spectators directly in front of her. Sabatino swung the car right, up and round the corner, giving her access to the pink surface of West Carriage Drive. The circuit, here, was straightish with a very slight meander in each direction for two hundred yards. Kensington Gardens were now over to her left.

Turn Sixteen was one of the features of this circuit, the Duchess of Cambridge Hairpin. Dropping down to second gear, Sabatino timed her entry. Despite the adverse camber of the corner, her feel from the car allowed her to apply massive acceleration through the apex, and gain a clean exit into the fast straight of North Carriage Drive.

In the relative inactivity of the next segment, she looked down at her steering wheel as she built up speed to two hundred miles an hour again. Everything was looking good. Up and over a very slight rise, with no more than a fifteen-degree right, she was able to relax her neck and shoulders momentarily, as she hurtled down past the public grandstands running parallel with – and backing onto – the Bayswater Road.

Turn Seventeen, the Cumberland Gate, gave onto the Marble Arch roundabout. This was a one-hundred-degree left-hander. The surface – where the organizers had removed some of the island bollards normally in the road – was a little uneven.

Taking off speed, she hung over to the right, lined up her entry, braked hard, and swung left onto the roundabout. The car was faithful, despite the rough surface, only giving one scintilla of instability – otherwise, she was round and through. There were seventy-five yards to run before she was into another corner. A sharp right-hander this time, joining the Bayswater Road. This turn, like Turn Ten around Hyde Park corner, had a favourable camber. Pushing in hard, she rounded it easily and hurtled on towards Oxford Street, with the Odeon to her left and Marble Arch to the right.

Then Turn Nineteen.

The last on the circuit.

She hung left, judged her moment – and sliced as tight as she dared through it, kissing the apex on the inside to perfection. As she opened the throttle heading south into Park Lane, she was ecstatic.

The car's set-up was magnificent.

She didn't think she could have driven any faster.

Crossing the line by the Dorchester and starting to wind down – ready to amble back on her in-lap – Treadwell's voice came up animatedly on the radio. 'Bloody terrific, Remy!' he yelled. 'You're fastest by nine tenths. *Outstanding.*'

Sabatino smiled and allowed herself to shut the FIA hearing, due to be held on Monday, out of her mind. For the moment, at least, she wallowed in being the fastest of the pack so far.

Qualifying Three had Sabatino set up for a two-stop strategy.

Her fuel load was similar to the faster laps she had done all weekend. She posted two flying laps in Q3.

The first put her point-three ahead.

On the second, with nothing to lose, she gave another scorching performance, not putting a wheel wrong – bettering her own time by a further five tenths.

She was on pole by over a second.

For the two Championships – the Constructors' and Drivers' – as well as for herself, she had done everything she could have hoped for.

But would it be enough?

FIFTY-NINE

Weather, on the Sunday, was as close to a perfect English summer's day as anyone could wish for.

Once the cars had formed up on the grid in the southbound carriageway of Park Lane, the great and the good were swarming all around them. The hooter went.

The engines started their roar.

All the media and hangers-on soon dispersed and, within a few moments, all that was left on the track was the might of fifteen thousand horsepower screaming for a fight.

The lights went on, and Sabatino pulled away, sedately leading the field off round the 3.75 mile circuit on the formation lap.

A few minutes later, Sabatino – on pole – was ready.

This was it.

The wait seemed interminable.

One red light came on.

The second red light.

Third, fourth and then the fifth.

The five lights seemed to burn for an age.

Then GO!

The roar peaked as twenty-two cars pulled off the line.

Sabatino, on the clean side of the track, got a blistering start. She was away well, and hurtling down to Turn One. Behind her off the grid was a Mercedes, not a contender in the Championship this year. Behind him – in P3 and very much a challenger – was Simi Luciano in the Massarella. Over Sabatino's right shoulder was her closest rival for the title, Paddy Aston in the Lambourn. Championship-wise, this race could see the leader board turned completely on its head. If she wasn't careful, she could be dethroned that very afternoon.

All of that pressure was hurtling down the road behind her – every pursuer hell-bent on taking her lead.

But Sabatino was focused.

Judging her line, she held her ideal position down Park Lane and got a clear entry into Turn One on Hyde Park Corner roundabout, kissed the apex, and exited powerfully into Piccadilly.

Those behind her weren't so lucky. There was a bottleneck. The Mercedes in second place was challenged by Luciano, which queered his entry into, and line through, the apex. In the exit, the Mercedes managed to hold P2, while Aston made the most of the enforced funnelling, getting a jump on the Massarella.

Sabatino snatched a glance in her mirrors. She saw the order between Luciano and Aston had been reversed. Damnit, she swore to herself. Paddy Aston's Lambourn was now up to P3. Her hope that Aston might be held up further down the field for a while had evaporated round the very first corner. Sabatino, now, needed Paddy Aston behind the Mercedes in P2 long enough for her to break away and establish something of a lead.

Reaching Turn Two, round Piccadilly Circus, Aston's purple Lambourn was in the Mercedes's mirrors and getting bigger all the time.

Sabatino pushed hard while her chance remained. She had a clear sweep through Turns Two, Three and Four – and could just about see the spat going on between Aston and the Mercedes behind her. She didn't want that scrap to end anytime soon. The Mercedes was a vital four-point buffer between her and the man who was only one point behind her in the Championship.

Round Turn Five, at the bottom of the Haymarket, and Sabatino was feeling confident. Her car was up to temperature and performing as well as it had all year. Passing Canada House, she had a one-second lead on the Mercedes, and could see how much of a challenge Aston was mounting behind him. Aston, very clearly, was not going to let Sabatino get away.

Down towards the bottom of Trafalgar Square.

Sabatino planned to take the left-hand option under Admiralty

Arch and set herself up accordingly. Looking back, though, she saw her unchallenged claim to the lead was about to end. The second-placed Mercedes was clearly following her route into the entry, but Aston was already swinging wider. He's going to cut in through the middle arch, she thought to herself as she lost sight of them both in her mirrors rounding the corner herself.

Lo and behold – as she screamed through under the arches into The Mall and looked back – she saw what she feared. The Mercedes was emerging through the left-hand arch, while Aston's Lambourn was coming through the middle one.

A little Scalextric-like, but that unusual split in the track had already livened up overtaking – while the TV shot along the length of The Mall to Admiralty Arch, with cars racing for position emerging through the different arches, was quite sensational.

Aston now had a clear track to his front. The Mercedes had lost its advantage: Aston, with the Lambourn's extra grunt, soon drew level and was past.

Paddy Aston was now in P2 and only a hundred and fifty yards behind Sabatino as they headed through Turns Seven and Eight, the chicane outside Buckingham Palace.

Sabatino breathed deeply, as she resigned herself to her closest rival for the Championship emerging from that squabble and mounting a serious challenge to her lead. If she wasn't able to pull away, she would have to drive error-free, defensively – resolutely, holding her rights to the line. This race, now, was far more than simply the London Grand Prix. It was, de facto, for the Championship. It was her or Paddy Aston. Only one point separated them on the Championship leader board. Sabatino could extend that to three points, if these positions were held to the end of the day. Or she could be a point behind him if the places were reversed. Her not finishing the race did not even bear thinking about.

The two gladiators raced on, lap after lap. Their relative positions held constant. At least for the moment.

Straker was watching avidly – and hearing analysis of her telemetry and performance throughout the race from the team in the
motor home. By all technical measures – as well as sporting ones –
Sabatino was driving with extraordinary sang-froid and consistency.

They were only ten laps in. There were sixty more to go. How
could she retain that level of concentration for that long? And under
that mental pressure – knowing that the tiniest of mistakes would let
Aston pounce and take advantage?

What *must* it be like in the cockpit? Straker wondered.

To the spectators, the tension heightened significantly during the
pit stops. After thirty laps, Sabatino and Aston were still only two
seconds apart on the track.

Any slip-up in the pits – a wheel nut that wouldn't budge, a wheel
gun that refused to work, a problem with the fuel rig, a misunder-
stood signal from the lollipop man, or a snatched start causing a stall
– could easily cost her two seconds. Thirty laps of brilliant racing
– not to mention the Championship lead – could be thrown away
that easily.

'Box this time,' came Treadwell's instruction over the air.

Sabatino, just passing the Serpentine, responded: 'What's my
lead?'

'Two-point-four seconds.'

'Okay, ask the guys to do this one for me!'

Straker held his breath.

Sabatino approached Cumberland Gate and Marble Arch. She
rounded Turn Eighteen cleanly and was pointing up to Nineteen.
Round there, she was about to re-enter Park Lane when, pulling
over further to the right, she threaded herself on round Cumberland
Gate before turning left into the top of the other carriageway of Park
Lane. There, she headed south down the pit lane in front of the row
of temporary garages. Flicking the limiter, she kept her speed down
– to an agonizingly slow – eighty kilometres an hour.

Her crew were out and ready.

She cruised down on the limiter. She swerved in and jammed on the brakes.

She was straight up on the jacks.

The wheel men went to work immediately.

Front right, off.

Front left, off.

Front right, on.

Front left, on.

She saw two horizontal arms held above each front wheel, indicating completion.

What about the rears? She grabbed a look in each mirror. Both their arms were horizontal too. The car dropped back down as the jacks were removed.

What about the fuel? She couldn't see the rigger from where she sat.

Come on! Come on! – she screamed to herself.

She felt the car jolt to the right. Let that be the rig coming off. She looked at the lollipop man. The sign was swivelling round.

Yes!

Revving the engine, she dreaded a stall. Then, the lollipop was being raised, shooting up and away. First gear, now!

The car jumped forwards. It kept running.

No stall!

She was away.

She swerved left and then right – almost under the compressed air hoses of the next team – as she regained the pit lane.

She was trundling along on the limiter. Come on! Come on! It seemed to go on forever – heading down towards the cut-through in the central reservation directly opposite the Dorchester Hotel. Feeding through there, and desperate not to cross the white line, she built up speed as fast as she could.

She screamed on down to Turn One. Ahead of her she found a Ferrari and a Mercedes jostling for position. *Not* what she wanted.

At all. To get past them would be for track position too – she wasn't going to get any help from blue flags. She would have to challenge these two for real. For position.

Adding to the pressure, she would *have* to take them quickly – otherwise, any hold-up on the next few vital laps, would kill her wafer-thin lead over Aston. Aston was currently out there on an uncluttered track with a lighter fuel load in a car with bedded-in everything, while she was on cold rubber and stuck behind two cars completely absorbed in their own little battle.

'Well done the lads,' she said over the radio. 'But we've blown the re-entry. How many laps do we think Paddy's got?'

'Three, max.'

'His times?'

'No quicker than before, thank heavens. He wasn't really in your dirty air.'

'Okay, I've got a spat in front of me. Hope it doesn't hold me up.'

'They're lapping point-nine slower than you. You *do* have a straight-line advantage – try and take them on the straight, rather than into a corner – at least until you get a feel for your tyres.'

Sabatino fought to remain cautious until the new boots were up to temperature. She stayed behind the Ferrari/Mercedes scrap all the way down to Turn Five, at the bottom of the Haymarket.

She had to get by soon – otherwise all of her lead over Aston would be gone.

Her eyes bored into the backs of the two cars in front. They screamed down past Canada House, one after the other – the blocked one swerving this way and that, trying to get by. Would they be so preoccupied with each other that they wouldn't see her coming? If they were, that could be both good news or bad.

Down towards Turn Six, at the bottom of Trafalgar Square, she was ready to put herself in a position to strike. Which way would the squabblers go through Admiralty Arch? Who would take the left arch? The Ferrari in the lead? Did that mean the Mercedes, behind, would automatically try for the middle one?

She had no way of knowing … yet. She got closer and closer, ready to pounce – praying for an opportunity.

Reaching the entry, it looked like the Ferrari at the front was going wider – through the left arch. But then he tried the element of surprise. At the last minute, he ducked inside, aiming for the middle one. It threw the Mercedes behind him. The Mercedes had clearly expected to be going that way himself. Momentarily, he had to lift off, for fear of running into the back of the Ferrari. But now, realizing his chance lay in going wide, he swung out to the left and tried to adjust his line. That change of direction, though, cost him a nanosecond's delay.

It was enough.

Now! screamed Sabatino to herself.

With the Mercedes's loss of pace at the element of surprise, she herself ducked *inside*, following the leading Ferrari – through the middle arch. Having taken that initiative, the Ferrari would still be travelling at top speed. Getting in behind him would be quicker for Sabatino than following the Mercedes who was probably still reacting from being wrong-footed.

She fought the wheel to keep the car heading straight through the incredibly tight fit under the middle arch. Applying the power – while still under the building – she emerged the other side, and, thrillingly, found herself drawing level with the wider-going Mercedes to her left.

She'd got past one of them already.

Now she had the Ferrari – only four lengths ahead of her.

Sabatino was quickly on terms – the Benbecular kicking out ten or so more horsepower – the difference beginning to show encouragingly soon.

They screamed on up The Mall, the scarlet Ferrari in front, the turquoise Ptarmigan behind. Two Formula One cars racing through London in front of the world-famous backdrop of Buckingham Palace.

As the Ferrari prepared for the chicane, Turns Seven and Eight, it pulled left, gingerly, so as not to open the door for Sabatino.

She couldn't challenge him there.

Up Constitution Hill, their line-astern formation resumed.

Turn Nine, onto Hyde Park Corner roundabout. She couldn't challenge him there.

Down the hill to Turn Ten and into Grosvenor Place. She didn't challenge him there, although encouragingly the Ferrari ran slightly wider and a little ragged. Was the pressure of her pursuit beginning to get to him?

She hoped so.

Up past the Lanesborough Hotel, to the right-hander – and she was still on his tail. She didn't challenge him there.

Round Apsley House and through the Queen Elizabeth Gate they raced. Nose to tail. Still no challenge.

Entering Hyde Park, Sabatino timed her moment to strike. The Ferrari ran a little wide on the exit of Turn Fourteen. Into the broad and straight Serpentine Road, Sabatino powered rapidly up through the gears, revs and speedometer until she was running flat out.

The gap started to close.

The crowds were treated to a five-hundred-yard head-to-head as the Ptarmigan mounted its inch by inch challenge to the Ferrari.

They swept up to and started rounding the lake as the battle fought on.

Sabatino pulled level.

By the time they passed the fake wattle and daub boathouse, she had gained the advantage – just about getting her wheels in front. There! She'd cleared the scarlet Ferrari. But she was pounding down to Turn Fifteen.

Losing shape into the right-hander, she breathed deeply as she fought to stabilize her line up and onto West Carriage Drive.

She'd done it, though – *and* made it stick.

She radioed Treadwell in the pits. 'Where's Paddy?'

'Well played with those two. He's gained two seconds on you since you pitted.'

'Damn that Ferrari. Any clue when Aston'll pit?'

'Can't be more than two laps from now.'

'Okay.'

Sabatino pushed hard. With the advantage, now, of a clear track in front of her, she gave the circuit everything.

Two laps on, she was rounding the Duchess of Cambridge Hairpin when Treadwell radioed her: 'You've shaved off a second. Keep pushing hard.'

There was a brief pause, then: 'Wait ... wait ... he's coming in! Aston's coming in!'

Sabatino didn't even reply. She dug deeper and hammered the Ptarmigan.

Screaming along North Carriage Drive across the top of Hyde Park towards Cumberland Gate and Marble Arch, she had to get round there – round the corner by Oxford Street, back into Park Lane and still get down to the Dorchester – in the time it would take the Lambourn to pit and re-emerge on the track.

Round Cumberland Gate, Turn Seventeen.

Up towards Bayswater Road.

Round Turn Eighteen, the back end was trying to step out despite the massively favourable camber – she was pushing the car *that* hard.

Up towards Oxford Street past the Odeon.

Hanging left, she soon sliced right through Turn Nineteen hammering on the power.

Into Park Lane.

She screamed up the gears. With Park Lane's slight kink to the left, she couldn't yet see its second half.

'Where is he?' she yelled into the radio.

'Coming to the cut-through.'

'I see him.'

She was four hundred yards back up the road and travelling, now, at over one hundred and eighty miles an hour. Aston was accelerating fast – up through ninety, hundred, hundred and ten.

The gap between them was closing.

Would it close fast enough? Could she get in front?

He was still inside the white line – the exit from the pits.

She powered on, willing her car to go faster. She hit the rev limiter. Aston was accelerating all the time. But he was on cold rubber. Their closing speed, though, was now slowing.

Down Park Lane towards the Hilton she screamed.

Aston was getting faster all the time.

She was just about pulling level, on the left – he to her right.

She powered on.

She was nudging past.

Was there enough of Park Lane left? She needed to be half a car length in front to have a legitimate claim to the line.

Hyde Park Corner loomed into view.

Had she done enough?

To be sure, Sabatino was going to have to be the last of the late brakers. If that threw her out of shape, she knew Aston would capitalize immediately. He would inevitably pounce, slip past, and take the lead.

She pushed on – with absolutely no let-up – nothing less than *full* commitment.

NOW – she hammered the brakes – as late as she dared. She had no time to look around her, to look in her mirrors.

She pounded into the double apex, the car sliding badly through the middle. A massive yaw. She fought to keep control.

Sabatino was *in* Piccadilly.

Where was he? Where was Aston?

She looked either side of her – couldn't see anything. She looked in her mirrors.

Couldn't see anything there either.

Then suddenly – there! *There!* She saw a wheel. He was back *there!* She'd done it. She was back in the lead.

'Bloody marvellous,' screamed Treadwell in raw Australian over the radio. 'Fantastic driving. *Magic* stuff.'

'Phew!' she yelled back as she raced up the gears and revs along Piccadilly towards the Ritz. 'Let's hope I can keep him back there for the rest.'

The crowds around Hyde Park went wild.

Twenty laps later, with Aston still breathing down her neck every foot of the way, Sabatino rounded Marble Arch for the last time.

She sliced into Park Lane and accelerated hard.

Moments later she saw the chequered flag.

It was waving for her.

She'd done it. Monaco, Singapore and now London. *What* a feeling.

Sabatino savoured the adulations from the crowds all the way round on her victory lap. She pulled up into Parc Fermé.

The very first to come over and congratulate her was Paddy Aston. 'Great drive, Remy. Great stuff,' he said. 'You are, undeniably, the street-circuit queen.'

The celebrations were immense.

Crowds of people flooded into Park Lane to watch the prize-giving on the podium set up outside and level with the first floor of the Dorchester Hotel. Both the Prime Minster and the Mayor of London were involved in handing out the numerous trophies.

The crowds loved anything that prolonged this moment.

Sabatino, once again, had captured everyone's imagination.

The win in London kept Sabatino in the lead for the Drivers' Championship, her ten points bringing her season tally now to 81.

Aston, in second, scored eight points, putting him on 78 – meaning Sabatino's lead had actually been widened to a still incredibly modest three points. Luciano, scoring six points for third, was up to 72. It was all extraordinarily close. Any one of the top three in the Drivers' Championship could still win the title.

Formula One was in for a spellbinding showdown in Brazil in two weeks' time.

In the Constructors' Championship it was a very much clearer story ... or was it?

Helli Cunzer's five points for fourth in the other Ptarmigan were all the team needed. Their combined points were enough – potentially – to win the Constructors' Championship. With only Brazil to run, Ptarmigan could not now be beaten.

At least, not on the track.

Despite all this triumph – not to mention the edge-of-your-seat excitement during the first running of the sensational London Grand Prix – the Ptarmigan Team were far from jubilant. Their Championship win was not a given. They were not celebrating.

They were mightily distracted.

Particularly Sabatino.

All were haunted by the spectre of the FIA hearing, to be held in London the very next day.

Would she – or the team – even get to *keep* the Championship points she had just driven so hard to win?

SIXTY

Straker couldn't sleep that night. The threat of injustice kept him awake. What if the FIA system failed? What if Ptarmigan weren't able to clear their name at the hearing?

Waking before five, annoyingly unrefreshed, Straker set out on a run, despite the residual discomfort from his attack in Leamington.

Turning right at Putney Bridge, and following the towpath along the Thames to the west, he tried to distance himself from everything – the saboteurs, the hearing, and even Remy Sabatino.

Straker wanted to blank everything from his mind.

The weather helped. It was one of those special summer mornings – absolutely still, not a breath of wind, already warm, hazy, with the sun barely visible through the mist and a spectacular day promising to burst through. Even the air smelled warm.

Straker ordered his thoughts for the hearing. He deconstructed and challenged the case they would make in front of the FIA later that day. Despite his exertion running, and the occasional distraction of an extra sprint or a bit of tricky navigation through a twisty or impeded section of the towpath, he went over and over their arguments. Would they be enough? How could he be sure?

An hour and a half later, running eastwards back along the south bank for home, Straker reached the end of the gravel track into Putney. Up ahead were the rowing club boathouses, enjoying the sun that had just starting burning through the haze.

It was quite a scene.

Down the wide slipway, a crew was carrying an inverted eight above their head to the water's edge – wearing body-hugging Lycra in the livery of their club and, incongruously, wellington boots. A coxless four was already out on the river, as well as several sculls – all gliding effortlessly along on the mirror-like surface of the Thames.

Putney suddenly seemed so restful, particularly for central London. Straker found himself dropping down to a walk to breathe it all in.

Everything about the place seemed different. Most obvious was the offer of a view – impossible in most parts of the capital. He could see for quite a distance in both directions along the river, inducing a relaxing feeling – a feeling of open space.

The multi-arched stone road bridge across the Thames also played its part, making the place seem more like a county market town, than the suburb of a frenetic metropolis. Adding to this impression, the architecture along the waterfront had a distinctive unregimented style, too, which suggested it was somewhere other than central London. And then, with the prominence of the boathouses, there was the very obvious devotion of the place to leisure and an altogether different focus of life. Straker realized for the first time how much Putney was content to live at its own pace, irrespective of whatever hubbub chose to go on around it.

He found it utterly calming.

He looked the place up and down, drinking in as much of the space and atmosphere as he could.

Catching his eye was a For Sale board in front of a stylish Georgian villa, right on the waterfront. Walking up to the front of the house, Straker took in its façade: fanlights over a heavy panelled door; large well-proportioned windows; and an elegant first-floor balcony edged by a set of ornate railings. Then, peering in through the windows, he tried to get an idea of the inside.

Straker was immediately hooked – on the house, its architecture, its outlook, position, the Thames – everything.

He ran on down the waterfront to cross Putney Bridge, making his way back to the flat in Fulham.

But as he ran across the bridge on the upstream side, he couldn't stop himself looking back across the river – to the slipway, to the row of boathouses, to the houses along the waterfront – and to that Georgian villa with the For Sale board out front. He found himself pulling out his phone and typing in the name and number of the estate agent.

The follow-up hearing of the Ptarmigan industrial espionage case was held at noon that day in the spectacular Edwardian clubhouse of the Royal Automobile Club in Pall Mall, London. Outside the RAC, there was the familiar press mob crowding the entrance.

As the Ptarmigan party arrived, they were met with the same baying and shouted questions – challenging, as earlier, the team's ethics and integrity. The excitement of Sabatino's drive and victory the day before did not seem to count for anything. Even so, she and Nazar chose, once again, to stand calmly in front of the journalists, allowing them to take their photographs – hopefully reflecting some dignity – before they went in.

Sabatino, Nazar, Treadwell, Straker and Brogan were met by an FIA official inside the RAC and ushered through the magnificent rotunda and up the stairs to the right. Around the gallery on the first floor, they were led to the south of the building and into the library. There, they were asked to wait until being called into the committee room next door.

To Straker, Brogan seemed almost agitated this time. It was unnerving. What did that mean? Was the barrister's demeanour giving away his true thoughts on the strength of their case?

Sabatino continued to express her fear of having points deducted because of the FIA inquiry, and harming her Championship chances. The expression on her face clearly showed that such anxieties were weighing heavily on her mind, completely overriding any buzz from her drive through the streets of London the day before.

Finally, the Ptarmigan party was called in.

The surroundings for this hearing could hardly have been more different than the last: there was none of the clinical starkness of the décor in the Paris Council Chamber. Here was London clubland at its finest. The committee room was magnificent. A high ceiling. Intricate and elaborate plasterwork. A marble fireplace. Portraits, in oil, of grand-looking men around the walls. In the centre of the large room was a highly polished antique table, across which were numerous silver models and statuettes of famous cars and their drivers since the dawn of motoring and motor racing. Directly above this was an eye-catching crystal chandelier. And incongruous to the Ptarmigan team's mood, bright sunshine poured into the room through the open double doors from the conservatory.

This time twenty people – including the thirteen voting members of the Council to make the meeting quorate – were sitting around the table for the follow-up hearing.

The President of the FIA, the Marquis of San Marino, as before, rose as the Ptarmigan party entered the Council hearing. 'Ms Sabatino, gentlemen. Please take a seat at the table.' The Massarella contingent was already seated, across the table to their left.

As proceedings began, San Marino said: 'Mr Brogan, may I assume that you accept this as a continuation of the FIA hearing, on 25th July in Paris, to assess Massarella's allegations of industrial espionage against Ptarmigan?'

'You can, Mr President. May I confirm that you have now received our revised statement of facts and that, on this occasion, you will also admit our counter-claim against Massarella's conduct this season?'

'You may. Now, Mr Brogan. We had established, in Paris, that an employee of your client, a Ms Charlotte Grant, had been in contact with Massarella. Would you care to comment on this – now that your client has had some time to consider it?'

Brogan opened up his notebook and straightened his pen on the RAC-embossed leather blotter in front of him. 'Indeed, Mr President. Can I first explain that Ms Grant was indeed an employee of Quartech, Ptarmigan's owner. She was on secondment to the team. I do not wish to slander the dead, but I need the Council to be aware she had already behaved in a disloyal fashion within Quartech – leaking top secret blueprints for a cutting-edge rifle system to a German rival. Mr President, I am prepared to elaborate further, but only to you, personally, in private session. I do not feel comfortable discussing her conduct, or the impact on Quartech's defence business, any further in a public forum. Quartech International is, after all, a publicly quoted company.'

San Marino's face registered some surprise at the revelations. Even so, he nodded his acceptance of Brogan's request.

'In summary, we would describe Charlotte Grant, therefore, as a rogue employee, Mr President.'

Straker looked over at the Massarella people. Van Der Vaal clearly looked disquieted. He wondered whether the South African was going to challenge either the description of Charlotte Grant or the imposed limit on discussing her any further.

Van Der Vaal seemed to be keeping quiet. For now.

'Mr President,' Brogan went on, 'this description of Ms Grant is offered to the Council to indicate that she had already attempted to do Quartech and its interests serious harm in one area. We contend that she was out to do my client serious harm in another. If I may, I'd like to refer, now, to my client's revised statement of facts in the light of this news. Under the new Tab 10, there are transcripts of some text messages we've recovered from Ms Grant's mobile phone.'

At this point there was a grunt and a growl from Van Der Vaal. 'Mr President, if we are not to discuss this Ptarmigan employee any further, how are we now able to discuss her mobile phone messages? Ptarmigan can't have it both ways.'

San Marino held Van Der Vaal's agitated stare. 'I am satisfied that enough information has been shared with the Council, without having demeaned or defamed someone who can no longer defend herself, Eugene. Please continue, Mr Brogan.'

'Thank you, Mr President. On page twelve you will see a number of SMS messages.'

Around the table members of motor sport's supreme governing body opened their folders and turned to the indicated spot.

'There is one message here of particular interest, which was sent to Ms Grant,' declared Brogan. 'It says, and I quote: *"Hope the ASD idea is going over well…"*'

One of the thirteen Council members present looked a little quizzical. 'ASD? Can you remind us what that means, Mr Brogan?'

'It's a reference to the technology in question in this allegation, sir,' answered Brogan politely and with deliberate patience – mindful that he might need this blazer's vote later on. 'ASD is Massarella's acronym for Aero-Spiral Device – the feature the Council has come to know as the spiral surfaces – and which Ptarmigan refer to as Fibonacci Blades.'

The Council member nodded his thanks.

'Mr President,' said Brogan, 'whoever sent that message is clearly prompting Charlotte Grant to promote the ASD. We submit to the Council that this clearly forms part of the information chain that led to this particular technology reaching and getting into Ptarmigan.'

'It would appear so,' acknowledged San Marino with a series of slow nods as he studied the text.

'So whose number is it that sent this message?' asked Joss MacRae from the side of the table. 'You've not identified it. How can this *possibly* constitute evidence?'

'A good point,' replied Brogan to the room with a slightly sly smile. 'You will notice that the number bears the international dialling code for Italy – and that it is a mobile phone.' Redirecting his attention to San Marino, he added: 'Mr President, during our previous session, you asked me to direct a question to another member present through the Chair…'

San Marino nodded.

'In that case, Mr President, I would like to ask whether Mr Van Der Vaal would comment on this number.'

San Marino's expression changed instantly, as did the mood in the room at this unexpected turn.

There was muttering for a few seconds.

'Well, Eugene?' asked the FIA President. '*Are* you able to comment on this number?'

Van Der Vaal's reaction was equally surprising. 'This has nothing to do with this case,' he growled. 'How are Ptarmigan allowed to use this kind of bogus evidence?'

San Marino then took everyone by surprise. Reaching forward, he grabbed the flying-saucer-like conference phone sitting on the table in front of him. Looking down through his half-moon reading glasses, he looked for the number on the SMS transcript and began to dial it out.

Van Der Vaal watched him – his expression that of someone with an increasing sense that he was about to be wrong-footed.

San Marino continued punching out the number.

Van Der Vaal's expression changed again. Quite markedly. Straker smiled inwardly. He stared at the Massarella team boss. Was the man finally coming to a realization?

Van Der Vaal let out a kind of growl. 'All right, *all right*,' came the guttural accent. Van Der Vaal paused. 'It's mine, okay. That's one of *my* phones.'

The Council was not able to control its reaction.

There was chatter and fidgeting all round.

'Mr President,' said Brogan commandingly – loud enough to be heard above the noise of the room and to be demanding of attention, 'this is hugely significant. And pivotal to this case. My client would like to ask a further question of Mr Van Der Vaal.' Brogan caught San Marino's eye as he looked up. 'Why was Mr Van Der Vaal clearly encouraging an outsider – an employee of the Ptarmigan Team, at that – to promote what we are now told was Massarella's proprietary technology?'

Noises of surprise continued to come from around the elegant RAC committee room.

At that point, Brogan just waited – leaving his question hanging in the air.

Still the rumble of noises continued.

San Marino simply said: 'Gentlemen?' to try and calm the room before looking over at Van Der Vaal. 'Eugene, I believe Ptarmigan have made a strong point. You need to explain this. It's one thing to be the victim of industrial espionage, and lose valuable information to a competitor. But quite another to be the apparent instigator of the transfer in the first place.'

Straker looked around the room, studying the faces of the Council members – trying to detect any change in their expressions.

'Eugene, you need to answer.'

Straker then looked across at Van Der Vaal. The arrogance – the brutish expression – was unwavering. Straker was staggered by the man's ego. He clearly wasn't conceding anything.

'What the hell is this?' barked Van Der Vaal. 'I reject this assertion, and reject evidence from a source that I am not allowed to challenge. In a proper court – of law – this evidence would be inadmissible.'

San Marino hesitated, switching his attention from Van Der Vaal back to Brogan.

'In that case, Mr President,' Brogan went on, retaking the floor, 'I would like to demonstrate to the Council that this encouragement to pass on ASD technology is by no means an isolated incident from the Massarella Team. Indeed, it is entirely consistent with a programme of intervention levelled by Massarella at Ptarmigan throughout this season. May I ask you to turn to Tab 15 of our revised statement of facts, which shows my client's new evidence. Which is substantial. I should explain, Mr President, that Ptarmigan's feeling of injustice over Massarella's conduct, and their lack of disclosure in this case, was so strong it prompted my client to take significant legal action. Ptarmigan applied to the British High Court – under the UK's Civil Procedure Act 1997 – for powers to search premises and to seize documents from two parties involved with Massarella's activities. On the strength of Ptarmigan's case, the Court granted permission. Tab 15 shows some of the records seized from the premises of Trifecta Systems and Mr Michael Lyons, formerly of the same, under the powers of the Search Order issued by the High Court.'

Some Council members looked clearly surprised by the extent of the legal processes Ptarmigan had invoked.

Brogan kept talking, though, almost as if he were chairing the meeting. 'In here, Mr President, you will now see batches of emails – between Mr Lyons and Mr Van Der Vaal. Extraordinarily, news is shared between the two men of the sabotage incidents since alleged by Ptarmigan. The first batch of emails relates to the jamming device placed in Ms Sabatino's helmet before Monaco – which interfered with a potentially race-winning transmission at the time of the safety car. The second set of emails discusses the sabotage of Helli Cunzer's exhaust in Monte-Carlo, intended to degrade his suspension – which it did at high speed, causing that horrific crash which nearly killed him. And the third batch refers to the device used by Adi Barrantes to remotely activate Ms Sabatino's engine limiter in Spa, which caused her to suffer that terrifying high-speed loss of control in the second round of Qualifying at the Belgian Grand Prix.'

Brogan stopped.

He sensed he had delivered quite a punch. There was a lot for the Council to absorb.

The room fell silent.

The news was sinking in.

Straker felt they might be approaching the crunch point in their arguments – and he did not want Van Der Vaal to have any room to wriggle out of this. None. Above all, he wanted Van Der Vaal to pay for having lied.

As the Council members were getting over their shock of this new evidence, Straker pulled a pre-prepared piece of paper from the top pocket of his suit, and slid it across the highly polished antique table to Brogan. Brogan picked it up and opened it. It said:

Call Andy Backhouse and ask him about the sabotage of Ptarmigan, NOW! It was was followed by a number.

Brogan was clearly taken aback. Forgetting the decorum of the meeting for a moment, he turned to Straker and said aloud: 'What? Are you *serious*?'

'Absolutely, Oscar. *Call* him,' Straker said with unequivocal conviction.

Sounds of their exchange attracted some attention from around the table.

'Mr President?' said Brogan to the meeting, more easily heard now that a number of people had turned towards him. 'Ptarmigan would like to call a witness.'

San Marino, distracted from the animated chatter among his Council members, said: 'Er, who would that be, Mr Brogan?'

'Mr Andy Backhouse, sir.'

San Marino looked considerably put out. 'Now? But we've not made any arrangements to have anyone here.'

Straker did not want this to stall. Catching Brogan's eye, he stuck his thumb and little finger out from a clenched fist, lifted it to his ear, and urged him to make the call.

'We can get him on the phone. We have a number for him, Mr President,' at which point Brogan looked at Straker for guidance. 'I gather he's available,' said the lawyer with interrogative intonation. Straker nodded his confirmation.

San Marino looked around the room to his Council colleagues as if to seek their approval. This meeting had been taken completely by surprise already. Either they were too shocked to object, or were simply too hooked on hearing the next unexpected twist.

There was no dissent.

'What are you doing calling one of my members of staff?' blasted Van Der Vaal.

'Do you object, Eugene?' asked San Marino quite sternly, given the other man's tone. 'This Council *does* want to get to the truth.'

For the first time Van Der Vaal looked like he didn't quite know what to do next. 'What the hell. He'll back me up anyway. Call him – call my mother, if you want.'

San Marino reached out again for the desk telephone in front of him and pulled it a little closer. Brogan read out the number, which San Marino tapped into the phone.

It was soon heard ringing over the loudspeaker.

Straker turned to look at Sabatino. Her face reflected complete bemusement and then serious concern. It seemed to ask: 'What the hell?'

The phone was answered. 'Hello, Andy Backhouse,' said the Brummie voice.

'Mr Backhouse, Bo San Marino, here.'

'Good morning, Mr President.'

'Andy, I'm calling you from a special hearing of the World Motor Sport Council – looking into allegations of industrial espionage by the Ptarmigan Formula One Team.'

'Okay.'

'We have a quorum of thirteen of our members, as well as other dignitaries present. We have members of Ptarmigan and a representation from the Massarella Team here. We would like to ask you some questions. But first, are you comfortable with the significance of this – and do you recognize the authority of this meeting?'

'Of course, Mr President.'

'Thank you, Andy. Go ahead then, please, Mr Brogan.'

'Mr Backhouse, Oscar Brogan – counsel for Ptarmigan F1 – here,' he said casting an eye down at Straker's note: 'I would like to ask you about the sabotage of Ptarmigan,' after which he looked across at Straker. He received a nod of reassurance.

'Certainly, sir. Has the Council been made aware of the various instances?' Backhouse asked.

'It has,' confirmed Brogan.

'Okay, then. Mr President, up until Spa, I was Remy Sabatino's race engineer. I feel personally responsible every time a driver gets into the cockpit of one of my cars and takes to the track. Travelling at two hundred miles an hour is dangerous enough. Add the combative dimension of cars racing wheel to wheel – a matter of inches apart – and the risks are multiplied. Sending a driver and car out knowing that someone was trying to thwart them – possibly even to try and cause them to lose control, as happened to Helli Cunzer in Monaco and Remy Sabatino in Spa – meant the responsibility was too much. I couldn't take it.'

The room was completely attentive listening to the dismembered voice over the loudspeaker.

'Hang on a minute, Backhouse. If you thought that Massarella were the perpetrators of this sabotage – as you alleged in Spa – why and how could you possibly leave Ptarmigan and go and join *them*? That's ridiculous. It makes absolutely no sense, at all.'

'That was a a question from Mr MacRae, Andy, the commercial rights holder,' offered San Marino.

'Thank you, Mr President. I'd recognize Mr MacRae's voice all right. It was actually *his* reaction to that high-speed sabotage in Spa – when we met him and yourself afterwards, Mr President – that convinced me there was something deeply unpleasant going on.'

Suddenly the room exploded. At the tone of the remark? Its personal nature? Its implications? Straker couldn't decide which.

San Marino called the meeting to order. 'I'm sorry, Mr Backhouse,' he said with a strongly disapproving tone in his voice. 'What *exactly* are you insinuating?'

'Mr President, the sabotage Ptarmigan reported to the FIA – to you in Monaco and to you and Mr MacRae in Spa – warranted far greater concern and action than it was granted. I fully accepted your assertion at the time, Mr President, that our evidence was tenuous. But when Mr MacRae said,' and here it sounded like Backhouse was reading: *"This is a business. Billions of dollars are at stake, and many thousands of jobs. The last thing Formula One needs, right now, is another scandal"*, I couldn't believe it. Ptarmigan needed to get to the bottom of the hideously dangerous sabotage it was suffering, but we were getting *no* help from the authorities. In the meantime, Remy Sabatino's life was clearly being put in danger. But no one would listen. We were helpless. There was nothing we could do about it. It was then that Colonel Straker came up with a plan.'

The room fell silent.

All eyes immediately turned on Straker.

San Marino also looked Straker straight in the eye. 'What plan was that?' he asked sternly.

Straker stayed silent.

In his stead, Backhouse replied: 'That I was to resign from Ptarmigan – and *defect* to Massarella. I was to rejoin Massarella; as I had been with the team for a number of years a while back, there was a logical fit there. Colonel Straker hoped that they might see recruiting me as a bit of a coup, hopefully even seeing me as a valuable asset. Once on the inside, he wanted me to try and gain their confidence. As it happened, that came more easily than we hoped – best illustrated by Mr Van Der Vaal's gloating and flaunting of me as part of the Massarella team in Monza and Shanghai. He clearly revelled in *winning* me away from Ptarmigan. That enabled Colonel Straker's plan to start working: I was to try and learn what I could about what was behind this extraordinary sabotage, from the other side – from inside the team we suspected of being the perpetrators.'

San Marino's study of Straker's face became almost chilling.

Straker held his stare, remaining impassive. While still maintaining eye contact with the President, Straker turned his head, indicating that this revelation might mean something significant to another person at that table. San Marino read the clue and followed it, looking away and turning his attention towards Van Der Vaal.

The Afrikaner looked fit to burst.

His face had reddened. The blood vessels stood proud in his neck, while the muscles in Van Der Vaal's shoulders, arms and fists were clearly clenched.

Backhouse continued: 'Mr President, once in with Massarella, I was told by Mr Van Der Vaal that Ptarmigan – particularly the arrival of Dominic Quartano on the scene – had ruined Mr Van Der Vaal's long-term ambition to succeed Bernie Ecclestone as the Tsar of Formula One. Massarella's attracting sponsorship by Obrenovich Oil & Gas, and the financial clout it brought, was to have been the launch pad for Van Der Vaal to mount a bid to be the new Tsar. To conceal his intentions, though, he wanted to stay on as a team boss for as long as possible – until his path to the top job was clear. So he did a deal with Joss MacRae. He offered to invest many of the oligarch's millions in his Motor Racing Promotions company – in order to carve up the commercial side of the sport between them. That included taking stakes in key businesses within the sport, such as Trifecta Systems. The more I heard and pieced together – with snippets here and there from conversations with Mr Van Der Vaal – the more I was able to confirm Colonel Straker's earlier findings and deductions.

'Mr President,' Backhouse said, 'Eugene then told me something deeply disturbing. He told me about his policy of *rectification* – which all began after Ptarmigan was hailed for its marketing genius. Media and public applause for Ptarmigan really got up Eugene's nose. As we all well know, our hiring Remy Sabatino – the first serious female racing driver – exploded in the press. There was another massive press explosion when Ptarmigan started discussions with Mandarin Telecom, about a sponsorship deal valued in the hundreds of millions of dollars. Both of these developments really irritated Mr Van Der Vaal. Eugene, in a fit of anger one night, told me how he detested all the attention of the sport swinging to Ptarmigan – away from himself and Joss MacRae. Those two men had clearly wanted that sort of publicity for themselves – let alone the Mandarin sponsorship money, which they also believed should have been going in their direction. Why else would MacRae have taken such an extraordinary position on Remy's high-speed sabotage in Spa, unless there was a conflict of interest somewhere – and that there was something else going on?'

San Marino, for all his patrician dignity and bearing, was clearly affected by this unexpected news. Surprisingly softly, he asked: 'What was this policy of *rectification*?'

'Sabotage, Mr President,' came the reply from Backhouse over the loudspeaker. 'Van Der Vaal's sabotage of Ptarmigan was very carefully planned out – and to be done completely invisibly. Deviously. It was clever – under the radar, like the radio jamming in Monaco. Or concealed as malfunctions, such as Helli Cunzer's suspension failure. Or simply actions that could be so easily dismissed as driver error, such as Mr MacRae did so emphatically with Remy's high-speed loss of control in Spa.

'Van Der Vaal's ultimate blow, though,' Backhouse went on, 'was particularly devious. It was to accuse Ptarmigan of industrial espionage. After the FIA, under a predecessor of yours, Mr President, fined an F1 team $100 million in the 2007 Spygate case, Van Der Vaal confessed to me over a beer in Singapore that his plan had been to inflict a similar fine on Ptarmigan. His ruse was simple. He aimed to get Ptarmigan to adopt some identifiable piece of Massarella's proprietary technology. It didn't really matter what – anything would do. The moment that happened, an accusation of industrial espionage could follow, which would inevitably land Ptarmigan in front of the World Motor Sport Council. Once there, Ptarmigan could be indicted and preferably hit with a similarly crippling fine – or at the very least be fatally stigmatized by such damaging accusations against its integrity. In other words, Massarella's accusation and the inevitable bad press stemming from it would knock Ptarmigan – and more importantly Dominic Quartano and his financial and marketing genius – out of Formula One.'

There was no attempt by anyone around the Council table to intervene in Backhouse's testimony.

'Van Der Vaal had an unexpected early bonus, Mr President,' he continued. 'You cannot imagine Van Der Vaal's jubilation when he heard that even the first inconclusive FIA hearing into this case prompted Mandarin Telecom to pull out of their sponsorship deal with Ptarmigan. Not only was his plan working earlier than expected, it also opened up the way, afterwards of course, for Massarella to try and pick up that potential contract for themselves.

'Charlotte Grant, God rest her soul, was complicit,' Backhouse added. 'She had already done bad things to Quartech, and was trying to do them again to damage Quartano's prized project – his F1 team – for her own personal reasons. But she would not have got anywhere without Eugene Van Der Vaal's initiating everything. I may well have blown my reputation and credibility for this deliberate deception, Mr President, but I *had* to do something to prove that Ptarmigan was the victim here.'

Backhouse had clearly reached the end of his testimony.

The room was aghast.

It stayed silent for quite a while.

It was strangely unnerving.

As if nobody knew what could possibly happen next.

Straker, too, was nervous. How would his subterfuge be received? Would *he* be censured for mounting such deception? Surprising himself, the first person he turned to for a reaction was Remy Sabatino.

She met his eye.

Her face seemed stern to him. Had he upset her again? Straker held her stare. Then, very slowly, Sabatino's expression broke, giving him the tiniest hint of a smile. It graduated into a smile of you-shouldn't-have-done-that-you-son-of-bitch-but-I'm-sort-of-glad-you-did. He gave her a smile of relief in exchange, before turning his attention back to the hearing.

San Marino now looked concerned. 'Mr Backhouse, thank you for that bombshell.' The President exhaled. 'Eugene,' he said with a strong hint of disdain, 'do you wish to reply?'

Van Der Vaal looked completely thrown. Straker had expected the man to explode with some blast of a defence – defiance – outright denunciation of Backhouse's testimony, perhaps, or even a direct attack on his character. But nothing came. Straker reckoned the blow inflicted by the surprise telephone testimony – that Backhouse had been a mole, not to mention the weight of the man's evidence – was probably too much for him to regroup that quickly.

Straker scanned the rest of the room, trying to gauge the reactions from other Council members. Were they glowering at Ptarmigan, ready to challenge and chastise them – over the deception and the nature of this testimony – or were they prepared to accept it?

He watched all twenty faces around the table turn in Van Der Vaal's direction.

They were clearly looking to *him* for an answer.

Not to Ptarmigan.

Not to Straker.

'Mr President,' said Brogan choosing this moment to step back into the discussion. 'Ptarmigan has made its case. We'd be very happy to take any questions.'

San Marino's attention, though, stayed trained on Van Der Vaal.

'We have some questions,' said a pronounced Finnish accent, sternly, from the far end of the table, 'but for … Eugene … and Joss.'

There were mutterings of agreement.

San Marino turned to address the Ptarmigan contingent. 'In that case, Mr Brogan, let me thank you and your client for your presentation so far. May I ask you and your colleagues now to leave the meeting?'

'Certainly. Do you wish us to remain in the building?'

'Yes, please,' said San Marino.

As the Ptarmigan party stood up to leave the magnificent plaster and chandeliered room, Oscar Brogan asked: 'Is it your intention to reach a judgment today, Mr President?'

'Ideally, yes,' replied San Marino looking at his watch. 'But after all this,' he said with a circular wave of his fingers, 'I'm afraid I have no idea when that will be.'

Having withdrawn from the hearing and returning to the library, Straker braced himself for an onslaught.

It came – but was surprisingly gentle.

'Why the *hell* didn't you tell us what you were doing with Andy?' asked Sabatino with a stern face but with a smile in her voice.

'Because of authenticity,' he said.

'Say *what*?'

'If I was to plant a successful mole in the Massarella camp, to combat the sabotage threat,' replied Straker, 'he *had* to be credible. I *had* to have you completely pissed off with Backhouse. The more you showed your disgust with him, the more Van Der Vaal would buy Backhouse's defection and credibility. Your faces – that time Van Der Vaal paraded Andy up and down the pit lane in Monza – were an absolute picture. Utterly authentic. *Utterly* invaluable. Anything less than the raw contempt and loathing you showed in your expressions, and Van Der Vaal would have suspected that something was up. I couldn't risk even your body language not conveying your disgust. If anyone had inadvertently given this wheeze away, Backhouse's cover – and therefore his value as an intelligence source – would've been blown.'

'So he wasn't the *insider* saboteur?' said Nazar.

'Good God, no,' replied Straker. 'He's one of the team. To his soul. He was the whistle-blower,' he said looking at Sabatino, 'helping us nail Van Der Vaal. *He* gave me that tip-off about Michael Lyons being sacked by Trifecta – and, vitally, that Lyons had hoarded documents and evidence as an insurance policy against possible accusations of sabotage.'

Nazar had to smile as he began to appreciate the fullness of what had been going on. He ended up shaking his head. 'Superb, quite superb,' he said in his crisp Indian lilt. 'It could so easily have *not* worked.'

Straker smiled. 'Tell me about it. My biggest risk actually came from above – from Quartano. I was quite sure the plan was all over when he started trying to slap an injunction on Backhouse. Thank heavens Andy's employment contract with Ptarmigan is so crap that Stacey couldn't enforce it.'

'You mean not even *Quartano* knew about the Backhouse ploy?' exhaled Sabatino.

Straker shook his head. 'No. No one did.'

SIXTY-ONE

The Ptarmigan team was recalled, but not for three and half hours. Its members re-entered the majestic committee room of the Royal Automobile Club and retook their seats at the antique table.

Straker was intrigued to see that the chair where Joss MacRae had been sitting was now empty.

San Marino then called for the Massarella team to appear.

Once Van Der Vaal and his people were back in their places, the President put on his half-moon reading glasses and addressed the Council.

'We have reached our decision,' he declared authoritatively. 'I will start with Ptarmigan, as this hearing originally related to allegations made against them. I will then address the new information about Massarella and the case they have to answer.'

'Understood, Mr President.'

'On the original allegation of industrial espionage – the charge that information was transferred from Massarella to Ptarmigan – we conclude that information *was* exchanged.'

The Ptarmigan team braced themselves and tried not to show too much of a reaction.

'As has been learned, however, Ptarmigan were ill-served by a member of their staff, who is now deceased. Nevertheless, the management processes at the team *did* allow for information to be fed in without being properly scrutinized or checked. While we are not prepared to punish Ptarmigan for the actions of an obviously rogue member of staff, we do believe Ptarmigan's internal processes were less than thorough. As described in Ptarmigan's revised statement of facts, however, it is clear that these processes are now much tighter. We are content to believe that this is not an ongoing risk. Nevertheless, wrong was done, for which we intend to fine Ptarmigan the sum of $100,000.'

San Marino looked up. 'Mr Brogan, is there anything you would like to say in response?'

Ptarmigan's barrister looked surprised that the President was inviting comments already. Brogan even seemed a little thrown. He took a moment to respond. 'What about Championship points, sir?' he asked tentatively.

San Marino shook his head. 'No loss of points in either Championship.'

So that – relatively modest fine – was *it*?

Straker immediately turned to look at Sabatino. She gently thumped the table top, smiled, and then affecting slow motion, punched him on the upper arm. Without wallowing in her reaction, Straker quickly pulled another piece of paper from his pocket and slid it straight across to Brogan. The barrister unfolded it and saw the suggestion; turning to Straker, Brogan nodded and smiled at the idea, before he readdressed the meeting:

'Thank you, Mr President,' said Brogan. 'I have no observations to make at this stage. May I reserve the right to speak, however, after your comments about Massarella?'

'Provided the comments are appropriate.'

'Of course.'

'Now we come to Massarella,' said the President, turning to face an extraordinarily unabashed-looking Van Der Vaal. 'An unexpected case has been made against you today. The Council has given you the chance to account for yourself. We appreciate that you were not granted as much time as you would normally be afforded. However, you *have* made a defence of your actions and I have to say that this Council finds it wanting. To have instigated a transfer of intellectual property with the sole intention of making it look like industrial espionage – so as to implicate the recipient – is scurrilous behaviour on any level. However, the Council is satisfied that this was not an institutionalized scam. Consequently, Mr Van Der Vaal, we hold you personally responsible and have arrived at a judgment accordingly. You are to be fined $2 million and banned from any involvement in Formula One indefinitely.'

Straker could not resist glancing over at Van Der Vaal to see how he was taking this. Straker allowed the unprofessional – emotional – side of him a moment to delight in having beaten this odious individual and in exposing him, publicly, for what he was: an over-ambitious common-or-garden thief and liar.

'The Council, of course, will grant you, Mr Van Der Vaal, the right to appeal this decision,' concluded the President.

Straker could not see any particular reaction from the Massarella boss. There seemed to be no change from the brutish expression. 'I *will* definitely appeal this fiasco,' he growled. 'You can count on it.'

San Marino gave the slightest of bows, as if merely to acknowledge his right to do so, before going on: 'Next, we consider Adi Barrantes, Massarella's Number Two driver. The Council has been in telephone contact with Mr Barrantes today, to question him about the evidence presented in this hearing. He has not denied his involvement in the engine-limiter incident in Spa. As a result of his unsporting involvement in the high-speed sabotage of Remy Sabatino at Spa, he is to be fined $250,000 and lose all his Championship points – Drivers' and Constructors' are to be taken away.'

Straker was staggered. Massarella may not have been punished directly, but the loss of the Constructors' Championship points would hammer the team's ranking and, therefore, hugely reduce its receipts under the Concorde Agreement. Massarella's revenue, this year, would drop by tens of millions of dollars.

'As I mentioned in respect of the judgment on Mr Van Der Vaal,' San Marino went on, 'Massarella and Mr Barrantes will also be granted the right to appeal these decisions.

'Finally,' said the President, 'this Council seeks to question the actions of certain employees of Trifecta Systems and Benbecular Engines, Mr Michael Lyons and Mr Jeremy Barnett. We demand their presence at a hearing in Paris on 5th December this year in order for them to account for their actions.'

San Marino stopped looking at his notes and lifted his eyes to address the room as a whole. 'You should also know – as you may have inferred from his absence at the table – that Mr MacRae has stepped down as head of the Sport's commercial rights holder, a move the FIA has welcomed.

'Now, Mr Brogan,' said the President removing his half-moon glasses. 'I think you wished to speak after you had heard the Council's full decisions. I ask you to limit your comments to Ptarmigan's interests only, please.'

'Thank you, and of course I will, Mr President. Clearly, I have not had the chance to discuss your judgment with my client, so reserve my client's right to appeal the fine.' Brogan then turned to Straker and nodded, as if to acknowledge his earlier written suggestion: 'Mr President, in the light of the Council's overall findings, I would ask whether the FIA might be prepared to write a letter on Ptarmigan's behalf?'

SIXTY-TWO

As the Ptarmigan contingent withdrew back to the library in the Royal Automobile Club, Sabatino's relief and jubilation bubbled over. 'We're Constructors' Champion!' she declared with triumph. 'From receivership to Champions in twelve months. *What* a result.'

The judgment also meant that, personally, her own F1 points were still secure – meaning she was still leading the Drivers' Championship. Tahm Nazar, Oscar Brogan and Straker were all swept up in Sabatino's moment of relief and triumph. There were hugs all round, with a theatrical one from her for Straker.

The now-jubilant Ptarmigan party readied themselves to leave the RAC. As before in Paris, they settled on an approach for handling the press and media outside. They all seemed happy to underplay the result of the FIA's hearing.

'The judgment says it all for you,' offered Brogan. 'You really don't need to say anything.'

'I agree,' said Straker. 'Its findings were so clear, there's no need to spin this. Much more dignified to show restraint – let the editors draw out the distasteful meanings and conclusions.'

As they exited into Pall Mall, their approach was well judged. Ptarmigan's vindication was clearly not the biggest news from this hearing and judgment. Instead, the banishment of Van Der Vaal, and the departure of MacRae as the CEO of the commercial rights holder, were seen as the bigger stories – and, therefore, the focus of media interest.

After only a few minutes in front of the press, cabs were hailed in Pall Mall.

Sabatino and Straker soon rode away up St James's Street together.

She looked at him with an expression of supreme happiness on her face. Soon, though, it gave way to a you-so-and-so smile, and then, surprising Straker, almost apology. 'That was ballsy stuff,' she said, clapping her hand down on his thigh several times.

'Planning and careful execution,' he said with just a hint of vindication in his voice.

Sabatino smiled. 'And you've had *all that* going on – as far back as Spa, just a week after that first sabotage incident in Monaco,' she observed, as if to herself. 'Without any of us knowing?'

Straker nodded dismissively. 'But it wasn't a certainty that it was going to work. I had to get lucky, too.'

Sabatino turned to face him. 'Talking of which…'

Bursting in through the front door of her suite at Claridge's, their hands were all over each other as they barely found their way to the bedroom. Sabatino set about ripping off Straker's clothes.

'Well, well, I see the Colonel's ready for action.'

'I hope your engine is in its operating window, too.'

'Oh yes,' she said licentiously. 'Hang on a minute.'

Surprising Straker further, he watched her almost jogging – naked – across the large room to the ceiling-to-floor windows. At each curtain on either side, he watched her unhook the luxurious silk tiebacks, with their large tassels, before closing back in on Straker. Pressing herself against him, kissing him, and, once again, cupping him and playing teasingly with one hand, she said: 'Tie me up,' and handed him the clutch of silk ropes with the other.

Straker could not suppress a smile. This woman was the stuff of pure fantasy.

Within a couple of minutes she was restrained – one curtain tieback securing each limb – spread-eagled on the bed, and "ordering" him to take her.

But with her now unable to move, *he* took control.

He started to tease and tantalize.

Beginning at her feet, he focused on stimulating her skin – kissing and massaging every inch of her with his tongue, mouth and fingertips.

She could hardly bear it. She started to writhe – but was securely bound by the silk ropes holding both arms and legs.

As he progressed, her anticipation and frustration increased. He kept going – for over an hour – moving inch by inch up her body. Sabatino began to pull maniacally against the restraints.

Teasing her – and denying her – he raised her to an extraordinary state.

Just before he finally complied, Sabatino was practically scream-ing at him to take her – the release, when it happened, a letting go of all her pent-up stress and uncertainty from the last three months.

After hours of physical passion, dinner, and more devouring of each other, Sabatino finally fell asleep in the crook of Straker's shoulder.

As much as he was contented by the outcome of the day, he still couldn't sleep.

Passing through the lobby of the hotel on their way to dinner, he had spotted a Late Night Final of the *London Evening Standard* – his eye drawn to its front page. It carried an article about the FIA disci-plinary hearing, screaming with the headline:

FORMULA ONE CLEAROUT.

The story did manage to convey some of the drama of the afternoon.

Straker was staggered, though, by the surprising comments made by Eugene Van Der Vaal, *after* the hearing. Direct quotes reported him as saying:

"I will appeal … monstrous decision … overturn the ban … FIA exceeded its powers … inadmissible evidence … defection con trick … Avel Obrenovich will pay to reverse this ruling … Avel will keep backing Massarella … avenge the wrongs inflicted on me…"

Straker had hoped the FIA hearing – and believed its judgment – would bring an end to the malicious interference from Van Der Vaal and Massarella. Sickeningly, he was not so sure now. In the light of

Van Der Vaal's defiance – and complete lack of contrition – Straker was troubled.

He had in his possession an email from the Massarella boss.

It had been discovered on Michael Lyons's laptop, following the seizure of his documents under the High Court Search Order. This email, though, hadn't made it into Ptarmigan's statement of facts or its bundle of evidence for the FIA hearing. He and Stacey Krall, Quartech's in-house counsel, had discussed the email at length, and had concluded its content was too far-fetched – and prospective – to help their cause.

He had chosen not to share the email with Sabatino either.

Given Van Der Vaal's comments in the press, though, Straker now wrestled with this view. Wasn't he duty-bound to tell her? Didn't those quotes from Van Der Vaal mean that he and Massarella were out to vindicate themselves – to even the score? Didn't it mean that they were harbouring thoughts of revenge?

And if that was the mood in the Massarella camp, what did it mean for Adi Barrantes – heavily fined and stripped of all his Championship points from this season? Didn't that mean he now had *nothing* to lose?

All this – going into Brazil, with the pivotal significance that race meant to Sabatino in the Drivers' Championship – was truly alarming.

The undisclosed email in question discussed a completely different degree of sabotage against Ptarmigan which – now used out of spite for the purposes of revenge – could yet come back to haunt them.

PART SEVEN

THE SENNA S

SIXTY-THREE

Dominic Quartano stood on the apron of Aeroporto de Congonhas, in the midst of the urban sprawl of São Paulo. With him on the ground were Tahm Nazar, Matt Straker, Remy Sabatino and Andy Backhouse. They were there formally to meet the passengers off a special flight.

Dr Chen, members of his Mandarin Telecom board and guests of the company had just landed – invited to attend the Brazilian Grand Prix.

Mandarin Telecom's CEO appeared at the cabin door and smiled genuinely as he saw the Ptarmigan party waiting to greet him at the foot of the steps.

'Dr Chen, welcome,' said Quartano. 'Excellent to see you again. You might remember some of my team?'

'Of course, Madam, Mr Nazar, Colonel.'

'I don't think you've met Andy Backhouse, though? Andy was instrumental in clarifying – at the FIA – the recent incident with one of our rather unsporting rivals.'

'No, I haven't. Mr Backhouse, how do you do? I have to say that I didn't much take to Mr Van Der Vaal, either.'

Backhouse smiled. 'Thank you, sir. We all take comfort that his garden will be well tended for the foreseeable future.'

Dr Chen, once again, found himself not quite understanding the English, but his expression didn't betray it. Instead he replied with: 'I am delighted that Ptarmigan has been well served by the process of law and justice under the sport of motor racing. The letter from the President of the FIA explaining everything was very reassuring. I and my board are thrilled that our sponsorship is still to proceed.'

'Likewise, Dr Chen,' answered Quartano. 'Now, permit us to

show you to your hotel. Then, we would very much like to introduce you to some of our friends and, afterwards, invite you all to dinner.'

Straker looked out on the five hundred guests who had congregated for the Ptarmigan reception in the large hospitality area within the Interlagos race track. He, Sabatino and Nazar were standing in the Ptarmigan receiving line by the main doors.

'This turnout is amazing,' said Straker. 'Are all these people really here to celebrate our Mandarin sponsorship deal?'

Nazar had to smile. 'We've got the Earl of Lambourn to thank for this,' he explained. 'Massarella's actions, and the complications with MacRae, incensed him so much that he took it upon himself to whip people here as a show of moral solidarity – to reassert the sport's integrity.'

'No man is an island,' suggested Sabatino mischievously as she raised a glass of orange juice in salute to the dashing Earl.

'Perhaps they aren't all piranhas? Maybe there are one or two dolphins around here – after all,' said Straker with a smile that acknowledged the line was corny.

A few minutes later Quartano appeared through the main entrance of the room. His upright bearing, mane of silver hair swept back off his forehead and handmade blue suit projected quite a presence. He was accompanying their guest of honour, Dr Chen of Mandarin Telecom. Although shorter, the Chinese CEO's dark hair, heavy-rimmed glasses and double-breasted charcoal grey suit gave him a powerful – but perhaps more of an understated – charisma. There was a warm round of applause as the two business leaders made their way through the guests to the Ptarmigan-branded stage arranged at the far end of the room.

The house lights dimmed and a spotlight fell on Dominic Quartano. Standing at a small lectern, the brightness of the lighting accentuated his rugged Mediterranean-seasoned skin and pale-blue miss-nothing eyes.

'Friends of Formula One,' he said, his rounded baritone

immediately holding everyone's attention. 'I am flattered that you should all have graced us with your company this evening. I am immensely proud to reintroduce you to Fi's new friend and partner, Mandarin Telecom.'

There was another burst of applause.

The lights dimmed further and the spotlight was extinguished. Over the audio system, a dramatic voice-over to a new spectacular five-minute video extolled the virtues of Formula One and the might of Mandarin Telecom. As well as a crisp, logical message for the allegiance of these two brands, Bernie Callom's visual imagery was intoxicating – even managing to impress the grizzled old campaigners in the room.

As the video ended, the stage started to move. A sloping trapezoid panel above the screen, apparently there to channel the eye, started to lower, hinged along the top of the screen. As it descended, a concealed display mounted on top of it came strikingly into view. Resting above it, slowly rotating down into sight, was next year's Ptarmigan Formula One car, dressed in the team's new Mandarin Telecom livery and markings. Its unusual colour became a talking point – introduced as qing. Mandarin Telecom explained this as the Chinese colour of renewal – the colour of vigour and vitality. Being a bluish-green, it wasn't that much of a transition from Ptarmigan's turquoise. High-intensity spotlights made it and the car seem to sparkle and gleam, while, underneath it, wafting dry ice cascaded down onto the stage.

As the display panel came to rest, showing the car off to the room, Quartano returned to the lectern and announced: 'Today marks the start of a new sponsorship partnership which, we believe, will benefit the Chinese business community as well as our beloved sport of Formula One. Ladies and gentlemen, I am proud to introduce you to Ptarmigan's new partner, Mandarin Telecom, and their Chief Executive Officer, Dr Chen.'

After a sumptuous dinner and only a modest amount of alcohol, the

Ptarmigan party bade the Mandarin Telecom directors good night. Quartano said his good nights, too, leaving Straker and Sabatino alone.

'It's getting late,' he said. 'We need to have you on song for practice tomorrow.'

'What are you, my Mama?' said Sabatino.

Straker shook his head.

'Don't go all coy on me,' she admonished.

Straker couldn't help but grin at the directness, there being nothing equivocal about her meaning and lascivious tone. 'Are you going to tie *me* up this time?'

Sabatino smirked. 'Now, there's an idea.'

SIXTY-FOUR

The excitement going into the Brazilian Grand Prix – the final round of the season – was that for the first time ever a woman was leading and could be about to win the World Drivers' Championship.

Sabatino's lead, though, was only three points – being on 81 to Paddy Aston's 78. The narrowness of that margin added another dimension of excitement to the build-up of this race.

With ten points for the winner, tapering down to one point in eighth, there was, under the then-format of the FIA scoring system, a matrix of outcomes for Sabatino to win the World Championship.

The clear-cut one was easy: for her to win the Championship outright, she needed to finish at least second in Brazil.

If, God forbid, she failed to score – through being lower than eighth, or being forced to retire – Aston would need to finish fifth or better to win the title himself.

Most people expected both drivers to score points. In which case, to be safe, Sabatino needed to finish the race – anywhere – better than Aston.

Whether the nuances or complexities of the scoring system fully registered with everyone or not, the motor racing audience was nevertheless hooked. They were content enough to be focusing on the drama of the Drivers' Championship going down to the wire. There was going to be excitement, whichever way it went.

Everyone was buzzing.

Particularly as the climax of this season's Championship was spilling over into the mainstream media around the world. The chance of a woman winning the Drivers' title saw estimates of the expected global TV audience doubling for this race – up to a staggering 800 million viewers.

It was a safe bet to assume that no one was going to be disappointed with the theatre of this event.

Straker, though, was finding it difficult to join in the excitement. Van Der Vaal's rejection of the FIA's findings – and apparent lack of remorse – meant he continued to brood over that secret email from Michael Lyons's laptop.

Walking into the Ptarmigan garage on the morning of Friday practice made Straker's unease all the more intense. Gangs of turquoise-liveried mechanics were working energetically around the two Ptarmigan cars. There was such a sense of purpose – an air of confidence among them that he had not seen since Monaco. Everyone was showing their relief at the lifting of the sabotage threat. Ptarmigan was clearly channelling that relief from their recent troubles into a focus on winning the Drivers' Championship for Sabatino.

How could he, Straker, now do anything to damage this potentially Championship-winning *esprit de corps*?

And yet what if something did happen – along the lines threatened in Van Der Vaal's email – and he had done nothing about it? How could he live with himself after that?

Despite the inspiring sight of the team at work, therefore, Straker had to pull himself away.

He resolved that he needed to talk to someone about his unnerving information.

He needed reassurance that concealing it *was* the right thing to do. Otherwise, the pressure of harbouring this snippet of threatening communication would continue to eat him up.

'Oh crap,' said Tahm Nazar when Straker finally told him and showed him the email. He and the Ptarmigan team boss were sitting in the private closed-off section of the motor home.

Nazar reread the key section of it from Van Der Vaal to Michael Lyons.

"Congratulations on your creativity. Your clandestine rectification is superb. Don't forget, if we run out of ideas or time, our comrade will always compensate Adi enough to invoke the 'collision option.'"

'Tahm, the mood of the team is so highly charged, I couldn't bear to dent it.'

'Particularly if this threat doesn't materialize.'

Straker then produced the front page of the *London Evening Standard*, with the key quotes from Van Der Vaal highlighted, and slid that across the table.

'Oh crap,' repeated Nazar. 'I wouldn't give him a snowball's chance … of overturning that judgment on appeal. But, as you say, what if he *is* that spiteful?'

Straker shook his head. 'What kind of team boss could instruct a driver to crash their car, anyway? Let alone given the danger involved?'

'Oh, you'd be surprised in this game – there's a very well documented F1 case from 2008,' said Nazar with a surprisingly resigned tone. He refolded the email and newspaper cutting and slid them both back across the top of the rosewood table.

'I feel a weight off just telling you,' said Straker. 'What would you prefer to do with this knowledge?'

'I completely agree with your reluctance to tell the team,' said the professorial Indian in his immaculately precise accent. 'It would inevitably put a dent in their collective spirit.'

Straker nodded, relieved he might have done the right thing to have kept it quiet thus far. 'What if something happens and precautions weren't taken?'

'Quite.'

'I've been trying to think this through,' offered Straker. His face seemed more determined than usual. 'When's a collision going to be the most effective?' he reflected almost rhetorically. 'Massarella would only get one shot at it – as any attempt is likely to take Adi Barrantes out at the same time. Wouldn't that mean it had to be *in* the race, when there's no chance of our making a repair – rather than in practice or Qualifying, when we could?'

'That's logical.'

'In which case, we probably wouldn't need to deploy any counter-measures until Sunday.'

'Okay. I can live with that. But,' said the team boss, 'you and I can't take any chances. I need you, Matt – without making any kind of show – to provide full comfort in the meantime. Call it extra team scrutiny for next year's car, or some such. But I'll need you to remain just as vigilant as you have been hitherto.'

Straker went straight to work. As well as his usual surveillance, his focus, this time, was shown in the bank of screens in front of him. He arranged a feed from every camera that covered Adi Barrantes. But – just in case the threat didn't come solely from Barrantes – he arranged similar coverage of the Simi Luciano Massarella, as well. Also, with Straker's primary concern being the relative positions of the two Ptarmigans and the two Massarellas, he set up a screen showing a graphic representation of the real-time positions of all cars on the track.

Quite clearly, the collision threat was only real when the tur-quoise and black cars were close together. That's when it could get really ugly.

Straker's biggest fear, therefore, was "proximity".

Sabatino's proximity to any Massarella was going to be the moment of highest danger.

SIXTY-FIVE

Qualifying One began on Saturday morning. The public, commentators, and audience were all focused on the fight between the two Championship contenders – Paddy Aston and Remy Sabatino.

Both drivers went through the first round of Qualifying without a hitch.

Q2 saw Aston make a mistake, while Sabatino lost the back end to a spin in Pinheirinho, Turn Nine – but both made it through easily to the top-ten shootout.

Then everything changed.

Thick grey clouds started forming over the lakes – the wind got up and rain was on the way. Everyone started agonizing. Would the weather change enough, or would they get away with it? And what of tomorrow? If it was going to rain for the race, should the teams rig the cars for Qualifying in a wet set-up, just in case?

To Sabatino, the choice was all the more heightened, given her standings in the Championship. In some ways, though, her decision-making was perversely easier. She was, in effect, only driving against one other competitor now. All she had to do was stay competitive relative to Paddy Aston and his Lambourn.

Backhouse and the whole team devoted their efforts to trying to work out what Aston and the Lambourn team were planning to do.

Qualifying Three started.

Grey clouds loomed.

The last ten cars set out on their out-laps in the final shootout.

By the time flying laps were attempted, the heavens opened. On drys, the teams were completely thrown. Inevitably, they were sliding about all over the place. Lap times were ludicrously high and completely unrepresentative of anything.

Aston tried to snake his way round, and slid wide in the middle of the Senna S. Sabatino fared only marginally better, tottering round while completely holding her breath.

Qualifying Three came to an end.

The Championship decider could not have been tighter. On much slower lap times than normally expected, because of the weather, Aston and Sabatino had ended up side by side – on the second row.

Sabatino P3, Aston P4.

Thankfully from Straker's point of view – and his threat of proximity – Adi Barrantes in his Massarella was well back behind her, down in P6. On their starting positions on the grid, therefore, Sabatino was well out of harm's way.

But then the order and the Championship were all about to be turned upside-down.

Everything changed on Sabatino's in-lap, while she was making her way back to the pits.

Inching slowly – because of the wet – she changed down as she approached Junção, Turn Twelve. Even at the virtual snail's pace of sixty miles an hour, that was plenty fast enough given the volume of surface water. Paddling for second gear, the Ptarmigan's rear wheels suddenly locked-up, taking her by surprise. Steering aggressively to correct the resultant slide of the back end, she managed to avoid a spin.

She slid to a stop.

Her first reaction – following the sabotage incident at Spa – was to look around her and in her mirrors. But there were no other cars in sight. Next, she looked down at the indicator on her steering wheel. Her gears had clearly jumped from third to first.

Not what she'd asked for at all.

Cursing mildly at the inconvenience, she revved the engine and paddled again. Nothing. The car was now not responding. Wouldn't accept any gear.

At all.

'What's up?' asked Backhouse over the radio.

'Gears, Andy. I changed down. She's jumped down two. That, on this surface, locked-up both rear wheels.'

'And now?'

'Nothing. I've got a box full of neutrals. Can't get her into gear at all. Anything showing on the telemetry?'

'Nothing.'

For two minutes Sabatino tried to engage a gear. Nothing would take. 'It's no good, Andy. I'm going to need recovering.'

Half an hour later Sabatino's forlorn-looking Ptarmigan was delivered to the pit lane on the back of a truck. It was hoisted off, hanging beneath a hydraulic arm, lowered to the ground, and quickly pushed backwards into the team garage.

Sabatino, still soaking wet from the rain, stood over the car, watching the guys take off the aerodynamic shell as they looked inside to see what was wrong.

'Go and change, Remy,' suggested Backhouse gently. 'We'll let you know as soon as we've fixed it.'

Straker's immediate concern was why the thing had failed. Was this an organic failure, or induced by interference. Were their ghosts already back to haunt them?

Sabatino returned fifteen minutes later. She was met in the garage by a troubled-looking Backhouse and a disheartened-looking Straker.

Reading the two men's faces, she asked seriously: 'What's wrong?'

Backhouse grimaced. 'The gearbox has gone.'

Sabatino's expression hinted at defiance. 'Fixable?'

Backhouse inhaled and shook his head.

In an instant, Sabatino seemed to buckle at the waist and half turned away. 'You're kidding! You're kidding me?' she screamed. 'You're *fucking* kidding!'

Backhouse shook his head with great sincerity. 'Remy, I'm sorry … it's got to be replaced.'

Sabatino, still agitated, turned to face the two men. 'That's a

ten-place penalty … that'll drop me *ten places* on the grid. TEN!'
she yelled. 'It's over, the Championship's fucking over.'

Straker stepped forward and tried to place his hands on each of
her shoulders. 'No, it isn't,' he said gently.

Disconcertingly, she shrugged aggressively, shaking his hands
away.

'That puts me down in thirteenth. Nine places behind Paddy.
Nine! I'm out of the points. He's on for *five*. It's his. The fucking
Championship is his.'

SIXTY-SIX

All afternoon Sabatino was impossible to talk to – to reason with. She scowled, fumed, and grumped her way through every meeting and conversation. Nothing seemed to placate her.

Straker decided to stand back, and let her rage play out.

Backhouse, working with a gang of mechanics in the garage all afternoon, gave the defective gearbox every last chance. He had it removed, placed up on a sterilized workbench, dismantled, and assessed for repair – component by component. But one of the gear clusters had failed; bits of it had worked loose, and, having caught between two moving parts, had ruptured the cassette. There was no way it could be repaired reliably enough to stand up to seventy-one gruelling laps in the race. Grimly, Backhouse instructed the gearbox be replaced and that the team file the change with Race Control.

Sabatino's ten-place penalty was announced in the paddock at four o'clock that afternoon.

She would now have to start from thirteenth on the grid.

Nine places behind her Championship rival.

The points Sabatino needed to secure the title were suddenly a long way out of reach.

Straker found Sabatino in the motor home. She was still sullen and uncommunicative. He tried twice to converse and be supportive, and both times she snapped back. After one more try, he stood up, grabbed his phone and, deliberately in her hearing, rang the team driver: 'Bill, can you come to the motor home, please – to take Miss Sabatino back to her hotel?'

She glowered at him critically, as if to challenge his right to make any decisions on her behalf.

Hoping she might still co-operate when the driver turned up,

Straker ducked out of the Ptarmigan motor home to find a little privacy – some distance away. On his iPhone, he searched the web to find a number. Using the link on the website, he dialled it. 'Could I speak to the manager, please?'

There was a pause – some clicking – some excruciating bossa nova muzak – before a Portuguese-accented man came on the line.

'João Asturias,' he said, 'how can I make your day better?'

'Mr Asturias, thank you for taking my call. I have an emergency – and I need your help.'

Asturias sounded suitably concerned and receptive.

Straker explained what he was after. 'Can you do all that for me – in a bit of a hurry?'

'Of course, Senhor, we can – and will – do it, with pleasure.'

Straker, thanking Asturias profusely, rang off and returned to the turquoise motor home in time to see Bill, the team driver, pull up alongside.

Climbing back into the Ptarmigan headquarters, Straker walked up to Sabatino, careful to take her firmly by the hand – not the wrist – and led her down the steps to the waiting car.

Her mood barely changed during the drive, or as they rode the lift up to her floor in the hotel. Taking the key card from her, Straker opened the door, and stood to one side to let her into her suite.

She was immediately taken aback.

The room was dark – not black – but dark – unlit by electric lighting. Instead, there was candlelight. Masses of candles flickered from every flat surface on the inside. Soft music – Dean Martin – could be heard wafting over the sound system. Sabatino was about to turn round and react to Straker, when a Portuguese voice came from inside.

'My lady,' it said, 'I am Senhor Asturias, the manager of the hotel. And I offer our compliments of the house,' and wafted forwards holding a silver tray on which stood a bottle of Taittinger, a flute already filled, and a half-pint glass of Guinness.

This greeting – from a stranger – took the puff out of Sabatino's reaction.

Almost automatically, she reached out for the Guinness, and took a sip. Her eyes becoming accustomed to the change in light, she noticed a padded massage table had been set up over by the drawn curtains, stacked with a number of neatly folded fluffy white towels. An immaculately dressed Chinese girl wearing a dark blue Nehru-collared silk jacket was in attendance. On a low table beside her was a small incense burner offering up an intoxicating scent – as well as several bottles of aromatic oils and a warming plate holding a collection of large rounded flat stones.

Asturias, having placed his tray of drinks down on a portable stand, proceeded to walk forward, and, with an outstretched arm, invited Sabatino to move into the bathroom. Here, again – with no electric lighting – the space was lit with hundreds of candles, spectacularly reflecting off the wall-sized mirrors. Next to the bath – filled to the brim and almost overflowing with white foam – was another portable stand, this one supporting a large tray. On it was a crisp white linen cloth hosting silver cutlery, and an array of plates with collections of exotic fruits, pastries, meats, cheeses, and four different types of chocolate. In the corner of the tray stood a slim and elegant silver vase holding a single rose.

Sabatino, turning round to face Straker, said: 'This is all a bit cheesy, isn't it.'

Straker exhaled with an exaggerated blow. Shaking his head, he walked forward and threw the electric light switch on in the bathroom and killed the music. Against the earlier dimness, the numeruos bright spotlights were almost blinding, even hurting eyes.

'Okay, João, take it all away,' said Straker and started indicating – with a series of wildly dismissive hand gestures – that Asturias should pick up all his cheesy paraphernalia. 'But … João, please leave *me* the chocolate … if you will?'

'Ah, er, hang on,' stammered Sabatino, spinning round. 'Hang on, a minute,' she said loudly, holding up a hand to try and halt the removal.

Straker glared at her, the diagonal folds of skin above his eyes intensifying his stare more than ever. 'You don't want it taken away then?'

Sabatino turned round to look back at the bath and the tray of goodies waiting beside it. Sheepishly, she shook her head.

Straker threw the bathroom switch back the other way, immediately restoring the room to the much softer and flickering candlelight, and re-engaged Dean Martin. 'Sense at last. João, thank you,' and turned away from the door, allowing the hotel manager to withdraw. As Asturias passed, Straker smiled, shook the man by the hand, and patted him on the shoulder as he let him out of the suite.

When the door was closed, Straker heard Sabatino say from inside the bathroom: 'This is okay,' – her resistance clearly de-energized since the Yes or No showdown of a few moments before – 'but,' she added, trying to restore her sense of control, 'you can let the Chinese girl go. I'll ask Colonel Straker to perform the massage, if he'll be so kind?'

After an hour in her bath – and a more spirited go at the tray of snacks than Straker had expected – Sabatino climbed out and walked through into the bedroom. There, she climbed up onto and lay face down on the masseuse's table. Straker, rubbing some oil on his hands, began his attempt at massage, hoping he'd be able to stretch out the limited number of moves and techniques he could think of.

The limits of his repertoire were never tested. Before he ran out of ideas, the gesture of the unsolicited pampering had finally got through to Sabatino. Fewer than twenty minutes later, they ended up in bed together. This time, they seemed to make love rather than – as on previous occasions – perform gymnastic sex.

Lying beside each other afterwards, they were both pretty near spent.

A matter of a few minutes later they fell into a nap.

Two hours on and they were bathed again and changed.

Straker, continuing his religious silence of the afternoon, said nothing about racing, the Championship, the Qualifying session, the gearbox, or her place on the grid. Sabatino began to show a little more appreciation for his attempts at a distraction. By seven o'clock, she was even enthusiastic about the idea of a light meal somewhere out, but nearby. Straker let the idea be entirely hers.

After supper, he walked Sabatino back to her hotel.

'I'm happy to go to my room,' he said as he kissed her gently on the cheek, 'to give you a decent night's rest before tomorrow.'

'Where's this Mama stuff keep coming from? I haven't finished with the Colonel, yet. Not yet. Not by a long way.'

With his efforts to distract Sabatino throughout that afternoon, evening and night, Straker was grateful to have also been distracted from his own concerns.

But lying in bed after she had dropped off to sleep, he couldn't calm his thoughts.

Following the official Qualifying session, Straker had been pleased and relieved. With Sabatino in P3 and Aston in P4, she had been well positioned for the Championship – staying ahead of Aston. And, from Straker's point of view, in P3, she would have been well in front of the suspected collision threat from Adi Barrantes – the proximity threat, as he called it, Barrantes being a long way down the grid behind her.

But now – with the gearbox penalty, and the ten-place drop to P13 – Straker could only fixate on Adi Barrantes' Massarella.

Barrantes was lurking there, now, in P6.

In order for Sabatino to get back up to the front of the pack – to get close to, let alone retake the advantage from Aston – she would have to get past the menacing black Massarella of Adi Barrantes.

The proximity threat was back.

And the risk – and stakes – were higher than ever.

SIXTY-SEVEN

Next morning the weather had cleared. None of the threatening clouds were left. Sublime sunshine bathed Interlagos – the land between the lakes – and Sabatino awoke refreshed and seemed completely refocused.

'Nine places? It's just nine places,' she said as they were both wearing white towelling robes and eating breakfast in her hotel suite. 'I've got a second advantage per lap on each car between me and Aston. This *is* doable,' she declared as if coming to an understanding.

Straker continued to say absolutely nothing. He was still distracted by the threat of proximity and intentional collision.

By mid-morning, the cars were out on the grid. Sabatino's Ptarmigan, now in P13, had its new gearbox. Exhaustive checks had been carried out overnight to ensure there were no possible complications or snags with the change of such a major component.

Sabatino walked onto the grid. While trying to get to her car, she was repeatedly bombarded with media interview after interview. It began to dawn on her the kind of a mêlée that would follow if she did succeed today. If the press were like this now, what would they be like if she actually won the World Championship?

Finally climbing into her car, she was grateful to escape the attention and to enjoy a moment's peace. Sitting there – isolated – with time to reflect, she suddenly realized that she *was* back in the zone. They, Ptarmigan, had rid themselves of all that trouble with Massarella, which removed a considerable amount of stress, and – today, now – she had become resigned to the ten-place drop for the replacement gearbox. This race might be tougher than needed, and certainly tougher than any of the team had expected, but she realized she *was* ready to take her fight to Paddy Aston.

On the hooter blast, her adrenalin started to kick in for real. The grid cleared and, with Sabatino's engine finally running, she absorbed the thunderous noise of the cars all around her.

She was grateful.

The intensity of the sound helped to occupy the entirety of her attention.

The lights came on and the Formula One runners pulled off on their formation lap for the last time this season. Round they went, all swerving, zig-zagging, accelerating, braking – every driver busily working temperature into their cars in their own way round the 2.7 mile circuit.

Sabatino spent half the lap changing up and down the gears, making doubly sure her new gearbox was working and reliable. It felt good – better, even, than the last.

After Bico De Pato, Turn Ten, she let the cars to her front pull away, to give herself a longer run on a stretch of clear track. Pumping her right foot, she accelerated hard and threw the car round Junção, Turn Twelve. She nodded to herself.

The car felt good.

The conditions were ideal, and her car's set-up was pretty much spot on.

Straker, back on station in the motor home with all his surveillance equipment, watched the field re-form, each car slotting into its designated place on the grid. He was completely focused on the two black Massarellas in P2 and P6.

Sabatino looked down. Her temperatures were all good. She blipped the accelerator. The Benbecular sounded fantastic and ready.

This was it.

One red light came on.

Sabatino felt her heart rate quicken.

Two red lights. She breathed deeply, and exercised her fingers.

Three red lights.

Four.

Five.

Wait … Wait! … WAIT!

GO!

The engine roar around her was deafening. Cars screamed forward off their spots. She hurtled forwards. Accelerating. Accelerating fast.

Suddenly, the car in front darted to the right. In nothing less than a reflex, Sabatino did the same. A Sauber had stalled on the grid. It was stationary. The cars behind had to swerve violently to avoid ramming straight into the back of it.

How didn't she hit it? – skimming past it by only a whisker.

In the run down to Turn One, and the intensifying bottleneck of cars all trying to squeeze through an ever-shrinking space, one part of her brain had already registered that the Sauber had held a place ahead of her but behind Aston.

She'd clawed back one place already.

She was twelfth.

Turn One, at the top of the upcoming Senna S, was *the* corner for overtaking on the circuit. To take the challenge to her Championship rival, this was where she was going to have to do most of the work that afternoon – to be bold – and to take every opportunity that came along, however tenuous.

But not this time.

In the mêlée of the start, she was happier to get round safely, and get herself under way.

Into the corner they ran.

Every car was now in, through, or half-out of Turn One. Front runners were already accelerating, streaming down the hill through the Senna S. From six rows back, Sabatino could see the field jostling and squabbling for position spread out down the hillside combination of turns – a right, left, then a more gentle left – below her.

Suddenly there was a smash.

Two cars had come together at the bottom of the first right-hander.

A Lotus had lost its back end – after being bumped? – and was sliding across the track. Then slam! Another car smashed straight into its back wheels. Debris flew outwards, right across the circuit.

Some of the debris was turquoise. Wouldn't that be Cunzer in the other Ptarmigan?

Sabatino flinched to find a way round these now-stationary cars and the lumps of wreckage lying slap-bang in the middle of the track. To avoid it all, she had to dive out to the left – wide to the outside. Holding her breath, she had no choice but to drop a wheel over the edge onto the grass. She prayed she didn't lose the back end. Exhaling deeply a second later, she fully regained the tarmac – keeping herself in the race.

She rounded Turn Three and pushed on down Reta Oposta. The long straight gave her time to think. Poor Helli going out – and the Lotus. But then she had a Darwinian thought – verging on *Schadenfreude*. Hadn't she just gained another two places? That smash, then – to her – was actually *good* news.

She cleared through the apex of Turn Five. She looked at the field down the track in front of her. There were two Red Bulls and a Mercedes. Weren't these guys – after the stalled Sauber and the collision of her teammate and the Lotus – now P7, P8 and P9?

Didn't that make her tenth?

She accelerated hard and chanced a look in her mirrors. There was a stretch of clear track behind – indicating no immediate threat of being overtaken herself.

She settled down to catching the cars ahead. The front runners were speeding down to Turn Six. Finally letting the Ptarmigan go, she realized the set-up and conditions were married up perfectly. Now she had to use them.

Immediately ahead of her was a Mercedes, currently in P9.

Radioing in, she asked: 'Is Helli okay?'

'He's fine.'

'Have they cleaned up the Senna S?'

'No.'

'Any sign of the safety car?'

'Highly likely. There's crap all over the road.'

Even better, she thought. The front runners may have built up the beginnings of a few seconds lead between them already. But the safety car would see them all bunched up again tightly – keeping her well and truly in touch with the leaders – at least for a little while longer.

Within ten seconds the letters SC appeared in the LED display on her steering wheel. Sabatino yelped in delight. A few moments later the field had been concertinaed up again – the first nine cars in front of her forced to crocodile round nose to tail – behind the safety car. Aston, still retaining P3, hadn't been able to get that far away from her. Not yet.

It took three laps for the marshals to clear the debris from the Senna S.

As the pack rose up the hill from Turn Thirteen the next time round, the lights suddenly went off on the roof of the safety car. Fifteen seconds later, it was ducking into the pits.

They would be racing again soon.

The Ferrari at the front accelerated hard into the long pit straight, aiming to get himself away from the bunched-up pack behind him and to re-establish his lead.

Being bunched up might make it easier to mount a challenge to the car in front, but exactly the same opportunity was created for the guy behind. There was some protection from this – being pro- hibited from overtaking, at least until they crossed the line. Once over it, though, all cars were free to mount a challenge – or be chal- lenged. Sabatino was pleased it was more the former. She took great delight in the Benbecular engine's furious purr immediately behind her, giving her all the power she wanted as she pelted up the long start/finish straight.

Crossing the line, her few extra horsepower were working to her advantage. The Mercedes, in front of her, was fast, but the Ptarmi- gan felt quicker. Using her speed, Sabatino closed in and right up to the Mercedes's gearbox. She started taking a tow.

The two cars crested the rise – when suddenly Sabatino reckoned she had a shot. Timing her moment to the last minute, she remained tucked right up – a matter of inches – behind the Mercedes. Three hundred yards from the braking zone, she swung left, out of the Mercedes's slipstream, setting her jaw at a move down the inside of him into Turn One.

Slowly but surely, she gained on the car in front.

She only had a few hundred yards to run before the corner.

Would it be enough?

Could she stake her claim?

Come on! she yelled into her helmet.

She powered on. With nothing less than full commitment.

'Lift, you bastard, lift!' she screamed at the Mercedes.

She held her nerve. But so did the Mercedes. They were side by side. Did she have the line? Would he concede? Would she have to lift off, after all?

She held out … And out.

She *wasn't* going to bottle first.

Then it happened.

He lifted.

The Mercedes lifted off!

It felt like she suddenly shot forwards, as the Mercedes – visible through her peripheral vision to the right – quickly dropped back under braking. But she was still going into the corner hard and fast. Could she control the car into, through, and round Turn One? Would the Mercedes just need to be patient, watch her run deep and wide – and simply cut back after the corner?

Watching all this on the monitors, the Ptarmigan team were holding their breath. Straker, on the edge of his seat, willed her car round the corner. From an overhead camera, the shot showed the turquoise car's sharper angle into the turn. A small puff of blue smoke came off Sabatino's front-left. Then was gone.

Would she get by on the first turn of this complex only to have the Mercedes come back at her through Turns Two and Three?

She felt the car go a little here and there.

Sabatino wrestled with the wheel, the brakes, and the yaw of the car.

She held her nerve.

She was getting round ... round? ... round!

She'd done it. She'd taken her man, fair and square.

With all the risks, she was now up to P9.

She was closing in!

Recovering down the hill on the far side of the corner, the Ptarmigan headed down the long straight, the Reta Oposta, flying back up to top speed. Ahead of her now Sabatino could see a Red Bull in P8. He was, maybe, one second further down the track. Along the straights, that length of time at this speed looked like a mile. But as they swung through Turn Six, and were soon in the succession of curves, sweeps, rises and compressions all the way from there to Turn Twelve, the gaps closed right up. But the design of the Interlagos circuit offered few genuine overtaking places through this section. A driver might make a mistake, and create an opportunity to pass, but at this late stage in the season, with the cars so well used to the Formula – and in the dry – it was going to be unlikely. By the end of this segment, as she rounded Subida Dos Boxes, Sabatino had nevertheless closed the gap and was all over the Red Bull's back end. After that turn, Fourteen, the Red Bull and she had the three-quarters-of-a-mile drag up the hill on the long left sweep until they reached Turn One again, where she'd just jumped the Mercedes.

Up the hill they raced, the Ptarmigan giving Sabatino all it had. But it wasn't quite enough. She didn't quite get the tow.

And so it remained for the next ten laps.

Sabatino was frustrated, but not despondent. A couple of times she radioed the pits, wanting to know where Aston was – how fast he was lapping – whether it looked like he was making any headway on P2, or whether, God willing, he might even be overtaken. But no.

Everything, for Aston, was running normally – all going his way to secure the World Championship.

Lap twenty and they saw the first of the pit stops.

To Sabatino's delight the Red Bull in front of her pitted earlier than expected. She hadn't been aware of his dirty air, but the moment he was out of the way, she found an extra couple of tenths per lap. So much so that when she pitted herself, five laps later, she was nearly up with the other Red Bull in P7.

Sabatino remained on the same compound tyre and was fuelled to lap fifty-eight.

Out she went again.

Re-emerging, though, she was met with a surprise. She found herself in front of a Lotus. What did that mean? Where was the Red Bull who'd been in P7?

She radioed Backhouse in the pits.

'He's about a second behind you.'

'*Behind* me? You're kidding?'

'No, he's just entering the pit straight.'

She looked back in her mirror. 'I'll be … Where does that put us, best guess?'

'Could be good for P6.'

'*P6!*'

'And where's Aston?'

'Still P3.'

Sabatino juggled the numbers – and yelled. 'That's good enough! We're only three points apart. We're equal – that would make us equal. With my number of wins, I'd be World Champion.'

'Just bring it home, Remy,' snapped Backhouse fiercely. 'There'll be time for all that later.'

Round they went. Sabatino continued to push hard. She was now bearing down on a Ferrari.

Lap fifty-one and the second round of pit stops began.

Aston came in and was out again in a phenomenally fast stop.

Two laps later Sabatino was in. Her boys had to get this one as right as right. They did – everyone beginning to sense the prize was within their grasp. They achieved their fastest change and refuelling stop all year. That and her next few lap times made a difference. By the time the Ferrari in front of her pitted, he re-emerged on the track behind her.

Didn't that give her P5?

But then the penny seemed to drop for Lambourn.

Aston suddenly dug deeper and found another level himself. Had he been coasting up till now, believing his margin to be big enough from the start?

In the next lap Aston's Lambourn shaved four tenths off her time.

The one after that another six tenths.

And then half a second in the next.

'He's closing in on the Massarella in P2,' reported Backhouse. 'He could be in a position to take him soon.'

Sabatino kept driving, but waited with bated breath to hear news about her Championship rival.

It wasn't long in coming.

And it wasn't good.

'He's taken Simi Luciano,' Backhouse announced. 'Aston's up into P2.'

'Oh, no,' bellowed Sabatino. 'Eight points to my three – would give him a five-point advantage – *and* the title.'

Sabatino pushed hard in response.

There was some distance between her and the next car down the track from her. With fourteen laps to go, she was going to have to dig in.

But this was the scenario that Straker had not even dared to imagine.

Sabatino had showed brilliant resolve to fight her way up the field, taking advantage of opportunities as they arose – gutsy over-taking – slick strategy – and well-timed stops which had gained her track position.

But now, she was entering the proximity zone that he had dreaded.

She was coming up on not one – but *two* Massarellas.

If the email Straker had recovered from Michael Lyons's laptop showing Van Der Vaal's readiness to pay for collisions was serious, then they were all coming up on *the* moment of danger.

Proximity.

SIXTY-EIGHT

Straker called up Tahm Nazar on the pit wall. 'Do you want to warn her – now – about the possible threat from the Massarellas?' he asked.

'Hold on.'

There was a moment's pause.

'Matt? I've just told Andy. He's got the relationship and the responsibility. I'll let him decide.'

On the other net, Straker heard Backhouse immediately radio Sabatino.

'Go ahead, Andy.'

'Watch yourself with the Massarellas, Rems. We think they could be out to bump you.'

'That's all we fucking need.'

For two laps Sabatino mounted a substantial charge, clocking up two fastest laps consecutively.

Aston responded in kind.

He, too, clocked up a fastest lap. This was now a psychological battle – played out on different parts of the circuit – each trying to undermine the confidence of the other, each trying to put the other under pressure.

'Aston's catching the race leader,' reported Backhouse. 'He's only point-four seconds behind.'

Sabatino, hurtling down the start/finish straight, saw the key data on her pit board, and breathed deeply. 'Shit. P1 to my P5. The Championship would definitely be his – if he gets past.'

Growling into her helmet, Sabatino pushed again, and flew round the exhilarating Interlagos circuit. Her sights were now set on Adi Barrantes, her saboteur from Spa, in the Massarella – in P4. 'How far am I behind him?' she asked.

'Three seconds. You can do it.'

Sabatino belted on round the track. She soon saw her quarry.

She was so nearly in reach. 'Can I turn up the mixture?'

Backhouse hummed. 'Not really – you'll be cutting it fine to finish.'

'Andy, a miss is a miss. Unless I take this guy, Aston's going to win anyway. Who'll care by how much?'

Backhouse paused. Straker wondered whether he was running the numbers again or weighing it up. 'Okay, okay. Turn it up a notch.'

Sabatino screamed to herself. 'Right, let's see what this brings.'

She felt the difference immediately. The car produced an extra point-five a lap.

In two more laps, she was ready to make her challenge.

Straker, on the edge of his seat in the motor home, stared at his surveillance screens until his eyes hurt – continuing to study every inch of the Massarella, looking for any sign that Barrantes was positioning himself to do her harm. He could hardly bear it. Radioing Tahm Nazar, again, he felt he had to say or do something.

The tension was too much.

'Tahm, are you up for putting on the show in front of the Massarella garage?'

'You think now's the time?'

'I've no idea. Nothing's happened yet. But for the sake of a moment's theatrics, might the deterrent be worth a shot?'

Nazar acknowledged the call.

Straker switched one of the two CCTV screens to show the pit lane. He saw the turquoise-clad Ptarmigan team boss quickly climb down from the prat perch on the pit wall and walk in the direction of the Massarella garage, two slots down. There, Straker could see Nazar stand and make a show of studying what the Massarella team were doing.

There were only ten more laps to go.

Sabatino had to get right up the Massarella's back end. Half a lap later she was there – starting to badger Barrantes for real – through the corners between Six and Twelve.

Out of Turn Fourteen, Subida Dos Boxes, she got a superb exit – immediately feeling she had the better start up the hill.

They screamed up and round the long left-hand sweep, and into the pit straight. She felt she had enough. The momentum was with her. The two of them, one behind the other, roared up the long straight – and across the line.

Five hundred yards to go to the corner – Turn One.

Sabatino looked for a tow.

She drew up to Barrantes's gearbox.

On they ran.

Now! She ducked to the left, ready to make a charge down the inside – just as she had against the Mercedes earlier.

The yards flashed by.

She drew level with the Massarella's rear wheels.

She willed the car on.

Did she have any more?

She was pulling forward by a matter of inches at a time.

Straker sat forward in his chair. Switching all of his screens to cover Adi Barrantes's CCTV feeds, he peered at the live shot of the Massarella driver's cockpit. Straker was looking for any untoward behaviour. The most obvious, though, would be for Barrantes simply to "close the door" on Sabatino too soon – driving across her path into the corner to claim the racing line. He could easily bump her – and take her out. He would surely claim he was unsighted – claim he thought he had the advantage, getting the collision dismissed merely as yet another racing incident.

Straker stared at the screen – studying both of Barrantes's hands on the wheel.

The two cars were going to have to brake. Who was going to blink first?

Sabatino held her position.

She was still hurtling into the corner. She was completely committed. It was now up to the Massarella. She was at the point of no return. If he didn't brake, now, she would end up losing her front end, sliding across in front of him, possibly taking him off with her. Straker suddenly realized that that would be an even cleverer way to take her out – to make it look like it was her fault.

'Arrgh!' she screamed as she willed her car on, willing him to brake, and waiting for the outcome.

Come on! Come on! Come on!

Yes? *Yes?* Yes! He blinked. Yes!

He blinked first!

Barrantes lifted off. She shot past him. She'd done it. She'd taken him down the inside.

Would she now be able to hold it together?

She fought on.

She *was* holding it together.

She was through!

But Barrantes was already retaliating. Slewing and wrestling his car as well, he flung the Massarella round the corner and pointed it down the hill of the Senna S, straight after her.

She stole a glance in her mirrors. She could see the black menacing shape of the Massarella behind her. It closed right up. It appeared in her right-hand mirror.

Then disappeared.

As she continued to accelerate hard, she suddenly caught a fleeting glimpse of the black shape in her other mirror. He was crawling all over her gearbox.

Sabatino reached her top speed, flying at full tilt down the Reta Oposta. Barrantes wasn't able to get any closer than that, though. She'd managed to hold the Massarella off against a counter-attack. She had taken P4. Not only that, she'd managed to make it stick. And P4 was good – it was good *enough*. Her P4 to Aston's P2 was back to a three-point deficit, and while that would put them equal in the Championships, her number of race wins would still see her ahead.

Distance, now, was what she wanted. As much distance from Barrantes – to neutralize any threat he posed from behind – and, at the same time, to close the distance on the car in front.

On they raced.

The Ptarmigan was performing as well as Sabatino could have prayed for. Her lap time was consistently quick – on or near the fastest times of the day.

Then something unexpected happened.

Sabatino started gaining on the car in front.

Substantially.

Point-six of a second on one lap.

Point-eight on the next.

She was gaining rapidly on the car in P3.

The excitement mounted. Could the crowds and TV audience be about to see another spectacular overtaking manoeuvre, right into the closing stages – not only of the race but of the Championship?

Sabatino pushed on.

Minutes later, she saw the back end of the car in front.

But this elevated Straker to a completely new level of anxiety.

The car she was closing in on was the other Massarella.

Calling up Backhouse on the radio, he asked: 'Is she that fast, or is Luciano slowing down to let her catch him up?'

Backhouse paused. 'Don't know.'

Straker breathed in. 'Where's Barrantes? How far behind her is he?'

'Two point two seconds.'

'If Luciano slows any more, he'll back her up to allow Barrantes to catch her. Remy'll be in a Massarella sandwich. Who knows what shit they might then try and pull?'

Tahm Nazar's voice came up on the radio. 'Andy, you'd better warn Remy what's happening. I'll go and make another show in front of the Massarella pit wall.'

Two laps later and Straker's worst fear was realized.

Simi Luciano, in P3, *had* slowed yet further, but not sharply enough to make it look like it was deliberate. Sabatino very quickly got on terms, moving into his immediate wake. His slower pace, though, was causing Sabatino to slow up too. Adi Barrantes, in the other Massarella, was bearing right down on Sabatino from behind.

Straker's heart was in his mouth.

If these bastards were going to do anything to thwart Ptarmigan's Championship chances, now was the time to do it. They could inflict the cruellest wound of all – just three laps from the end of the season.

Straker thought that as an act of revenge, it would have little to parallel it.

SIXTY-NINE

Sabatino was rounding Subida Dos Boxes, Turn Fourteen, with both black cars looming large in her forward and rearward vision. From that exit, the three of them began their long uphill drag, sweeping left-handed all the way into the end of the pit straight. Nose to tail. Sabatino got a good exit. But so did the Massarella in front. She kept in touch as they raced up the hill. Then, looking in her mirror, she saw that Barrantes had had an even better launch behind. He was right up her tail as they passed through Turn Fifteen.

Sabatino watched the car in front, desperate to see any sign that Luciano was lifting off, and trying to back her up into the other Massarella. She could benefit from slipstreaming Luciano, but so too could Barrantes take a bigger tow by being behind both of them.

Straker watched the Massarella sandwich as the three cars raced at full throttle up the hill in line astern and crossed the finish line. He found himself holding his breath – yet again.

Sabatino had to remain hyper alert and be ready to react to any action against her – whether that came as tactical manoeuvrings, field of play or foul play.

Unless she took the initiative…

Sabatino decided to make her move.

As before, she ducked out quickly from the slipstream to the left, setting up for a lunge down the inside of the front Massarella.

But Luciano reacted rapidly and moved across, forcing her even further left. The circuit was wide enough for her not to be pushed into the wall, but she was well off the racing line and onto the dirty part of the track.

This veer across her front had taken some of the steam out of her attack.

Looking into the mirror on each side, Sabatino was now desperate to know where Barrantes had gone.

She couldn't see him.

She kept to the inside of the leading Massarella as they both hurtled towards Turn One. Again, Sabatino looked for Barrantes.

Then she saw him. There he was. Behind her, to the right – and the distances between them were only a matter of feet.

Sabatino looked at the road ahead. The corner was looming. The gap was beginning to close in front of her. She would have to move out, to the right, to regain the racing line if she was to maintain her speed into and through this corner. She looked in the mirror to see Barrantes. He was right there on the outside of her, overlapping her rear axle with his front wing.

She was boxed in. If she moved out now, wouldn't she hit him? If she moved out now, would he yield?

She hinted at making a move. Barrantes didn't budge. He was holding his ground. Sabatino moved back. She was completely hemmed in. If she didn't want to be penalized for any collision, *she* would have to do the yielding. Which would cost her the place. And that, with only three laps to go, would easily cost her her title.

Sabatino was running out of road.

Luciano, in front of her, secured his claim to the racing line and cut in front of her – right to left – towards the apex. Sabatino wanted to do the same, but was still being fenced in by Barrantes – forcing her into a much tighter angle. If she maintained her current speed and line she would corner too deep, particularly on the exit. And that would be exactly what Barrantes wanted – allowing him to slip in down the inside as she went wide, on the far side of the turn.

There was no time left.

Sabatino had to decide.

Lift off and give Barrantes the place or keep on, run too deep – and give Barrantes the chance to cut back on the far side of the corner and *still* take the place.

Both options sucked.

Straker, Nazar, and the entire world watched this high-speed bottleneck, all at the limit of their nerves.

Sabatino acted instinctively. When cornered, lash out.

As the distance to the corner closed down, she resolutely maintained her position. That would surely put Barrantes a little on edge – being that ballsy.

Then, exactly when she expected Barrantes to be thinking about braking, she flicked the car as violently to the right as she could – for an instant – checked that lock and swung the wheel back to the left. It was not dangerous as she never encroached on Barrantes's line. It was just an extremely aggressive insinuation. The sharpness of the flick, in the confines of their convergence, was startling.

Barrantes couldn't *not* react. He *had* to flinch.

And he did – a little more than Sabatino had even hoped for, flinching out to the right.

The moment he'd done it, she turned her wheel quickly, immediately filling the space – the line – Barrantes had just vacated. She was now further to the right than she had been before. While not exactly on the racing line, she *had* given herself a better angle into the corner.

Would it be enough?

She maintained her pace into the apex.

On her outside, Barrantes was still feeling the effects of destabilizing his line so close to the corner. He, now, was going too fast on an angle that was wide of the entry. It was his turn to stab at the brake and try to rebalance his car and approach. But that's when it went wrong for him. Barrantes locked-up his front left. Losing grip at that critical moment, he started running even wider. His front right then ran off the clean line of the track and rolled onto the dirty part. Braking now, that tyre could only lock-up too. He was suddenly in recovery and survival mode.

Poetic justice! His intimidation had been thwarted by Sabatino's reply in kind.

She was soon in the midst of the corner.

She fought herself round Turn One. Inevitably, she ran slightly wide, but with Barrantes fighting his own battle with the corner away to her right, she could use the full width of the circuit without fear of his cutting back inside.

Sabatino found stability and was back on the power. But Luciano in front had got the cleaner exit and was already charging down the hill through the Senna S below her.

Even so, she'd *done* it.

She'd defended P4.

How the hell had she got out of that? She looked in her mirrors for comfort. Barrantes was a good way back, still recovering from his flinch-induced error. She looked forwards to the other Massarella: Luciano looked like he was racing again, now that his wing man had failed in his assisted attempt to get by. Luciano's attention had clearly switched from team tactics to maintaining his own position, P3.

It afforded Sabatino some time to settle herself.

'Well played!' yelled Backhouse into the radio. 'What a game of chicken!'

She shouted back, 'Where's Paddy?'

'Still in P2.'

'To my P4?'

'Correct.'

'His eight points to my five? We'd be *level* on points.'

'Points, *schm*oints. You've got more wins this year than he has.'

'I'm still on for the Championship, then?'

'You are.'

'How far back is Aston from the leader?'

'A good eight seconds.'

Sabatino looked down at her steering wheel display.

There were only two laps to go.

Aston couldn't do it, could he? He couldn't make up eight seconds *and* take the leader? Not with only two laps remaining.

'You should be okay,' said Backhouse reassuringly. 'Hold steady. Lean off the mixture.'

'Two more laps.'

'Two more.'

'Oh my God!'

SEVENTY

Sabatino breathed deeply. Two more laps. Less than six miles. Could she really *be* it? Was she *really* about to be World Champion?

Only two laps to go.

Then one lap to go.

Could she hold this together?

Sabatino forced herself to concentrate on the road, and on making no mistakes.

She crossed the finish line once again. This was it, now – the last lap.

She tried not to think about it. Less than three miles to run.

After the twenty rounds of Grands Prix this year – the hundreds of laps – the pressure – the distances flown – all the sabotage bollocks from Massarella. Was it all about to pay off?

Round Turn Five.

Through the succession of corners through Six to Twelve.

Keep it on the road. *Keep* it on the road.

She didn't know what had happened until she'd rounded Junção, Turn Twelve.

She wasn't told immediately.

Up ahead, on the outside of Turn Thirteen, she could see a yellow flag being waved. An obstacle of some kind. Something blocking the circuit.

What could it be?

Who could it be?

She rounded Turn Fourteen – and saw the reason. There was a Ferrari on the inside of the track. Stationary. A Ferrari. But whose?

Wasn't that the race leader?

'Andy, Andy? What's happened to the race leader?'

Sabatino knew instantly from Backhouse's tone. 'Looks like he's out – we think he's run out of fuel, half a lap from the finish.'

'So I'm third? P3?'

'Yep.'

'That's good, isn't it?'

There was an ominous pause on the radio.

'*That's good, isn't it?*' she repeated.

Sabatino screamed into the end of the start/finish straight.

Up ahead, the chequered flag was being waved. The race was over. Hadn't she won the Championship?

Why wasn't the radio going mad?

'What's wrong?' she called. 'Aston wins. I'm P3?'

'Correct.'

There was silence over the air.

'Oh no! NO! Fucking *no*!'

'Afraid so.'

'Aston wins – ten points – to my six?'

'*Remy…*'

'I've missed it by one point? One fucking point.'

Sabatino screamed to herself in the cockpit. 'All that way, *all* that success. And we miss it by … *one … fucking … point.*'

SEVENTY-ONE

Sabatino ambled round the circuit on her in-lap. Her frustration was stratospheric. One point. That was all. She thought about what might have been – had the saboteur not destroyed her Qualifying run in Spa, had she not taken Luciano off in Monza, had she not flat spotted the front right in China causing that unscheduled pit stop, had she not lost her gearbox here in Brazil. An absence of any one of those incidents could have given her the damn title. How could she have come so tantalizingly close? As a thwarted competitor, her instinctive soul-searching was now starting in earnest.

But all that was about to be blown away.

It started as soon as she came to a stop.

She heard it the moment her engine powered down.

There was cheering. Triumphal cheering.

Sabatino pulled the steering wheel towards her, removed it, and climbed out of her car.

As she straightened up, and looked around, there was an immediate disconnect. All that cheering was focused on her – and not just from her own team. From everyone, everywhere.

Sabatino scanned the other cars and drivers in Parc Fermé.

What?

Aston's Lambourn wasn't even there.

It took some time to sink in. This adulation was for *her*. It was Sabatino who was being hailed. Film crews appeared and trained their cameras on her. Even when Aston's Lambourn eventually pulled in, the attention stayed on her.

This was weird.

In a breach of all press protocols, a female TV presenter scrambled over the barriers and came charging over, thrusting a microphone towards her. Sabatino hadn't taken off her helmet yet – and wouldn't until she'd weighed in – but she still managed to catch some of the questions yelled at her over the noise of the crowd.

'What does it feel like to be the most successful woman driver *ever*?'

Another journalist appeared.

'How does it feel, as a woman, to have come that close to winning the World Championship?'

Whether she wanted it or not, Sabatino was being dragged out of her post-result sulk. She couldn't believe it. These people – the TV, the press, the crowds – were projecting an entirely different outcome of the race – the season, even – from her own interpretation.

They were not saying: "You've been beaten", "You came second".

They were not commenting on the result at all.

This realization hit her even harder when she stepped out onto the podium. From two storeys up above the track, it offered her an extraordinary view. She looked out on a sea of faces stretching off for hundreds of yards up and down the Interlagos pit straight in each direction. It seemed as if every spectator from all round the circuit had congregated below. Even at that distance she couldn't fail to get the message – it really couldn't take long for it to dawn on her fully.

Paddy Aston may have won the race, and snuck the Championship from her at the very last minute, but the predominant colour over the heads of this massive Brazilian crowd was a clear surprise.

It was turquoise.

Turquoise!

For *her*.

Any vestige of doubt was then dispelled completely, as the crowd began a rhythmic chant: '*Remy, Remy.*'

She was given no chance to dwell on what might have been in this race or the Championship. This acclamation snapped her right out of that.

Sabatino's standing in the sport was being hailed – unmistakably.

Moving to the front of the podium, she registered her appreciation of the moment. She beamed a large smile – and gave the crowds a two-handed wave. A crescendo of support came back in return.

Paddy Aston, trying to revel in his triumph having achieved the pinnacle of any motor racing career, couldn't miss the centre of gravity of this crowd. Not only that, he was aware of the iniquitous – even life-threatening – interference his principal rival had suffered during the season. He couldn't – and wouldn't – deny he had benefited unwittingly from Sabatino's misfortune. Technically, with his tally of points, he was unquestionably this year's winner but there was a part of him – articulated by the mood of this crowd – that felt his standing, even legitimacy, as World Champion was suspect.

Realizing these factors, Aston walked across the podium to Sabatino, offered his hand, and then raised their hands together above their heads. Aston shared the remaining moments of his triumph with an arm across her shoulders. He made her feel just as much a champion.

Perhaps, somewhere in the crowd, Dr Chen was watching and shaking his head, again, at his continued incomprehension of the English.

After the race, Quartano and Straker were hosting Quartech's and Mandarin Telecom's guests within the Ptarmigan hospitality area in the paddock.

The room was crammed with people. Straker was able to catch glimpses of Quartano as he worked the room, introducing himself, introducing others, clearly buzzing with the possibilities of each conversation, each new relationship.

Straker gravitated towards Nazar, Backhouse and Treadwell – keen to enjoy their moment of triumph at the end of a remarkable season. To be Constructors' Champion, when, a year earlier, the team had been in the hands of the receiver, was an achievement worthy of some celebration.

Having witnessed Quartano's engagement with their guests, Straker was surprised the tycoon soon came looking for him. 'Matt,' he said turning gently away as a cue for Straker to follow him. In a relatively quiet hole in the throng, he said: 'Well done – truly. Another *outstanding* assignment. Without identifying, purging and eliminating the saboteur threat, Ptarmigan wouldn't be Constructors' Champion – and Remy wouldn't be such a phenomenon. Worse,' he said with a gesture around him, 'we'd have lost this relationship with the Chinese. Three organizations here are looking to put a payload into space in the next six months, and I'm having the conversations. None of this breakthrough with the Chinese would be happening without your fiendish coup,' he said and looked Straker directly in the eye to reinforce his compliment.

Straker was not sure what to say.

'You saved this contract. And it's turned out to be an even bigger opportunity than I hoped,' added Quartano with a smile. 'Ptarmigan's new relationship is a case study in the extraordinary value of sponsorship's "convening power". This tie-up with Mandarin has *already* created opportunities I would have to price in the billions of dollars.'

'Great news,' agreed Straker.

'It is,' said Quartano instantly sounding serious, 'which is why I need you – by Friday at the latest – at our satellite launch site in French Guiana. Something troubling has been going on in the Quartech space programme, and I need you there to investigate it. In the meantime, well done with all this,' he said patting Straker on the shoulder before breaking off to interact with more of his guests.

The reception erupted when the Ptarmigan drivers appeared. Having been doused in champagne up on the podium, Sabatino had showered to wash the fizz out of her nut-brown hair and changed into one of her clean turquoise racing suits; now, she barely showed any sign of having been through a gruelling and emotionally draining last two hours.

She was fêted, and gushed at, as she made her way around all of the room, saying hello to everyone.

After a while she made her way into the Ptarmigan team gaggle where there was much hugging and emotion at the outcome of the season.

Sabatino soon spotted Straker watching her discreetly from a distance. She broke away to approach him.

He leant down to kiss her gently on the cheek. 'Well done. I'm sorry you didn't clinch it this time. One point, eh?'

She almost dismissed the condolence. Sabatino seemed to be buzzing. 'I was *that* ready to go into the mother of all sulks,' she said, 'but how could I now? Did you *see* the crowds? The result of the race – or even the Championship – didn't seem to matter to them, at all. This woman thing – and my status as some sort of "hero" – has completely hijacked the competition story.'

They both took a fresh flute of champagne offered by a waitress.

'I'm mighty relieved you *did* get that big a reception,' he said with a confessional smile and a chink of her glass. 'The team and I could have made a case to persuade you to see the scale of your achievement this year, but you would undoubtedly have ignored us all. Not even you, though, can dismiss the views of two hundred thousand Brazilian fans. At only twenty-two, you've got ages to clinch the title many times, yet.'

Sabatino looked up into his eyes and smiled gratefully at his understanding. 'If I'm being rational,' she said, 'I have no reason not to be upbeat: Ptarmigan is easily the best team, with – thanks to Mandarin Telecom – the biggest backing the sport has ever known. From an earnings potential, I own the media gold mine of being the only woman in the malest of sports. Double the usual TV audience tuned in to watch the first woman, *me*, try and win the Championship today? 800 million people! What could that be worth when I do win?' she asked. 'I know I shouldn't get hung up about one point, really!'

'Oh, you should *always* get hung up on one point,' he admonished firmly, 'otherwise you wouldn't be a competitor. But ... you should never let professional disappointment threaten your next step forward.'

Sabatino nodded emphatically. 'And I *am* looking forward, I am. But then – because of today's reaction – I get hung up about that too.'

Straker looked mildly disapproving.

'I can't help thinking that this whole "hero" thing, and my gold mine, makes me more vulnerable than ever – when I think of Van Der Vaal's chauvinism.'

Straker was surprised how seriously she said this. He shook his head. 'You should be sabotage-free, at least while Van Der Vaal's in exile. Unless by some miracle he wins his appeal, I suppose.'

'After all that's happened, and has been written about me,' she said with a shake of her head, 'I can't get away from the feeling that some people won't like it: a celebrated woman in masculine Formula One? Standing to make a fortune? I dread the resentment it might create. At least say you'll be there for my first race next season – just in case?'

Straker smiled trying to conceal his surprise. 'When and where's that?'

'Melbourne, first weekend in April.'

Straker nodded and chinked her glass. 'Of course I'll be there.'

She smiled back, looking as if she was actually relieved. After taking a big gulp of champagne, she asked: 'So what's next for you, now?'

'I wasn't sure – until a few minutes ago. DQ's just asked me to go to French Guiana and look into an incident on the Quartech space programme.'

'Wow, that's different.'

'Certainly is.'

'When do you go?'

'Friday.'

'You going home between times?'

'Haven't thought about it yet. I don't think French Guiana's that far from here, actually – just over Brazil's northern border, isn't it? Home would be a long way to go before flying straight back again.'

'Mm,' she said looking intently up into his eyes. 'How about we stay local and I keep you company?'

'Sounds like fun,' he said unable to stop himself smiling at the idea. 'What d'you have in mind?'

With a flash of her dark brown eyes she looked up into his and asked: 'Ever been to Rio?'

The End

Acknowledgements

I am so grateful to Mike Chanides and Joe Ellis for their patient help, as I am to Jamie Pursaill for his early editorial encouragement.

I would also like to acknowledge the support of the Hanbury Agency. Getting a 'break' is everything in life; the publication of this book is entirely down to the support, guidance and generosity of Maggie Hanbury and Henry de Rougemont.